I0779265

VOIDLIGHT

BLADES OF HEAVEN AND HELL

BOOK TWO

AARON HODGES

Edited by Elo Quence
Proofread by Sara Houston
Cover Illustration by Efosa Promise
Typography by Nikko Marie

ISBN: 978-1-991018229

ABOUT THE AUTHOR

 Aaron Hodges was born in 1989 in the small town of Whakatane, New Zealand. He studied for five years at the University of Auckland, completing a Bachelors of Science in Biology and Geography, and a Masters of Environmental Engineering. After working as an environmental consultant for two years, he grew tired of office work and decided to quit his job in 2014 and see the world. One year later, he published his first novel - Stormwielder.

FOLLOW AARON HODGES…
And receive TWO FREE novels and a short story!
https://aaronhodgesauthor.com/newsletter

ALSO BY AARON HODGES

The Sword of Light

Book 1: Stormwielder

Book 2: Firestorm

Book 3: Soul Blade

The Legend of the Gods

Book 1: Oathbreaker

Book 2: Shield of Winter

Book 3: Dawn of War

The Knights of Alana

Book 1: Daughter of Fate

Book 2: Queen of Vengeance

Book 3: Crown of Chaos

The Evolution Gene

Book 1: Reborn

Book 2: Havoc

Book 3: Carnage

Descendants of the Fall

Book 1: Warbringer

Book 2: Wrath of the Forgotten

Book 3: Age of Gods

Book 4: Dreams of Fury

The Seventh Realm

The Hawthorne Effect: a form of reactivity in which subjects modify an aspect of their behaviour, in response to their knowing that they are being observed or studied.

PROLOGUE

Fifteen weeks before the Festival of the Satana

Arimus Shore sat slumped in his chair, chin resting against his hand. His fingers tapped gently against the table as his advisors argued amongst themselves. He was only half-listening. They were droning on about provincial taxes and merchant turnover and the rate of crime in the south. Just as they did in every meeting.

He stifled a sigh, allowing the monotonous voices to fade into the background. By the Emperor, he was spoiling for a proper fight. It had been almost two years now since he'd end his service with the Gurrian Legions after their victory against the rebellious armies of Ressi. He had even been the one to cut down the Ressian Prince and finally put an end to the decade-long conflict. If he'd known this dreary place would be his reward, Arimus might have stayed his hand!

Instead, the snivelling brat had died, and Arimus had been made governor of Skarta. The last governor was growing old, ready for retirement, and a youthful face was needed to ensure order in the farthest province in the Gurrian Empire. Many would have given their firstborn child for such an opportunity.

Unfortunately, the reward turned out to be a poisoned chalice. His predecessor had been an incompetent buffoon. The streets and canals of the river city were rife with crime, its alleys full of the poor and homeless. Arimus's last two years had been spent trying to round up the riffraff. But the cancerous underbelly of Skarta was well established, and every attempt to snuff it out only saw fresh growth appear elsewhere. There was even a group who dared to call themselves the Skartan Resistance. They might have even provided Arimus with a bit of entertainment, if the bastards didn't spend all their time skulking in the shadows. Instead, they were a constant thorn in his side, either stealing from the Gurrian aristocrats or making life for everyone unpleasant by disrupting supplies to the city.

There had been another attack just last night—a grain store, owned by a Gurrian merchant, burned to the ground. The fools had even claimed responsibility in giant words painted on the neighbour's shopfront. Well, maybe their popularity would finally end when the populace discovered the shop had been responsible for supplying a third of the city's bread. With it in ashes, starvation would increase.

His advisors were even now arguing over a tariff on the local farmers to cover the shortfall. The discussion had already stretched past half an hour. Taken by a rush of impatience, Arimus slapped a hand down on the table, cutting off the conversation.

"I agree," he growled. "Let the measure be set at ten percent. And make sure the people understand exactly who is responsible. Let's see how many doors are left open to those bastards when a loaf of bread costs a silver penny."

His advisors hesitated at the outburst, before nodding their agreement and turning to the next subject on the agenda: meat imports. The Dean of the Skartan University was surprisingly vehement on the subject, his jowls practically bouncing with enthusiasm. It took all Arimus's will not to groan out loud.

Fate be damned. If only they'd had word about the situation in the north! He knew in his gut the Highlanders were up to something—that clansman, Jaxon Daniyal, in particular. The Darkstrider. Arimus snorted. The man was a traitor, no more, no less. He had come to Gurria and fought in their armies, learned their trade, and built himself a legend, only to return to his backwater clan and begin training an army of his own.

The arrogance of the man, to think no one would notice. And maybe they wouldn't have, if the old governor had remained. But Arimus had actually *read* his intelligence reports. He had put together the threads of the plot.

First had been the gang of bandits raiding merchants in the north of Skarta—before their mysterious disappearance. A suspiciously similar group of Ressian men had then been noted by observers in a Malesie village, not far from the border. And who did they work for, but the fabled Darkstrider?

Another report made mention of the growing number of Pathfinders in the retired soldier's company. Men and women of extraordinary ability, with the power to shape the world to their liking.

The final nail in the old man's coffin had come when Lieutenant Ting had reported the presence of an *Offworlder* in the same village. An actual Offworlder. The kind women told tales of to their children to scare them after they had misbehaved. A gods' honest Destroyer, come amongst them.

And Jaxon Daniyal, the Darkstrider, had been secreting him away from the world.

Arimus had immediately sent Lieutenant Ting with a Force of soldiers to deal with the situation. Eighty men—including four Pathfinders of their own—should have been more than enough…

…only they had never returned. In fact, there had not been so much as a whisper from the north in the weeks since. Not a single soul had returned. Just…silence. It was as though Ting had marched his men off the face of the planet.

It was concerning, to say the least. Though…there could be a silver lining, if it meant Arimus got to deal with the threat himself. He still had the better part of a Battalion in the city. Whatever force Jaxon had secreted away in the Highlands, it would not be enough to stop eight hundred battle-hardened soldiers of Gurria.

He just needed permission first.

"Excuse the interruption, Jon," he said, interrupting the old windbag from the university, who was still lamenting the loss of quality beef from the north. As the man stammered to a halt, Arimus pressed on with his question: "Has there been any word yet from the Emperor?"

"Ah, no, sir," the dean said belatedly. "No word yet about your request."

Arimus grunted. "Then out with you, all of you. That's enough bureaucracy for one day."

Most of the men and women rose immediately. The dean grumbled a few last words before following. Arimus remained in the council chambers, happy for them to clear out so he could steal some peace and solitude for himself. After this, he would have to spend the afternoon in the grand hall, listening to petitions from the public. He wasn't sure which of the duties had taken more years from his life—though both were undoubtedly greater than any wound he had received in battle.

Stretching his arms with a groan, Arimus rose and wandered over to one of the enormous stain-glass windows that adorned the chamber. The building had once been the cathedral of Skarta, and this window depicted some holy being in the sky swinging a mighty blade. Arimus knew the story from his childhood nanny, who had been Skartan herself. Arimus could not recall the name of the entity, but the story went that with a single swing of his blade, he had created the mountainous crags of the Desolate Alps to Skarta's south.

The window itself was probably considered a work of art, with its twisting swirls of coloured glass. All Arimus saw was a weak point that would immediately be exploited by an enemy army intent on taking the building.

Art. He snorted. What use was art in this violent world? It could not shield him from his enemy's blows, nor steady his hand in battle. Give him a sword to swing or a stone wall to stand on any day.

"I'll admit, I did not expect to find Skarta so…decadent," came an unexpected voice from behind him.

Caught off-guard, Arimus spun to find a young woman standing in the doorway. His heart dropped into his stomach as he recognised the speaker. Alyina Sorulus, princess of Gurria. The woman was an enigma, stunningly beautiful, cunning, and one of the most powerful Pathfinders in the Empire. Some even claimed she might have eclipsed her father, though that was only spoken in whispers.

What was not debated was her rank of General over the Legions of Gurria. If she was here…

"I suppose they were our rich neighbours, a long, *long* time ago," Alyina continued, wandering around the council table towards him. "That probably explains why it's all so *old*. Not like Gurria and our modern civilisation."

"Princess," Arimus rasped, his mouth parched. "What… what are you doing here?"

He had seen her once or twice during his time in Ressi. But he had never been *this close*. Just her presence set his heart racing. Piercing emerald eyes studied him as she approached, auburn hair tumbling down around her shoulders. Today she wore a dress of flowing black silk, but he had seen her just as comfortable in leather armour, when she had fought at the head of the Gurrian Legions. Small she might be, but no one would ever describe Alyina Sorulus as fragile.

A smile flitted across Alyina's lips as she came to a stop before him. "Why, Governor, was it not you who sent for me?"

"I…I only asked for permission…to deal with a minor bit of unrest in the Highlands."

The princess laughed. "If my dear Jaxon Daniyal is involved, then there can be nothing *minor* about the situation."

Arimus swallowed, searching for the right words. Her relationship with Jaxon had been an open secret during the Ressi campaign—but that did not mean people actually *spoke* about it. A Gurrian princess bedding with an uncivilised clansman? No, it wasn't worth a man's life to have those words on their tongue if it ever got back to her father.

"With respect, Princess," Arimus said carefully, "he is but one man."

At that, Alyina Sorulus threw back her head and truly laughed. "Ah, but you are cute with your words, Arimus." Raising a hand, she rested it against his chest. Her fingers were adorned with a dozen golden rings inset with gemstones. Arimus swallowed as the scent of wildflowers overwhelmed his senses. The skin beneath his tunic was hot where her hand rested, and he could feel the pulsing of heat against her hand, the rushing of blood in his ears…

Rising onto her tiptoes, she brushed her lips over his ear. "You can relax, Governor," she whispered. "My father does not care whose company I enjoy." She stepped suddenly back from him. "He cares that I see his enemies crushed."

"That's…that's good," Arimus said, regathering some of his lost wits from where he had spilt them on the floor. Licking his lips, he eyed the woman. "Does that mean my covert mission to deal with Jaxon Daniyal and his friends has been authorised?"

His thoughts were already rushing ahead to the confrontation. To meet Jaxon Daniyal himself, blade to blade…the Darkstrider was said to have been a swordsman without peer in his youth. He had been a Silver ranked Pathfinder when he'd left Gurria. Arimus wondered if the old soldier had found the spirit to reach Gold in his retirement. Otherwise the matchup could only prove to be a disappointment against his own Gold tier abilities.

"No, quite the opposite, in fact."

"*What?*"

Alyina's eyebrow arched. "Are you questioning me, Governor?"

"I…no…I mean…" His heart lurched in his chest. Quickly he bowed his head. "My apologies, Princess, I did not mean—"

Laughter rang in his ears, rich and full of mirth. "So formal! Aren't you just the perfect little soldier." She wore a mischievous smile on her lips when he looked back at her. "Not like Jaxon. There is nothing polite about that man."

"What are your plans for him then, Princess?"

"First of all, there will be no more underestimating our Highland enemies," she said, her voice growing serious. "It seems that army you sent north was defeated by a group of clansmen half their number."

"What? That's impossible—they're savages. It would take *twice* their number to defeat our soldiers."

"My father believes the Offworlder had a hand in it." She was watching him again. "The Offworlder you were meant to deliver to us."

Arimus swallowed at the sudden coldness in her eyes. "Ting failed…"

Alyina waved a hand, dismissing his words. "What's done is

done. His survival may ultimately be to our benefit, if he does indeed possess the knowledge of another world."

"If he is working for our enemies, I do not see how that could be to our advantage."

"Then you do not see half as much as you think, my dear," Alyina said, reaching up to pat his cheek. "No matter though, I'm here! And I have a plan."

"Which is..."

"You are to send the Offworlder an invitation to join us in Skarta for the Festival of the Satana."

"What possible reason could he have to accept such an invitation?"

"Peace," she replied easily, "and the chance to learn more about his own kind." She grinned. "I hear the Skartan University has a great selection of works on Offworlders."

"And what then, if he accepts?"

"Then he will join our cause." The princess smiled. "Or he will have a little accident and never return to his friends in the Highlands."

Arimus frowned. Her plan made little sense to him. He couldn't see a few books convincing anyone to risk venturing into the territory of an enemy with only their word as a shield. Especially one under the tutelage of someone like Jaxon Daniyal.

"With respect," he said carefully, "I think your vision is clouded."

"Oh?" she asked, eyebrow arching dangerously once more.

He swallowed, but he *was* still the governor of this province. His father would look on him with scorn if he shirked his duty because he was *afraid.*

And so he asked: "Are you sure this has nothing to do with Jaxon Daniyal? He was your lover, after all."

The slightest hint of a smile touched Alyina's lips at that. "Jaxon Daniyal means nothing to me now."

Arimus licked his lips. A nervous tick he had never quite shaken. "I don't believe you."

Alyina's smile grew as she stepped towards him. "Is that so?" Her hand rested against his chest again; her fingers toying with the buttons of his shirt. Pupils dilated to slits, she looked up at him with hunger in her eyes. "Well then, let me prove it, Governor."

1

Present Day

Mikael Heaton staggered to a stop in the middle of the road and just stared. He couldn't help it. Half a year had passed since he'd torn open a portal between dimensions and entered a strange new world the locals referred to as the Seventh Realm. A place filled with magic and gods and demons. Six months in which he had grown accustomed to its eccentricities—or so he'd thought.

Apparently not.

An enormous creature lay on the banks of the river, its long, *long* neck stretching from its partially submerged body up onto the sandy shore. Its appearance was reminiscent of a Plesiosaurus back on Earth—or at least, an artist's reimagining. He could just make out the enormous flippers beneath the muddy currents, and that long neck had *dinosaur* written all over it.

However, instead of scaly skin, this creature was covered in a pelt of short, thick fur, like that of a seal. And when it opened that enormous mouth, row upon row of herbivorous molars were revealed, instead of the jagged blades of a carnivore.

Not that this made the behemoth any less intimidating.

"What is that thing?" Mikael whispered.

"A leviathan," Jaxon Daniyal grunted.

The man was unruffled, as per usual. Jaxon Daniyal, the Darkstrider, was a legend amongst his people, a warrior of unmatched skill and a Pathfinder of significant power. He stood at ease beside Mikael, hands on his hips as he studied the beast.

"Don't usually see them this far north. Don't worry, it won't bother us."

The sun was high in the sky behind them. They were just leaving the Highlands on their journey south to the city of Skarta. A journey they were only taking because of an invitation sent by a man who just a few months ago had tried to have them both killed. Mikael tended to take that kind of thing personally; but Jaxon had insisted they accept. And given it was the lives of *his* people at stake, Mikael had relented.

Though he still had his doubts. It was not that he thought Jaxon naïve. The man possess more experience than Mikael could hope to gain in a lifetime. But he was also desperate to avoid a war between the Highlands and Gurria. Too desperate: he would do anything to avoid that fate, and their enemies knew it.

It was likely a trap. This Arimus Shore had guaranteed their safety—something Jaxon claimed the Gurrians took seriously—but his word had already proven treacherous once, when his lieutenant tried to poison Jaxon under a banner of truce.

Truthfully, this entire endeavour was probably a fool's game. But Mikael had his own reasons for the journey, not the least of which was curiosity. He needed to learn more about the enemies he would face in this world. The Gurrian Empire had opposed his very existence from the beginning, sending first their hunters, and then an army, to eliminate him. He had expected a full-scale invasion to be next. So to instead receive an invitation from the very man responsible for those acts of violence…

Yes, he was curious.

"Come on," Jaxon grunted, already halfway across the ford. "You can gawk while you walk. I want to reach Skarta sometime this week."

Mikael raised an eyebrow at the gruff words, but Jaxon had already turned his back. His powerful legs carried him confidently through the swirling currents to the other side. There were the beginnings of grey in the man's dark hair and wrinkles on his forehead, but Mikael had yet to meet anyone who could match him with a blade.

There was a power about the man, a sense of indomitability that lifted Jaxon's abilities above the good to the exceptional. On Mikael's first day in this world, he had watched Jaxon walk through a circle of armed men, all intent on murder and mayhem. Not one had dared to challenge him —not even when Jaxon removed their leader's head.

A natural-born killer indeed.

Letting out a long breath, Mikael followed the man into the river—and immediately began to curse as the icy water filled his boots. This river ran directly from the ice-capped mountains looming behind them. He had to admit, he was looking forward to the milder climate of the lowlands.

His attention returned to the behemoth as he crossed. Its sheer size still had him on edge; such a creature, even a herbivore, could be dangerous if it became territorial. At least in his universe.

His power stirred instinctively. On his first day here, Mikael had inadvertently tapped into the foundational power of the Seventh Realm by manifesting an Essence—what the locals considered to be gifts from their gods. By absorbing its power, Mikael had become a Pathfinder himself, able to draw on the foundational forces of this world.

He used those forces now. Some would call it the soul, others his spirit. He didn't like to think about the implications of those terms. He simply thought of it as Aura. An energy stored *within* him that he could use to influence the external world. Or allow him to see it in a new light.

Aura Sense activated.

The creature on the beach flickered and changed, so that it seemed that Mikael viewed it through a kaleidoscope of overlapping colours. It took a moment to make sense of what he saw, so overpowering were the interlocking hues, as though he was not looking at one creature, but many…

He saw it then. The colours clicked into place. A soft turquoise surrounded the beast, indicating calm and tranquillity. Reassuring, to say the least. Overlapping it, though, were other colours—the scarlet of frenzied activity, the emerald of life, the pink of passion. These were smaller creatures, he realised. Insects and larvae and grubs. An untold wealth of life teemed within the pelt of the leviathan.

Satisfied that the creature was unlikely to come charging in his direction, Mikael let the vision fade. Emerging from the river, he paused long enough to remove his boots and shake out the water, then set off quickly after Jaxon. They were officially in enemy territory now, and they both needed to be alert for tricks.

Fortunately, they would be arriving...unfashionably early. The invitation had been for the Festival of the Satana, which marked the summer solstice and the return of the fiery heat of the hells—at least in Skarta. They would reach the city a full week before the festival. Hopefully that would put a torch to any plans the governor had brewing around their visit.

Mikael also had contingency plans of his own back in the

Highlands. While they were in Skarta, his friends would be journeying to the other clans to enlist their help. If war was brewing, the Malesie would need allies. Not even all the forbidden knowledge he had brought from Earth would allow them to stand alone against the Gurrian Empire.

His stomach clenched as he thought of those he had left behind. Young Fiachson and his curious mind. He would go to the Izolu, his father's people, who lived apart from the other clans, high in the rocky crags of the Highlands. They were said to be an eccentric people. Mikael hoped that Fiachson could bring them to their cause.

Then there was Conner. He had been Mikael's rival before the Gurrian army had come. It seemed foolish now, their bickering, like a stick fight between children when exposed to the cold reality of war. They had fought side by side against the enemy, the day the attack had come. There was a respect between them now, if not friendship. Conner he had sent to the Fushore on the northern coast. They would need their ships, if the worst came to pass.

And finally there was Lunden Marcs. The man from Ressi who had lost his home and his people, even his honour. Lunden had been amongst the bandits that had attacked Mikael on his arrival in this world. Mikael was not generally a forgiving person, and if it had been up to him, the lot of them would have hung for their crimes. Instead, Jaxon had offered them a chance for redemption. And when the Gurrians had come, Lunden Marcs and the other former bandits had stood with the Malesie against the invaders.

Since then, Mikael had come to see Lunden in a new light. The man had a way about him, a sense of steadiness that inspired faith. Men followed Lunden out of respect, not fear. So it was to Lunden that Mikael had entrusted the training of the new Highland army. The man might not be a clansman, but he thought perhaps an outsider was needed if the clans were to learn his new way of waging war.

There were others, of course. Roalin and Maria, even Scott Sobotta, the boisterous twin that had fought with Conner. The man hadn't been the same since losing his brother. Steven, and so many others, had fallen in that final battle. It hurt, thinking of them. They had stood with Mikael, defended him when it would have been so easy to give him up instead. Mikael owed them a debt for that, one he would do everything in his power to repay.

There was another, of course. A name that was never far from his thoughts. *Isabel.* The young woman with whom he'd grown close to over his months in Sarton. Jaxon's first apprentice, she was a powerful warrior and Pathfinder, capable of extraordinary things. There had been something between them once, or so he had thought. But that was before Isabel learned he was an Offworlder and not just an eccentric foreigner from a faraway land. Given his kind were considered this universe's version of the Bogeyman, their relationship had soured after that.

He'd hoped their relationship had been mended after the battle for Sarton, but while things were at least civil between them now, she had refused to join them on this journey. Mikael didn't blame her, but that did little to numb the pain of the rejection.

Still, at least he knew she was safe. She would be far from any battle in Sarton. Or at least, he hoped.

Standing on the rise, Isabel watched with twisted lips as Jaxon and Mikael entered the river. She waited until they had crossed and set off along the road to Skarta before starting down the slope herself.

If someone had asked, she could not have said why she was avoiding them. Not really. On the battlefield outside Sarton, Isabel had realised that she cared deeply for both men. Jaxon had been like a father to her in the years since his return from Gurria, and Mikael...

A night beneath the stars, the heat of the bonfires against her skin, and Mikael close, spinning, dancing in the square of Sarton, his hands firm around her waist, his head tilting, their lips pressed against one another's...

In a flash of anger, she shoved the image away. Her cheeks were hot from the memory. But that had been before she had discovered his lie. Both their lies. Both had spun tales to deceive her, to hide the truth that Mikael was from another world, that he might carry the seeds of their destruction within.

The knowledge was still a burning pain within, a betrayal so vast, she had hated them both for a time. And now...well, now, she still needed space. Time to resolve the conflict in her own heart.

But that didn't mean she would allow the idiots to go marching into enemy territory without her. This was Mikael Heaton and Jaxon Daniyal they were talking about. The pair were like dirty dogs to fleas when it came to attracting trouble.

So here she was, shadowing carefully along behind them, employing all of her skills to avoid their notice. It helped that Jaxon had taught her everything she knew about tracking—she understood him, when he would pause to check his back trail, where he would look to camp...

Isabel felt a pang in the pit of her stomach, as though she had eaten something foul. She stood on the banks of the river now. Its waters bubbled, the pebbles rumbling as they shifted beneath the currents. This would be the farthest she had ever been from home. Another land awaited, an unknown city, filled with hidden dangers and enemies.

And she was alone.

She glanced back at the mountains of the Highlands. The peaks soared into the sky, jagged and broken stone, with ice glistening high above in the spring sunlight. They had shadowed Isabel her whole life. Beyond the river, she saw no mountains, just an endless plain of rolling grass, with only the occasional hill to break the open ground.

Had Jaxon felt this dread when he had first ventured south to explore the world beyond their mountains? She could not imagine the stoic Jaxon Daniyal fearing the unknown.

Isabel straightened her shoulders. So neither would she. She was powerful, armed with steel and her bracers, which she unravelled to become a whip. And she was a Pathfinder with Bronze rank abilities. What did *she* have to fear from the uncultured people of the south?

"Your mother never told you where your father came from, did she, child?"

A shudder ran down Isabel's spine as she recalled the seer woman's words. Vinnie. For years, no one had paid the woman any heed. Her prophecies always spoke of doom and destruction, and none had ever come to pass.

Then she had called Mikael a "Destroyer" and named him the Voidlight. Blind as she was, she had seen through the lies and the deceit when no one else had.

Just yesterday, before Isabel had set off for Skarta, the old woman had come to her and spoken of her father—her true father. She had never known the man, for he had not bothered to stick around for her birth. Gladly, others in the clan had stepped in to fulfil the role. First, the kind baker, Dario, and later Jaxon…

…but that did not remove the hurt of his rejection. All she had of the man was an image in her mind—not even of her father himself, but from a painting. Her mother had painted it herself, long ago on a warm summer evening, and kept it all those years.

Until the fire.

Clenching her fists, Isabel felt the Mana gathering in her palms, the flickering of heat. The flames—her ever-present companion since the day she had lost everything.

"Why should I care a damn about him?" she had said to the woman. "He never cared about me or my mother."

"Because you have questions, my sweet Dawnbloom."

"I don't."

The old woman had not responded for a moment. "You wish to know where you came from," she had said at last. "Your story. The blood that runs in your veins. The Paths that came before you."

Isabel could not renounce the words, for with them, she had felt again the void, the emptiness of her past. The piece that had been missing all her life.

"You could tell me." She had said instead.

"I could," the woman had replied with sadness in her eyes, "but then you would not be where you need to be."

"And where is that?"

"Skarta."

"Jaxon and Mikael are going to Skarta."

"And so must you."

"Why?"

"So you can seek out the place called Silvercrest."

"What will I find there?"

"Your Path, child. Your Path."

The woman had walked away at that, leaving Isabel standing in the field of Jaxon's farm, a dozen questions spinning in her head that she had no idea what to do with.

And so here she was, following her friends, determined to protect them in the big city…

…and afraid of what she might find when she got there.

"No," she said softly, looking beyond the river at the distant plains. Jaxon and Mikael had already disappeared over a rise. "I won't be afraid."

Stepping into the river, Isabel set off after her friends. She did not look back this time—and so she did not see the old woman standing at the top of the rise. There was a sad look on her aged face, and while her eyes were a milky white, they tracked the young woman as she set off after the two men.

"I am sorry, my dear Dawnbloom," Vinnie whispered to the winds, "but you are the only one who can hold him to the light."

With a final sigh, she turned and set off on the long path back to Sarton. She would play no further role with those who ventured beyond her lands. Perhaps her sister would care for them. Perhaps not. Their fate was no longer Vinnie's concern. But there were others in the Highlands she could help. Others who might yet change the fate of her children.

2

Damp cobblestones glistened beneath Kat's worn boots as she darted through the streets and intricate bridgeways of Skarta, her breath misting in the darkness. The street urchin clutched a burlap sack to her side, heart pounding in time with the thud of footsteps from behind. Moonlight shimmered off water as she leapt across a narrow gap in the canal.

Shoulders hunched, her eyes darted from shadow to shadow. When she came to an intersection, she barely paused, her path guided by a childhood spent on these harsh streets. It was her greatest advantage against the Gurrians who had subjugated her city. Kat had been born in these alleyways, knew every bridge, every elaborate bend in the canals better than the scars left by her Gurrian schoolteachers on the backs of her hands.

The darkness seemed to whisper its encouragement, the gloom speeding the little thief on her way. She'd glimpsed three guards outside the warehouse. Hired brutes whose strength lay in their muscle. She hadn't checked their Aura, but none of them had been built for speed. There was little chance of them catching her now.

Her confidence growing, she allowed herself a smile as she slid through the gap between two poorly constructed buildings. The occasional *thud* and grunt of her pursuers still whispered from behind, where the fiery light of the burning warehouse lit the sky, but it was clear the men could not keep pace with their wily prey. A few more scaled walls and vaulted waterways, and she would be clear.

Kat pressed on. Silence descended over the sleeping city, the humid air covering the world like a blanket. Finally she slowed to a brisk walk, sweat beading her brow. Speed would only draw further attention now. Her breath came easier, the burning in her lungs fading. The weight of the sack seemed lighter, despite its contents. Her smile broadened as she crossed another bridge. The gold and silver she'd taken from the safe would fund a whole cache of weapons for the resistance.

That, and the message she'd left with the burning warehouse, would make Jon proud. This was meant to have been a hit-and-run job. And the others *had* been in and out. Probably why they'd gotten away without being noticed. But after spotting the safe, Kat couldn't resist. She almost laughed, imagining the resistance leader's face when she showed him the contents of her sack.

But that was why he valued her, wasn't it? She was no ordinary thief. The Elohim themselves had blessed her with an *Essence!* She was only a Copper ranker, but still! Her ability to spy Gurrian traps and pick out their hidden places—even avoid their most dangerous servants—was invaluable to the resistance. The safe hadn't even been locked, they thought it was hidden so well!

The joke was on them. Now she had evaded the last of the guards—

The faint scrape of a boot was Kat's only warning before the figure struck, detaching itself from the shadows to slam into her side, driving her to the ground.

"I got her!" a woman's voice shrieked in the darkness. "Help, before she gets away!"

A shout answered her call, followed by the crash of bodies barrelling through the debris-strewn alleyways. For the first time that night, fear touched Kat. She snarled as the older woman clasped at her wrists, trying to pin her to the cobbles. Colours flashed in her vision as her *Aura Sense* ability activated, revealing her attacker's swirling Aura.

Another Copper! Probably with an *Aura Sense* ability like herself, to have found her in the maze of canals. She'd been so busy concentrating on the brutes, Kat hadn't considered who else might be in pursuit. Thankfully, Coppers only got one ability—otherwise she'd be as good as dead.

Unfortunately, the woman didn't have to beat Kat. She just had to hold her until the others arrived.

"Stay…still," the woman growled as Kat thrashed, trying to break her grasp.

Ignoring the command, Kat slammed her elbow back and felt a satisfying *crunch* as it connected with something soft. The woman cried out and her grasp loosened.

"Godsdamnit, get *off*!" Kat snarled.

Twisting, she managed to get her leg between them and kicked with all her strength. The woman hurtled backwards into the wall of the alley. Gasping with exhaustion, Kat stumbled to her feet. The pounding of boots were close now, closing in from all directions.

No time to think.

Kat chose a direction at random and darted for the shadows. Or at least, she tried to—before a desperate hand caught her by the ankle and sent her crashing back to the ground. The impact drove the breath from her lungs. Choking, she kicked herself free of the blasted woman and scrambled to her knees—

"I don't think so," a cruel voice spoke as a hand as thick as iron shackles closed around Kat's arm.

She screamed as the thug of a man loomed over her. A second appeared, followed by a third. Colour flickered as she checked their Auras. They were all scarlet with rage, deeper than ordinary, like a pool in one of the fast bends of the Skartan river. Dangerous—and Copper rank. All of them. From there size and the power in her assailant's grasp, they probably all had abilities that enhanced their physical bodies.

"Where do you think you're going, missy?" the brute holding her sneered. At some point in his life, someone had made a decent attempt at slicing off his nose. His fingers dug into her bicep.

"By the Emperor, about time you lot arrived," the woman muttered, picking herself up from the ground. "The little bitch almost got away."

"We're stumbling around in the dark out here, Sophie," Noseless replied.

The woman called Sophie snorted. "She shouldn't have got by you in the first place." She gestured in the direction of the warehouse, where the light of the fire only seemed to have grown brighter. "Believe me, it's not going to be *me* explaining that to the boss."

Kat glared daggers at the woman but held her silence. Everyone knew not to antagonise a Pathfinder. It was rare for people to advance beyond Copper, which meant only one ability, but that was more than enough to cause problems. Piss off someone with *Might* or an *Enforced Body*, and you were sure to end up in pieces. Worse still were those with *Elemental Manipulation*, who could turn the very forces of nature against you.

"Not a talker, ay?" the woman grunted. "Well, you can tell us who sent you now, or after the boss is done with you. Either way, you'll talk." She gestured to the three brutes. "Come on, let's take her in. Casoway is gonna have questions."

Snarling, Kat struggled in the grip of her captor. These people, they acted like Gurrians, talking about the Emperor and all that, but they couldn't hide the harshness of their accents. They were Skartan like herself, clear as day. People got like that, thinking they were better than the rest of them, just because they got to work for the Imperialists.

"Ain't no one sent me," she said, "please, was just a prank. Just…please, let me go…"

Pinching her thigh, she got her eyes watering, and blinking, she felt a hot tear streak her cheek. She even managed a pretty convincing sob—even as her free hand felt for the dagger in her waistband.

Unfortunately, these bastards didn't care one bit for her act. The hand around her arm remained like iron. But even an *Enforced Body* could bleed. If she took down the man holding her, she might be able to slip away before anyone else got a hand on her. Unless one of these bastards had the *Movement Surge* ability…

"Excuse me," a voice spoke suddenly from behind them, "sorry to interrupt, but I was hoping you might be able to offer me some directions to the library."

The men spun to find a young man leaning against the wall of the alleyway. He wore a leather jerkin and dark pants of homespun cotton, along with a thick woollen cloak checkered in red, green and blue. A sheathed sword hung from his belt, shorter than the longsword popular with the Gurrian nobility —who were the only people allowed to wear a blade in Skarta.

A long second passed before anyone spoke.

"It's the middle of the night…" Noseless muttered.

"Obviously," Sophie snapped, pushing past the three men. "I think you'd best be on your way, stranger." Her gaze slid to the weapon. "Unless you'd like the City Watch to join us."

To Kat's surprise, the man chuckled. Pushing himself off the wall, he cast his gaze over Kat's assailants. She shivered as the golden eyes settled on her. There was an intensity there that set the hairs on the back of her neck to tingling.

"Sure," he said easily, "but why don't I take the girl with me?"

Kat felt a chill at his words. The men stilled while she silently opened her *Aura Sense*. Her heart began to palpitate. The stranger's face revealed nothing, but the swirling of his Aura was an open book. Its colours changed almost faster than Kat could track. Red to white to black. Dense. Powerful. *Angry*. The Aura of the other men were like shallow puddles compared to the depth of this man's soul.

Steel rank.

Momentarily forgetting the hand that held her, Kat tried to back away, only for a tug from her captor to pull her up short.

"Who do you think you are?" Noseless snarled.

"He's a Steel ranker," the woman murmured. She had the same vision as Kat.

The others stilled.

"Someone who doesn't take kindly to bullies," the stranger answered, his eyes unblinking.

The men hesitated. Kat could see them calculating the odds. Steel rank outclassed any one of them—even the most ignorant commoner knew that. But there were four of the Coppers and just one of him. The difference was not insurmountable. In fact, given their size…

"Or what?" Noseless challenged, apparently deciding to call the man's bluff.

"Or you will not live to see the sunrise."

Silence fell over the alley. The threat was spoken with such confidence that it even seemed to penetrate the thick skulls of Kat's captors. They exchanged uncertain glances, clearly unnerved. Kat dared to hope they might release her and retreat.

But four against one?

It was poor odds, even for a Steel ranker.

"You know what I think, stranger?" Sophie shot back. "I think you're her accomplice, trying to bluff us into letting her go. Why don't you show him who rules this town, boys?"

Kat's heart thundered like her father's old wagon across the cobblestones of the marketplace. The two men not holding her hefted their clubs and started towards the man. Being servants to the Gurrian nobility didn't give them an exception to bear blades of their own.

"Last chance," the stranger warned, hand resting on the hilt of his blade. "Drop your weapons and release the girl, and I'll let you live."

The pair laughed, convinced now that the man was bluffing, and continued their advance. Noseless lingered with Sophie, still holding Kat. Her hand drifted to the dagger, ready should a chance present itself.

It didn't take long.

Thump. Crack. Thwang.

The sounds of combat reverberated through the alley as the men met with the Steel ranked stranger. In the flurry of movement, it was impossible to follow the flickering silhouettes, but Kat sensed her captor's grip loosen as he took an instinctive step in the direction of his comrades.

She didn't hesitate.

Twisting, Kat drew her dagger in one fluid motion and slammed it into the man's thigh. He howled, releasing her and clutching at his leg while Kat tore the blade loose.

"Damn you!" he cursed, swinging his club at her head.

But Kat was already gone, tearing off down the alley in the opposite direction of the fight. She burst into a moonlit street. Speed was everything now and the broad avenue beckoned. Time to put as much distance between herself and her assailants as possible…

Instead, she hesitated, glancing back at the dark mouth of

the alley. Suddenly, the night was silent. A tremor ran down her spine. She'd left her nameless rescuer for dead.

Well, it wasn't *her* fault he'd bitten off more than he could chew. Not like she'd asked him to intervene! More fool on him if he thought she'd go back…

It was so *quiet* though. Surely there should be *some* noise. Kat cursed beneath her breath. Typical, letting curiosity get the better of her. She slipped back through the shadows and peered into the alley. It took her eyes a moment to adjust from the moonlight…

An involuntary gasp escaped her.

Three bodies lay on the ground. The thugs. Only the woman remained. The stranger stalked towards her, sword in hand.

Sophie held a dagger towards the golden-eyed stranger. It didn't seem to faze him. No kidding—he'd just taken out three Coppers in as many heartbeats. Her hand trembled, before releasing the dagger with a jerk. It clattered to the cobble-stones. The man paused, his head inclining to the side.

"I surrender," she said. To her credit, Sophie's voice was steady. "You said if we surrender, we live."

"I did say that," the man murmured, his gaze on the fallen dagger.

Sophie's shoulders slumped with relief. In that moment, the stranger's hand snapped up. Through Kat's *Aura Sense*, she saw the energy drain from the world. Mana. The fabric of creation. In a matter of heartbeats, it gathered in her benefactor's outstretched palm. A crackling light appeared, burning away the shadows of the alley.

There was a moment as realisation dawned in the woman's eyes, a split second where she knew…

…followed by the deafening *boom* of thunder.

Kat staggered back with a scream, tripping on a brick as lightning seared across her eyes. Terrified, ears ringing, she struggled back to her feet. Over the roar, she heard the whisper of approaching footsteps. Panic. Still half-blind, she stumbled and spun…

…and came face to face with the golden-eyed stranger.

The pair stared at one another in stunned silence, then…

"You killed her!"

The words burst from Kat's lips before she could contain them. Her heart was pounding and blood thundered in her ears.

The slightest of frowns crossed the man's lips. "I am a man of my word."

"You said you'd spare her!"

What was she doing, arguing with a madman? She needed to run.

"*If* they released you." He smiled. "You released yourself."

She swallowed at the matter-of-fact way he spoke about killing four people. "Right." Her mouth was parched. At least her heart was slowing…marginally. She didn't dare look away from those golden eyes. "And, ah, who…who are you?"

"Your world has many names for me," he replied, a smile twitching at his lips. "I seem to get a new one every week. But I quite like the one given to me by a Malesie Seer. She called me the Voidlight."

"The Voidlight?" Kat blinked. "What kind of name is that?"

"The kind you give a man destined to tear your world in two, I guess."

"Ah…ha…"

"I mean, she wasn't entirely wrong," the man continued, looking sheepish as he scratched the back of his head. "My arrival did inadvertently lead to the Gurrian Empire invading the Highlands." He paused. "And your world being infiltrated by one of your so-called-gods."

Kat stared at the man. "Ah…" She glanced around, feeling

the strange need to check that the world did indeed remain whole. "Right…" She subtly began to back away.

The man, whose face had taken on a distant look, blinked and flicked a glance in her direction. He grimaced.

"You think I'm completely insane, don't you?"

Her heart was racing again. She held up her hands. "Ain't my place to say, Mr. Voidlight."

The man chuckled. "I like you, kid. Glad I rescued you."

"Yeah, thanks for that." She hesitated, searching for the right words to extract herself, before coming up empty. "I'm, ah, gonna go now."

"Wait."

She paused. The golden eyes studied her, seeming to look deeper than just her appearance. "What was your name?"

Frowning, she opened her mouth to lie, before deciding better of it. You never knew what strange abilities an unknown Pathfinder might possess. "Kat."

"Nice to meet you, Kat."

She started to turn away, but lingered. The cloak the man wore was strange, but those were Highland colours, from the three clans. "What you said about the Empire…invading the Highlands…is that true?"

He shrugged. "As true as everything else I've said."

A frown touched Kat's lips. "Then why are you here?"

The man blinked at the question. His forehead creased, his face darkening. When he looked at Kat, she saw the darkness there, saw the man who could casually cut down four strangers in a dark alley.

"The Gurrians tried to kill me and my friends," he said quietly, his voice filled with rage. "So I've come to teach them a lesson." He smiled, but there was no mirth in his eyes this time. He looked around, surveying the dark streets. "I've come to burn their Empire to the ground."

3

Mikael watched the girl bolt away into the night. She was filthy, her face streaked with dirt and dark hair slick with oil. Her clothing was little better than rags and her shoes looked about two sizes too small. She was obviously used to living rough and in desperate need of a good meal. The sound of her broken shoes slapping against the cobbled streets faded as she disappeared around a bend, but words were still whispering in the back of his mind.

User: Katherine Delinghy. Rank: Copper. Body: 5. Aura: 21 Mana: 2. Abilities: Aura Sense.

Interesting. What twist of fate had made a Pathfinder out of a street rat? And what had she done to attract the attention of those men?

He'd almost bit off more than he could chew back there. None of them had shown anywhere near the skill as those who'd trained him, but the narrow alley had limited his room to manoeuvre. He rubbed his shoulder where the stray swing of a club had clocked him.

Muttering a curse, he set off in the direction of the inn,

remaining on alert as he went. The girl and her assailants were not the only dwellers of the night in Skarta. He spied one man asleep in the lee of an old bridge, and a woman and her children tucked into the corner of an alley. Yet another man was passed out with a bottle on the edge of a fountain.

Strange. There was poverty in his own world, of course, but this was the first time he'd seen it in the Seventh Realm. True poverty, at least, where people were so obviously going without. After his time in Sarton, he'd begun to think it didn't exist.

It made him wonder. Was it because the Empire had conquered this city, consigning its citizens to a life of hardship beneath the yoke of their new masters? Or was it something more intrinsic than that, the natural outcome of human nature, of a species that lived as a community but which also strove for individual excellence over the collective?

Something to think about. He wiped a trickle of sweat from his brow. Those questions had never bothered him before he'd come to this place. Before the construct, before the portal, before…

The body of a woman lay on the floor, eyes open, staring, empty, accusing.

Mikael staggered to a stop on the arch of a bridge, a sudden pain in his chest. With the image came a sense of loss, of being cast into an ocean of pain. Slumping against the railings, he dragged in breath after breath of humid air, seeking to regain his equilibrium, to…to escape the pain of what he had done.

The woman was his mother. She had helped him, worked alongside him to create the construct that would tear apart space and time and bring him to this world. Why they had sought such a miracle…strangely, that knowledge still eluded him, like there was a block in his mind.

But he knew at the end his mother had turned against him. Betrayed him.

And in return, he had killed her.

Your own mother.

Why? The question lingered in his mind. The decision had seemed so logical at the time. He had known with certainty she would do it—and had planned out the consequences to the smallest detail. There had been no regret then, no sadness or uncertainty. Just a cold, calculating will to succeed no matter the cost.

It was strange, thinking back to the time before. Those memories were a part of him, but something in the journey, or perhaps it was his time in this world before he recovered his past, had changed him. The memory might have returned, but the person he was *now* felt strangely decoupled from the person he *had been.*

Though…there had been something else, at the end. It hung with perfect clarity in his mind. That he would return to Earth and save her…somehow.

Shuddering, he pushed the thought away. Dark water swirled past beneath the bridge. It had taken a week to reach the city, and the climate had changed markedly since crossing the icy mountain river. Away from the Highland crags, the sun beat down on their backs, baking the earth beneath their boots. The journey had been a dusty, sweaty haul, even once the rolling hills gave way to open plains. Golden crops of maize and wheat had appeared, swaying in the humid breeze blowing in from the west.

But finally they had arrived and looked upon the walls of the Skartan capital. The city sat in the centre of a broad river on a collection of tiny islands, each joined together by canals and bridges and artificial waterways to make up a single city.

Very reminiscent of Venice, he couldn't help but think,

leaning against the stone railings. Hopefully it offered a similar level of civilisation. He had felt a strange sort of relief on their arrival. This would be the first true city he had visited since arriving in the Seventh Realm. Sarton, the town where Jaxon had trained him, was quaint and peaceful, its people welcoming, but it was little more than a waystation on the road to greater places. And while the clans apparently had a few cities deeper inside their territory, Mikael had not been able to visit them.

After all this time, he was very much looking forward to a few luxuries of civilisation.

Although knowing this world and the enemies he faced, Mikael would have little time to enjoy them. Even the dark waters probably concealed fresh dangers. Imagining a leviathan concealed below, he decided to move on.

There was a third option for all the misery in the multiverse, Mikael considered as he stepped onto the street leading to his inn. All the poverty, all the suffering on Earth and the Seventh Realm and however many other worlds there were out there, it could all be by *design*. All because someone, or *something*, wanted things this way.

He knew better than anyone that larger forces were at play in this world. Forces with their own agendas, that may not have the best interests of humanity at heart. They could be shaping events even now, manipulating chance encounters…

Mikael came to an abrupt stop in the middle of the road. The girl…could she have been placed in his path? To set him against the Empire, perhaps? Or to put Mikael in their sights, now he was in their territory? His heart began to race. If that was the case—

"No," he muttered out loud, cutting off the thought.

That rabbit hole could only lead to madness. Divine forces, demons and angels and fate, whatever you wanted to call them, Mikael Heaton would not be played like a fiddle. He was his own man and would make his own decisions. The girl had been in trouble, so he had helped her. Nothing more than that.

Though…a smile touched his lips as he started off again. Jaxon would not be pleased. They had not even been in Skarta for a single day and Mikael was already stirring up trouble. But it wasn't like he'd gone looking for it. Unable to sleep in the soft beds of the inn, he'd decided to take a midnight walk to centre himself a little. Not his fault he'd stumbled into some thugs looking to rough up a girl.

Hell, it had been Jaxon's own code that had spurred Mikael into action:

I swear to guard the weak against those who would do them harm and fight evil wherever I find it. To never use my powers for personal gain, nor allow temptation to lead me down the path of evil.

Mikael hadn't spoken the words himself. There was too much on the line. The Malesie, his friends, they were relying on him to win the coming confrontation with the Gurrian Empire. He couldn't afford to bind himself with scruples like the vague concepts of good and evil.

Especially after the glimpse he'd had beyond the veil.

His footsteps grew lighter as he reached the busier end of the street, where music and laughter spilled from nearby taverns and lanterns cast back the shadow of midnight. He drew the folds of his cloak about himself, covering the hilt of his sword. His invitation had included an exception that allowed him to carry a blade, but on a dark night like this the authorities were more likely to shoot first and ask questions later—so to speak.

Thankfully, no one bothered him, and within a few minutes he was slipping through the front door of the Dancing Donkey, one of the few inns they'd found with rooms available. Just about every other place in the city was apparently packed to the rafters and beds were at a premium.

Inside, Mikael was greeted by the familiar scents of smoke

and ale. A few patrons still lingered at the bar, but most had already staggered upstairs for the night. Jaxon was not amongst those who remained. No surprises there; the man made a habit of retiring early.

He took the stairs two at a time, the wooden boards creaking beneath his boots, before creeping down the corridor and into his own room. The sounds of voices carried up from below, and outside he heard the occasional bought of laughter, but hopefully after a bit of midnight exercise, he could finally sleep.

Or not.

Removing his cloak and draping his sword belt over the dresser, he sank onto the bed. The weight of what was to come lingered in his mind. Tomorrow they would present themselves to the Governor of Skarta. The same man that had sent eighty Gurrian soldiers and a Silver ranked lieutenant to kill him.

Blood began to pound in Mikael's ears. But it was not fear. It was…exhilaration. Maybe he hadn't wanted to accept this invitation, but now he was here…walking into this city was like the rooster striding into the fox den and declaring himself dinner. Suicide, surely. Unless he played his cards right.

Mikael was just reaching out to shutter his lantern, when he sensed something…amiss. He frowned, glancing around. They had each rented simple rooms in the upstairs section of the inn—little more than a single bed and dresser to place his few belongings. Nothing leapt out at him as dangerous.

Pursing his lips, Mikael hesitated, wondering what had changed. It was another moment before it came to him. The silence. There were no more voices, no more laughter. Even the soft creaking of floorboards beneath sleeping bodies had vanished. The night was still—unnaturally so.

He lurched for his sword as the eyes appeared in the darkness. Glowing, scarlet, slitted eyes. They were followed by a twisted face and phantom lips and a mouth filled with row upon row of daggerlike teeth. Twin horns twisted from the mutated skull, shining as they reflected the lantern light.

"Gidday, mate." A voice like death itself spoke.

4

Mikael crouched, one hand wrapped around the hilt of his sword, too terrified to drag it from its sheath. Fear had frozen the breath in his lungs. All he could do was watch in terror as the creature loomed in the tiny room.

Then…then he felt something from the sword. The blade that was not a blade, but one half of a construct—the machine he had built back on Earth to forge a path between worlds. The hilt warmed, vibrating with a gentle, almost indiscernible power. He didn't hear the voice in his mind like he did when examining other Pathfinders, but there was…something there, and he found his fear receding.

Still gripping the blade tight, he exhaled, and his wits returned.

"Azaroth," he said, surprised at the calm in his voice. "I didn't expect to see you again."

He had tried to forget. To purge their last meeting from his mind. The day that time had stood still. The Day That Had Never Been—as Jaxon had taken to calling it.

Azaroth and Dagon.

Four months ago, the forces of heaven and hell had

stepped through a rift. The power wielded by the pair had made the very mountains tremble, had torn the skies asunder.

Two infinite forces, one of the light, the other darkness.

First had come the being of brilliance, Dagon, who had called himself Elohim. Strange, to find that old name here. It suggested a connection between their worlds. But if Dagon had any relation with the old scripts of Earth, it was as a vengeful deity. The being had begun a merciless slaughter as it preached of its cleansing gift.

And then Azaroth's arrival had saved them. Dante's beast. The demon behind the veil. And the monster that now stood before Mikael. Just being in the presence of this creature felt blasphemous, like it could corrupt his soul with a look.

You know, if Mikael had believed in that kind of thing.

"Ah, I'm hurt, mate," the creature's words reverberated through the room, though its hideous mouth did not move. "Thought we made quite the team, didn't we?"

"…team?"

This time the jaws moved, the pale lips drawing back into a toothy smile. "Yeah, mate, you made me a lot of credits last time."

Mikael swallowed. A pit opened in his stomach, threatening to swallow him whole. He had allowed himself to believe these creatures were a distant threat, that only his original interference with the nature of the Seventh Realm had drawn their attention.

If only he could be so lucky.

"That is…nice to hear?" he said, keeping his voice steady.

A howl of laughter came from the creature. "Oh, believe me, it is," Azaroth said. "You shoulda seen Leviathan's face when you showed up at the river. Priceless."

"Leviathan…" Mikael frowned. "As in those things from the river?"

"Ba! Nah, those are just something he left behind. Made in

his image and all that. Unfortunately for you, the wily bastard is nothing like those dumb imitations. He's like me: an administrator, only he's got the Fourth Circle."

"Right."

Despite his terror, Mikael tucked that piece of information away for later. He needed every advantage he could get. His fist clenched tighter around the hilt of his blade. Azaroth had tried to take the construct from him last time. Illegal contraband or something, the demon had claimed. But the machine had been bound to Mikael's soul during the passage between worlds. Removing it had crippled him, which for reasons he was yet to understand, was a big concern for these beings.

So instead, the demon had transformed Mikael's construct into a pair of swords. It had left Mikael with one, while banishing the other to gods—or demons, he supposed—only knew where.

He planned to find that sword, once the immediate danger posed by the Gurrian Empire passed. Though now Azaroth had reappeared, Mikael found himself revising those priorities. He didn't know exactly what the construct was capable of— he'd only used it once—but if the demons didn't want him to have it, it was vital he reunited the twin blades as soon as possible.

"I'm glad to have been of service," Mikael said carefully, "but, from what I understood, our bargain is…complete?"

After the infringement of the Elohim into the Seventh Realm, Azaroth had reset time, rewinding the day so it could unfold the way it had been "planned." But the demon had made a deal with Mikael—it would leave him his memories, so long as he survived the new day. Apparently, someone, somewhere had gambled against Mikael's survival. And lost.

The thought made him inexplicably angry, clearing his mind further. He was Mikael Heaton, damnit. *No one* controlled him. Not kings. Not governments. Not even so-called gods and demons.

"Yeah, about that." The demon somehow managed a sheepish look as it used a clawed hand to scratch its ashen chin. Flesh peeled away, releasing a burning red light. It quickly blinked back out, as though something had sealed it. "Went and got greedy with my winnings, didn't I?" It grinned. The sight was pure terror. "I am a demon, after all. Gotta have my vices. Anyways, you're going to need to live a little longer, if it's all the same to you."

Mikael's mouth was suddenly parched. "I…wasn't planning on dying anytime soon, if that's what you're worried about."

"Yeah, that's why you're in a city run by the same man who tried to kill you last time, right?" Azaroth pursed its almost inexistent lips, then sighed. "Sorry, that was harsh. Just, you gotta try *extra* hard to live, alright? Cause Leviathan is gonna do everything he can to put you in an early grave."

"What?"

"Oh, relax, he can't come for you directly. That'd be too obvious. The producers would obliterate him. He'll probably just send some Gold-ranker to kill you."

"A…Gold-ranker," Mikael rasped. "Great, not concerning at all."

He'd learned a lot more about Pathfinders and their ranks in the past few months. At lower ranks—the base metals—they remained more human than not. They might be particularly strong, or have access to a few Mana or Aura-based abilities, but it was not outside the realm of possibilities for a skilled non-Pathfinder to best them in combat.

But beyond that? Things changed. Beating a Bronze ranker was more than just pushing the realms of impossibility. They were just stronger, faster than your regular human. And the power of their abilities was magnified as well.

At Gold…

Jaxon was Gold rank. In six months of sparring, Mikael had never once landed a hit on the Highland man. The gap between them might as well have been the Grand Canyon when it came to power.

"Oh *relax*," Azaroth muttered, rolling its scarlet eyes. "That's why I sent the girl."

"The girl?"

"Kat."

"Kat…you mean the *Copper ranker*. How is she going to help me fight a *Gold?*"

"Saving her life should put you in the good books of some important people here in Skarta." The demon paused. "And the bad books of a few others. But as they say on your planet, can't make an omelette without breaking a few eggs, right?"

Mikael blinked. It was beyond weird to hear an old Earth saying come from the mouth of this monstrosity. "Does your kind, ah, eat?" He spoke the first thing that leapt into his mind.

"'Course we eat," the creature grunted. "But never mind that. Concentrate. Kat. You'll be seeing her around. Make sure you keep an ear out."

Mikael groaned. "Seriously, that's it? You're giving me a Copper ranker when this other dude is going to send a Gold after me?"

"*Probably* going to send a Gold. You never know—he might find a Royal somewhere."

"What in the ever-loving-god is a *Royal?*" Mikael closed his eyes, dragging in a breath. "You know what, never mind. Are you sure there's *nothing else* you can do?"

"Believe me, if there was, I would! I got a lot of credits on you, mate. But Skarta is prime time viewing. Barely got in here on an interdimensional black spot. Speaking of which." The creature cursed, the terrible head whipping around. "Oops, okay, I gotta go. Good luck, mate. Look out for Gold-rankers.

And remember, eternal damnation if you die before the Festival of the Satana!"

"Wait, that's only a week—"

Too late. Azaroth was already gone. Mikael sat, staring at the darkness where the demon had been. There was a pounding in his mind, a thundering like a V8 engine at full tilt. That…that…

His eyes fell to the sword in his hand. The festival was just a week away. That meant this Leviathan creature, or demon, or whatever it was, had plenty of time to make its move soon. He cursed.

Calm, Mikael. One thing at a time.

He exhaled. It was okay. This changed nothing. He just needed to stick with his plan.

And pray to the forces of…*hell* that the governor didn't just kill them on sight.

CHARCOAL CRUNCHED BENEATH THE BOOTS OF ARIMUS SHORE as he moved through the wreckage. Acrid smoke hung in the air and there was still the occasional *pop* of dying embers. Everywhere he looked was devastation. The warehouse had been completely gutted by the flames and every inch was covered in a thick layer of ash.

Another attack. They were growing bold, these rebels. This time it had been a chemical store. The fumes would have been enough to make a mortal gasp and choke. Even at Gold, Arimus's eyes were watering at the potency. He continued through the wreckage, seeking out any clue the culprits might have left.

But flames were good at covering tracks, and the chemicals had burned with such intensity that even the stone walls had begun to slag and crumble. At least it had not been another food store. The last thing he needed was to cut rations further in the soup kitchens. The last reduction almost started a riot. It had taken every single one of his seven hundred soldiers to clear the streets.

Still, this incident would not be without cost. These chemicals had been destined for the city's forges and bricklayers, as well as the hospital used by the Skartan public. They would be short of medicines now.

The locals would be angry. Hopefully that anger would be directed at the true culprits, but he knew from the past two years it was unlikely. People had a habit of blaming those in charge for their hardships, rather than looking to their own houses.

By the Empire, he hated this place. And now Alyina Sorulus was here. His blood raced a little faster at the thought of the cunning princess. Her presence was a complication, although over the past few weeks, one he had come to…tolerate.

Though now their time was running short. The Festival of the Satana was less than a week away and the Offworlder was expected any day now. Arimus's doubts remained about the plan. Legend and superstitions existed for a reason. They were a warning. Playing nice with Offworlders had only ever ended in tragedy.

The sundered Detian Isles were testament to as much. A thousand years ago, the great island known as Deti had embraced a woman from another world as their queen. A short time later, an explosion of such enormity ruptured their land, splintering it into a thousand broken, barren pieces.

And now Arimus had invited another into his city. He might not be an academic or a politician, but even he could see the risk that entailed.

But Alyina was his princess and his general, and nothing Arimus said would change that. So he would just have to keep faith that whatever benefits she foresaw outweighed the risk to this land.

Which, Arimus considered as he wiped tears from his stinging eyes, might not be such a loss after all, given its nigh ungovernable peoples. If this was the kind of behaviour the last governor had faced, then perhaps Arimus had been too hasty in his assessment. Sadly, it was too late to revise his feedback to the capital. The man had already been arrested, hung, and quartered for failure of duty. Such was life.

Emerging from the warehouse onto the docks of the canal —or what remained of them—Arimus continued his assessment. Not even the canal boats that ferried supplies from the warehouse around the city had been spared. Several had been moored overnight and now lay half-submerged in the murky waters, hulls scorched and twisted from where flames had leapt from the burning building.

His eyes narrowed as he counted the boats, before turning at the sound of approaching footsteps. A pair of sergeants approached: the men he had placed in charge of investigating these attacks.

"Get your soldiers to dredge the canal," he ordered before either could pepper him with pointless questions. "There was nothing inside. But they might have dropped something into the water that points to them."

"Yes, sir!" the first shouted, offering a crisp salute before turning and barking orders to his Unit of eight.

The other lingered. Arimus waved for him to speak.

"There was another incident last night, sir," he said quietly. "Not far from here. Four Skartan Pathfinders. All dead." His eyes flickered to the burnt-out warehouse. "Thought they might be connected, so I spoke with the merchant. Apparently he had four guards on duty last night."

Arimus pursed his lips. There had been no human remains inside. He'd assumed that the merchant had ignored his warnings about attacks. But if the resistance group had managed to slay not just one, but *four* Pathfinders, they were far better funded than anyone realised.

"Good work, Sergeant…Bolt, no?" The man nodded and Arimus continued: "Very well, let's see these bodies."

Offering a salute, Sergeant Bolt spun on his heel and set off through the confusing network of canals and back alleys that formed the unkempt underbelly of Skarta. It only took a few minutes to reach the site of the massacre.

"Their ranks?" Arimus asked as he approached the bodies.

They lay in the shadows, not far from the rumbling of carts and bustle of morning traffic in a nearby avenue. Three were large men, brutes wearing the harsh rough-spun wool of Skartans. A quick look over their bodies showed they had been killed by quick, piercing thrusts of a blade. Strange. The ban on any blade longer than a hand for Skartan citizens was strictly enforced.

"All Coppers, sir," his sergeant replied. "The men with *Enforced Bodies*, the woman…" His voice trailed off as he glanced at the last body and swallowed. "*Aura Sense.*"

Arimus could understand his unease. If not for his years on the Ressi campaign, he himself might have balked at the sight of the woman. Unlike the others, she hadn't been killed by mortal means. Something of incredible heat had struck her, scorching her flesh and melting her silk tunic until it stuck to her skin. The result of an *Elemental Manipulation* ability, if ever he'd seen one.

"Ask around," he said at last. "Find out if anyone saw something. Good work on this, Bolt. Keep it up."

Bolt nodded his thanks before retreating. Arimus wandered back in the direction of the warehouse. Even from this distance, the air was thick with the acrid tang of burning chemicals.

He clicked his tongue in frustration. Maybe Alyina was

right and he needed help dealing with these scum. They were like rats fleeing a sinking ship. Whenever he found one of their little hideouts, they scattered, only to reappear someplace else weeks later and begin the attacks all over again.

"Sir!" one of the soldiers working at the canal called as he emerged from the alleys. "Sir, come quick. Think we've found something!"

Returning his face to a neutral expression, Arimus moved quickly to join them. He hoped for a body—that was usually the best way of tracking the rats, watching to see who appeared at a memorial—but instead the privates were gathered around a damp-looking sack on the sidewalk. They backed up as he joined them, allowing him to kneel and tug open the drawstrings, revealing a sword.

Frowning, Arimus removed it from the waterlogged cloth and held it up to the light. The hilt was plain enough, leather wrapped without a handguard and a basic steel pommel rather than the jewel-encrusted variety favoured by their nobility. It was shorter than your regular Gurrian longsword as well— barely longer than a hunting knife, really. *Well-balanced though*, he thought as he weighed it in his hands. Whoever had forged it obviously favoured practicality over appearances.

The leather scabbard was still soaked from its time in the water. He was about to draw the blade, when shouts broke out amongst his men as they scattered away from the canal.

Arimus tensed, before relaxing as he saw the enormous body slipping through the dark waters. Just some of the local longnecked wildlife. A big specimen, admittedly, but the leviathans were supposedly harmless. Being fish eaters for the most part, they had no interest in humans. Although…it was a little unnerving, the way this individual's beady eyes seemed to be watching them. He swallowed, before retreating a step from the edge himself.

A splash came from the waters as the enormous creature

sank beneath the surface, disappearing into the dark. Arimus shook his head, irritated to find his heart racing.

"Almost as pretty as the local lasses, ay Governor?" one of the men said, producing a round of nervous laughter from the others.

Arimus grunted. "You're not wrong there," he muttered, before glancing at the sky. The morning mists were beginning to dissipate, beckoning in the heat of the day. A sigh slipped from his lips. He was due for another council meeting. "I'll leave you lads to finish up here. Sergeant, report your findings to me at the end of the day."

"Yes, sir."

On another plane of existence, Azaroth carefully pulled the dimensional door closed behind him. It disappeared with a flicker of light and soft crackling of Mana. Just in time too, as a second door appeared, lines sizzling to life as though someone had taken a blade of burning hydrogen to the fabric of the universe.

The demon-faced Satana stood, enormous arms folded across his twisted chest, as Leviathan slipped through the door, stealthy as could be, and closed it silently behind him. For a moment, all was dark in the control room. Then Azaroth coughed.

Leviathan practically jumped out of his reptilian skin. The Satanic monstrosity spun so quickly he must have gotten whiplash in his overly elongated neck.

"Azaroth!" the other Satana exclaimed. "Didn't see you there. Why, what are you doing out and about at this dimensional hour?"

"I was going to ask you the same thing, Leviathan."

The two stood staring at each other for a long time. A *very* long time. Somewhere beyond the universal compendium, a star was born, blooming to a brilliant, fiery glow, then brighter still, its supernova form consuming an entire solar system—before collapsing on itself in the fiery, everlasting blackness of death.

"What did you do?"

"What did *you* do?"

Another long silence. Another star was born. And died.

"If they catch you…"

"Ha! I'm not the one leaving mortals with memories of gods and demons." Leviathan smiled, revealing an enormous row of teeth filed to points.

Azaroth glowered. "The bet is off if you've gone and killed him."

"That would *definitely* tip production off now, wouldn't it?" He folded his neck. "I'm not that foolish."

Azaroth snorted the fires of hell. "So you say." They glared at one another, before Azaroth rolled his eyes. He gestured to his operating console. "Come on then, let's see what the little brat does next."

5

"I need your help."

Jaxon looked up from his meal with raised eyebrows. He sat in the corner of the Dancing Donkey inn at a table laden with an assortment of cured meats, freshly toasted bread and some kind of Skartan potato omelette. The hour was early and the inn was still quiet, though a couple of guests were beginning to make their way downstairs to take their places at the breakfast tables, where similar spreads had already been prepared.

Their table was alongside the window looking out onto the street, rather than the ones lining the inn's courtyard. It gave him an eye on the entrance—an old habit from his soldier days. On campaign, even in a supposedly friendly village, you never knew when trouble would come knocking.

Mikael stood over him, looking like death warmed up with his golden eyes ringed with shadow and stubble on his normally clean-cut chin. Even his clothing, a thin cotton tunic and leggings, was somewhat in disarray. Had he managed any sleep last night?

Jaxon felt a pang of guilt. Mikael hadn't wanted to come here—it had been Jaxon who'd convinced him to accept the governor's invitation. Now the young man was a long way from friendly territory, surrounded by enemies far more powerful than himself. It didn't take much to predict what he might want.

"Let me guess," Jaxon said with a grimace. "You want to know how you can get stronger?"

They were both Pathfinders, but the difference between Mikael's Steel and Jaxon's Gold rank was as vast as the Desolate Alps.

Slumping into the opposite chair, Mikael grimaced. "Am I that transparent?"

"Not usually, no," Jaxon grunted.

"So, can you help me?"

"I wish I could, Mikael, I really do. But advancement cannot be rushed. You could damage your soul—then you won't be good to anyone."

Mikael snorted. "I'm not much good dead, either." He pursed his lips, eyes looking distant. "The first time…it was because I accepted something about myself."

Jaxon nodded. Back in his early days in Sarton, Mikael had picked a fight with Conner Spears—another of Jaxon's apprentices. Conner had been dismissive of the weaker young men and women of the village, preferring to train only the strong in the way of the Malesie warrior. Mikael had objected on their behalf.

A magnanimous act, although his interjection had come only after Conner judged him as one of the weak. After weeks of division within the clan, Mikael had finally admitted his motivations were less than pure—if only to himself.

That moment of personal enlightenment had been enough for him to break through the barrier from Copper to Iron.

"Then…when Ting came with his army…" The young man swallowed.

Jaxon frowned. "You've never said what pushed you forward during the battle."

"I remembered something." There was a haunted look in Mikael's eyes as he looked up at Jaxon. "Something about myself, from before. Something I wanted to forget."

"I see," Jaxon didn't press the matter. Revelations tended to be a deeply personal matter, especially at the base metal ranks. The amount of introspection required was the reason so many Pathfinders failed to push beyond their initial limits.

"So, advancing to Bronze…I need to accept something *else* about myself?"

"Not exactly…"

"Then what, Jaxon?" Mikael asked wearily. There was no anger in his voice with the question, just a resignation. And that look in Mikael's eyes…what exactly had happened to his friend last night?"

"Mikael, there's a reason why I never told you about these things before they happened," Jaxon said reluctantly. "If I tell you, the very existence of that knowledge could form a block in your mind…"

"I don't care," Mikael insisted. "I need to know if it's possible."

They stared at each other for a long moment, and Jaxon was relieved to see a glint of Mikael's fire return.

"Very well," he relented. "Advancing to Bronze and the other precious metals…it requires more than just an inward perspective. You need to find your place in this world."

Mikael snorted at that. "Great," he muttered. "Given this world thinks I'm the Bogeyman, I'm sure that'll work out just fine." He waved his hand as though to place the matter to the side for the moment. "Sorry. Guess I woke up on the wrong side of the bed. What's the plan with the governor?"

Jaxon eyed the young man, trying to read those indecipherable golden eyes.

"I thought we'd walk up to the citadel gates and announce ourselves," he said, still watching for a response.

It was remarkable, thinking back to the innocent young man he'd first encountered eight months ago, dangling in the grasp of the brutal bandit leader. It was like looking at a completely different person. Mikael had changed since the battle to protect Sarton. He was a harder man now. Darker. Jaxon couldn't help but wonder again just what his Steel rank revelation had been.

After a moment's silence, Mikael began to chuckle. "I like it."

Jaxon blinked. "Come again?"

"It's simple," Mikael said with a grin, "and about the last thing they'll be expecting if they've really been setting a trap for me."

Jaxon fixed his apprentice with a glare, waiting for the 'but'. Once such a look would have had the young man shrinking in his seat. Not now.

"You don't have any objections?"

"None."

"Not even if Alson Ting is there?"

That got a reaction. The smile on Mikael's lips faltered. He shifted nervously in his chair. "Ah, yeah, about that…"

Jaxon glowered across the table at Mikael. "What is it?"

Alson Ting had been an old comrade of Jaxon's from his time serving in the Gurrian army. More recently, however, the man had led the eighty-man-Force that had attacked Sarton. He'd also invited Jaxon to parlay before the battle—and poisoned him in an act that broke every law of etiquette of the Gurrian Empire. Jaxon had only survived because Isabel, in her desperation to save him, had advanced to Bronze and developed the Healing Touch ability.

After the battle was won, Alson Ting had been taken prisoner—then released along with several other survivors and sent back to the Empire with their tails between their legs. Or so Jaxon had believed.

"He's, ah, dead," Mikael said sheepishly.

"*What?*"

"They didn't deserve mercy after what they did," Mikael replied coldly. His eyes glinted, hard as stone. "Not to mention, they would have revealed our secret to the empire. You know, the handy bit of military brilliance that might be the only thing that saves the Highlands from an invasion."

Jaxon stifled a curse. *Of course* Mikael had gone after them. The man could not leave well enough alone. He forced himself to exhale. *Calm.* Mikael had not been the only one to regret the release of those prisoners. It had been Conner who had shown mercy, after taking command at the end of the battle. But with so many Malesie dead, even Jaxon had to admit the man deserved death. Just...not out loud anywhere in earshot of Mikael Heaton.

"That was not your decision to make, Mikael," he said instead.

"Maybe not. But it *was* the right one."

Jaxon clenched his fists, hands trembling with suppressed rage, but before he could say more, Mikael started. His bloodshot eyes blinked rapidly as his head swung around.

"Hey, what's that smell? Is that..."

He rose abruptly, chair scraping against the stone floor, and moved towards the kitchen, leaving Jaxon sitting alone at the table. He watched the young man wave down the innkeeper. The two spoke for a few minutes before Mikael returned with a steaming mug in hand.

"Coffee!" he declared, a look of absolute joy on his face. "I can't believe it! I didn't think it even existed in your world!"

Jaxon held his glare. "They ship it from the south," he said shortly. "It costs a fortune getting it through the Desolate Alps."

"Money well spent," Mikael declared happily.

The money had no doubt come from the small fortune Mikael had collected his first day in the Highlands, when he'd inadvertently robbed a bandit gang. Those same bandits would have killed him for it, if not for Jaxon's intervention.

"Awful stuff," he growled.

"Well, get used to it," Mikael declared. "Cause Rob over there is going to see if he can get me a few kilos to take back with us." He paused. He held one of the beans from the terrible drink, rolling it between his fingers. "Actually, there's some other things I wouldn't mind asking about, you know, before we go tempt fate. If you'll excuse me!" He didn't wait for an answer before scampering back to where the innkeeper was polishing glasses behind the bar.

"Wonderful," Jaxon muttered, wrinkling his nose as the smell drifted across the table.

Though he couldn't keep a smile from his lips at the glimpse of the goodhearted young man he'd met in the Highlands all those months ago. He could try to hide it all he liked, but there was more to Mikael Heaton than the hard-eyed man he presented to the world.

Mikael returned a short while later with one of those dangerous smiles on his face. Before Jaxon could ask what he'd done, however, the Offworlder gestured towards the door.

"Right!" he said. "Now that's done, shall we go greet our hosts?"

With a sigh, Jaxon let the matter of Alson Ting drop —for now.

And so they set off for the citadel, taking care to bring the papers the governor had provided, which granted them the right to carry their swords in the city. Hopefully they would be a deterrent against any overeager guards they might encounter along the way.

The citizens of Skarta were already out and about en-mass as they navigated the twisting streets and bridges. Thankfully though, the roads remained pleasantly clear of wagons and horses, with most goods being transported around the city by canal boat. As the sun crept above the three-storey-skyline, however, the shadows disappeared and sweat beaded Jaxon's brow. He might possess a magically *Enforced Body*, but that did not make him immune to shifts in the climate.

In truth, Jaxon had been yearning for the Highlands since practically the day they'd left. He'd never been fond of Skarta, where the air was so heavy with moisture, just walking its streets could feel like you were drowning. With the hour still early, this was the busiest time of day, as the city's occupants tried to complete their business before the arrival of the sweltering midday heat. By the afternoon, the city would be silent as its denizens sought solace behind thick walls of stone.

Though wandering through the labyrinthine network of passageways, Jaxon noticed many even lacked that luxury. There seemed to be a beggar on every street corner. Wrapped in thin blankets, many were still asleep, taking advantage of the slivers of shade to escape the sun. Others extended emaciated hands and rasped out a few beseeching words for coin.

It was a grim sight and a shocking change since even five years ago, when he'd passed by the city on his return to the Highlands. It made him glad such sights were uncommon back home, even in the Malesie capital. Amongst the clans, men and women of every age and ability had a part in society, a contribution to make to the whole. And when one fell on hard times, others were there to pick them back up.

That was not to say that poverty and crime were non-existent. But as he stepped around yet another sleeping body in the street, Jaxon couldn't help but think that something had gone irrevocably wrong here in Skarta.

It was an hour before their destination came into view. Marble towers stretched high into the sky ahead, every inch of stone etched with intricate murals, the details of which were lost to the distance, but which Jaxon knew depicted tales from the time the Elohim had walked the Seventh Realm. The building had once been a cathedral, a place of worship for the peoples of Skarta. But when their nation had fallen to Gurria, it had been repurposed. The polished spires now stood as testament to the might of the Empire.

There were several men dressed in the familiar uniform of the Gurrian army standing outside the gates of the citadel, spears in hand. But it was a young woman who emerged from a booth to the side of the entrance that addressed them as they approached.

"Names?" she asked, frowning at a list scribbled on a scroll in her hand. "Do you have an appointment?"

"No," Jaxon replied, "but I believe the governor is expecting us."

"Sorry," the woman replied. Without looking up, she started back for her booth. "Only those with appointments are allowed today. You'll have to visit the town hall to petition…"

She trailed off as Jaxon stepped into her path.

"My name is Jaxon Daniyal, and this is Mikael Heaton. Now, I suggest you pass our names onto your boss before you say anything more, lass."

He gave the woman his best glower…which turned out to be completely unnecessary. The blood had already drained from her face at the mere mention of his name.

Clearly his reputation preceded him.

Which was somewhat gratifying. Even before recent tensions, his name had held power. As a youth, Jaxon had left the Highlands in search of glory. He'd found it aplenty serving in the Gurrian army, where his prowess with the blade had caught the attention of a certain princess.

Even now, his stomach twisted at the memory. The rush of battle. The heat of their passions. The shame that stained his soul.

The fear in the eyes of the young woman was obvious. She stared up at him, practically quaking in her boots and obviously at a loss for words. Some of the nearby guards had the presence of mind to reach for their weapons, but they froze as Jaxon turned his steely eyes on them. Silence. Then…

"You," Jaxon growled, nodding to one of the older men. There was more white in his beard than black, but he was one of the few who had kept his wits about him. "Go and tell the governor his guests from the Highlands are here to see him." He paused, before adding: "Better mention we come in peace."

At his side, Mikael gave a dry chuckle, while the older guard drew himself up and offered a salute. Jaxon grunted his approval as the man departed, before turning his eyes to the others. As a group, the soldiers took a collective step back. They knew his name—and what they were up against. There might be a dozen of them, but none were Pathfinders. They wouldn't last more than a few heartbeats against Jaxon's Gold ranked abilities.

Mikael began to pace as they waited while stealing glances in the direction of the citadel. The actions betrayed his nerves. The gates opened onto an interior courtyard, where a handful of stairs led up to the ornate iron doors of the stone building.

Thankfully, the old soldier's absence proved short, as a few minutes later the doors cracked open and he reappeared, scuttling down the stairs and crossing the courtyard. He approached Jaxon with his head bowed respectfully.

"The governor will see you, sir."

"'Course he will," Jaxon rumbled.

"I will show you the way—"

"Don't trouble yourself, son." Jaxon interrupted. The man's head jerked up in surprise, but Jaxon was already pushing past him, gesturing for Mikael to follow. "I've been here before; we'll find our way."

6

ser: Jaxon Daniyal. Rank: Gold. Body: 47. Aura: 43. Mana: 37. Abilities: Enforced Body, Movement Surge, Might, Aura Sense, Spirit Attack, Shield.

Blinking, Mikael dismissed the stats, relaxing just a little. They were inside the citadel. If he was honest, he was a little surprised they hadn't been shot down on sight. Jaxon could insist all he liked that Gurria treated their word as sacred, but Mikael was no fool. He remembered the red wedding…mostly.

So as the stone walls swallowed them up, he couldn't discount the possibility they were being lured into a trap. Though as they started down a long corridor, Mikael was relieved to see this place was not like the grim old castles and forts from his world. There were no murder holes watching them from above or portcullis to seal them within. In fact, this building seemed more like a church than a fortress, with the intricate decorations etched into the marble walls and stained-glass windows casting coloured light across the polished marble floors.

Stifling a sigh, he forced himself to follow Jaxon's lead. It was difficult. Jaxon Daniyal might be the most powerful man Mikael had ever met, but the Gold ranker viewed the world in black and white. Accepting the invitation of an enemy in the hope of peace? Sure! But kill a man in cold blood? *Never.* Not even if that man had the blood of your friends on his hands.

That was why Mikael had waited to tell him about Alson Ting. Even now, the memory of the man—and those they had lost in the battle—had Mikael trembling with rage. Barta the huntsman and Taldar the stonemason. Steven Sobotta, forever separated from his twin. And Derric, the only member of Mikael's inner circle to fall. Just a few weeks before the battle, he had finally tied the knot with his love, Maria. Now Derric lay in the cold ground and Maria was alone.

All because of Alson Ting. And Jaxon dared to *lecture* him for killing the man?

Coming to the end of a corridor, Jaxon strode towards a massive set of doors. They were made of a reddish wood reminiscent of mahogany and were strangely plain compared with the intricate murals and carvings that decorated the rest of the building.

"They were replaced after the war," Jaxon grunted, as though reading Mikael's mind. He grasped the handle, before pausing to glance back. "I do the talking."

Mikael raised an eyebrow. "You know the invitation had *my* name on it, right?"

"Did you serve for a decade with the Gurrian Legions?"

"Point taken."

The Gold ranker eyed him another second before turning to the doors. They swung open with a push. Inside stood a row of men in baked-leather armour. Each held an iron-tipped spear, currently pointed in their direction. They wore purple cloaks and leather helms with metal nosepieces. Each also had a sword sheathed at their side.

The sight of the armed men had Mikael's hand twitching

for the hilt of his own blade, but he resisted the urge. By the look of things, these men wouldn't need much provocation to start something. They were already eying Jaxon nervously, though to their credit, they stood their ground as the Gold ranker approached their line.

"Is this how Gurria greets its guests nowadays?" he asked, coming to a stop with a grunt.

Several of the soldiers exchanged glances. Meanwhile, Mikael swallowed as his gaze swept over the giant chamber. A gallery lined one side of the room, the balustrades of which were lined with more soldiers—but these held crossbows, all pointed directly at Jaxon. They seemed to be ignoring Mikael for now.

So much for peace.

His throat tightened, but he did his best to keep the panic from his face. That…that was a lot of men. Thankfully, according to his *Aura Sense,* most were normal humans, but there were still too many, even for a Gold ranker. And why hadn't he sensed them earlier? Were the stone walls too thick for his *Aura Sense?* Had Jaxon known they were waiting for him? The man seemed unnaturally calm—even his Aura was settled, though Jaxon always maintained an iron discipline over his soul.

"Jaxon Daniyal," a voice spoke from the other end of the chamber, where a circular table sat on a raised dais, surrounded by yet more soldiers. "Strange, I do not recall inviting you to my province."

A trickle of sweat dripped from Mikael's brow, despite the cool air inside the stone walls of the citadel. He tried to make out the speaker. There was a commotion amongst the men and women sitting around the table as one among them rose.

The blood drained from Mikeal's body and settled in his boots as he viewed the man with his *Aura Sense.* His soul *shone,* burning with a deep, powerful glow he had seen in only one other man—Jaxon Daniyal.

User: Arimus Shore. Rank: Gold. Body: 52. Aura: 38. Mana: 42. Abilities: Elemental Manipulation, Ardent Onslaught, Enforced Body, Might, Movement Surge, Shield.

A stone settled in Mikael's stomach as his suspicions were confirmed. Gold rank. He struggled to contain the chill that seeped through his limbs. Could this man be more powerful than Jaxon? And just what the hell was that ability, *Ardent Onslaught?* He would have to ask Jaxon later. If there even was a later.

The man himself was surprisingly young, no older than thirty. He wore a close-fitting tunic of violet cotton and carried a sword in a gold-clad sheath.

"The invitation mentioned I could bring my companions," Mikael spoke, drawing a glare from Jaxon. He offered the man an apologetic look.

Moving through his ring of guards, the man Mikael presumed to be the governor descended to the floor of the chamber. "Ah, you must be the famous Mikael Heaton," he said softly. Hands clasped behind his back, Arimus approached the line of spearmen. "You know, it's considered somewhat of an insult for guests to bring weapons into the house of a friend."

"Perhaps you'd like to try and take them from us," Jaxon rumbled.

To Mikael's surprise, a smile tugged at the governor's lips. "No need for that, I'm sure," he murmured. "Though, perhaps the Darkstrider would care to trade pointers with a young warrior during his visit. I heard you were a legend...*once.*"

Mikael winced. There was no missing the inflection on that last word. He jumped in before the dark look that flashed across Jaxon's face could be translated into words.

"I'm sure the Darkstrider would only be too happy, once we are settled," he said quickly. "And you have of course our apologies for the discourtesy. Though, I must apologise a second time…to whom do we have the pleasure of speaking?"

Laughter rasped from the man's throat. "They warned me you had a quick tongue." He dipped into a shallow bow. "My apologies, Mikael Heaton. I am Arimus Shore, Governor of Skarta. I was pleased to read that you had accepted my invitation for peace talks," he paused, eying the pair of them. "Though I'll admit, your sudden arrival at my gates has caused some…disquiet in certain quarters. You are rather early."

"A tradition from my world, I suppose," Mikael replied with a smile. "We call it being fashionably early."

The governor arched an eyebrow, before his eyes were drawn to the sword on Mikael's belt. "An interesting design," he murmured. "Very unlike that of your Highland companion. Another tradition from your world?"

It seemed like an offhand remark, but there was something in Arimus's tone of voice that immediately had every hair on Mikael's body standing on end. A tremor went through his core, a flicker of disquiet that would have revealed him to anyone watching with an *Aura Sense* ability, before he recovered his control.

"Oh, we have little use for swords in my world," he said with a laugh.

The governor continued to study him, the slightest of frowns on his lips, before turning to the soldiers and giving a wave. There was a rattle of steel as the spears and crossbows were withdrawn, followed by the thump of boots as the men retreated to the edges of the room.

"Some greeting party," Jaxon said with a smirk, "if I didn't know any better, I'd say you were afraid, Arimus."

"Maybe next time you could give us some forewarning."

"Just thought we would repay the favour shown by the last Gurrian visitors to grace our Highlands with their presence."

Silence fell as the two men glared daggers at one another. No one could have mistaken their mutual dislike. Mikael wondered if it was personal, or more of an instinctual rivalry between two powerful Pathfinders. Eventually, someone back at the table on the dais coughed. The sound seemed to break the tableau between the pair.

"It was with regret that I learned of the…misunderstanding with Lieutenant Ting," the governor said at last. "I take it he is dead?"

There was a flicker in Jaxon's eyes at the mention of his old friend's name. Mikael saw it as his opportunity to jump in.

"He is," he said quietly.

"May I ask how he died?" Arimus asked.

Mikael clasped his hands behind his back. "No."

The smile faded from the governor's face as, for the first time, he truly seemed to appraise Mikael. "I will admit, I had some misgivings, inviting you to my lands, Mikael Heaton," he said at last. "It has been many centuries since an Offworlder graced these halls. The last is not remembered fondly."

Behind the governor, whispers rose from the table, spreading through the hall, even to the rows of previously unflappable soldiers around the gallery. The term *Offworlder* didn't exactly pass for a compliment around here.

"So I have heard," Mikael held his nerve.

"I would consider it a gesture of goodwill if you were to tell me what became of Lieutenant Ting and the Force of eighty men that marched with him. It would go a long way towards mending relations between the Empire and the Highlands."

Mikael arched one eyebrow. "I had thought our invitation was about the *Empire* making reparations for the dozens of Malesie citizens killed by your rogue officer."

The governor's cheek twitched. "Yes, yes, of course," he

said quickly. "Ting was never meant to engage in any violence against the clans."

Beside him, Jaxon snorted. Mikael wasn't buying it either, but he flashed his friend a look that said *be quiet*, before returning his eyes to the governor.

"Yes, I had a chance to speak with him, before his passing. Strange, he seemed to be under the impression that your emperor wanted me dead." Mikael inclined his head to the side. "So imagine my confusion when I received your invitation."

His words were calm, but inwardly Mikael's heart was racing as he met the governor's gaze. Jaxon might believe in Gurria's sacred concept of hospitality, but tradition was a thin shield against the power of an Empire.

It was terrifying.

And strangely exhilarating.

Thankfully, the governor clearly wanted him alive. It wasn't difficult to guess why, but for the moment Mikael held his tongue, happy to watch the man squirm.

"Ting was clearly disturbed," Arimus said at last. "You must understand, there are many in this world who believe your kind to be destruction incarnate. The emperor sent those soldiers to ensure your safety. We are not so superstitious here in the empire, but we feared our neighbours to the north might do you harm."

Mikael feigned a sigh of relief. "I am glad to hear it. I would have hated to make an enemy of the Gurrian Empire." He paused, before continuing. "I'll be frank, Governor. I believe I have a lot to offer this world. Knowledge that could advance your civilisation by decades, if not centuries."

"Mikael…" Jaxon sounded a warning, but Mikael ignored the big Highlander.

It was pretty obvious to him why he had been invited here. Arimus Shore could talk about missing soldiers and forging fresh relations between Gurria and the Highlands until the cows came home—at the end of the day, the only reason either of them were still alive was because Mikael had something they wanted. Knowledge. Someone in a position of power clearly realised that Alson Ting and his soldiers hadn't been defeated by conventional measures. And they wanted a piece of the action.

The reaction of the governor did not disappoint. His face remained carefully neutral, but there was no mistaking his change in tone. "Such knowledge has proven dangerous in the past," he said, "it must be shared carefully, with the right people, lest we invite disaster."

"That's why I am here," Mikael paused, offering a smile. "To decide whether you can be trusted with that knowledge."

Arimus stood still, dark eyes regarding Mikael. "And what might a humble servant of the emperor do to earn such trust?"

"A new peace must be negotiated with the Highlands."

Was it Mikael's imagination, or did the governor's jaw tighten at those words?

"Of course," Arimus replied, his easy words dismissing the moment of tension. "The Highlands have long been a friend to the Empire. As a matter of fact, dignitaries in the capital are even now drafting a new peace treaty. We had hoped to share it with you during the Festival of the Satana, but I fear your early arrival has caught us somewhat unprepared."

"And when might it be ready?"

"These are delicate matters. Misunderstandings aside, a Force of Gurrian soldiers was killed. Eighty men. Such an event will cause unrest in the capital. The emperor must take care to balance peace with the fears of his citizens. However, I expect the documents will arrive in a matter of days. A week at the most."

Mikael pressed his lips together in a thin line. That would bring them perilously close to the festival. Arimus was clearly buying time for *something*, but he'd played his cards well. They couldn't simply turn around now that a peace offer was on the table—however fleeting it might prove to be.

"Very well, a few days it is," he said, feigning irritation. "Should we be needed, you can find us at the Dancing Donkey."

Mikael turned to leave, taking the opportunity to conceal his smile. It was an old negotiating technique, asking for more than you were really hoping for. But it was just as useful here as it had been in the bazaars of Istanbul. He didn't want to *leave*. Azaroth had made it clear he would not be getting out of Skarta without a fight. He needed those days to get the lay of the land and find these allies the Satana had promised.

But let Arimus think he had the upper hand. The man had every reason to be confident, after all. Mikael was only a Steel ranker. A child playing in the big leagues. Outclassed. Everyone expected him to run—perhaps even this Leviathan character playing against him.

Well, that was just fine. Let them underestimate him. He was not the innocent Mikael who had first arrived in this world, without his memories or knowledge of Earth.

He was Mikael goddamn Heaton.

They would never see him coming.

7

I sabel stood in the middle of an empty street, staring at the decrepit old building on the corner. A sign out front read in flaking paint: *"Silvercrest Manor"*. Clenching her fists, she cursed the mad old woman from Sarton.

It had taken her most of the day to track the place down. She'd started at Skarta's city hall, but when they had turned out to be entirely unhelpful, she had moved onto the library. Unlike most cities, knowledge in Skarta had always been shared and anyone could enter to peruse the books. The staff were even friendly towards her, though they were no more the wiser as to the location of this Silvercrest place. Their only suggestion had been to browse the section on local architecture.

Isabel would have consigned herself to a long and fruitless search, but for a happy twist of fate. Amidst the dusty shelves, several of Skarta's less fortunate denizens had taken to lingering during the day, and one had overheard her enquiry.

"Bit old for Mother Marta, aren't ya?" a man had asked, approaching only after the librarian moved away.

Isabel had frowned in confusion, but the man had just chuckled before offering directions and good luck.

Now she knew why. Whatever this place had been, it was long abandoned. The former manor loomed over the garbage-strewn street, its windows boarded over and plaster crumbling from its clay-brick walls. Even the roof looked to have partly fallen in on the upper stories. Whatever Vinnie thought she had seen, the old hag had obviously seen it wrong. Isabel wouldn't be finding anything in this old wreck.

She felt a pang of pain in her stomach. She might as well go and check whether Mikael and Jaxon had gotten themselves into trouble yet.

Yet she hesitated, peering at the shadows behind the broken windows. This was it. Her one fragile connection to her father. Godsdamn Vinnie. She didn't care. Hadn't. What did it matter that the man had abandoned her mother? Had abandoned her? What use did Isabel have for a father? She had her duty to the clan…

…except she knew now that was not enough. Not anymore.

She swallowed the lump caught in her throat. That had been her revelation, the thing that had pushed her beyond the limitations of Steel and catapulted her to Bronze.

That she could no longer *just* be a weapon for her people to use. Not if it meant losing everyone who mattered to her along the way. She needed to be more, a *shield* as well as a blade. So instead of the power to destroy, her soul had given her something else. *Healing Touch*. The chance to be something more.

And now…now Isabel was trying to live up to that potential. To learn more about her place in this world, about where she came from, what had made her.

Except she had fallen at the first hurdle. Casting one last glare at the abandoned manor, Isabel turned to leave—and caught a flicker from one of the windows. Furrowing her brow, she paused. The sun was beginning to set and this didn't look like a safe neighbourhood to linger in after dark. But if someone was inside…

Making a decision, Isabel pushed open the rusting iron gate and started up the path towards the house. This time she was watching for it. Sure enough, something moved behind one of the shuttered windows—as though a watcher had just pulled away from the boards.

Someone was home after all.

Probably more of Skarta's less fortunate, judging by the neighbourhood. Was that what the man in the library had meant? Well, if they had been in the building for a while, maybe they could tell her something about the manor's prior inhabitants. Any morsel of information that put her on the next step towards her father would be welcome.

As she approached the rotting steps leading to the entrance, the front door swung open with such force that it slammed into the wall behind it. Yet more plaster crumbled from the bricks. Isabel jumped, reaching for the bracer on her arm that unravelled into a whip.

She also reached instinctively into the world around her, where swirling knots of energy filled the air and ground and vegetation of the overgrown garden. Mana. The ethereal forces that made up everything in this world. It came to her easily, and her soul crackled as the fresh energy filled her. Heat gathered in her palm as she readied herself for a fight.

Sparks were just beginning to form when an old woman stepped into the fading light. Weathered and worn, she leaned against a twisted cane that had been repaired a few times too many. Two young boys shadowed her, tattered clothing clinging to their skinny frames. Their faces wore mean looks, and each held a cudgel.

"Away with ya!" the old woman screamed. "Find ya own

spot ta crash. This here place belongs to Marta. Ain't no shadow weaver gonna take it from us!"

Somewhat confused and struggling to understand the accent, Isabel raised her hands. "I mean no harm to you or your children."

"Ay, just what a shadow weaver would say," the woman muttered. "Before ya weave us into 'em cloaks!"

"I'm…ah, sorry, what exactly is a shadow weaver?"

"Ha, like you don't know!"

"I really don't," Isabel replied, her confusion growing. "Though I'm pretty sure I'm not one."

"Yeah?" the woman snapped. "And what if I don't believe ya?"

Isabel sighed. The woman was clearly mad. She contemplated walking away again. But…she still wasn't ready to give up on her hunt. Not yet. Not when a door to her father had quite literally opened in her face.

"Please, I was just wondering about the people who used to live in this place?" she ventured, choosing her words carefully.

The woman's scowl deepened. "Ain't never been no one but Marta and her kids." She spat on the steps leading up to the door. "And the shadow weavers trying to eat 'em."

Isabel hesitated. Could her father have been raised by this madwoman? It seemed unlikely. Who knew if she'd been in this place for a day, or a decade? With a sigh, she gave the woman a nod to show her gratitude and resigned herself to defeat.

The old woman's gaze lingered on Isabel as she turned to wander away. "Young thing, ain't ya?" she observed, concern on her wrinkled face. "Barely older than me oldest. Be getting dark soon. Streets ain't no place for a pretty face like 'at. Shadow weavers 'll get ya." She shuffled back a step and gestured to the door. "Suppose Marta could let ya stay one night. *One night*, mind! Already got enough mouths to feed!"

"It's okay, really…" Isabel said hesitantly.

"Mila!" the woman shouted, ignoring Isabel's feeble objection and shuffling back into the house. "Put another bowl on the table. We got a guest!"

Isabel sighed. But it *was* growing dark, and she noticed a few silhouettes shifting in the shadows of a nearby alley…

…perhaps spending the night in the rundown manor wouldn't be the worst decision in the world. Besides, maybe it really did hold clues about her father. Vinnie had to have sent her here for *some* reason. Striding up the creaking steps, she nodded to the pair of boys, who shot her still-suspicious looks, then stepped into the shadows of the old manor.

Arimus's fingers drummed gently against the table as he considered the sword they had dredged from the canal outside the gutted warehouse. To the naked eye, it appeared like any other weapon. Even beneath his *Aura Sense* there did not seem to be anything remarkable about the naked steel. And yet…

…something about the blade called to him. Each time he touched the worn hilt, he felt a jolt, as though this were some legendary weapon of power, drawn from the stories of the ancient Pathfinders and the Elohim. Removing its sheath had revealed a steel blade as dark as the night's sky. And the more his eyes lingered on it, the more unnatural it seemed. The way the firelight did not flicker from the steel, almost as though the blade was drinking the light. And its Aura, well, only living things possessed an Aura. Inanimate objects appeared as a plain grey to his *Aura Sense* and this weapon was no different… or was it darker, *emptier* than the rest of the table…

Arimus blinked, surprised to find his fingers gripped around its hilt. Shaking himself, he released the blade and stood, turning his back on the weapon. Its discovery was strange in one other important way. Plain as the blade was, the short length and guard-less design was unique. He had not seen it's like in any of his many battles.

Until the Offworlder had come marching into his meeting hall this morning, wearing a *matching* sword on his hip.

He clenched his fists as he recalled the encounter. First, Jaxon Daniyal had come striding into his citadel like the man owned the place—then the damned Offworlder had gone about dropping his little threats and warnings. The arrogant bastard was only Steel rank, but had faced Arimus like there was no difference between them. If Alyina hadn't *ordered* him to play nice…well, the Offworlder would have discovered just how vast the chasm between Steel and Gold was.

Though Arimus's doubts had only grown about her plan after the meeting. Mikael Heaton had seemed amenable to an arrangement with the Empire—but then there were these swords. One found at the scene of a resistance attack, a second of identical design in the hands of the Offworlder. The blade would certainly match the wounds left in the dead guards. It could not be a coincidence. He grimaced. It meant that the Offworlder—and most likely the Highland clans themselves— were involved with the Skartan Resistance. No wonder they had been so hard to put down.

Making a decision, Arimus crossed the room and pulled open the door. It was late and he had retired hours ago to his private residence—an old manor his father had purchased decades ago. A member of the emperor's inner circle, Jasper Shore had been placed in charge of Skarta's economic integration decades ago, when it had first become a province of the Empire. Arimus himself had been left at a boarding school in Gurria. To be raised as a proper gentleman, as his father liked to say.

Truth was that the man had little interest in his only child —except to berate Arimus for his choices. Apparently being a common soldier wasn't good enough for the Shore name nowadays. Never mind that soldiering was how they'd earned their position in the first place. Arimus was quite sure that his father had had a hand in his appointment as governor.

The night was silent as Arimus moved through the long corridors, the servants all having retired hours ago. There would be soldiers on the grounds, though, along with those on the gates. They would have to do.

Passing along the path through the gardens, he kept alert for the dozen or so men patrolling the grounds of the manor. There weren't many hiding places amidst the roses and manicured lawns, but he saw nothing but the occasional flicker of a shadow beneath the tall walls that surrounded the manor. He could have opened his *Aura Sense* and picked them out in no time, but he made for the gates instead.

He was satisfied to find the four soldiers alert and at their stations around the iron gates, which were the property's only entrance.

"Good evening, soldiers," Arimus said as he approached.

Despite their alertness, the men jumped at his announcement. Little wonder—at Gold rank, his *Enforced Body* was so finely tuned that he instinctively moved without so much as a rustle of clothing.

"Sir!" a man wearing the badge of a sergeant exclaimed, offering a salute. Arimus was pleased to recognise Sergeant Bolt, the man he'd placed in charge of finding the killer responsible for the four dead Pathfinders. "What brings you out at this hour?"

"Your investigation, sergeant," Arimus said without preamble. "Did your men find anyone who witnessed the attacks?"

The man shook his head. "Not yet, sir," he grunted. "You know these local sorts. Don't like blabbing on their own."

Arimus pursed his lips. That was certainly true. Though

perhaps if it *wasn't* one of their own? And it didn't have to be related to the attacks. Jaxon Daniyal and the Offworlder were staying at the Dancing Donkey—an inn located in a more lively part of town.

"Very well," he mused. "In that case, sergeant, I'd like you to take a couple of the privates off the gardens and ask around the local taverns. Don't mention the attacks, but if anyone happened to see a man in a tricoloured cloak out and about late last night…"

"Of course, sir," Bolt saluted and set off.

Satisfied that he'd done all he could for the night, Arimus wandered back through the grounds. The lanterns were burning low in their brackets as he returned to the manor, and the sound of his footsteps echoed loudly in the empty hallways. By the Emperor, he hated this place. So decadent, so wasteful. So very like his father. Arimus would rather a campaign tent and the comradery of a Legion on the march any day, than this pointless display of power.

The fire had burned low in its grate by the time he entered his personal chambers. Dismissing the dying flames, he made for his bed, when a voice spoke from the shadows.

"This is an interesting piece of work, my love."

Arimus spun, heart thundering in his chest, only to find Alyina Sorulus sitting in the chair he had occupied just half an hour earlier.

"Alyina," he breathed. "How did you get in here?"

A smile toyed at the woman's lips, but she did not answer. Instead, she gestured to the blade from the canal, which he had left on the table. "Where did you acquire such an interesting weapon?"

Exhaling his panic, Arimus found his heart did not slow as he approached the table. Alyina was wearing a dress of pure white. Its soft silk seemed to shine, highlighting the curves of her body beneath, even in the dying light of the fireplace.

"It was pulled from the canal after the attack on the warehouse," he rasped, before hesitating. Considering her fixation with the Offworlder, he decided not to mention Mikael's matching sword. Instead, he nodded to the blade. "Do you sense anything…strange about it?"

Arching one eyebrow, Alyina reached out and lifted it from the table. The dark steel rippled in the light from the embers. A flicker passed across her face and she frowned, but finally with a shrug she offered the sword to Arimus.

"Nothing but empty steel."

Licking his lips, Arimus accepted the blade. It felt strangely heavy in his hand this time. Looking from the sword to Alyina, a flicker of his anger returned as he recalled Jaxon Daniyal standing in the citadel.

"The Darkstrider is here with the Offworlder."

"Naturally."

He scowled. "You didn't think to warn me?"

Alyina's inclined her head to the side. "And why would I do that?"

Clenching his fist around the hilt of the blade, Arimus—

Suddenly there was darkness. A void pressed down on him, a hunger unlike anything he had ever felt, raging, burning. Screaming to be sated. Something within Arimus withered before that desire. His soul shivered as the void lashed at him, tearing away chunks of light.

Fear shook Arimus, threatening to overwhelm him...but he was no Copper ranker, and he gathered his power in response. A shield of burning Aura swept out, forcing back against the void. For a moment it resisted—before abruptly it collapsed, and went rushing from him, vanishing as if it had never been.

Arimus returned to himself with a gasp—and found himself pressed up against Alyina, the sword in his hand resting against her throat.

The princess had not moved an inch, but in his mind's eye,

he felt the power gathered within her, like a deadly blade ready to strike. She arched an eyebrow as their eyes met.

"I know I like a little spice, my love," she said quietly. "But let us not get too excited, shall we?" Slowly she reached up and touched a finger to the blade.

Arimus shuddered, allowing her to push the sword away. "I'm sorry," he rasped, staring at the weapon in his hands. "I don't know what that was."

Her lips were pursed as she studied the blade anew. "For a second, I felt something…"

"Like the void?"

Alyina nodded and he swallowed. Carefully, he replaced the dark sword on the table. "But now…it feels like nothing."

Licking her lips, Alyina moved alongside him. "Like any other normal weapon," she agreed. For a long moment, she stood studying the weapon. Finally though, she shook her head, as though to dismiss the entire incident. Her smile returned. "Are you sure it wasn't a flash of jealousy for my former lover, Governor?"

Arimus scowled. "Of course not."

There was a twinkle in her eye as she took a step closer, until her body brushed up against his. "Are you sure, my love?" she asked, fluttering her eyelashes innocently.

"The man is dangerous," he grated.

Her laugher pealed in his ears as she threw her arms around him. "Jaxon Daniyal, dangerous?" she giggled. "Once upon a time, maybe. But haven't you heard? The man lost his stomach for war years ago. He's a wolf with no teeth now."

Unamused, Arimus scowled and Alyina laughed louder, until he realised she was playing with him.

"Relax, my dear" she said, rising on her tiptoes to brush her lips against his chin. "Why don't you leave the scheming to me?"

"Because Jaxon Daniyal is a soldier, not a politician!" he growled. "You should let me deal with him."

"And just how would that look?" Alyina laughed. "The Governor of Skarta cutting down an invited guest?"

Her face hardened and suddenly Arimus felt the weight of her Aura crash down on him. Any scrap of anger he had left fled as an iron vice closed around his soul with the promise of an inexorable, inescapable doom. He bowed his head. Even Gold rankers had to answer to someone.

"We are Gurrian, Arimus," she said, her lips moving to his ear. "We look after our guests. Poisoning someone over a cup of tea is for lesser civilisations. Or did you forget that?"

Arimus's heart hammered in his chest. *She knew.* Months ago, when he had sent Lieutenant Ting to deal with the Highlanders, he had given the man a potent poison and ordered him to do whatever it took to deal with Jaxon Daniyal. The man had obviously failed—but knowledge of the incident had somehow reached the royal family anyway.

"Such a bad boy," Alyina chuckled, before waving her hand. "Oh, very well. You think Jaxon is dangerous? I think he is an opportunity."

"What do you mean?"

"As I said, he's gotten old. He doesn't want a war. He'll jump to whatever we say if we dangle peace in front of his nose."

"Does the Emperor really want peace with the Highlands?"

Alyina snorted. "Of course not," she said. "It would be madness to leave a violent, uncultured collection of clans on our border. But we must play nice, at least until the Offworlder comes around to our way of thinking."

"And what if he doesn't?" Arimus asked, thinking of the investigation he had just started into the Offworlder. If Mikael Heaton was already involved with the resistance, it seemed unlikely that he wanted anything to do with Alyina and her father.

Alyina smiled sweetly and fluttered her eyelashes. "You think he could resist my charm?"

"I think we should not underestimate him," Arimus insisted, not to be deterred.

Laughter rasped from deep in Alyina's throat. "Of course, my dear. Do not worry. I will go to the Offworlder. See if I can't soften him to our cause." Her face hardened, her lips narrowing into a thin line. "And if he refuses to see reason, then I will surrender them both into your tender care."

8

Twelve weeks before the Festival of the Satana

Conner Spears stood in the entrance to the longhall, taking a moment to compose himself. The low buzz of conversation carried from within, where various dignitaries and members of the public had gathered. The dignitaries would be there to plead the cases of various lords, merchants and traders to the Highking, while the public came to stand in witness. Some might have a petition of their own, but these would only be heard after those in line—if there was time.

There was always an order, a system, with his father.

He drew in a breath. Within the open doors, he could see the gilded decorations of the Highland throne room—such as it was. The walls were adorned with ancient tapestries, each telling the story of a different clan hero. There was Balidor, a Highking from the Fushore, whose clan had been forced from their lands by Detian raiders—the ancient enemy of the clans. Wielding their traditional greatsword, Balidor had forged an alliance with the other clans and led a counterattack, driving the invaders back to their broken islands.

Similar stories were depicted on the tapestries throughout the hall. Each a warrior. Each a leader. These men and women —whether Malesie, Fushore or Izolu—had led the Highlands against those who sought to destroy them. All of them heroes.

Conner felt a churning in his gut. His mind, as it so often had these past few weeks, returned to the battle for Sarton. To the screaming of men and women and the stench of blood, to the darkness that had clouded his mind. All his life he had dreamt of that day. To lead his people against a terrible foe. Yet when the moment had finally arrived, there had been no exaltation, no joy. Only terror. And pain. And sorrow and fear.

There was no glory in war.

He returned his gaze to the throne room. His father waited within. Denether, Highking of the clans. He let out a sigh.

"No time like the present," he muttered before stepping inside.

Lunden Marcs followed on his heels. For a moment, no one seemed to notice their approach up the centre of the hall. Then someone amongst the crowd shushed their neighbour. A slow, inevitable silence fell over the crowd as they turned to stare at the newcomers. Conner and Lunden approached the wooden chair that served as the Highland throne. The simple chair was a symbol in itself—that the man who sat upon it was not above the laws of their land, but rather an adjudicator of them.

Not that the man himself would agree.

Denether Spears sat, one leg crossed over the other, his enormous arms resting in his lap. Only Conner's father could manage such a stately pose while seated in that stupid chair. He wore a plain leather vest and heavy woollen leggings. The silver circlet resting on his head was the only marker of his rank, though an enormous greatsword did rest point down alongside him. His hair was grey with age and there were more wrinkles on his face than Conner remembered, but Denether's sapphire eyes remained as clear as the day he had sent his son away to be trained by the legendary Darkstrider.

"Father," Conner said, falling to one knee as he reached the throne. At his side, Lunden did the same. "I greet you as a loyal son and a warrior of the Malesie."

Two empty chairs were placed to either side of his father—one each for the chieftains of the Izolu and Fushore, though neither leader had taken their seats in a generation. The Fushore would never settle for a position beneath the Malesie, while the Izolu were entirely uninterested in the contest.

"Son," his father rumbled, voice echoing from the log-round walls, "welcome home." The king studied Conner. He did his best not to squirm beneath that gaze. "Rise," finally came the command. "I have had word from the Darkstrider. It seems we have much to discuss."

As if by some prearranged command, the dignitaries and other members of the public began to file from the room. Conner rose slowly to his feet, clothes rustling as he met his father's eyes. Neither spoke as they waited for the room to empty.

When the last of the crowd had departed, a man stepped from behind the throne. Conner offered Brandon Thorn, his father's bodyguard, a nod of greeting as he strode the length of the hall and closed the wooden doors, before retreating to his king's side.

"Welcome home, young prince," he said with a smile as he passed. "It is good to see you again. I will be interested to see what the Darkstrider has taught you."

Conner suppressed a smile of his own. Brandon was almost as famous as the Darkstrider himself. He had been Conner's swordmaster in his formative years, before Jaxon Daniyal returned to the Highlands and Conner's father bid the man to train his son. Conner had had mixed feelings at the time. Sure, the Darkstrider's prowess in battle was legendary, but for some strange reason the man had decided to retire to a nothing village in the south. Training with him meant giving up the luxuries of Furness and the keep of the Highking. Though…

"He taught me much, sir," he replied. "Like when to avoid a fight I cannot win."

The muscular bodyguard chuckled at the response. Conner's father was less pleased.

"Had I known I was sending you to learn from a coward, I might have paid your arguments more heed."

"Jaxon is not a coward."

"No?" Denether grunted. "He did not have the nerve to destroy the Offworlder when I commanded it. Look at where that has gotten us."

Conner's stomach tightened. "If not for Mikael—the Offworlder you speak of—Sarton would have been razed to the ground, its people killed." He paused, eyeing the man on the wooden throne. "*I* would have been killed."

"If not for the Offworlder, Sarton would have never been threatened in the first place."

"Jaxon believes it was only a matter of time before the Gurrian Empire turned their greedy eyes to our lands," Conner countered.

"Ay, on that much we are agreed." Grimacing, the king rose from his chair. "But it is a war our people cannot win. That is why I have spent the last decade trying to prevent it."

Conner frowned. "What do you mean?"

The king waved a hand. "The past is not important now," he replied. "Time is short. I already have reports of strange movements with the Legion stationed in Yarrin."

"Yarrin?" Lunden spoke up finally as Conner's fears returned in a rush.

"Ah, finally the man from Ressi speaks," Denether murmured, his gaze turning on the ex-soldier. "According to the Darkstrider, you came to the defence of my son in his hour of need. For that you have my thanks."

Lunden nodded. "The Darkstrider gave my people a second chance at a home," he replied. "A man must defend his home."

Lunden and those who followed him had once been bandits. Desperate men driven from their homes by war or poverty, they had followed a truly evil man by the name of Bjorn Cresswell. After Jaxon Daniyal had slain the man, he'd offered the others a choice: join him on his farm as workers or leave the Highlands forever. Every one of them had chosen the first. Then, when the Gurrian soldiers had threatened to slaughter everyone in the Sarton, they had made a last-minute charge that changed the course of the battle.

The king eyed Lunden, considering his words. "They say you were a soldier?"

The man nodded his agreement. "Fought to the end for Ressi."

"Yet you're alive."

Lunden's lips twisted into a scowl. "My squad was out scouting the enemy position. We thought we had them licked, but their leader was a crafty bastard."

"Aylina Sorulus," Denether offered. "A crafty witch indeed."

Lunden grunted. "Whoever it was, they had a few stragglers set a false trail, while the bulk of their Legions slipped around us. Cornered the prince against the river." His eyes stared into space, and it seemed the man was watching something no one else in the room could see. "Lost a lot of friends that day. Didn't think there was much point throwing away the lives of my squad on a lost cause."

Denether nodded. "And what now, then, Marcs?" he said softly. "The creature that consumed your first home turns its eyes on the Highlands. Will you fight for us?"

Conner shivered at the look in his father's eyes. There was a power there, a furnace that demanded others bend before his will. To his credit, Lunden Marcs met that gaze without flinching. He had faced powerful men before and would no longer be cowed.

"Did the Highlands fight for Ressi in our hour of need?" he asked instead. "When our king called for your aid? When my prince begged you?"

"We did not." Denether stepped up to the man, so they stood face to face. "I did not wish to throw Highland lives away on a lost cause."

The breath caught in Conner's throat. Silence fell across the chamber, so sudden he could almost hear a ringing in his ears. The Highking and the Ressian man stood staring at one another, each unmoving, unwilling to blink…

"I serve Jaxon Daniyal and the people of Sarton," Lunden said at last. "I serve the Voidlight." His face did not so much as flicker.

Conner could not see the man's Aura, but he imagined it must be a picture of chaos. And his father…he tensed, expecting the man to rage and scream.

To his surprise, Denether chuckled. "It seems even in his old age, the Darkstrider still inspires loyalty." Shaking his head, he sank back into his chair. "When we were young, I once watched him leap from the riverbank onto the deck of a Detian longboat. He was only Iron rank back then. Suicide, I thought—until the rest of my men followed him." Denether's ocean-blue eyes shifted from Lunden to Conner. "I never understood it. But I will use all the weapons in my armoury to defend the clans."

Conner nodded. "He and Mikael will journey south. They have an invitation from the Governor of Skarta. Jaxon hopes he can prevent war altogether."

"Suicide. You destroyed a Gurrian Force. Eighty men. The

Empire must present itself as all-powerful, or the continent would soon sunder back into its little city-states," Denether chuckled as he leaned back in his chair. "But what do I know? Still, if his efforts fail, we must be prepared."

"Mikael has a plan," Conner said quietly.

The king raised an eyebrow. "Oh?"

Puffing out his cheeks, Conner nodded. "That's why he sent me here," he replied. "To prepare the clans for war."

***

Fiachson Payne stood nervously outside the Longhall of Furness. Despite the spring sunshine, the air was still cool to the breath, the shadow of the ice-capped Ryntirax stretching long over the city. Men and women gathered around Fiachson, their faces nervous as they waited on the Highking's decision. From the older Roalin, his beard with more streaks of grey than red, to the ferocious Maria, to the grief-hardened face of Scott Sobotta, every one of them had come to Furness for one reason, and one reason alone.

Mikael Heaton.

To others, their loyalty might seem strange. Mikael was an Offworlder, after all, destined to wreak havoc across their world. And perhaps that was his destiny. That thought still weighed on Fiachson at times, when he doubted himself.

But in the end, they were Highlanders, all of them. They followed their traditions, leant upon one another in the hope of building a better world for those that came after—just as those who had come before had done. You could not judge a man on what one day might come to pass, but instead on his actions today.

And Mikael had more than earned their loyalty. For Fiachson, and many of the others, it was because he had believed in them when no one else would. The kid that was smaller than his peers, the man past his prime, the young woman with a fire burning in her soul. Mikael had seen their value and shown it to the world.

And the world had reacted.

Fiachson thought back to the day of the battle, to the light that had gathered over the bloody field when all was said and done. A multitude of Essence had manifested that day. A sight unlike anything seen in centuries. And Fiachson would know— he'd read more history books than anyone north of the Torviam Gulf. Such a manifestation had not been witnessed since the days of Balidor and Sordyx—the Highkings that had ruled during the sundering of the Detian Isles.

Whatever the reason for it, the outcome had been incontrovertible. Fiachson and every other Highlander who had fought and survived that day became Pathfinders. Wielders of power. Guardians of the Highlands. His heart still swelled with pride when he recalled the words Jaxon had asked them to speak:

"I swear to guard the weak against those who would do them harm, and fight evil wherever I find it. To never use my powers for personal gain, nor temptation to lead me down the path of evil."

It gave him a chill thinking of them. Though…his conscience struggled with what had come next: following Mikael into the night, hunting down the survivors of the Gurrian army. Cutting down unarmed men did not feel like fighting evil, even if those same men would have slaughtered them all if they'd had the chance.

But that was the loyalty Mikael inspired.

Even Conner had been persuaded to follow the Offworlder, though they had been bitter rivals before the battle. And now he stood within the longhouse, arguing for others to be given the same chance that Fiachson had been offered. Together they would become a force unlike any the Highlands had seen in generations.

If Denether could be convinced.

The others around Fiachson shifted, their heads turning as first Conner, then Lunden Marcs, emerged from the longhall. Fiachson held his breath. If he was honest, he did not expect much. Denether was well-liked among the Malesie, but he was a hard man. Much like Conner, he was a warrior with little patience for weakness.

That was why Mikael had asked Conner to make the proposal. If anyone could convince the Highking, surely it was his own son.

Conner's face was grim as he crossed the street and drew to a stop before the warriors of Sarton. He drew in a breath, scanning the faces of those gathered.

"He said yes," the words came at last. "The call will go out tonight." There was no sign of joy on Conner's face as he met each of their eyes, before his gaze turned to the great mountain peak that soared above the city. "May Ryntirax watch over us. Tomorrow, the war begins."

9

Present Day

Kat lingered in an alleyway near the front gates of the citadel, watching the entrance for signs of commotion. She had only gone a few blocks last night before doubling back to shadow the man with the golden eyes. Only when he'd led her to his inn had she returned to the hideout and reported the events to Jon—the man who had spearheaded resistance efforts in Gurria for the better part of a decade.

As expected, he'd been more than a little aggravated about how close she'd come to capture. Lost agents tended to lead to raided bases and further losses of personal. He was somewhat appeased by her impressive haul of coin, though. The more funding the better, given the Festival of the Azaroth was fast approaching.

But what had *really* appeased him was the news she brought of the Highland man calling himself the Voidlight. Especially the part about him wanting to burn the Gurrian Empire to the ground.

Which was why he had instructed Kat to learn more about

the man and any of his companions in the city. Thus, her lingering in an alley outside the citadel. That part was bound to be less welcome news for Jon. Because if the Highlander could walk so easily into the command hub of their mutual enemy, maybe his grievance with Gurria wasn't as grave as he'd made out.

For now though, the Highland pair were yet to reappear, and the walls of the stone building were too thick for her *Aura Sense* to penetrate. Hours had passed and there was still no sign of either of the men.

Bored and starting to sweat in the sweltering heat, Kat kicked a stone deeper into the alleyway and resettled herself onto the discarded crate she was using for a seat. What the hell were the two doing in there? It was common knowledge in the city that there had been tensions with the clans recently. Rumours were rife of a potential uprising, or that a war was imminent. Hell, she had seen the hatred in the man's eyes last night.

But if they were still inside...even she was beginning to wonder. Could they actually be stupid enough to bargain with the godsdamn Gurrian Empire?

Any bum from the streets could tell you how bad an idea *that* was. Most had been working men just a decade ago, with their own business and trades. All that was gone now, united under the banner of prosperity the Gurrians had flown when they'd first arrived as so-called-benevolent-conquerors.

Kat snorted.

If only someone had seen it sooner. Her father certainly hadn't.

He had been a tinker when the last of Skarta's armies had fallen twenty years ago, travelling the countryside mending pots and wagon wheels in towns too small for their own black-smith. That was some years before Kat's birth, but back then, most Skartans had been at best indifferent to the sporadic skirmishes of the three city-states. Tensions between Skarta, Yarrin, and Gurria were customary, after all. It was not uncommon for the pressure to boil over into war on occasion.

Those conflicts inevitably ended in new treaties, a few redrawn borders, and peace. Not this time. This time, Gurria was led by Orson Sorulus. A man determined to rule the world. With his Pathfinders, he had swept across the continent, bringing Skarta and Yarrin to heel and building himself an empire.

But what did one man's ambitions matter to a tinker? One king or another, it mattered little to the common people—or so he had told her as a child sitting fondly on his lap. When all was said and done, people would still need their pots fixed and troughs mended.

At first, his words had proven true. Five years passed, and another five, before Kat's mother had passed. The plague, they said. All ten-year-old Kat had seen was her mother wasting away before her eyes.

In the days and week after, she'd finally begun to notice the changes.

Her father had been good at his work. So good he'd caught the eye of their Gurrian overlords. A man named Jasper Shore had been the first to approach with an offer—to partner with her father and create a proper establishment, with new tools and supplies and assistants. Her father would no longer need to travel across the province offering his services—instead, his clients would come to him.

He was growing old by then, tempted by a stable life. Kat couldn't see why. The thought of travelling the land, every day setting her eyes on a new view, a new wonder, set her blood racing. Better than eking out a living on the stinking, sewage-ridden canals of Skarta, that was for sure.

Whatever the reason, he'd accepted the offer. For a time, the orders had poured in from around Skarta as people flocked to the new workshop. Kat still remembered sitting quietly on her father's worktable as he mended a barrel or pot or an old temple bell.

They were her last fond memories of her father.

Because not long after that, her father had noticed the changes around his workshop. New artisans whose work wasn't up to standard. Larger orders, rushed jobs, new suppliers, and materials arriving of poor quality. Suddenly products barely lasted a year without needing repair, rather than the decades they should have.

Being an honourable man, her father had gone to Shore, of course. People chose him because they trusted the quality of his work. But Shore had disagreed. The changes allowed them to lower their prices and provide their products to every citizen in Skarta—rather than just the better off.

The next day when her father had appeared for work, he'd been greeted by a clerk from the town hall and a contract to buy out his share of the venture. Shore had offered a piddling amount, and enraged, he had told the clerk exactly where to shove his papers.

That same night, Kat had woken to smoke and flames. Her father had barely gotten them out alive before the entire house was consumed. No one doubted who was responsible. But there was no proof. And when their complaints went ignored, her father had finally been forced to accept Shore's offer.

The money kept their heads above the canal waters for six months. But by then, every artisan shop in the city was owned by the Gurrians. And each and every one of the bastards had blacklisted her father from their establishments.

Her father had finally resorted to begging in the streets just to put food on their plates. He had died a few years later, a broken man.

And Kat had been left alone.

Those had been dark days. After a few months, she'd found

shelter in the broken-down home of a mad old woman, but she would never forget those cold winter nights huddled beneath a bridge or an alleyway, nor the pain in her stomach when the only thing she'd eaten for a week was a mouldy crust of bread.

She hadn't thought beyond her next meal those days, or where she was going to sleep that night. But one image, one face, remained burnt into her memory like her father's mark on one of his pots. *Jasper Shore.* He had left the city not long after that, his conquest of their miserable lives apparently complete—until just over a year ago, his *son* had been appointed as the Skartan Governor.

Her fists clenched at the thought. She had never lain eyes on the man, but she knew he was powerful. It didn't matter. His father had destroyed her life. One day soon, she would have her revenge. And it would not just be on the family that had stolen everything from her. She would destroy their whole damn *system.*

I've come to burn their Empire to the ground.

Kat jumped as a gust of wind swept through the alley, carrying with it sounds from outside the citadel. Her eyes hardened as the pair of Highlanders emerged from the gates.

Her suspicions immediately spiked. They'd both entered the belly of the beast—and now they had emerged alive. Either this Voidlight was a much smoother talker in the light of day compared with his ravings last night, or they really were here to broker peace.

Lips pressed tight, Kat slipped into the street after them. The crowds had thinned as the sun crept into the afternoon hours and its heat sent citizens indoors. As she crossed the arch of a bridge, laughter came from the canal below, where children leapt into the cooling waters. She almost paused to watch them, her heart twisting with a childhood of lost joys.

Instead, she continued over the bridge, eyes locked on the retreating backs of the Highlanders. The Gold ranker was an older man, his skin tanned and face all harsh edges, as though chiselled from granite. He wore the deep blue cloak of the Malesie clan and moved with smooth. The footsteps of a warrior.

She shivered. His age did not fool her. When she'd first set eyes on his Aura, a chill had swept over her and she'd almost abandoned the pursuit back at the inn. Gold rankers were not to be trifled with.

The Voidlight had donned the same checkered cloak of red, blue, and green from last night. He held his shoulders straight and moved with stiffer steps. Where his older friend seemed at ease in the sweltering heat, he wiped sweat from his eyes, clearly ill at ease. Not a warrior then. He wasn't even watching his surroundings—a perilous mistake in some parts of Skarta.

No one bothered the pair, however, on their return. Lips still twisted in distaste, Kat was about to call it a day. But when they reached the inn, instead of entering, her rescuer from the night before bid his companion farewell and continued down the street. Cloak drawn tight, he cast furtive glances over his shoulder as he crossed a bridge, heading in the direction of the marketplace.

"What's this, now?" Kat muttered to herself, her heart beginning to race.

She slipped from the shadows, racing to catch up. By the Elohim, he was terrible at this subterfuge stuff. All that looking around. If anyone else was following, they would have known he was up to something instantly. And he was never quite looking in the right place. Always at the vendors and people coming down the road—never the shadows, or the ones wandering the streets seemingly at random.

Though—damnit, the bastard could move! Turning a corner, she *just* caught the flickering of the multicoloured cloak fluttering around the next. Throwing caution to the wind, Kat gave chase, her worn leather boots blessedly silent on the bricked streets. If the golden-eyed man was meeting with someone, she needed to know who! What if they were planning their own attack on Skarta? Maybe the resistance really could find a common cause with him. But first—

Kat scrambled to a stop as she barrelled into a fresh street, only to find her quarry standing directly in front of her, arms folded across his chest.

"Hello, Kat."

The breath caught in her throat. She reached for her dagger, but the golden-eyed man was faster. In one languid movement, his hand snapped out to catch her by the wrist.

"Easy," he said with a smile that showed teeth. "I come in peace."

"Then let me go!" she spat, struggling in his grasp.

To her surprise, he obeyed, retreating a step and raising his hands to show they were empty. "Peace, as I said," he repeated, "but I need to talk to your boss."

"My boss?"

The Highlander raised an eyebrow. "Don't play dumb, Kat. I did some digging about our…encounter last night. Some kind of warehouse fire? Missing gold? Doesn't sound like the work of a common thief to me." He grinned. "Then there's the part where you're following me."

Blood was hammering at Kat's skull. She stared at the man, mind racing, trying to work out a path of escape. She couldn't take him to Jon. They'd both be killed if she walked in with a stranger. But if he really *was* working against the Empire…Jon wouldn't want her to antagonise him.

"What's your real name?" she asked, her voice soft. "My 'boss' likes to know who he's dealing with. Unless you really go around calling yourself 'Voidlight.'" She raised an eyebrow at that last part.

"I was being a little melodramatic, wasn't I?" He actually

managed to look sheepish. "Sorry, I thought I'd try the secret identity thing. Seems like you already found me though, so I suppose you'll find out soon enough. It's Mikael Heaton." He held out his hand in some strange custom she assumed was a greeting.

She eyed him closely. "Did you really mean what you said last night? About bringing down the Empire?"

"Every word."

"Good." She couldn't take him straight to Jon, but there were ways of getting word to him. "Then follow me."

10

The streets grew quiet as Mikael strolled after the girl, hands deep in the pockets of his breeches. It was the heat that had driven away the crowds, he assumed. He could understand why. The sun beat down on his head with a fury that suggested a thinner ozone layer in this world than Earth. The humidity only made the situation worse.

His clothing was less than ideal for the climate. The rough spun wool of the Highlands was harsh enough at the best of times—now his sweat had glued it to his skin like clingwrap. Truth be told, he still hadn't grown accustomed to the local clothing. He would have to pay a visit to the market at some point to see if cotton existed in this reality.

Thankfully, the street urchin kept to the shadows, rather than the open pavement where the sun was brightest. She'd been easy to spot that morning. Her Aura control was excellent for a Copper—to the point it was difficult to distinguish the denser glow of her soul from others in the crowd. But forewarned by Azaroth, Mikael had been watching for her from the moment he left the inn. Once he'd confirmed she was there, he'd put on a show of ignorance so as not to scare her off.

Then he'd waited until he could ditch Jaxon before initiating the encounter. After their meeting with the governor, the man was in high spirits and would have no interest getting involved with a local resistance group. Mikael didn't have that luxury. He already knew from his encounter with Azaroth that their efforts here would fail—at least as far as *his* life was concerned. Which meant he needed to be productive with the week they'd been given.

Meeting the enemy of his enemy would be a good step. Or at least, he hoped. Mikael wasn't so naïve as to believe these people would be his friends solely because they shared a mutual enemy. This world was superstitious, to say the least, when it came to his kind. He needed to be careful.

So, carefully, hoping it would go unnoticed by his keen-sighted guide, he reached out with his mind, to a world awash with colour. The greens of life beneath the waters of the canals, and the soft blues of sleeping souls inside the nearby buildings, even the violent red heat of the sun. Mana. He drew a little from each, filling his soul with its power.

Only when he felt his soul straining did Mikael exhale. Now he was ready. If the situation deteriorated, he would unleash hell and bolt.

They passed over another canal and entered a large plaza through an arch of the scarlet sandstone common around the city. This seemed to be the centre of the settlement, but with the distinct lack of shade in the open plaza, there was also a distinct lack of people. Which made the enormous bronze statue of a man rising from the middle of a fountain in the centre all the more striking.

Pausing in his stride, Mikael studied the effigy. Several soldiers stood guard around the fountain, but being cast in bronze, it was likely a replica. Back on Earth, a mould of plaster would have been created from the marble original, into which liquid bronze would be poured to form the copy. Yet the detailing was impressive, the beginnings of wrinkles on the skin, the shaping of muscles so fine it seemed the work could come alive at any moment. Like in the old Greek works of Earth, the man stood naked and proud, though there was one oddity about the piece of work.

"The…crotch is tarnished," he muttered.

Kat snorted. "That's the emperor," she explained. "We have a legend here in Skarta. If a thousand people touch his cock, the emperor's reign shall end in ruin."

"I see." Mikael raised his eyebrows. Now the soldiers made sense. "And how many would you say have, ah, done so?"

"Millions," came the street rat's reply.

She was probably right. He'd seen similar tarnish at statues in popular tourist spots—though the tradition was usually about good luck rather than the destruction of an Empire. An interesting development. Jaxon had said there was little dissent here against the Gurrians. The statue suggested otherwise. He could work with that.

They moved on, leaving behind the larger canals and entering again into the alleys and little waterways he had visited the night before. Here the shadows were deep, but the scent of rotting garbage and stale water became suffocating. It took all his willpower to keep the look of disgust from his face.

Despite the discomfort, he remained on high alert. Azaroth said he could trust this girl—which was good reason to be wary. His hand rested on his sword, where it remained hidden beneath the folds of his cloak, and his *Aura Sense* probed the shadows ahead.

There was plenty of life in these alleys, somewhat to his surprise. A dozen shades of green Aura lit up the shadows, where mould and fungi thrived in the dampness, and even the smallest of waterways teemed with tiny creatures.

Nothing as large as the leviathans from what he could see, thankfully.

After some twenty minutes of winding through the maze—at which point Mikael was well and truly lost—Kat finally led him to a tiny room concealed behind a pile of decaying wood. As they entered, Mikael prepared to speak, but the girl raised her hand.

"We should wait until Jon arrives."

"Jon?"

His heart sped up. He hadn't noticed her signalling anyone. The square maybe, when he'd been distracted by the statue? Maybe. Either way, it was impressive. And dangerous. He eyed the girl and allowed himself the possibility that she had *wanted* him to notice her. Could this all be a trap?

He dismissed the idea immediately. What was there for her to gain? And her surprise had been genuine. He was sure of it.

Even so, he stretched his *Aura Sense* to the limits of his perception, seeking the approach of another Pathfinder. Nothing. The only souls nearby were those in the adjacent buildings—

A man stepped through the sagging doorway.

Mikael stifled a curse. *How?* He hadn't sensed his approach *at all*. Eyes narrowed, he focused his ability on the newcomer. Still nothing. Not even the Aura of an ordinary man. If not for the fact he stood in front of Mikael, it would be as though he did not exist.

Fortunately, *Aura Sense* was not the only tool in Mikael's cabinet. He activated his Offworlder ability.

User: Jon Sorrow. Rank: Silver. Body: 21. Aura: 49 Mana: 20. Abilities: Aura Sense, Spirit Attack, Healing Touch, Mute, Ardent Onslaught.

Mikael felt a chill run down his spine. This man's Aura was on par with Jaxon's—despite being an entire rank lower. He also had several Pathfinder abilities that Mikael had never heard of. He would have to ask Jaxon if he knew about these *Mute* and *Ardent Onslaught* abilities. Jaxon had *Spirit Attack*, an ability that allowed a Pathfinder to attack another Pathfinder with their Aura, but Mikael had yet to really witness him using it.

"Mikael Heaton," the man spoke softly. "My name is Jon. It's nice to meet you. I hear that thanks are in order. Kat is a valued member of my team."

"Think nothing of it," Mikael replied with an easy smile.

He needed to tread warily here. He hadn't expected anyone nearly as powerful as Silver rank. Though to the naked eye, few would have considered this man a threat. With his bulging waistline and retreating hairline of blond locks, Jon was the antithesis of a warrior. His faded robes were torn and streaked with dirt, suggesting a life on the streets like Kat.

Unlike Kat, however, his skin was clean, and Mikael caught the distinct aroma of soap about his person. This was a persona he put on, rather than his true appearance. He wondered if Kat knew.

Regardless of his appearances, there was no mistaking the glint in the man's emerald eyes. The glint of a predator.

"I saw someone in trouble and decided to help," Mikael said easily. The man was still masking his Aura—presumably with that *Mute* ability—so Mikael needed to play along as though he remained ignorant to the threat standing before him.

"So I'm told." Jon took a step towards Mikael, so that they stood eye to eye. They were about the same height, but Mikael felt a tremor within, a flicker of fear. "Is that why you are here, Mikael Heaton? To help?"

"I'm here because the Governor of Skarta invited me."

"Oh?" Jon raised an eyebrow. "And why would he do that?"

"I won't pretend to know the mind of a man like the governor." Mikael smiled. "But if I had to hazard a guess, I'd say it's because someone powerful in the empire wants something from me."

Walking in a circle around Mikael, Jon paused to study him, before his emerald gaze shifted to Kat. "You can leave us."

The girl's lips thinned, but her Aura reflected nothing of her displeasure. She slipped out the door without even a goodbye—though with his *Aura Sense*, Mikael saw that the street urchin did not go far.

"You're an interesting man, Mikael Heaton," Jon murmured after the girl had left. "The Offworlder adopted by the clans. After all this time with them, perhaps you could settle a mystery for me. Some time ago, a Gurrian Force marched north into the Highlands. They never returned. Do you know what happened to them?"

"Of course. I killed them."

The man's thin eyebrows arched, wrinkling his forehead. "Really? Then pray, how did you leave the citadel alive? Arimus Shore is not a man known for his mercy."

Mikael eyed the man, aware of the peril of his situation. There would be no fighting back against those Aura abilities if Jon turned them on him. He could lie, but…this man clearly already knew things about him.

"As I said, they want something from me."

"It must be pretty valuable."

"I would say knowledge from another world is priceless, would you not?"

There was no reaction from the man—though given the level of control he seemed to exert over his Aura, that was little surprise.

"Priceless indeed," was all he said. Letting out a sigh, he stepped closer, so they were face to face, and reached out to rest a hand on Mikael's shoulder. "Do you know who I am?"

Mikael pressed his lips into a line. Another test, clearly, but what was the right answer? There was a weight to the hand on his shoulder, like a barely veiled threat, so with a shrug, he went with the truth. Or at least a version of it.

"If I had to guess? I'd say you are the leader of the Skartan Resistance."

It was the wrong answer.

The easy smile left Jon's lips as his fingers tightened on Mikael's shoulder. A flickering of fear swelled in Mikael's chest —then spiked to terror. Terror that flowed like ice along his veins, rending and tearing, until he struggled just to breathe. Those eyes…the power in those awful depths, this man could break him. With a snap of his fingers, he could take everything and everyone that Mikael had ever known.

"Tell me, Mikael Heaton," Jon said softly. "Just how you would know that?"

The Satana told me!

He wanted to scream it at the top of his lungs—but something, some tiny, fragmented piece of him resisted. Something was wrong. This fear…he shuddered, a groan slipping from his lips. His knees were wobbling more than the time he'd been forced to give a speech in front of half his school. That was a long time ago, just before his father…

"Speak or die," Jon Sorrow growled.

A knife appeared in his hand. It seemed comically small in his meaty hands, yet the blade glinted in the light of his flaring Aura, razor sharp…

His Aura!

A rasping breath hissed from Mikael's throat. He tried to retreat, but cold bricks pressed against his back. It helped. He swallowed, mouth parched as he struggled to gather his wits. This man…he was doing something to him with his Aura. Something to *make* him afraid.

Unfortunately, realising just what was happening did not

really help. Cold sweat dripped from his brow as he looked into those unforgiving eyes. Mouth pressed into a thin line, Jon raised the dagger.

Some instinctive part of Mikael reacted, his hand sliding through the folds of his cloak to clutch the hilt of his sword—

Warmth flooded him, a surge of…not power, but something else. An energy, almost like another Aura, like when Isabel had used her new ability to heal him after the battle for Sarton. The terror that had paralysed him fell back before this fresh force. He gasped and his knees sagged with the sudden relief.

Jon mistook it for a plea. "Last chance," he growled, pointing the knife at Mikael's chest.

"I made an educated guess!" Mikael blurted out, making his voice seem panicked.

Jon clearly didn't realise his ability had been neutralised and Mikael wasn't about to let him in on the trick. Though what exactly had happened…his fist tightened around the hilt of his sword. The sword that was not really a sword, but his construct, a powerful artefact reshaped by the magic of the Satana. Well, maybe it did something after all. That would require further investigation.

"I'm listening."

Jon towered over him, Aura still soaking the room. Despite the warmth of the sword, Mikael couldn't help but shudder at the depth of the man's soul. Jaxon's Aura was powerful, sure, but it had a raw edge to its depth, like he was using a sledgehammer to perform open heart surgery. But this man, the way he had drawn out Mikael's terror without him even realising what he was doing, he was a surgeon with a scalpel.

"Kat asked me about the Highlands, whether the rumours about war were true," he explained. "I already figured she worked for someone. I doubt those subjects are high on the list of interests for a local crime lord."

The man pursed his lips and seemed to consider Mikael's words. "Very well, let us say I believe you." He crossed his arms. "And let us say I *am* the leader of the Skartan Resistance. Tell me, Mikael Heaton, why should I let you leave this place alive?"

This time when the chill ran down Mikael's spine, he knew it had nothing to do with Jon's *Spirit Attack*. He swallowed, having no trouble feigning fear now. He might have found a way to neutralise the man's assault on his emotions, but this was still a Silver ranker he was dealing with, and in close quarters at that. The man could probably snap his neck without working up a sweat.

Damn Jaxon. Why couldn't he just *tell* him how to get stronger? *You need to find your place in this world.* What the hell kind of advice was that. He needed to progress, or he was going to remain a pawn in other people's games for the rest of his short life.

"Because the governor offered peace—but he's a liar. War is coming, for Skarta and for those I care about in the Highlands."

"You said the governor wanted your knowledge. Seems like a good reason to dispose of you."

Mikael offered a grim smile. "Except I have no intention of ever giving it to him," he said. "In fact, I plan on using every scrap of knowledge and power I have against them."

Jon studied him for the longest time, eyes burning into Mikael as though seeking some hint of deception. Mikael stared back, unblinking, until finally a grin broke out on the fat man's face.

"In that case, Mikael Heaton," Jon said, "I would say we have much to discuss."

11

Ten weeks before the Festival of the Satana

Seated in the stern of the little riverboat, Fiachson watched as the land drifted past. The trees were already beginning to thin as the valiant efforts of the polemen carried them ever upstream. The four men were impressive as they worked together, one near the stern with Fiachson, shepherding the craft around rocks and other obstacles, while the others powered the vessel forward.

Fiachson's gaze travelled down the valley, to where the distant point of Ryntirax could just be glimpsed above the verdant green of the spring canopy. Furness had long since disappeared from sight, but his gaze lingered on the mountain.

Ryntirax.

Like every clansman, its twisted horn had loomed over his entire life. Always watching. Accusing.

Ryntirax, who had once been the Sword of the Elohim, greatest of their order. The god who had ruled the Highland clans, fuelling their warrior spirit, demanding their sacrifice. And bringing shame to those who failed to pass his ordeals.

Even after his fall, those expectations had remained. For the longest time, Fiachson had counted himself amongst the inept. Too small, too weak, *too weird* to be a proper member of the Malesie.

Too busy in his books, others whispered.

But not now. Now he was a soldier of the Highlands. A follower of the Offworlder. The Voidlight, as the other members of their team were now calling Mikael. Fiachson felt a swell of pride. He was amongst the elite—one of those who had stood against a Gurrian army and *won*. And he had been rewarded with an important task.

The others from the team had remained in Furness to help train the budding Malesie army, which would be led by Lunden Marcs. But Conner and Fiachson were to bring the other clans to their cause. Conner was even now sailing for Pine Harbour, where he would meet with the Fushore Chieftain. Fiachson did not envy him—the Fushore were great rivals to the Malesie and would resist any suggestion for their peoples to fight side by side.

Fiachson had the easier mission, though there were still butterflies aplenty in his stomach whenever he considered it. He was headed upriver, into the steeps of the endless mountains, on his way to speak with the Izolu.

His father's people.

A lump lodged in his throat as he thought about the man he had never known, yet who had shadowed his entire life. Raiders had killed Hanequin when Fiachson was just a babe.

His gaze returned to the distant Ryntirax. The horn of the Highlands. He had read every story of the ancient Elohim, every interpretation of the god's fall. Conceit, ultimately, had led to his death. Ryntirax, it was said, had collected power only for himself. Jealous, his brother had gathered others amongst the Elohim who desired Ryntirax's strength. A terrible battle had ensued amongst the gods, sundering the lands and costing the lives of untold millions.

Ryntirax had finally fallen here, amidst the broken mountains of the Highlands. As he lay dying, he had looked around and finally saw what his greed had cost, how the world had suffered for his folly.

And so the immortal Ryntirax had done what no other had done before him. He had released his power, allowing his Aura and Mana to wash across the Highlands, bathing the land in a flood of magic unlike anything ever witnessed in this world. The land had been healed, and Ryntirax turned to stone, becoming the mountain that stood alone amongst the verdant valleys of the Malesie.

In the end, Ryntirax had given his life for the world he had sworn to defend. Some claimed it was only out of spite, to deny his brother the power. Fiachson did not know whether that was the truth. But as he watched the mountain disappear around a bend in the valley, he wondered if this would be his last glimpse of its icy peak. If he followed Mikael's plan, and events unfolded as the Offworlder expected, he would not return by this route.

Letting out a little sigh, he sank into his seat and turned to his mother. Maisiwan Payne, the blacksmith of Sarton, sat nearby, back resting against the hull of the boat. After his father had fallen, she had become a warrior herself, helping drive the Detian ships from their waters. She was everything Fiachson was not—much to his shame. All rippling muscle and harsh edges, she was a Steel ranked Pathfinder like Conner and Isabel and even Mikael now.

Today his mother's scarlet eyes were distant, watching the trees, just as he had been until now. Fiachson wondered how it must be for her, returning to the Izolu after all these years. He swallowed. Few amongst the other clans had visited their territory, due to its isolation high in the rugged land to the east.

Even the hardiest of Malesie adventurers were known to become lost in these mountains—only for one of the Izolu to appear and lead them to safety.

They would not have that problem, or so Fiachson hoped. His mother claimed to know the way—though she had spoken little of their destination so far. She had been strange, since the battle for Sarton. He'd hoped that seeing him fight, or his ascension to Pathfinder, would mean she finally saw him as a man, but…

He sighed. At least Mikael saw his worth. The Offworlder was gambling everything on their success. Even as he recalled his friend's words, Fiachson felt a sense of urgency. Mikael thought the governor's invitation was most likely to be a trap. If something went wrong—which if he was being honest, seemed to be a regular occurrence with Mikael Heaton—the Offworlder was relying on Fiachson, Conner, and Lunden to come through for them.

"That's a strange look on your face, son," his mother spoke up, stirring from her own thoughts.

"Just thinking about…about how it'll be…meeting Dad's people." He stuttered, caught off-guard. "Did you go to his homeland very often?"

They'd rarely spoken of his father. He had never understood why. But the look that came into his mother's eyes whenever he mentioned Hanequin…it hadn't taken the young Fiachson long to learn not to mention him. Now though, he was surprised to see a smile touch his mother's lips.

"Just the once, actually," she said softly. "Hanequin…he loved his people, but he wanted to see more of the world." Her eyes grew distant. "They're a peaceful people, for the most part."

Fiachson sat up straighter in his seat, his interest aroused. "And they're really nomads?"

"Some."

"And what do they think about us?" he quizzed, before clarifying at his mother's frown. "About the Malesie?"

The smile returned. "They don't think much about us, to be honest."

"What do you mean?"

"The Izolu pay little attention to the comings and goings of lowlanders."

"Lowlanders?"

His mother chuckled. "That's what they call the other clans."

Fiachson raised his eyebrows. "But what about the Highking? If they think so little of us, why did they bother voting for Conner's father?"

"It did not sit well with them when the Fushore refused to send their warriors against the Deti when they raided our lands," she answered, her face hardening. Little wonder. His father had died in those attacks. "The Izolu have fought their own battles with the Deti over the years. They consider the islanders their mortal enemies."

"Do you think they'll listen to the Highking's command?"

"Not if you put it to them like that."

"Why not?"

"The Highking has little real authority. The role was only ever to fairly adjudicate disagreements between the clans. Given their isolation, the Izolu aren't really worried about that."

Fiachson grimaced. "But we need them."

Maisiwan did not reply for a while, though the twist of her lips said she was thinking. "Your father's people are no fools," she answered at last. "They may not raise great cities or build libraries like our neighbours to the south, but they are a… studious people. Philosophers. Hanequin used to study the stars, the patterns he saw in the sky, how they changed over the years."

Fiachson's head perked up at the mention of his father. He barely dared to speak, lest his words snap his mother from the memories and she stop…

"He took me from the village one night, when we were still courting, and told me to look at the sky over Ryntirax. I asked him why, but he shushed me." There was a softness to her face as she told the story, one Fiachson had rarely seen. "We sat there for an hour, cuddled beneath the blanket, watching the stars, before it appeared."

"What?"

"The Devil's Maelstrom." Her smile grew. "A comet. For three days and nights it hung above Ryntirax like another sun in the sky. But we were the first to see it dawn."

"How did he know it was coming?" Fiachson breathed. His mind was already racing ahead. Had his father read the prediction in a book, perhaps, or been told by a Seer?

"Your father had been studying his histories. The Izolu record much of the past in song. There was one record in particular that fascinated Hanequin. The sundering of the Detian Isles a thousand years ago, when a second sun dawned over the land. We understand so little about that time, but the story reminded him of another tale—one from his father's time, of a second light in the night's sky, as bright as the moon."

Fiachson frowned, trying and failing to understand the connection.

"Curious, he went further back, and found another reference. And another, and another. He traced them back a few centuries and began to notice a pattern between the sightings. I will not pretend to understand his calculations, but from the positions of the stars recorded in their tales, and those he had been observing, he managed to calculate the comet's return down to nearly the hour."

"That's…incredible," Fiachson breathed. "How long ago was this?

"Thirty years ago, must have been." She gave a wry smile. "We were so young back then. A pair of love struck fools."

Fiachson swallowed at the distant look in his mother's eyes. He tried to imagine the study his father had put into such a project, the research and calculations. Could he replicate it? If only… "Do you…do you have any of his notes?"

He held his breath, expecting her to turn him down, like she had with so many other inquiries about his father. Instead, she smiled.

"Histories are important to the Izolu," she said, and while there was sadness in her voice, it was…different. More hopeful. "Every one of their children must learn them. It would have hurt Hanequin greatly, knowing he passed before he taught you his." She paused, turning again towards the mountains. "I do not know his songs. But perhaps, now we are coming to them, one of his people might teach you."

A lump lodged in Fiachson's throat. He followed her gaze to the lands ahead. The stone blocks of a watch tower rose in the distance, where the last of the trees gave way to alpine tussock. That would be Eastmore, the last outpost of Highland civilisation. Beyond, the mountains were like a wall across the world, so imposingly vertical, it seemed impossible that anyone could pass them.

Yet somewhere amidst that stone and ice, his father's people waited. His *past* waited.

"I think I'd like that," he said at last.

12

Present Day

Isabel sat at a long mahogany table set for some thirty people in the middle of a dining room larger than most houses back in Sarton. She had been given the position of honour—or so the old woman claimed—right in the centre of the table, with fifteen boys and girls squeezed in to her left and right. Isabel didn't feel particularly honoured. In fact, she was wondering whether she had bumped her head on a brick outside and was now trapped in some kind of fever dream.

The laughter of thirty children—none of which could be older than fifteen—rang from the high ceilings, where cobwebs as thick as drapes covered the plaster. A chandelier had hung there once, but all that remained of it now were the twisted wires that had once held the crystals and candlesticks. The flickering lanterns cast the shadows of her dinner mates dancing across the crumbling plaster walls.

"More food, Isabel?"

Isabel glanced at the girl next to her, who held out a stained porcelain plate with a few scraps of meat and old tubers. Her stomach rumbled. She had hardly eaten after seeing the condition of her dinner mates. How could she? The girl was more skeleton than flesh, her cheeks sunken and her eyes like little stars in her pale face. Yet she wore a smile as she offered the last of her food to Isabel.

"Ah, it's okay," she said, waving for the girl to eat.

Her eyes brightened and she set about devouring the scraps.

Isabel sighed, guilt settling in the pit that was her stomach. She was uncomfortably aware of the silver pieces in her wallet —and the gold coin tucked beneath the sole of her boot. It would be enough to feed these kids for a month…well, maybe a few weeks, she reassessed, considering the way the kids had devoured the mad old woman's scavenging's.

She would offer Marta a silver for the meal, Isabel resolved. The rest she would need for if she lingered in the city. Hopefully Jaxon and Mikael were already on their way back to the Highlands tonight after negotiating a successful peace agreement. She almost snorted. That was a fever dream for sure. Though Mikael and that silver tongue of his…

Her stomach twisted thinking about the Offworlder. A pang of yearning, a flush of warmth to her cheeks as she recalled a certain night beside the flames of the winter festival…

"…and the baker on Golem street, if ya help 'im keep an eye out for thieves, he'll slip some food for ya." The boy beside her was recounting his tales from the street.

Isabel nodded earnestly when she noticed him watching her, expecting a reaction. Grinning, he dove into a fresh tale about the time a nobleman had given him an entire silver piece for guiding him back from the bar one drunken night.

It was a strange sort of civilisation, this city of stone. Merchants always spoke about the glories of the Empire as they passed through Sarton. Of the wonderful roads that carried their goods so efficiently about the continent, the riches of choice when it came to clothing and food and materials. And it was true. There were no mansions like this in the Highlands—and certainly none in such a state of disrepair.

But nor did children go starving in Sitton. Even after her mother had died and Isabel was on her own, others amongst the community had cared for her, offering shelter and food and kindness…

Isabel clenched her fingers until her nails bit into flesh—an impressive feat with her *Enforced Body*. She had not come here to address the injustices of a civilised society. A Pathfinder she might be, but she was still a speck compared to the might of the Gurrian Empire.

So she looked around the room instead, trying to imagine what it must have been like before being abandoned by its prior owners—whoever they might have been. She pictured the mahogany table set with satin cloth and silver cutlery, the chandelier shining brightly, casting aside the shadows, and a young family sitting around the table talking about trade routes and the local gala…

Isabel snorted to herself and decided she preferred her present company.

Then jumped in her seat as a door banged open and a young woman marched through. Marta, who sat at the head of the table, looked around at the intrusion, a scowl deepening the wrinkles on her face.

"Kat!" she called. "Girl, ya late for supper!" Rising, she started bustling about the table, gathering whatever morsels had escaped the attention of the others. "Why didn't ya tell me you was coming? Look at 'em bones. Old Jon not feeding you…is he? The glutton, keeping all that food for himself."

Isabel missed the rest of her muttering as her attention was drawn to the newcomer. She was older than the other kids, closer to Isabel's twenty odd years if she was not mistaken.

Kat made it halfway down the table before she noticed Isabel. The easy smile fell from her lips, her jaw growing hard.

"Who's the new girl, Marta?" she asked, voice hard as iron.

"Dunno," Marta muttered. She was still rummaging about the table and did not seem to have noticed the change in the girl's demeanour. "Showed up this afternoon asking strange things—*there!*" She made Isabel jump again as she pushed aside one of the boys to make space beside Isabel. "All set. Now sit and eat, before the shadow weavers make a meal of ya."

Kat eyed Isabel, before relenting with a nod. She moved around the table and took her place, staring all the while. Did they not teach people that was rude here? The girl was acting like Isabel might pull out a blade at any moment and murder them all.

Maybe she saw Isabel as a threat to her place in the… would this be an orphanage? Travellers passing through Sarton had occasionally offered to take Isabel south to one of those places, where she would apparently have been taken care of. If they looked anything like this, she would be forever thankful that Dario, the village baker, had taken her under his wing instead. Still, if this girl thought Isabel was trying to force her out, there was no reason for tension.

"My name is Isabel, by the way," she said with a smile.

"Kat." Was all the girl said.

Still watching Isabel from the corner of her eyes, she began to eat. Isabel frowned. The young woman was tense as a spring, her fists clenched around the knife and fork like she was preparing to use them in a fight. Clearly Isabel's presence unsettled her.

Pursing her lips, she tried again to ease the girl's fears. "Sorry for the intrusion. I really didn't mean to be here, but…Marta insisted."

Still nothing. With a sigh, Isabel surrendered to the inevitable and returned to listening to the young boy—who was now ecstatic to be able to tell his tales to not just one, but *two* older girls.

Another half hour passed before the kids began to yawn and Marta declared it was bedtime. She herded them out of the room, Kat included, before returning for Isabel. Rising, she moved towards the woman, intending to give her the silver coin and take her leave.

"This way, this way," the old woman said instead, before Isabel had a chance to speak. "Had the kids keep a corner clear. Know how ya older girls like your space. Come on."

Isabel tried to object, but Marta pretended not to hear. After facing down bandits and soldiers and Pathfinders, Isabel found herself at a loss as to what to do as she was pushed into a dark room.

Thankfully, the eyes of her *Enforced Body* adjusted quickly to the dim light and she saw at least a dozen children sleeping beneath several scraps of blanket. Most were sharing, but there in the corner a single blanket lay untouched.

"Good night, luv," the woman declared. "Break ya fast at first light, then off with ya, you hear!" Despite her words, there was a jovial tone to Marta's voice as she shuffled from the room.

Then she was gone, leaving Isabel alone amongst the sleeping bodies. With some hesitation, she seated herself in the corner. Looking around, listening to the sleepy mumblings of the children, she felt the inexplicable beginnings of tears.

This...this could have been her.

Anger touched her, and she found herself clenching her fists again. Why was this world so cruel? This city, this Empire, it was meant to be the pinnacle of human civilization. Surely it didn't have to be like this—the less fortunate clawing at the detritus of the powerful to scrape together some form of existence. There had to be a better way.

Exhaling, Isabel wiped the tears with the back of her hand.

A part of her, the part that had awoken when she had seen Jaxon dying, wanted to do more than just protect these youths. She wanted to heal them, make a better world for them.

But for all her power, what could she do? There was no sickness or injury for her *Healing Touch* here, and even if there was, there were too many for her fledging Aura anyway. This city, she could spend a lifetime burning her own soul and still be nothing but a drop of water in the endless ocean of suffering.

Sitting in the darkness, listening to the whimpering of the hungry children, Isabel Fields felt as she always had. Ever since the night her life, and her future, had been burned away.

Helpless.

She rose suddenly. Her chest was tight and she struggled to breathe. She couldn't stay in this room a second longer. Silently she slipped between the sleeping bodies, back into the hall. There, she finally exhaled. Her heart was pounding. She clenched her fists and sucked in a deep breath.

Shivering, she straightened. The hallway was silent. It ran the length of the dining room, with the doors on her left opening into the great hall. Those on the right, she assumed, held other sleeping children. She recalled their happy, starving faces from around the table. So many. She swallowed, sorrow rising in her throat. If this was the Empire, she wanted nothing to do with it.

Isabel had just resolved to leave and her father be damned, when she sensed the shifting of air behind her. An ordinary person might not have detected it. And without an *Aura Sense* ability, Isabel was blind to the souls of others. But her *Enforced Body* did enhance her normal senses.

Enough that she spun in time to block the dagger that slashed for her throat.

Her eyes widened as she caught the wrist of her assailant. It was the girl from the dining room. Kat. "*Wha—*"

The question was on her lips, when the girl released the dagger, allowing it to fall—only for her left hand to snatch it from the air. Snarling, she drove it at Isabel's stomach.

Her *Enforced Body* might have been tough enough to survive the blow, especially from the awkward angle, but Isabel didn't take any chances. Releasing the girl, she twisted out of the way. Pathfinder or not, the blade would still cut. Perhaps not *badly*, but then again, this girl was clearly more than she seemed.

But so was Isabel.

As the dagger slashed through the space where Isabel had been, she threw a blow of her own. Caught off-guard by Isabel's speed, her fist struck Kat full in the chest, doubling her over. The colour drained from the girl's face as she wheezed, while the dagger struck the ground with a *thud*.

Plucking it from the floorboards, Isabel advanced. "What the *hell?*"

Eyes watering, Kat clutched at her chest. Her mouth opened and closed as she struggled to draw breath. Isabel rolled her eyes. Jaxon hit much harder than that when they trained together. Still…

Stepping forward, she laid a hand on the girl's shoulder. Kat flinched, but Isabel grasped her tightly, turning her vision inwards. She couldn't see Aura like those with *Aura Sense*, but she could still use her own. Her soul had brightened these past few months, as she practiced Jaxon's meditation techniques.

Gently, carefully, she teased the swirling light of her Aura and let it flow through her fingers into the choking girl. Immediately, Kat drew in a great gasp of air, then began coughing as her lungs convulsed with the fresh breath.

Crossing her arms, Isabel gave her a moment to recover.

"You're a *healer?*" the girl said finally, looking up at Isabel from the floor with tears in her eyes.

Isabel's lips thinned into a line. "It's a recent development."

Drawing back her cloak, she showed the girl the blade on her hip. "I'm more of a warrior, usually."

Kat flinched, freezing halfway to her feet. "Please, don't kill them." She gasped. "I know Marta and the kids aren't meant to be here, but they have nowhere else to go!"

"What?" Isabel blinked. "Why would I want to kill them?"

"Why else would a godsdamn *Bronze ranker* be in Marta's house?"

This time Isabel didn't respond immediately. She stared at the girl. Kill them all? She said it as though that was not something out of the ordinary here. A Pathfinder showing up and slaughtering a house full of children. She shuddered. What kind of monsters…

"I'm not here to kill anyone," she said softly when she saw the girl still had the wide-eyed look of someone about to do something reckless. "And wait, how did you know…" Her eyes widened. "You're a Pathfinder as well, aren't you?"

"Barely," Kat muttered.

"Copper?"

The slightest nod. Her fingers drummed rhythmically against the hilt of her sword. Now it all made sense. With an *Aura Sense* ability, Kat would have noticed Isabel's power the moment she set eyes on her. It wouldn't have even been hard. Isabel had neglected her Aura for years, preferring to train her Body and Mana. She was getting better, but she hadn't even thought to conceal her strength in a place like this.

"How did it happen?" she said after a while. "Your Essence manifestation, I mean."

The girl stared at her, eyes wide, as though she had expected anything but that question. Isabel understood that well enough. An Essence didn't just appear at your fifteenth birthday party. Some form of trauma was usually involved. Leaning against the wall, Isabel sank to the floor and drew her knees to her chest.

"For me, if was my mother," she said quietly. "They could never figure out exactly how the fire started, you know? Most said it was one of her clients." She shrugged. "I didn't see anyone that night. All I remember was mum shaking me awake and dragging me from my bed."

Kat was staring at her now with wide eyes. "She…"

Isabel shook her head. "Last I saw her, she was shoving me out the second storey window. Just as…" she trailed off with a gesture to her face, where the flames had licked along her chin and neck.

The same flames that had consumed her mother.

"Broke my arm in the fall, but I hardly felt it. I just lay there and watched my home burn. The Essence appeared soon after, this big light in the sky. I don't even remember accepting it."

"That's…" Kat swallowed visibly. Moving to the opposite wall, she slid to the ground. Silence stretched between them, deep as the darkness inside the rotting mansion. Nothing disturbed the night now, as in the rooms nearby, the children slept.

"It was my father for me," Kat said at last, voice barely rising above a whisper. "He…used to be someone in this city. The Gurrians took everything from him. But he wasn't the kind of man to bend to evil. He worked odd jobs around the city, repairing old wagon wheels others said were unfixable. Changing out drainpipes. Whatever he could find. And when he couldn't make ends meet, he begged for coppers on the street."

"It was the odd jobs that killed him. The man who took his business didn't like the competition. Dad was trying to teach me the trade. One day we showed up for a contract, but instead of the shop owner, men with clubs were waiting for us. They beat him badly. I tried to stop them, but…" She shook her head. "What could a twelve-year-old do?"

A tear streaked her cheek. "He was still alive when they stopped. I ran for help, but…" She swallowed. "The only doctors left for the likes of us are the clinics. They told me to bring him there. By the time I got back…"

Kat gave a soft shake of her head.

"I screamed and screamed and screamed…" She shrugged. "Until I guess the gods heard me."

Isabel gazed into space. That was the story. That an Essence was a gift from the gods for enduring such pain. She didn't know if it was true anymore. All she knew was that the suffering had not stopped since the day her mother died.

For so long, she had not thought it mattered. That she deserved the pain. Afterall, there must have been something wrong with her, if her father did not want her, and the gods had seen fit to take her mother as well. The pain became a part of her, something that gave her strength. It let her keep everyone else away, so she could concentrate on what was important. On becoming a weapon.

But it didn't have to be that way. If she could heal others, surely she could heal herself.

She would start with her father. She would look the man in the eyes and *show* him it didn't matter that he had left. *She* still mattered. She meant something in this world.

"So why *are* you here?" the other girl asked at last.

"I'm looking for my father," she answered truthfully. "I was told I would find him here. Or…perhaps that he *used* to live here." She looked around. "But…so many kids. If my father was one of them…" she trailed off with a shrug.

Kat, however, had a thoughtful look on her face. "Do you know his name?"

"Mum would never tell me." Isabel furrowed her brow. "He…wasn't around."

"What about a painting?"

"I…had a drawing." Her mother had sketched it for her

when she was just a girl and wouldn't stop asking about her father. It was her only memory of him. But… "I lost it though, in the fire."

"So you know what he looked like?" Kat continued, unperturbed.

"Yeah. That, and this house were all I had to go on." She sighed. "I know, I don't know what I was thinking."

To her surprise though, the girl rose and offered a hand. "Don't give up yet," Kat said with a smile. "Marta keeps… well, she keeps good records. You might not be at a dead end just yet!"

13

Mikael yelped as Jaxon's greatsword hissed for his head. Only at the last moment did he manage to duck, twisting away with a piece of gymnastics only made possible by his *Enforced Body*. A grin appeared on the lad's face as he brought his shortsword around for a strike of his own—

"*Ow!*" Mikael howled as the flat of Jaxon's blade slammed into his elbow. The shortsword struck the sand with a dull *thud*.

"Thinking too much again," Jaxon grunted.

He rested his sword against his shoulder, waiting for Mikael to recover. The Offworlder shook his hand, muttering words beneath his breath that Jaxon did not recognise, but which he assumed were curses from Mikael's world.

Jaxon stroked the stubble on his chin. The boy was getting better, but he still struggled to comprehend the ability of his *Enforced Body*—or that of his opponents. He should have avoided the first blow with ease. And he should have known Jaxon had the strength to reverse his swing and bring his blade back around. But Mikael had had his abilities less than a year. He was used to training with the likes of Isabel and Conner, who had first developed abilities as children.

They were sparring on the mudflat of the river, purportedly so they could train outside the city. The governor had made it clear that their permission to carry swords within the city should not be abused, so the excuse was as good as any. It wasn't a bad spot either. The mudflats were more sand than silt, meaning the ground was firm and did not slip beneath their feet. And there was plenty of room to move in the shadow of the city walls—essential given the heat of the sun at midday.

It also gave them the chance to examine the city's defences. The parapets of Skarta were nothing like the behemoths the emperor had raised around Gurria, nor the old fortifications in Yarrin, where Detian raiders had once been a constant threat. Old Skarta had seen less conflict than either throughout its history, and when it had, the river had formed its primary line of defence. But the province was now entering its fifth year of drought, and the once-mighty river had been reduced from numerous intertwining channels to a single, narrow stretch of water in the centre of the old riverbed. It would be a simple matter for an army to span the gap and march up to the front gates of the city—if one had an inclination for invasion.

Of course, neither training nor the fortifications were the real reason for their choice of training ground. Knowledge was the first objective in any war, and Jaxon's time serving in the Gurrian Legions had taught him well the capabilities of their observers. But out here, no one was going to be overhearing their conversation.

"Ready?" he asked finally.

Mikael clenched and unclenched his fist, testing whether feeling had returned to his fingers, before offering a nod. Jaxon had to admit, he had made remarkable progress with his swordsmanship. But Mikael was still just a Steel ranker. That progress would need to be nothing short of extraordinary if he wanted to match Jaxon someday.

He started forwards, only for Mikael to raise a hand. "I met with someone yesterday."

Jaxon paused. "What?"

"A Pathfinder, though I wouldn't have known it from my *Aura Sense*. I had to use my *other* ability." Jaxon frowned. Mikael's Offworlder ability was a mystery, though he suspected the Offworlder himself knew more about it than he let on. "*Mute*, the ability was called."

"I've heard of it," Jaxon mused. "It relies on Aura. A Pathfinder can use it to conceal themselves—physically as well as their Aura."

"He was Silver rank. But his Aura grade was stronger than yours."

Jaxon muttered a curse. "I think you'd better start from the beginning," he said quietly, sheathing his sword. "Just who was this man, Mikael?"

By Ryntirax, this kid attracted trouble like flies to cow dung. A Pathfinder with that kind of Aura control was concerning to say the least. In fact…narrowing his eyes, Jaxon drew on his own *Aura Sense*. The world flickered into a complex whirl of blue, red and yellow. He glared at their surroundings, concentrating all of his consciousness on the task, but nothing changed.

Satisfied they were in fact alone on the shoreline, he exhaled. This unknown man might have a powerful *Mute* ability, but it was doubtful his skill could evade the direct attention of a Gold ranker like himself. The ability was powerful, but it couldn't do all the work. A lesser Pathfinder might be tricked, so that his eyes would pass over the man without actually triggering his consciousness, but Jaxon should be powerful enough to pierce the illusion. At least out in the open like this. In a crowd…

"Before I answer," Mikael said evasively, "there was one more ability. One you've got, actually. *Spirit Attack*. When he used it on me, it felt like he was using his Aura to attack me directly. I didn't think Aura could do that."

"What made you think that?"

"Ah…Isabel, Maisiwan…" He shrugged. "Pretty much everyone mocked me when my first ability was *Aura Sense*."

"Which is very much not the same as *Spirit Attack*."

"I see," Mikael pursed his lips and seemed to consider something, before shaking his head. "This Pathfinder, he went by Jon. He's one of the leaders of the Skartan Resistance."

"*What?*"

Mikael had barely been gone *for an hour* yesterday. How in the Seven Hells had this happened?

"Hey, not so loud," Mikael hissed, glancing in the direction of the city, where the occasional guard patrolled the ramparts.

"Oh, *now* you're concerned about secrecy?"

First the business with Alson Ting, and now this? Jaxon seethed. One day soon, Mikael's meddling was going to get all of them killed. He'd had it.

Jaxon activated *Movement Surge*.

The gap between them disappeared in the blink of an eye. Mikael tried to flinch away, but he caught the boy with a fist of iron strength "What game are you playing at, Mikael?" he hissed through clenched teeth. "Explain, before I reconsider sparing your damned life."

A year ago, he had stumbled across the freshly arrived Offworlder in a cave in the Highlands. His kind were prophesised to be Destroyers. World Enders. The bringers of the void. Yet in Mikael's first moments in the Seventh Realm, he had placed himself in great danger to help others. Jaxon could not bring himself to act pre-emptively against him.

That day, at least…

He activated *Spirit Attack,* pressing his Aura down on Mikael's own, carving chunks from his soul, crushing, squeezing like a vice…

A strangled cry tore from Mikael's throat—but only for a second. As his hand fell to the hilt of his sword, the tension that had appeared in his stance vanished. Jaxon blinked. His Aura still *seemed* to be crushing down on Mikael, but now the Offworlder glared back at him with those golden eyes. And it was not fear he saw there, but anger.

"I'm trying to survive," Mikael snarled. "I'm trying to make it so we *all* survive?"

Despite his shock at the young man repelling his ability, Jaxon would not be deterred. Not this time. "By talking with the Skartan Resistance?" Jaxon spat. He released the Offworlder in disgust. "Do you know what happened the last time the Skartans tried that crap?"

"I could probably guess," Mikael muttered, rubbing his arm where Jaxon had grabbed him.

"The Emperor brought in an entire Legion to put them down. Not just the resistance—the entire city. Anyone even *suspected* of an association were dragged to the hangman's block and left to swing."

Silence fell between them as they glared at one another. The wind swirled across the shore, sending sand whipping at their flesh. Jaxon barely felt it. He was so angry, his entire body was trembling. He knew he wasn't thinking straight. But they had come here to make peace—not incite a revolution. Yet Mikael didn't seem willing to back down.

"Another war crime for the empire; why am I not surprised?" the Offworlder advanced a step and Jaxon was surprised to see his Aura flaring, burning bright, as though preparing for an attack. "What *does* surprise me, more and more, is how you could have *fought* for them all those years, Jaxon? All those atrocities, all those conquered lands, and yet there you were, right along with them."

The words took Jaxon off-guard. For a second he just glowered at the young man. He wanted to continue his tirade, to lash out at Mikael for daring to impugn his honour...

...except the little bastard was right.

"Because I was a fool," he said, turning away.

"No," Mikael brought him up short. His boots crunched in the sand, before a rough hand caught him by the shoulder and spun him. Shocked at his audacity, Jaxon just stared as Mikael jabbed a finger at his chest. "No, you've said that before. I want to know *why*."

Jaxon blinked. "You want to know why?"

He rubbed his temples, rolling the question over in his head. Why *had* he fought for Gurria? At first it had been for glory, that was easy enough to admit. He'd been a young man, still growing in power and eager to test his skill against the champions of this world. Gurria had been struggling with civil war in the provinces—he had seen more action in a single year than a decade in the Highlands.

And then...then he had *believed*. He had been awestruck by the wonders of the Gurrian capital, with its soaring towers and paved streets and running water. Sleek ships unlike anything the clans could tack together floated in its harbours, and there was a new food for sale on every corner. His purse heavy with his soldier's wage, the impressionable young Darkstrider had lived like royalty. And when he'd heard the mad king of Ressi wanted to burn it all down, Jaxon Daniyal had only been too eager to offer his sword.

He should have seen it then, the greed of the empire, the way it fed, how it *needed* to expand to fuel the wealth of its capital. When the destruction of the mad king's army had seen Gurria pushing into Ressi instead of bringing an end to the war, he should have known. Instead...

"I met a woman," he said softly.

Alyina Sorulus.

Even now his blood raced at the memory of the Gurrian

Princess. The woman was like bottled flame: a seething vessel of passion and desire, ready to burst at any moment—either to ravish the object of her attention, or to destroy them utterly if the mood so took her.

The young Jaxon Daniyal had been utterly enthralled by her smile and her witty jibes, by her skill on the battlefield and her passion on that other field of engagement.

It had taken a long time, and the slaughter of an entire town, for him to realise just how utterly evil she was.

"Ah," Mikael murmured when it became obvious he wasn't going to continue. "Now I understand."

Jaxon blinked. "You do?"

"All is fair in love and war," Mikael said with a sad smile. "There's an old story from my world, about a man and a woman who ran away to be together. Helen and Paris. Only she was already married—to a king. He followed them with an army. And so began to the Trojan war. It ended with the destruction of an entire kingdom." He laughed. "Or that is the Odyssey, at least. I'm afraid any truth was lost to time and tale..."

Silence returned as the Offworlder trailed off. A knot twisted in Jaxon's heart as he considered the story. Alyina Sorulus was just the kind of woman who would glory at the thought of two men going to war over her. Had it really been love that doomed the ill-fated couple, or had Helen known *exactly* what she had been about?

"Regardless of my past, it does not change facts, Mikael," he said at last, quietly. "Only a fool would pit themselves against Orson Sorulus."

Jaxon had met the emperor only once. The man had been cold, his eyes emotionless. But he was powerful, of that there was no doubt. Jaxon had felt his Aura—a prod to his soul, nothing more—but in that moment, he had been as a pebble before the might of the ocean waves. Alyina was powerful, but this man eclipsed anything that Jaxon had sensed before or since.

Eternal.

The Pathfinder rank was spoken of only in whispers, more rumour or legend than something that actually *existed*. But Jaxon had felt it. He knew it was real. No wonder the man was conquering the world.

"It wasn't me that wanted to come here, remember?" the young man said wearily. "But you and I both know the governor isn't just keeping us here to sign some peace treaty. I can't sit around and do nothing while they put the noose around my neck."

"I know," Jaxon sighed. Dropping the tip of his greatsword to the sands, he leaned against its hilt. "So, what did this man from the resistance have to say, then?"

Mikael pursed his lips. "They're looking to make a move soon, I think," he replied. "We didn't get to talk much more than that." He paused, eyeing Jaxon. "But I'd like to speak with him again. If it does come to war, we're going to need friends, Jaxon."

"Allies," Jaxon sighed and rubbed his face.

It was risky. If the governor found out they were speaking with his enemies, any hope of peace went out the window. He would claim the Highlands were conspiring against the empire and use it as justification for an invasion, just as he had with Alson Ting's little incursion. But…he cursed softly. In his heart, he knew Mikael was right.

Not that he would ever admit it.

"Talk. Nothing more," he said softly, before adding. "And Mikael, one more thing."

"Oh?"

"When the time comes, and the decision must be made whether the Malesie march to war." His face hardened and he took a step closer, pressing down on the Offworlder's flickering soul. "It will not be you who makes that decision. Understood?"

There was the briefest flicker in Mikael's face. A flash of guilt. Then it was gone, and his face turned hard.

"Okay, Jaxon."

The golden eyes met his, and despite the disparity in their strength, Jaxon couldn't help but shudder at what he glimpsed there. There was so much light inside Mikael, sometimes it was easy to forget the darkness that resided alongside it. The hard, unflinching soul that could hunt down a group of unarmed men and slaughter them in the night without a second's hesitation.

"I will not let you lead the Malesie down the path of darkness, Mikael."

Mikael held Jaxon's gaze, the muscles of his jaw clenched, eyes burning with that uncanny strength…

…and then he nodded, his face relaxing into a smile. "Fair enough."

14

"Sir?"

Arimus looked up at the interruption. Around the table, the various advisors and diplomats of his council frowned, their disapproval at the interruption clear. Ignoring them, Arimus looked around to find Sergeant Bolt standing uncertainly in the doorway to the council chambers.

"Sorry to interrupt," the man continued, "but you said to come immediately if we found anything."

"A witness?"

The man nodded. "Maybe more. Says he heard something of a commotion that night."

"Excellent." Rising, Arimus waved to the councillors with a smile. "Excuse me, sirs, we will have to reconvene tomorrow."

"But sir—"

Their complaints fell on deaf ears—Arimus was already halfway out the door, gesturing for the young man to go ahead.

"I brought him along to the citadel," the sergeant explained as they walked. "Wanted you to be the first to hear his story."

"What did he see?"

Bolt hesitated. "He's been…tight lipped. Best you ask him yourself, sir. This way."

Together they stepped into one of the many private rooms lining the corridors of the citadel. Once they had probably been used for prayer and private contemplation, but superstitions about long departed deities held little interest to the citizens of the empire. One of his father's acts while running the city had been to convert the old cathedral into its seat of government. It was a good way of breaking a populations connection with their past, apparently.

Inside the room, he found a thin man seated at a table. Sweat dripped from his brow, though the stone of the citadel kept the chamber cool. From the heavy reek lingering in the air, it was not an unusual sight for this character. Arimus wrinkled his nose. Hadn't these brutes figured out how to bathe yet? Why else had his predecessor spent so much on the public bath house?

"This is Jameson Sky," Sergeant Bolt announced. "Mr Sky, the Governor, as you requested."

"Ah yes, sir," the man said, rising from his seat to give an informal bow. "A pleasure."

Arimus's fingers tightened around the hilt of his sword. He had taken to carrying the blade they'd dredged from the canal. He couldn't say why, but he found himself drawn to its dark steel. It gave him a strange sense of satisfaction, holding that plain hilt in his hand. There was a secret there, he knew. He just had to wait for it to reveal itself.

"Mr Sky, I have been told you saw something on the night of the warehouse attack?"

"Well, I dunno about that. Was just having a little nightcap at the pub, wasn't I?" A sly grin crept across the man's lips. "Unless you're saying there's some kind of reward?"

Arimus's jaw hardened as he stared down at the man. Why wasn't he surprised? A murder had been committed and important chemicals destroyed, and all these bastard Skartans could think about was the coins for their next meal. He stood there for a long time, until the naked greed in the skinny man's eyes shrivelled, to be replaced with the hint of fear.

"Is that so, Mr Sky?" Arimus asked, leaning down so they were face to face.

The Skartan swallowed, sweat springing to his brow. "I mean…only if…it would be nice—"

His words cut off as Arimus's hand snapped down, catching the back of his chair and yanking it back. The man cried out in terror, arms windmilling, but it was already too late to halt his momentum. He tumbled to the ground, the chair twisting beneath him as Arimus's knee slammed down onto his chest, pinning him against the tiled floor and driving the breath from his lungs.

Suddenly the black blade was in Arimus's hands. He couldn't recall drawing it—but now that he had, he pressed it to the Skartan's throat. It seemed the correct course of action. He could feel a hunger growing within, the desire that had consumed him for so many months now. For battle, for action, for *death*. This man wanted a reward? That could be arranged…

"Ah, sir?" A voice interrupted his thoughts. "I think he's ready to talk."

Blinking, Arimus found the Skartan weeping pitifully beneath him, blood seeping from a shallow nick in his scrawny throat. Sergeant Bolt stood nearby, one arm extended, as though he'd been about to intervene, before remembering just who he was dealing with.

"Please, please," the Skartan was gasping. "I'll tell you, please, just spare me!"

Growling his frustration, Arimus dragged the pathetic excuse for a man to his feet and shoved him into another chair.

"Consider this your last chance," he snarled. "What did you see?"

"I was just taking a piss, I swear. That's it! Had nothing to do with the girl."

Arimus stilled. "What girl?"

"The one those dead men were after," the Skartan blubbered. "Saw 'em grab her and knew nothing good could come outta any of it."

"Describe her."

"A slip of a thing. Street trash, you know the sort. Was carrying some kind of bag. The guards said something about 'er being a thief."

Arimus tapped his chin with a finger. This could be the thief behind the warehouse attack. But it still didn't explain how four Pathfinders had ended up dead. "And the man with the cloak?"

"What about 'im?"

"You told my sergeant here you saw a man in a multi-coloured cloak that night, did you not?"

"Yeah, but not until I hightailed it back to the pub. Not messing around in Gurrian business, am I?" He seemed to have regained some of his nerve now. "Saw your man a little later, wandering back to the Dancing Donkey. Pretty memorable, that cloak."

Arimus pressed his lips together in a thin line. *Mikael Heaton.* So the Offworlder *had* been there that night. Between the dead Pathfinders and the strange shortsword found at the scene of the crime, it was all becoming too much for coincidence.

"Very well, citizen," Arimus said softly. "It would seem you have earned your life."

Patting the man on the shoulder, he waved the man from the room. The man practically sprinted from the room. Arimus waited a moment before addressing the sergeant.

"What do you make of that?"

"Sir?" the man asked, a look of confusion crossing his face.

"You did good work, Sergeant Bolt, finding him," Arimus explained. "I'd like your opinion on his story."

The sergeant licked his lips. "I've learnt to trust these Skartan scum about as much as a viper's kiss."

"Oh?" Arimus questioned, his curiosity piqued by the look on his subordinate's face."

Bolt hesitated, before offering a shrug. "Let's just say if you bring one of their women home, you'd best expect to be missing more than a few coins the next morning."

"She found your purse?"

"*And* the coin I had stashed in my bedpan," the sergeant replied bitterly. "What kind of lass checks a man's *bedpan*?"

Arimus chuckled. "I like you, Bolt." His gaze returned to the drops of blood his talk with the Skartan had left on the floor. "So, you think our man was lying?"

Bolt pursed his lips. "Given your methods…I would say he was telling the truth."

"And what conclusions would you draw then?"

The man swallowed. "I would say the Highlanders and their Offworlder are involved with the resistance, sir."

"My thoughts exactly," Arimus mused.

"What will you do?"

That was the question, wasn't it? He couldn't make a move against the man, not with Alyina determined to win over his affections. But if Mikael Heaton really *had* dipped his toes into the cesspit that was Skartan politics…

…well, they'd never found an active member of the resistance before. Maybe he was viewing this the wrong way. It could be an opportunity.

"How many Pathfinders are left in the Skartan Battalion?"

"I believe there are a dozen of us left."

"Any with the *Mute* ability?"

The sergeant shifted uncomfortably. "Just myself, sir. May I ask why?"

"That's excellent news." He clapped the man on the shoulder. "What was your full name again, soldier?"

"It's Bradley Bolt, sir."

"Well, *Lieutenant* Bolt, I have a new assignment for you. Think you can handle it?"

The man straightened at the words. "Of course, sir!"

"Good." The grin on Arimus's lips grew. "Because I think it's time we uncovered exactly what that Offworlder is doing in our city, don't you?"

15

"What's this box?"

Kat jerked awake on the rotting sofa where she'd been dozing in the corner of the records room. She didn't know what Isabel's father looked like, so there was no point in *her* losing sleep on the never-ending search. She frowned at the Highland Pathfinder, still struggling to gather her wits.

"Whatyousay?" she mumbled.

The strange woman was sitting amidst a pile of discarded papers that were Marta's 'records'. It was a strange custom. The crotchety old woman had every newcomer to the manor sit for an hour while she sketched them. She was actually pretty good, Kat thought, despite making do with the discarded graphite and paper scraps she scavenged on her shuffling journeys about the city.

After the sketch was done, she would also ask her various orphans for details about their lives—names, ages, birthdays, parents. Useless crap like that. It was a strange custom, but customs usually were, in her experience.

Afterwards, the records would be placed lovingly in the disordered stacks of Marta's record room—and promptly forgotten. When she'd been younger, Kat and the other urchins would sometimes come here to gaze at all the faces that had come before them and wonder what had become of them. Kat hoped they had found a good life, though in the pit of her stomach, she knew most were more likely to have ended up at the bottom of a canal.

"This box," Isabel repeated, holding up an old wooden crate. "What's this?"

Kat blinked at the box in the woman's hand. She'd never noticed it before. It was easy to miss things in this room, considering some of the paper stacks came up to her shoulders. Leaving the sofa, she knelt on the floor with the other Pathfinder.

"Where'd you get that?"

"It was tucked at the back, buried in papers."

Dark rings shaded Isabel's eyes, and she looked about ready to collapse. Kat could see there was light outside through the cracks in the boarded-up window. The poor girl had been going all night.

"Here," she said, carefully pulling the box towards her. "Let me have a look."

Dust swirled through the room as Kat removed the lid. She waited for it to settle before peeking inside. Yet more records. Why wasn't she surprised? But then she saw that these were different. The paper was thick and waxed, with the words inked by brush. Though as she turned one over, she realised the sketches could only have been done by Marta's hand. They had the same way of bringing their subjects to life with brush-strokes as the old woman managed with her graphite.

The kid in the sketch, however, wasn't dressed like any street urchin Kat had ever met. He wore a fine shirt and breachers, almost like…

"What in the Seven Hells?" Kat muttered, as Isabel picked up the next paper. "These must be from…"

"…before," Isabel finished with a nod. Fresh energy seemed to infuse her as she started on the new pile.

Kat just continued to stare at the page in her hand. This…Marta had always played the fool when asked about the old occupants of the house, calling them shadow weavers and worse.

But that clearly wasn't true. This place might have been abandoned a long time ago, but clearly Marta had been a part of its original purpose, whatever that had been. A boarding house for rich bastards like the one in her hand? Foreigners, maybe? Long before the Empire had formed, Skarta had been the capital of knowledge and learning, its university renown across the continent, respected even by the rival city states. People had travelled from all across the continent to study here.

"That's…" Isabel interrupted Kat's thoughts. She held up a fresh piece of paper, about halfway through her pile. "This is him."

Her interest piqued, Kat held out her hand for the paper. The girl didn't seem to notice. Her eyes had taken on a strange sheen. She sat staring at the page, her lips moving as she read the words. A smile tugged at Kat's lips.

"At least tell me his name."

Isabel blinked, glancing up, then back to the page. Her brow furrowed. "Cor…Jasper Shore. Looks like…"

Kat didn't hear anything more over the ringing in her ears. Suddenly her heart was pounding, as across her body a thousand needles prickled at her skin. She stared at the girl sitting in front of her, and suddenly she saw it. The sharpness of her face, the sun-kissed skin, despite the Highland upbringing, even the eyes. That dusty brown…

Dark brown eyes looked down at the broken body of her father. "Should have accepted my offer, old man."

Jasper Shore. The man who had ruined her father. The evil bastard responsible for ruining her life.

"…ever heard of him?"

The ringing cut off. Isabel was still talking. She stared at Kat, eyebrows knitted together in a frown, as though waiting for a response to a question.

The daughter of my enemy.

A shiver swept through Kat. It wasn't true, of course. Jasper probably didn't even realise Isabel existed. That was the way with these Gurrian bastards. They did whatever they wanted, with whoever they wanted, and accepted no consequences. Isabel was no more Jasper's daughter than Kat…and yet…

She imagined her blade slamming into Isabel's chest, the sudden fear, the pain…

No, that was foolish. That would not be justice, but misdirected revenge. She drew in a shuddering breath.

"No," Kat rasped, her throat inexplicably dry. She paused, unsure why she had lied, other than to buy herself time to think. "I can ask around about him, if you like?"

Isabel smiled. "I would like that very much," she said softly. "Thank you, Kat," she added, reaching out and embracing her. "Truly, I…" A tear streaked her cheek as she drew back and looked at the paper again. "It's foolish, I know, but…" she trailed off, a sad smile on her lips.

Kat swallowed. Rising, she placed an awkward hand on the Highlander's shoulder. "You should get some rest," she said. "I've got a few errands to run, but I'll be back this evening with news."

Isabel nodded, the shadows beneath her eyes seeming to grow deeper. "Yeah," she breathed, rising as well and moving to the sofa. "That's…a good…"

She was asleep before she could finish the sentence.

Kat stood, staring at the girl for a long minute, wondering…

…before moving back out into the corridor and closing the

door carefully behind her. She hadn't lied. She had promised Jon she would keep an eye on the Offworlder. And this time he *would not* see her.

Though as she slid through the large manor door into the streets of Skarta, Kat's mind was on anything but the task ahead. She was lost in other possibilities.

Like what to do with the bastard daughter of her mortal enemy that had just suddenly shown up on her doorstep.

Eight weeks before the Festival of the Satana

"No."

Conner flinched as the refusal echoed across the waters of the bay, resounding in its finality. Yiva, the woman who had spoken it, leaned against the railings of a galley that was currently docked in Pine Harbour. Her hair rippled in the ocean breeze, despite the braids holding it in place. A few traces of silver threaded their way through the raven-black, but otherwise she showed no outward signs of her age.

This woman had been chieftain of the Fushore clan since the last Detian invasion some fifteen years ago. She was also the woman he had come to negotiate with. Unfortunately, judging from the distasteful twist of her lips as she watched him, she found the very sight of Conner offensive.

"But your king commands—"

The woman snorted. "Denether can take his titles and his commands to the Seven Hells and make a deal with the Satana for all I care."

Conner clenched his fists, frustration boiling up inside. He reined it in. This was not the kind of situation he could afford to let his temper cloud his judgement. Not with the fate of his people resting on his shoulders.

There had long been a rivalry between the Fushore and the Malesie. While the Malesie ruled the valleys, the Fushore mostly kept to the coasts around the peninsula. Earning their livelihood in fish and trade through the port at Pine Harbour, they did not have to deal with the harsh winters in the mountains, nor the fear of losing their entire herd to the winter snows.

They did, however, have to endure constant raids by the seafaring Deti. Usually they struck the smaller coastal villages, but they had been known on occasion to attack Pine Harbour itself. Only once had the Malesie been attacked by the raiders, when they had slipped past Pine Harbour and sailed upriver to strike directly at their heartland.

That had also been the day the Fushore had refused the Malesie's call for aid. Conner did not know the whole tale, having been just a boy at the time, but he knew Yiva had recently been made chieftain after the death of her father a year before.

Drawing in a breath, Conner met the eyes of the hateful woman. That refusal had cost thousands of his people their lives. Even the Izolu had come, despite their isolation. But not the Fushore. Now the same woman would deny them again. Conner could not let it stand.

"Yiva, the Empire marched an *army* into our lands."

"Into *Malesie* lands," the woman snapped back.

Conner glared into her emerald eyes. Yiva did not blink. So hard, so unyielding. Undeterred, he tried again.

"We're facing an enemy that will see our very way of life destroyed."

"Do you think me a fool, son of Denether?" Yiva growled. Pushing herself back from the railing, she moved to the gangway and stomped down to the docks. Only when she stood eye to eye with Conner did she speak again. "I am not blind to the Empire's hunger. But I also remember the past."

"This is no time to cling to old rivalries!" Conner snapped. "We must stand together, or we'll fall one by one."

"Old rivalries?" Yiva's lips drew back in a snarl that revealed yellowed teeth. "Denether never told you what he did, did he?"

Conner opened his mouth to speak, then noticed the look on the woman's face. A vein bulged in her forehead, and her jaw was clenched so tight he could almost hear the creaking of her teeth. He swallowed. Yiva was furious.

"Tell me what?" he asked softly.

Pursing her lips in a thin line, the woman shook her head. "Ask him when you return to Furness. Alone." She started to turn away.

"No." Conner grated. "I won't."

The clanswoman frowned as she glanced back. "You do not have a choice, *boy*."

"Are you truly so selfish?" Conner snapped, throwing caution into the icy depths of the harbour. "You would condemn both our peoples to extinction because of a grudge with my father?

Yiva's step faltered. He saw a flicker in her face and her eyes grew distant, as though she were truly considering his words this time.

"Some grudges run too deep, Conner," she said at last. "My father trusted Denether once. He paid a heavy price. I will not make the same mistake."

Conner silently cursed his father. The man had warned him they had a history, but had refused to go into detail. What had he done all those years ago? Looking into Yiva's eyes, he could see her hatred. Whatever Denether had done, this woman would never forgive it.

But Conner couldn't turn back now. If he did, the Malesie would stand alone against the might of the Gurrian Empire. Mikael and Jaxon would be forsaken, trapped in the heart of enemy territory. No one would be coming for them. And not all of Jaxon's power or Mikael's cunning would be enough to save them.

He needed the Fushore. He needed their ships.

He did not need Yiva.

"Very well," he said, his voice suddenly harsh. "Then I challenge you, Yiva."

There was a collective gasp from the deck of Yiva's ship where her crew had been watching on with amusement. On the docks, Yiva's face hardened. Her emerald eyes flashed as she started back towards him. He hadn't noticed before, but she stood a full inch taller than him.

Suddenly, a weight like a sledgehammer slammed into his soul. *Spirit Attack.* A knot tightened around Conner's chest, but his training with Jaxon served him well. He did not flinch.

"On what grounds?" the woman demanded.

Conner met the woman's gaze. The assault on his Aura might not have troubled him, but what he saw there left him unsettled. That spite. That hatred. His father's work. His same father who had warned him this might be necessary.

Conner Spears didn't want this. He had seen enough of their people die in Sarton—and many more would perish in the coming months. He had seen enough of death. He spoke the words anyway.

"You hold a grievance against my father. It is preventing you from doing your duty to our people."

"Choose your next words carefully, Son of Denether."

He met the woman's burning gaze. "By the ancient law of the Highlands, let this grievance be resolved in combat. I will stand as champion for Denether, our Highking. Who will stand for you?"

"Don't be a fool, *boy*. You are not responsible for your father's crimes."

"Nor are my people, yet you would condemn them all the same. I repeat, who stands for you?"

"Enough with this nonsense," the chieftain started to turn away. "I will not fight a child."

"I am no child," Conner snapped. "I am heir of the Malesie, and I demand the right to settle your grievance against my people!"

"Fine!" Yiva roared. Spinning, she drew her greatsword. "But when I send you back to your father in an urn, by the eyes of gods and men, let no one doubt that this was *your* doing, Conner Spears."

With that, she *Surged* towards Conner, the silver blade flashing for his throat.

"You really expect us to fight with these? My steak knife is bigger!"

Laughter echoed around the campsite where the warriors of the Malesie clan were gathering outside Furness. Hundreds of men and women from the surrounding countryside had already responded to the call of their king and hundreds yet were expected. It was more than Lunden had hoped for when Mikael had first come to him after the battle for Sitton.

He had to admit, the Offworlder had some balls. Sending Conner to speak with his father had been a stroke of genius, but even then, he'd expected Denether to reject the plan to put Lunden in charge of the new Malesie army. If Lunden was honest, those doubts were part of why he'd agreed so readily when Mikael put the proposal to him. After all, what king would name a foreigner as High Commander of his army?

Denether Spears, apparently.

Looking around the circle of laughing faces, Lunden felt a pang of regret. They were smiling now, these men and women of the Malesie, but soon those smiles would turn to tears and sorrow.

He hadn't wanted another war. He and the other Ressian men had already fought a bloody, decade long war against the Empire. Now they were being asked to do it all again. To fight a new war, for a new home.

Lunden didn't plan to lose a second time.

Though he wished he could understand why people kept looking at him to lead!

Letting out a sigh, Lunden held out his hand for the blade the man held. Reluctantly, the Malesie handed it over. It was one of the original shortswords that Maisiwan had designed for the practice games Mikael had staged for the Festival of the Elohim. Even now, a hundred blacksmiths in the city were working on forging thousands more—along with the squat, square shields young Fiachson had designed.

Holding the shortsword in an easy grip, Lunden spun it in his hand. It was well balanced, though the tip and edges had been blunted for today's purposes.

"You are all warriors of the Malesie, are you not?" he asked the gathering.

A rumble of agreement rose from the crowd.

"And what would you say is the greatest advantage the Malesie have in battle?"

Reaching up to draw the greatsword from his back, the man who had scoffed at Lunden stepped forward. "This!" he bellowed. "Our enemies fear us because we are real warriors, with real weapons!"

Lunden pursed his lips. "What is your name, soldier?"

"Renard," the man grunted. "And I am no soldier. That is a Gurrian title. The Malesie do not make a life out of war."

"Ay, my people were the same," Lunden said sadly. "Now we are mostly dead, or enslaved in our own lands."

That stilled the crowd. Men and women shifted uneasily on their feet, but he pressed on, unwilling to linger on the past.

"If your clans wish to survive, you will have to adapt. I fought the Gurrians for nigh a decade. I know their tactics, how they think. That is why your Highking asked me to prepare you," he paused, his gaze lingering on the crowd. This time no one spoke. "So from this day forth you will be soldiers of the Highlands. Your days will be spent training, so that when the fight comes you will be ready. I plan to make the Malesie the most fearsome fighting force on the continent—but it will take time. That is why you must all remain here in Furness for the spring."

The crowd stirred.

"What about our lands?" one of the women called out.

"And our families? Our crops?" called another man.

"Taxes will be collected from those who remain," Lunden replied. He surveyed the crowd again, his face grim. "That money will be used to support your farms and your families while you are away."

The rumble of disapproval grew louder. The big man who had disagreed earlier stepped forward.

"Renard needs no other man to provide for his family." He glared down at Lunden. "Your people were weak, little man, and the Malesie are already the greatest fighting force on the continent!"

He raised his greatsword into the air with a shout. Several other men and women roared their agreement.

Lunden stood, lips pursed, watching them silently. When he raised his hand, he was surprised when they actually fell quiet.

"You *are* fearsome warriors," he said softly, "no one disputes that. But could you march across these mountains for weeks on end, eight hours a day, in leather armour carrying your shields and your greatswords and your food, then fight a pitched battle against a fresh force?" He waited, letting the words sink in. "If an enemy surprised you from the rear, could you turn as one and face them, or would you descend into chaos?"

His eyes surveyed the men and women, and not a one of them spoke this time.

"Because the Gurrians can," he continued. "Every day, for months on end, their soldiers are trained to fight together. To obey commands instantly. They have discipline, and endurance built from years of training. The Malesie are powerful warriors, yes. One on one, I would place my money on a Malesie over a Gurrian any day. But in battle, victory takes more than just great warriors. It takes soldiers."

A long silence followed his words. The crowd was watching Renard, as though his response would decide their reaction. Lunden ignored the big man and held his gaze instead. He was aware of his status as an outsider, but he did not stand alone. Behind him were the men and women who had fought with him in Sitton. Each of them held a place amongst Malesie legend.

"Alright, little man," Renard grunted at last, somewhat surprising Lunden. "Let us say you have convinced me about this soldier nonsense." He pointed his greatsword at the blade in Lunden's hand. "You still have not explained the pig sticker."

Despite himself, Lunden found himself smiling. "I could explain it, but I doubt you'd believe me," he said. "So why don't I show you?"

17

Present Day

It was strange, now that he had his memories, Mikael could see the similarities between this world and Earth. Like the smell of books. That strange mix of mustiness and worn paper, it was absolutely unmistakable. If you had ever stood in a library, surrounded by row upon row, shelf upon endless shelf of books, you knew that smell, though perhaps you could never hope to describe it.

Strange, when you thought about. This library was public, but curated and overseen by the Skartan University. Its scent was the same as any he had visited on Earth. And yet, the knowledge contained in its shelves were utterly different from those of his home.

Moving through the shelves, Mikael ran his hand along the spines of the books, scanning the titles for hints of his research subject. Most were fairly innocuous. *Radoor's Techniques for Forging Iron, A Thousand Ways to Cut an Enemy,* and…Mikael chuckled at this one: *Savages and How to Kill Them.*

None hinted at the topic that had drawn him to these halls.

The Twin Blades.

Back on Earth, he had forged a machine by mixing ancient, unknown materials with the technological advances of his people. When he had activated the machine, it had awoken as planned, becoming a construct that would help him breach the fabric of reality and navigate the universe beyond with relative safety.

Relative being the key word.

Both he and the construct had survived the passage between worlds, but *something* had seen them—and followed them to this world. Something calling itself Dagon of the Elohim—one of the gods of this realm. That creature had been a murderous angel, intent on cleansing this world of life, and had only been stopped by the arrival of one terrifying, hellish demon that went by the name of Azaroth.

The rest, as they say was history.

Azaroth had reset that day, but had allowed Mikael to keep his memories in order to win a bet with this other creature, the Leviathan who was apparently still gambling on Mikael's death.

And more importantly, Azaroth had taken Mikael's construct from him. Or more accurately, the demon had reshaped the construct, reforging it into two swords: one, the silver shortsword that hung from his belt. It seemed to have no real power—except that it had protected him first from Jon's, and then Jaxon's, *Spirit Attack.*

Then there was the other half. The black-stained blade that Azaroth had sent hurtling away into the ether. Mikael had a feeling that alone, neither sword contained the power he needed to save himself. Otherwise Azaroth would have never left him with one. But if he could reunite them…

…which was why Mikael was here. Azaroth had claimed the magical blades were more 'on brand'. If Mikael was interpreting that correctly, it meant his swords were not the first magical weapons to exist in the Seventh Realm.

Unfortunately, none of the tomes he had flicked through so far mentioned anything about magical swords. The librarians had been helpful enough, welcoming Mikael without a second glance at his Highland colours. They had even offered their services should he have a particular area of research to investigate. He'd unfortunately had to decline—it wouldn't do for word of his investigation to get back to the governor.

But as the sun set behind the pane glass windows and the librarians set out their lanterns with the greatest of care, Mikael was beginning to grow desperate. Only four days remained now until the Festival of the Satana, and he had just lost an entire day on this fruitless hunt. He should have been contacting Jon again, so they could plot the downfall of the governor, rather than wasting his time on these dusty old books.

"You must be the Offworlder." Mikael jumped as a woman spoke from behind him. "The librarians said I might bump into you up here."

Frowning at the interruption, Mikael turned to reply—only for the breath to catch in his throat as he laid eyes on the speaker. She was easily the most beautiful woman he had ever seen. Her eyes were a brilliant emerald green and her auburn locks shone brightly in the lanternlight. She wore a dress of scarlet silk of the strapless variety favoured by the locals, though the way hers hugged her figure was just a little more… revealing than most. It also barely reached her thighs.

For the hot weather probably, Mikael thought with a nervous swallow.

"I…Offworlder?" he stuttered, stumbling over his own tongue before recovering his wits. "Yes, that's me. What can I do for you, My Lady?"

"I thought perhaps that I might help you," she replied,

wandering down the aisle of books towards him. "I might be a touch rusty, but I was a student here once."

"But not anymore?"

A mischievous smile played across her lips. "Even the most studious of academics should live in the real world eventually, don't you think?"

"I suppose there is truth in that," Mikael replied with an arched eyebrow. They were on the third floor of the library, near a railing that looked over the ground floor, where the librarians went about their business. Mikael gestured to those below. "I'm not sure the old grey-hairs down there would agree."

Snorting, the woman joined him at the railing. "Ah yes, my esteemed professors. They always did have interesting ideas about how the world should work."

"Oh?"

"Perhaps it is a Gurrian thing," she mused. Her eyes seemed to look past him for a second. "We stopped believing in higher powers long ago."

"You don't believe in the Elohim?"

"My, my, you have read up on our world, haven't you, Offworlder?"

"My friends call me Mikael."

Her eyes danced. "Alyina."

"Very nice to meet you, Alyina," Mikael replied with the slight bow that was customary here, though…that name, it had a familiar ring. He pursed his lips. *Where had he heard it before?* "If you are Gurrian, how is it you came to study in Skarta?"

"Before the Empire formed, young people with a thirst for knowledge travelled to Skarta from all across the continent." She chuckled. "Things didn't change just because someone went and named himself emperor. I came here at fifteen, thinking I knew everything there was to know about the world.

My father considered it prudent to show me the error of my ways."

"A wise man."

"Some say so." Alyina leaned against the railing with him. "I'll admit to being curious about you, Mikael."

Mikael's treacherous heart was racing again. She smelled of wildflowers and honey. "How's that?"

"The man from another world. Destined to be a Destroyer, according to most of the scripts from our past. So why is it that so many are whispering that you could be different?"

"Are they?"

The woman only smiled. "So tell me about it," she said instead, straightening to look him in the eye. "Your world, is it wonderful, like I've heard?"

Mikael pursed his lips, considering the question. "Earth is very different from this place. Safer, for the most part, I think. There's no magic, and many nations have been spared from war for a generation or two. We have technological wonders— buildings as tall as your mountains, capable of housing thousands, and devices with all the knowledge of our society in the palm of your hand."

"That sounds...amazing." Alyina said breathlessly. Her eyes were bright with interest. "There is no poverty, or death then, surely?"

Mikael replied with a bitter laugh. "Alas, I have come to think that suffering is an inevitable part of the human condition," he said quietly. "A hundred years ago, my world suffered a war that engulfed the entire planet. Tens of millions perished, killed in battle or by starvation." He fell silent, before adding. "And then we had a second."

"But now there is no war?"

"For some," he murmured. "And you want to know why? Mutually assured destruction. Our scientists and leaders created weapons of such untold devastation, no country since has been mad enough to attack another with those weapons, lest they wipe one another off the map."

Mikael sighed, his hand falling unconsciously to the hilt of his sword. A tingling of alarm shot through his soul. What the hell was he thinking? Nuclear weapons were *definitely* off-limits. Shaking himself, he cursed his weakness for a pretty face and quickly diverted the subject.

"Have you ever wondered if it is by design, our endless wars?"

"Design?" Alyina pursed her lips. "No. I think it is our nature. All living things strive to survive, for more resources, the chance to grow. Bears battle for the best choice of cave in winter, and the lion pack drives all competitors from their lands. It does not make them evil."

"And what of your wars?" he asked, genuinely curious. "You are Gurrian, right? Your people conquered this city, this land. Took it from the Skartans. Was that not evil?"

"Do you think the continent was a peaceful place before Gurria rose to supremacy?"

Mikael shrugged. He had not read that far back yet in his studies of the books Fiachson had given him. Alyina offered a knowing smile. Her hand slipped over his on the balustrade.

"Before the Empire, the four cities of Skarta, Yarrin, Gurria and Ressi were in a state of constant conflict. Peace never lasted more than a decade, with alliances forming and crumbling over weddings and dinners. Thousands died as the cities were sacked by one neighbour or another. Gurria was once even occupied by the soldiers of Skarta."

"And now Skartans go hungry in the streets of their own city, while Gurrian citizens debate the advantages of their conquest with strange men from other worlds," Mikael replied, smiling to take the sting from his words.

Alyina threw back her head and laughed, the sound tolling from the high ceiling. "Oh, you are a darling, aren't you?" She smirked and he caught a flicker of fire in her eyes. "Very well, let us change the subject, shall we? Perhaps I could help you find what you're looking for? The librarians mentioned you'd been floating around these shelves for a few hours at least."

Mikael puffed out his cheeks, wondering how much he could trust this strange woman. Not much, probably.

"We were speaking of the Elohim earlier?" he asked at last, deciding to sate a bit of harmless curiosity. The very name 'Elohim' suggested a connection with his world.

"What about them?"

"I've heard some stories from the clans." He had to be careful here. These Elohim were revered as gods in this world. That was why he had told no one about the true nature of Dagon and the angelic being that had tried to kill him. "The Malesie speak of them as though they once walked this land. I'm interested to learn whether other cultures have a similar belief."

"You shouldn't believe everything you hear," Alyina said with a wink. "The clans are superstitious, but if you want to learn about the old gods, you should follow me."

Mikael nodded, gesturing for her to lead the way. She set off through the endless shelves until they found a staircase, where she led him up several flights to the top floor of the library.

"The histories of the Pathfinders," Alyina explained as she made her way through the shelves.

Here at the top of the building, the outside walls sloped inwards, meaning things were *tight* on this floor, the shelves crammed so close together there was little room to manoeuvre. Mikael bumped into Alyina as she came to a sudden stop and turned. His cheeks burned as he found himself pressed up against her.

"Sorry," he rasped, taking a quick step back.

Her eyes danced in the light of a single lantern burning

nearby, but she didn't reply. Instead, she reached out and pulled a scroll from the nearest shelf.

"Here," she said. "The Seventh Realm hasn't always been like it is today. It has been changing, the magic draining from the world. There are some who say we are now at the end of the Era of the Pathfinder. But a thousand years ago, the air was said to be so thick with Mana that most of our population were Pathfinders."

Mikael frowned as he accepted the scroll. "What does this have to do with the Elohim?"

"Everything!" Alyina's eyes glinted with excitement. "Pathfinders back then wielded untold power compared to those of today…" She licked her lips. "Power that could make the very world tremble. Enough to level cities, or heal thousands in the space of a single heartbeat. Here." She pointed to a passage in the scroll Mikael held.

Dutifully, Mikael read it out loud:

"Our records suggest that King Vysan ruled present-day Skarta some ten thousand years ago. While today Skarta is a lush land of rich soils and sheltered plains, in those days it was recorded to be a harsh and barren place, deficient in anything resembling cultivation.

However, legends recall Vysan as a mighty Pathfinder, and when he came to power he swore an oath to bring glory and wealth to his kingdom. Taking up a sword of ancient and untold power, King Vysan strode the land, carving great troughs through the harsh soils, until he came to the foothills of the Desolate Alps. There he found the waters of a mighty river, trapped by a narrow gorge that sent it twisting through the hills towards the northeast and away from these lands.

Vysan, in his wisdom, determined to make this river a gift to his people. And so, raising his ancient blade, he smote the mountains, tearing the walls of the gorge and releasing the power of the river, whose waters spilt forth over the lands of Skarta. Spreading over the barren plains, the mountain waters brought magic to our soils, and from that day forth, life sprang readily from even the most neglected of our lands. Eventually the waters settled into a new path—becoming our mighty river Skarta."

Blood was pounding in Mikael's ears by the time he finished the passage. A magical sword. A weapon of untold power. It was scribbled right there, as though its mention was no more unusual than a being capable of rending the earth in two with just his hands. Looking up from the text, he tried to keep the excitement from his face.

"You see?" Alyina asked.

Mikael forced his own heart to calm. "There's still no mention of the Elohim in this."

"There is not," Alyina replied, "unless you consider it carefully. It mentions the king, Vysan, correct?" She plucked another book from the shelf. Licking a finger, she flicked through the pages until she found what she was looking for. "Here, a story from the Malesie, about their patron god, Ryntirax."

"He was slain by another of the Elohim," Mikael murmured as he read, his heart beginning to race. "called... *Vesryn.*"

Holy crap. That meant...

"Vesryn. Or, by the Skartan tongue, Vysan!" Alyina grinned. "You see, one and the same. This is why my people no longer believe that the Elohim were gods at all, but merely Pathfinders of extraordinary ability. They took on legendary status as magic faded through the centuries and oral histories twisted their story." She tapped a finger on the scroll in Mikael's hands. "But the truth remains."

Mikael swallowed. This meant the Elohim had been *mortal.* Could that mean...it was the same with the Satana? Crap. If that was true, how had they become so powerful? Was it the atmospheric Mana levels, like Alyina claimed, or something else? Something like this ancient weapon the king had used...

"You really are a scholar," he croaked.

Alyina smirked. "Glad you think so," she said, lifting her chin. Her hands, already resting on the scroll, closed around his own as she stepped closer. "I have a curious mind," she continued, her blue eyes swallowing him up. "About magic, and philosophy, and other worlds. I wish I knew more about yours."

"I…" Mikael swallowed, struggling for words.

Damnit, his mind had turned to mush again with her proximity, and the warmth of her hands around his own, the press of her body against him in the tight space…

"Maybe…sometime, over a drink?" he managed at last.

Alyina leaned in close, her lips brushing against his cheek. "How does *now* sound?" she breathed.

Mikael practically groaned as her hand brushed his cheek. As it did so, the hilt of his shortsword bumped against the shelves. He quickly shifted it to the side, but as his hand wrapped around the hilt, a fresh bolt of sanity struck him.

And this time, he realised what was happening.

It was just like with Jon. Something—or someone—was afflicting his mind. But this time it was not fear, but…desire, distracting him, making him drop his guard. And the sword, somehow, was countering it. So he did what he should have done immediately—but had been unable to *think* enough to manage. He activated his Offworlder ability.

User: Alyina Sorulus. Rank: Royal. Body: 63. Aura: 73. Mana: 67. Abilities: Enforced Body, Spirit Attack, Ardent Onslaught, Invulnerable, Aura Sense, Illusive Image, Kinetic Force.

An icy cold spread down Mikael's spine as he looked into the glittering eyes of Alyina Sorulus. He *had* heard her name before. Of course he had. She was the princess of Gurria, daughter to the fearsome Emperor Sorulus, General of his armies.

And she had a Pathfinder rank beyond anything he had

even *heard* about in this world. She was strong enough to crush his throat with her pinkie.

She was also very, *very* close to him.

"I'm sorry," he choked out the words, struggling to control his fear. Hopefully she mistook it for the effects of her *Spirit Attack*. "I'm...not meant to share...about my world."

A long silence followed—or maybe it only felt that way because he *knew*. Knew that if she wanted, this woman could take him to pieces bit by bit and there was not a single thing Mikael could do to stop her. Not unless his blade revealed a whole lot of special abilities *real* quick.

She smiled. Such a sweet, innocent smile. All the more terrifying because of the monster that hid behind it.

"Fine then, mystery man, keep your secrets," she said, eyes dancing. "Perhaps you'll tell me more the next time we meet."

Was it just Mikael, or had the edge of a threat crept into her words?

If so, he didn't get the chance to respond, as standing on her tiptoes, Alyina kissed him softly on the cheek. Then she spun and strode from the room, leaving him alone once more in the rows of books.

Mikael stood there for a long time afterwards, blood pounding hard in his skull, muscles tense, his entire being trembling. He tracked her departure through the library with his *Aura Sense*. Only when she finally left the range of his senses did he allow himself to breathe. Exhaling, he slumped against one of the shelves. That had been *far too close*.

Though at least he had confirmation as to why he was here.

The same reason as always. He was an Offworlder with dangerous knowledge from another world. Only this time, instead of wanting to destroy him for it, they wanted the knowledge for themselves.

He would not, *could not* let that happen.

Drawing in a breath, Mikael made his way down the stairs and out through the ground floor into the street, where he set off through the winding sidewalks and bridges in the direction of the inn. He needed to fill Jaxon in about what he'd learned. The man might be a paragon of virtue and righteousness, but he knew more about the players in this game than Mikael ever would.

Consumed with his thoughts, he never saw the shadows that detached themselves from the wall behind him—nor the face of the man who threw the bag over his head. Before he could so much as open his mouth to cry out, the club came down, and all he knew was darkness.

CROUCHED ON A NEARBY ROOFTOP, KAT WATCHED WITH sadness as Jon's people dragged Mikael away. She had followed him dutifully, just as Jon asked, shadowing him to the library and lingering outside all day, waiting for *something* to happen.

She just hadn't expected that something to have the Aura of one of her night terrors. Seriously, what the hell even *was* that woman? Kat had never felt anything like it—but she knew she wanted nothing to do with it.

Except that wasn't her duty, was it? So she had crept closer, slipping through the shadows of the library until she had seen the truth for herself.

Alyina Sorulus.

She had never seen the princess, but her likeliness was everywhere in Skarta, if you looked for long enough. Paintings and statues dotted around the plazas, even those tacky mugs they sold as souvenirs in the marketplace. She was the princess, General of the Gurrian Legions, the Conqueror and the emperor's right-hand woman.

And Mikael Heaton was working with her!

Kat had no choice. She'd gone immediately to Jon and told him everything. And now, well, now Mikael Heaton was going to tell Jon the truth about what he was doing here. And then he was going to die.

At least it made Kat feel better about her plans for Isabel. If the Highlanders really were scheming with Gurria against her people, well then, the young Pathfinder deserved exactly what she got.

Speaking of which, the woman would be waiting for her. Time for Kat to put her *own* plan into action.

18

Crouched on a rooftop, Isabel studied the walls of the complex across the street. They stretched almost to the height of her own vantage point, making it impossible to see the grounds within. The walls themselves were massive and topped with razor spikes designed to tear the flesh of anyone foolish enough to climb them—if they got that far. The architects had taken advantage of the city's natural defences, building in the divergence of two canals, meaning the only entrance was a bridge leading to the main gates. There, two Iron Pathfinders had been stationed as guards.

Isabel had had a run in with the pair earlier in the day, after Kat had told her about the manor. *Her father's manor.* She shivered. The thought still made her stomach churn. The man that had wanted nothing to do with her.

She squeezed her leather bracers. The guards on the gate had dismissed her without a second glance. And when she'd tried to insist, they'd only been too happy to threaten violence. Both were giants, at least six feet tall and rippling with hardened muscles. Isabel was quite sure she could have given them a lesson or two, but starting a fight with the men would have only drawn unwanted attention.

Besides, leaving a trail of dead bodies in her wake might not be the best of introductions to her estranged father. I mean, she wasn't *entirely* opposed to the idea. The man *had* abandoned her. It might be worth the look on his face, walking into his mansion with blood dripping from her sword.

Jasper Shore.

The name filled her gut with an icy dread, like she'd swallowed snow from the frozen summit of Ryntirax. A nobleman—a *Gurrian* nobleman—according to Kat. One of many that had come to Skarta after the war, using their power and wealth to establish themselves as oligarchs in the newly acquired province. Kat hadn't offered much more than that, though the edge to the girl's voice when she spoke about him suggested there was more to the story.

Regardless, according to Kat, her father was *here*. And whether he was a beggar or a nobleman, Isabel would not be deferred from her course now. Not when she was so close. She would finally meet the man who had spurned her…

Her stomach churned some more, but she pushed down the wave of doubt. She needed to do this. When she stood and looked the bastard in the eyes, she would know what to say.

Darkness had already set when Kat finally returned. The young street urchin had warned her that the guards wouldn't let her near Jasper Shore. He was an important man. They couldn't just let anyone in to see him. The men had laughed in her face when she'd tried to explain their connection.

"What did you see?" she asked as the street urchin settled on the ledge beside her.

The girl had been gone most of the day and wore a strange look on her face now, like she'd seen something terrible with her *Aura Sense*. Maybe her father wasn't here after all? A part of Isabel felt relieved at the thought of postponing their meeting.

"He's there," the girl said distractedly, though she didn't seem to be watching the complex at all.

Isabel frowned, concerned that her accomplice was having second thoughts. "Are you sure you're alright with this? I can go in without you if you want." Without the girl's *Aura Sense*, she would be going in blind, but Isabel wasn't exactly powerless.

"What? *No!*" the girl said sharply. She shook herself and forced a smile. "I'm good. Just nervous. Let's do this." Her eyes narrowed as she studied the complex in earnest now. "I can only see through the stone as far as the gardens," she replied. "Plenty of guards, mostly regulars, a few Coppers scattered around for good measure."

"We'll be able to slip past them?"

Kat nodded. "So long as you can keep quiet."

"I can." She watched the girl for a moment longer. "Are you really sure you want to go through with this? If not, I can find another way…"

Hell, this was probably a bad idea anyway. What was she going to say to the man after sneaking over his wall and past his guards.

Hi, I'm the long lost daughter you never wanted. I just wanted to see—

"Why do you want to see him so badly?"

Isabel startled at the question, before pursing her lips and considering it. The whole thing was folly, she knew. Pure self-ishness. A Gurrian army could march on the Highlands and fall upon the Malesie any day now, and what was she doing? Playing lost daddy with a street urchin in Skarta. The old Isabel would never have been so self-serving. She would have sacrificed everything for her people.

But that Isabel had been stunted. Broken. She could not grow like that. Could never become someone like Jaxon, *truly* capable of protecting those she loved. So here she was, doing something for herself and the world be damned. She just hoped it would be worth it.

"Because he should know who I am," Isabel said at last. "Because whether he likes it or not, I *exist*."

"Well, after this, he's sure as hells going to see that much." Kat snorted. "Though you should know…these noble sorts, it's not exactly unheard of, them having a few kids on the side."

Isabel grimaced. "I figured. But it doesn't matter. I still want to look the bastard in the eyes."

"I guess I get that," Kat murmured, before her face hardened. "So, what are we waiting for? Let's go pay the bastard a visit."

19

"Now?" Isabel whispered.

Kat held up her hand for the Highlander to wait. She was using all her focus to pierce the wall with her *Aura Sense*. On the other side of the thick stone, a Copper guard was making his way through the garden. She waited for him to disappear from her senses before giving Isabel the okay.

With a nod, the woman crouched—then combining the strength of her *Enforced Body* and her *Movement Surge* ability, launched herself at the top of the wall. The razor wire waited at the top, but at Isabel's rank, that probably wouldn't even pierce her skin.

Kat waited, crouched in a dry section of the canal that surrounded the property. With the river so low, many canals had been reduced to muddy ditches. It was a disaster for those who made their living ferrying people around the city—not that someone like Kat would ever enjoy that luxury—but it served their purposes tonight perfectly.

Or rather, it served Kat's purpose.

She felt a pang of guilt at the deception. Only a pang, mind. Isabel's people were still working with the Empire. That might not make *Isabel* a terrible person, but it did sooth Kat's conscience somewhat.

She *had* done what she'd promised, asking around after Jasper Shore. This *was* his mansion, but he was not inside. He wasn't even in Skarta. Better profits to be stolen in new territories like Ressi, Kat guessed.

So there would be no reunion tonight between Isabel and her father. It was probably for the best. Isabel seemed like a good enough person, but her father was pure evil. Best she didn't have to face that.

But what the esteemed Bronze ranker *could* do was help the resistance break into the home of the all-powerful Skartan Governor. Because while Jasper Shore *senior* was away, *Arimus Shore* was very much in the city. And like father like son, he had been making life miserable for Skartan citizens ever since. Not content to just take his stolen pay check and broker backroom deals like his predecessor, he'd even started coming after the resistance.

According to her sources, he would still be in the citadel at this hour, working no doubt on his vile schemes to crush the last embers of freedom from the Skartan people. And while he was *there*, she had the help of a Bronze ranker to slip through his defences.

Kat was very much looking forward to robbing the man blind.

The whisper of metal being torn from stone carried from above. Kat held her breath, but no one in the gardens moved in their direction. Shortly after, a knotted rope trailed down to the moat. Grinning, Kat grasped it in both hands and began to climb.

Alighting atop the wall, she crouched alongside Isabel in a gap torn in the razor wires. Neither spoke while Kat surveyed the situation below. Inside the walls was a large garden, lush with rose bushes and duckponds covered in lily pads.

Apparently, no one had told the governor's gardener that Skarta was in a drought.

And here and there came the bright glow of a human soul as they moved through the plant life. Kat frowned as she counted them. There was a surprising number, even for the house of the governor. Could they have been warned somehow? Impossible! She hadn't told anyone. Not even Jon. He was going to be pissed when he found out what she'd done. This kind of job would even make him hesitate.

She glanced at Isabel, wondering if she should say something. Nah, let the Gurrians play their tricks. This time, she had a godsdamn Bronze ranker on her side. With that kind of power, the pair of them could have strolled through the front gates!

Removing a second rope from her backpack, she managed to wedge it around the stones and broken wires and tie it in place. Then with a final check for guards, she tossed the bundle of rope over the side.

"Come on," she said, slipping over the side of the wall.

She dropped into a crouch as she reached the ground, then darted for the nearest shrub, eager to be out of the open before the next guard appeared. Isabel followed, barely making a noise as she alighted on the soft grass. That was good. Everything depended on making it through the garden without detection.

Kat was about to dart to the next bush, when she sensed another group of guards approaching. Grasping Isabel by the scruff of her neck, she dragged the woman back down, then held her breath as they waited for the men to pass. One was an Iron ranker. Sensing the density of his soul, Kat supressed a shudder. Someone that powerful would normally have her fleeing for her life. Knowing the tastes of the Gurrian nobility, the man probably had two Body-based abilities—making him strong enough to tear her in two.

Let the bastard try it! Today, she had a Bronze ranker on her side!

Kat released her breath as the last of the men moved past. Pressing a hand to her chest, she whispered a prayer of thanks that the guards weren't particularly alert tonight. This lot had been chatting as they walked, not even glancing at their surroundings. Clearly they thought the place was secure.

See, no need to worry, Kat! she told herself.

Now they had an opening, the pair darted towards the manor, keeping low and using the bushes as cover from prying eyes. Clouds obscured the moon. Kat had them pause whenever a sliver of light slipped through their veil. You never knew what eyes might be watching from the house.

Within a few minutes, they were pressed up against the wall beneath a large window. The shutters had been drawn, barring entrance against unwanted visitors. Supposedly. They wouldn't deter Kat. Drawing a hammer and chisel from her pack, she wrapped a piece of cloth around the head of the hammer and handed them to Isabel. She was the muscle, after all.

"Here," she said. "I'll keep watch."

The woman pursed her lips, but she accepted the tools and went to work. The cloth did a decent job of muting the noise, but Kat still held her breath as she waited, her *Aura Sense* strained to the limit keeping watch for guards.

The wooden panels made the slightest *crack* when Isabel finally broke through, but with no one nearby, it went unnoticed. Isabel pulled the broken panel loose, allowing Kat to reach inside and quietly lift the shutters enough for them to slip underneath. She left them open as an escape route, hoping the inattentive guards wouldn't notice.

Kat turned to survey the room. A glow came from beneath a nearby door, granting them enough light to see. And what Kat saw made her smile. Rich violet drapes—the colours of Gurria, of course—hung across their window, while the room was furnished with a pair of ornate leather sofas and a coffee table of polished wood, probably from some distant land like Ressi. Even the air tasted rich—like sandalwood. Trust a Gurrian to have servants burning expensive incense when they weren't even around. An arrangement of roses and lilies had been set out on the table, their fragrance adding to the ambience, while the lush carpet of Yarrish wool was soft beneath their feet.

By the gods, the contents of this room could have funded the resistance for a year. The carpet alone would probably pay for a small cache of weapons. A shame she couldn't carry any of it out of here. She needed to figure out where the governor kept his gold.

"Well?" Isabel asked.

Kat felt a pang in her stomach. Guilt again. Now they were actually in the act, she felt bad, even knowing the Highlands were working with Gurria. Too bad. It was too late to turn back now. They were inside, and it was time to get to work.

She reached for her *Aura Sense* again. It took a moment this time for the colours to impose themselves over the world. She didn't usually use the ability this much, and her soul was feeling the strain. Exhaling, she focused the power, expanding her senses through the manor.

It was mostly empty, as she'd expected. A cluster of Auras were scattered through the rooms to their left. The servant's quarter, she assumed. From the muted colours, they were all fast asleep. They could discard that part of the citadel. No way a Gurrian stored their wealth anywhere near a bunch of Skartan peasants. She turned her *Sight* in the other direction—

And just about had an aneurysm—whatever that was. Terror sank its teeth into her guts as she stared at the brilliant, burning Aura. It lit up her *Sight* like a tiny sun in the heart of the complex. That…that was…

She cursed beneath her breath.

Gold. The governor was here after all. No one had told her that he was *Gold*.

"What is it?" Isabel asked sharply.

"He's here," Kat rasped. What else could she say?

She felt a tremor in her soul. A part of her—the little girl she had locked away all those years ago to survive—screamed for her to run, to wrap her arms around herself and flee the monster lurking in this dungeon. Gold rank? Another tremor. The sheer weight of his Aura pressed against her lungs—or was that just her panic?

What had she been thinking?

All she'd wanted was a little measure of revenge. To spit in the eye of the man who'd ruined her life. But Gold rank? Kat felt her courage creaking. She knew Pathfinders were not the immortal, unstoppable killing machines that commoners believed they were. They were mortals. A knife to the heart would kill them as dead as any other man on the street...

Kat stilled, her heart throbbing in her chest.

Arimus Shore was mortal.

And he was sleeping!

Did she really have the nerve? It was suicide, surely. But... she sensed no guards around the cursed governor. He was alone—and why not? The guards they'd passed should have been more than enough to prevent anyone reaching the manor.

Kat shivered, but this time it was not fear. She imagined standing over the black-hearted bastard, blade extended. A quick cut with a steady hand, and he would die choking on his own blood.

"...really here?"

Kat blinked, realising that Isabel had been speaking. The clanswoman's eyes were wide. She read the mixture of fear and anxiety in the woman's Aura, the tension after what Kat had said. What *had* she said?

"Yeah," she said softly, shaking off her nerves. "He's here."

What did one more lie matter now? Isabel might not deserve this, but here they were. Kat drew in a breath, steadying her resolve. There was a monster in this house. And she was going to slay it.

"This way," she said quickly, before her courage fled.

They slipped out the door into a dimly lit hallway. It seemed to run the length of the building, with doors leading off from either side. Polished lanterns of silver and bronze hung at long intervals, their partially shuttered flames providing the only source of light. The scent of roasting meat was heavy in the air, no doubt the remains of Arimus's dinner. So much for his unyielding work effort. The man had clearly retired early from the citadel for a feast.

Her stomach rumbled as they slunk from shadow to shadow. She'd missed dinner at Marta's. Maybe her *last* dinner at Marta's, if this went wrong…

Her soul flared, bringing Kat to a halt. The governor's Aura was close now. Just a few more doors. Desperately, she tried to hold herself together. What did Arimus Shore know of hunger? Had he ever suffered like Kat and her father had suffered? The thought poured anger on her soul. She grasped at it with desperation, using it to hold her fragile courage together. She sensed Isabel behind her and knew she had to move.

She moved.

To her relief, the Golden Aura remained calm. He was still asleep. She drew to a stop as they approached the door and turned to the clanswoman. She couldn't have Isabel in there with her. The Highlander would stop her.

"Wait here," she said as softly as she could manage, "I need to check for traps."

She slipped through the door before Isabel could object.

Within, the air practically bubbled with the strength of the

Gold ranked Aura. Even asleep, Kat felt his power pressing down on her. Even when she cut off her *Aura Sense*, she could still feel it, like a corrosive force against her soul.

The room was black as tar. Kat had to wait for her eyes to adjust, stars dancing across her vision from the lanternlight outside. As they dissipated, she saw him. A mound beneath twisted sheets. A solitary figure.

Arimus Shore.

A trickle of sweat ran down Kat's back. Her brow was slick with it. She shuddered, fear clawing its way back up her throat. She swallowed the scream. It was too late to turn back now.

She stepped towards the bed and her foot connected with something solid. Stifling a curse, Kat sucked in a breath and eyed the bed. The man did not stir. Carefully she crouched to check what she had struck. Her hand closed around the leather-wrapped hilt of a sword—

Darkness. Time stands still. A void, filling her, sweeping her away. The world holds its breath. Forever. Unending, swirling stars…stars that become eyes…and in the black, a voice speaks one word.

KILL!

Someone was screaming. *She* was screaming. Why would *she* be screaming? Where was she? Darkness clung to her still, but it was not the infinite that she knew, but a darkness rich with existence. With life.

"Kat, no!"

Light spilled into the world as the other voice spoke. Recognition tugged at her mind, a distant memory of a girl, of a time…*before.*

Then came another movement, a burst of energy, a blurring of the world.

Hunger tugged at her. Not the mortal sensation, that dull yearning she remembered from so long ago. This was far worse. Like someone had carved out a void inside her. A hole she needed to fill. To consume.

As the world moved, she swung.

Steel connected with flesh.

A voice screamed and energy flooded into her. Power. A taste unlike anything the girl had ever known. She gasped at the ecstasy of it.

Crack.

Something slammed into Kat, hurling her from her feet. Something was torn from her grasp...

...and she was Kat again.

She looked around at a scene of horror.

Light from the corridor caught the face of a young man as he staggered, blood pouring from the terrible gash in his chest. And his soul...his soul was *leaking.* Torn, like...like the claws of some ethereal beast had hacked through it. He stumbled a step towards her, hand extended, but his legs gave out and he crashed to the ground.

Kat stared at him. That...that was Arimus Shore. The governor. *What had happened to him?*

Above her stood Isabel, and her soul shone with *rage.* Her eyes burned as she glared at Kat, and she thought for a second the Highlander would strike her down.

But then Isabel turned and cursed, and instead she fell to her knees beside the injured man. Light bloomed around the woman, swirling from her soul and pouring into the Gold ranker.

Kat couldn't believe it—Isabel was trying to *heal* the monster. She wanted to shout for her to stop. But everything hurt. Her eyes fell to the sword. Isabel had tackled her, knocking it from her hands. What in the Seven Hells *was* that thing?

She shuddered, recalling the darkness. How long had she drifted there? And that hunger, that voice, what...

A groan came from nearby, snapping her back to the present. With all the commotion, the guards would be coming.

If they caught her, it would be death. She had to go. Gritting her teeth, she staggered upright. Isabel, intent on her *Healing*, did not notice. Kat took a step towards the door, before she remembered the sword.

Her eyes fell on the shining blade. Or rather, the dark blade. Unsheathed, it lay on the floor. It seemed that even the light from the corridor was consumed by it, drawn away to some other place. Her mouth was dry as she considered it. With one swing, it had incapacitated a Gold Pathfinder. She couldn't leave it.

Quickly she grabbed a handful of sheets. They were damp with blood, but she didn't care. Praying it worked, she clutched the sword with the linens. Nothing happened. Exhaling her relief, Kat slipped the blade carefully into its case.

Abruptly, the world grew still. It was a moment before she realised the governor was no longer groaning.

That was bad.

Isabel was still pouring her Aura into the unconscious man. She wouldn't leave. Kat could see it in the steely rage of her soul. This was all her fault. She had fooled the Highland woman, led her here. And now…

"I'm sorry," she whispered, knowing in all likelihood that the Highland woman would be blamed for what Kat had done.

Then hurling aside her regrets, Kat darted for the door. There was nothing she could do to help Isabel now. Hopefully her connection with the man on the ground—her brother— would give her some measure of protection.

In her heart, Kat knew that was folly. Gurrians were not a merciful people. But it was too late for second thoughts now.

It was time to go.

20

Eight weeks before the Festival of the Satana

Lunden Marcs would never admit it, but he felt a certain degree of satisfaction to see the surprise on Renard's face as he landed on his ass, having just received a solid blow from the rim of Lunden's shield. The Highlander's friends were already down, while Lunden and the Sarton woman who fought with him, Maria, remained unscathed despite their supposedly inferior weapons.

The Malesie man stayed on his back for a minute, puffing heavily as he regathered his breath. Finally though, he rose, face dark with anger.

"You cheated! You're both Pathfinders."

"We are," Lunden admitted, "but we didn't use our abilities."

"I don't care—"

Renard broke off as one of his friends placed a calming hand on his shoulder. This was Scott Sobotta. And he was almost as large a unit as the other man. While Scott came from

Sarton, he had volunteered to lend his strength to the other side in the interest of fairness, since he was a recent Copper ranker himself.

Both Scott and Maria had been amongst those blessed with an Essence after the battle for Sarton. And both had lost far more than they had gained. Scott, his brother, and Maria, her recent husband. Lunden had not seen either of them wear a smile since that fateful day.

It made Lunden's heart hurt. The war had barely started. Others like Renard might jeer and brag about their skill, but these two knew the cost they would all pay before the end. The friends and family they would lose. But here they were, willing to make the sacrifice anyway.

"The only trick is that we fought as one," Lunden said decisively. "Your greatswords are a powerful weapon, but they need space to swing, which means you fight separately. Each time you attacked our shield wall, you fought as individuals and were immediately outnumbered, one against the two of us."

There was a moment's silence as the big clansman seemed to consider his words.

"This is how you beat them?" he grunted at last, scratching his beard with a meaty hand. "I thought for sure it was just some rumour put about by Denether. But it is true, is it not? You defeated a Gurrian army."

Lunden grimaced, but to his surprise, it was Scott who answered. "We did," he said quietly. "Though it cost us gravely."

Renard turned to the man, seeming to weigh him up. "How many did you lose?"

"Twenty eight brave men and women." He paused, jaw tightening. "It would have been more, if not for the gods."

That was true—if you accepted that Essence came from

the gods. In the aftermath of the battle, the glowing lights had appeared before each of the survivors. Upon accepting them, the transformation to Pathfinders had healed even the gravest of wounds.

But not even the power of the gods could bring back the dead. For those twenty eight others, the fallen like Scott's brother and Maria's husband, the Essence had been too late.

The big clansman was nodding. "They shall be honoured," he said quietly.

"Good," Scott grunted. "You can start by listening to Lunden—because he is right. Those men were skilled. They did not panic, or buckle, or try to flee, even when they were losing. They fought together, mustered around their commander when he launched a counterattack. We very nearly lost that day."

"How many came against you?"

"A full Force," Maria entered the conversation. "Eighty men. We were only forty."

That got a response from the crowd. Whispers of disbelief spread through the clansmen and women as they turned to one another. Maria held their gaze.

"We lost many good warriors that day. But we would have all perished, if not for these swords." She raised her short-sword. "If not for our training."

A silence fell over the crowd then, heavy with the weight of her words. They might have all heard the whispers, might have even *wanted* to believe them. But they hadn't—not really. Not until right now, listening to two of their own who had been there.

A Gurrian army had attacked their lands—and been repelled.

The enemy could be beaten.

But it also meant the danger was real. This was no game,

to be played by those bored with their work in the fields. The hounds of war bayed louder with each passing day. And soon it would be more than just the bark. The jaws of death would close around their lives, and the world would never be the same.

But they were Malesie. They would not bend.

Renard was the first to step forward. Grim-faced, he held out a hand for the shortsword. Wordlessly, Lunden handed it over.

"Still think it's too small," the man grumbled as he took a few practice swings. "How am I meant to take a man's head off with a bloody toothpick?"

"You really want to learn?" Lunden asked softly.

The man nodded. "If it'll help us gut those Gurrian bastards, I'm in."

There was a rumble of agreement from the others around him.

Lunden smiled. "Then here is your first lesson," he said, taking the fresh blade that Maria offered him. "You won't be taking off any heads with one of these. But you don't need too. Mikael had a simple way of putting it: all you need to kill a man is to stick him with the pointy end…"

The others gathered around, some fifty men and women, as he began to run through the basic stabs and blocks that he and Mikael had practiced over the autumn. The lesson lasted several hours, at the end of which he left each in the crowd with a sword of their own. There would be plenty more where those came from, if Denether was doing his part organising the city's blacksmiths.

As Lunden moved away from the practice field towards the growing city of tents, he spotted a familiar face moving along the path from the city. It was Brandon Thorn, the highking's bodyguard. Waving a greeting, Lunden diverted from his path.

"Well met, Marcs," the man called as they met on the hillside. His gaze swept passed the Ressi man, to where his first group of students were still practicing with their new weapons. "I must say, I'm surprised. I didn't expect the Malesie to take so willingly to your methods." The wrinkles on his brow deepened. "Hells, is that Renard? How did you convince *him* to give up his greatsword?"

Lunden chuckled. "I put him on his ass—how else?"

The warrior grunted. "That would do it."

An uneasy silence fell between the pair as they studied those below. Lunden flicked the man a glance, noting the tightness on his face, the way his fingers lingered on the hilt of his greatsword.

"Well, what is it then?" he said at last.

Thorn pressed his lips in a thin line. "Who says there is something?"

"You didn't come all the way from the city just to make pleasantries."

"No, I did not." There was a long pause, before the man continued: "Something strange is going on with Denether."

"How so?"

"A messenger arrived yesterday. He was shown to the Longhouse in secret. Denether has been in talks with him ever since."

"War is coming. I imagine there is much to keep the highking occupied."

"That's just it, Marcs," the old soldier said quietly. "The messenger came from Gurria."

A pit opened in Lunden's stomach. "I see," he said quietly, "and might I ask: Why are you telling me this?"

"Thought you should know," came the reply. "What will you do?"

Lunden's eyes didn't leave the Malesie practicing below. "Nothing," he said calmly, though his pulse was racing.

"Mikael and Jaxon are journeying south at the governor's invitation. Maybe this is connected."

"I hope you're right, Marcs," Thorn said. "I'd best be getting back to the city." He turned and started back up the hill towards Furness without another word.

21

Present Day

Mikael woke to a sharp stabbing pain behind his eyes. Stifling a groan, he tried to sit up, but instead found his hands bound behind his back in iron shackles. *What?* The last thing he remembered was a conversation with the terrifying presence that was Alyina Sorulus. Had she decided his freedom was too much of a risk after all? Then why the subterfuge? It made no sense.

Which meant someone else was behind his current situation.

Great. Who had he managed to piss off this time?

He didn't have to wait long to find out, as the grinding of a door opening screeched in his ears. Awkwardly using his feet and bound hands, Mikael scrambled to his knees. His vision swam as he tried to get his bearings. Hell, his head was pounding like a Christmas Nutcracker and stars were dancing in his eyes, but he seemed to be sitting on the floor of an empty grey stone room that was just a bit too reminiscent of a prison cell for his liking. A pair of silhouettes approached through the stars.

"Get up," one ordered. Still struggling with his cognition, Mikael couldn't quite make out his face. His voice sounded like he'd gargled nails for breakfast.

"How about you tell me just who—"

Red exploded across Mikael's vision and the darkness churned again, threatening to swallow him up. Choking, he clung to the dim spark that was his consciousness…and found himself lying face down on the cold stone. He braced himself as he heard the shifting of boots, but there was no second blow. Instead, hands grasped him beneath the arms and hauled him up.

That was almost enough to do him in. The nutcracker went…nuts, pounding away at his skull like it had replaced bangers for hammers. A distant part of his mind worried what the repeated blows to his head since arriving in this world were doing to his future intellect.

Maybe he should ask Isabel to check him out when he saw her next. A warm feeling fluttered in his gut at the thought of the unfathomable clanswoman. *Where was she now?* he wondered. Safe in the Highlands, helping Lunden train the rest of the clan warriors, he hoped. Knowing her, though…

His vision cleared and Mikael found himself being half-carried, half-dragged up a final flight of stairs, then through a short corridor, before his captives stopped before another iron door. One of the men released him to pull it open.

With some of his wits recovered, Mikael triggered his *Aura Sense*. His heart fell. Both men were Iron rank—weaker than him, but given his arms were pinned and his current state, they would cut him down like a pair of rugby props smashing the opposition flyhalf.

He could try using *Elemental Manipulation* to hurl lightning at them, but he was still having problems concentrating. He would probably fail miserably to gather any Mana, or accidentally burn down half the city. So for now he did the only thing he could—nothing.

The door swung open and a cloud of steam came billowing out into the corridor. Seeing that he could stand on his own now, the men did not drag him this time, just held him by the arms and pushed him forward.

The steam swallowed Mikael up and for a second all he saw was swirling white. But with the door still open behind him, it quickly dissipated, revealing a large pool of turquoise waters in the middle of the room.

And there, massive arms spread on either side of his pudgy body as he reclined in the pool, was Jon Sorrow.

"Ah, Mikael, so good of you to join me," the man announced, waving to the guards in a gesture that had the flaps of skin beneath his arms wobbling. "Please, remove his bonds."

One of the men produced a key. Mikael sighed as the manacles clanged to the ground, stretching his arms and rubbing his wrists until the circulation returned. Sleeping—or rather, lying unconscious—for hours in those things had left his arms aching.

"Jon," he said at last, trying to hold his nerve. Something had obviously gone wrong if the leader of the resistance was meeting him like this. And without his sword—they must have taken it from him while he was unconscious—Mikael felt terribly exposed. "I was hoping our next meeting would be a little more…mundane."

"As had I," the man said coldly, "but it seems circumstances have changed. Please, join me. I am told you had a busy night."

Little pinpricks of warning tingled across Mikael's scalp, but he didn't have much choice but to obey. Not with the two brutes looming behind him. So he gingerly removed his clothing, careful not to bump his aching head, and descended the steps into the water. The pool only came to his waist, but he sank to his knees, letting out a sigh as warmth swallowed him up.

For just a second, he forgot his peril and basked in the pleasure. Hot water! He hadn't had a hot bath in almost a year. It was something he'd missed at first—especially during the horrible winter months in the Highlands—but eventually he'd come to accept the cold baths. Only now did he realise how much he'd *really* missed them. He would have to ask Jaxon if Skarta had a public bathhouse like this—if he survived the next ten minutes, of course.

"I'm guessing this has something to do with Alyina Sorulus, then?" he asked, taking a stab at the truth. He'd already caught the resistance watching him once.

"Oh, yes," Jon said softly. He didn't move from where he lounged at the side of the pool, but suddenly the weight of his Aura was pressing down on Mikael. "I had not even realised she was in the city—so imagine my surprise when Kat came and told me that the woman was meeting with you—and in *my own university.*"

Kat had been watching him? Damn, apparently she'd upped her game!

"I was somewhat taken aback as well."

"Perhaps you'd like to explain yourself before I have your throat cut."

Mikael swallowed, struggling to keep his cool between his pounding head and the pressure on his soul. "No need for threats." When Jon didn't respond, he licked his lips and continued: "She wanted to know about my world."

"And did you entertain the good princess's curiosity?"

"Of course not." Mikael scowled.

"I see." Water splashed as Jon let his arms fall from the sides. "And is that all you spoke about?"

"The only thing that—*blofdaggjf!*"

The rest of his words were drowned out as powerful arms gripped Mikael by the shoulders and forced him beneath the surface. He choked as water flooded his lungs, turning them to molten agony. The pounding redoubled in his skull as his eyes burned from the acidic waters. He thrashed against his assailants, struggling to break free, but their flesh was like steel. In flashes of colour, he saw their souls burning as they used the *Might* ability to overpower him.

His only hope was Mana, but as he tried to draw on the ethereal power, his soul recoiled as though struck by a hammer. The swirling lines of Mana flickered and died, slipping through his grip. Another mouthful of water flooded his throat and a deathly agony followed. His thrashing grew weaker, his energy fading and lactic acid creeping through his limbs. Strangely, there was no fear as his vision began to fade, only regret…

A man smiled down at him, a familiar face, like staring into a mirror, only this face was older. Grey streaked his beard and there were lines around his eyes, wrinkles upon his brow…

"Don't worry, son," the man said. "I'll be back soon. They promised." He smiled sadly, even as a crackling energy began to form around him. "Look after your mother for me."

ERROR! Unknown Temporal Distortion Detected. Detainment Protocols Activated.

BOOM!

The vision vanished as the iron hands released Mikael. Suddenly free, he found a last scrap of strength to push off from the bottom. Bursting through the surface, he threw himself at the side of the pool, clutching at the stone like it was his long lost father…

"I suggest you do not lie to me again, Mikael Heaton." Jon had not moved from the other side of the room, but his thugs loomed over Mikael, arms crossed, faces hard. "Or next time I cannot guarantee they will stop."

Mikael swallowed. His heart raced in his chest like a truck with its breaks cut and every muscle in his body burned with the buildup of acid. He should have been terrified.

Yet looking into the hard eyes of the fat man lounging in the thermal pool, he felt only rage.

"I offer you my friendship," he said quietly, "and this is how you repay me?"

"Friendship?" Jon hissed. "Just this morning, *another* Highlander arrived in the city and went straight to the citadel. I hear whispers about a peace treaty for the Highlands. And now I learn that you are meeting with Alyina Sorulus—the Emperor's personal executioner." His jaw was hard and his eyes burned with fury. "Is *that* the sort of friendship you speak of, Mikael Heaton?"

Mikael met the man's eyes. "I already told you about the peace treaty. It is as false as the beggar's identity you wore when last we met."

"And the princess?"

He shrugged. "If I had to guess, she's the real power running the show here in Skarta."

Jon leaned forward, the mist swirling around his body. "Pretty words. But they're just that at the end of the day, are they not? How can I be sure you are not planning to betray me, Offworlder?"

Mikael scowled. "That's easy."

"I have already warned you once, Mikael. I find myself short of patience this morning."

"Very well," Mikael said, his voice edged with danger. "You can trust me, because if I really was working with Gurria, I would have already told them your true name…Jon Sorrow."

Silence. It was a gamble—but a calculated one.

"How?" the resistance leader rasped, clearly shocked by Mikael's declaration.

"You have your secrets, I have my own, Jon," Mikael replied. "What's important is that we understand each other. I have no interest in working for people like Arimus Shore or Alyina Sorulus. My only interest is protecting the people of the Highlands."

Jon studied him, his lips pursed, and Mikael could see the man was weighing his options. "Why?" he said finally. "You are a stranger in this realm. Why such loyalty to the clans?"

"Because they stood up for me when no one else would." His face hardened. "Now, perhaps you will share something with me, Jon. You are clearly an important man here in Skarta. Someone in a position of power. Why would you risk it all, building an organisation like the resistance?"

"Because I am *Skartan*," the man growled, surprising Mikael with his vehemence. "I might have my riches, and power, but these luxuries only exist with Gurria's blessing." His gaze took on a distant look. "So I have made myself useful to them, offering my services and my wealth, all the while propagating the image of a harmless sycophant." His lips tightened. "All this, so they will not see the viper in the grass before it strikes."

Seeing the fire in the man's eyes, Mikael couldn't help but believe his words. "Then maybe we can still become friends, Jon," he said with a smile. "And if I am nothing else, I am loyal to my friends. You should remember that next time you consider kidnapping me."

To his surprise, the Silver Pathfinder chuckled. "Perhaps I will."

"Then may I take my leave?"

Jon nodded and Mikael rose from the water and climbed the steps. A servant, unseen until then, stepped from the swirling steam and offered him a cotton towel. Patting himself down, Mikael glanced back at the resistance leader.

"I understand you have a plot to dispose of the governor. It may be that my own plans can assist with that task."

A smirk crossed Jon's lips. "Thank you for the offer, but I have the situation well in hand."

"And the princess?"

The smile faltered. "She complicates things, but powerful as she is, we have strength in numbers."

Mikael eyed the man. "When?"

"Soon."

Nodding, Mikael finished dressing himself. He hadn't expected Jon to give out any more details, but he had his suspicions. Given the man's elevated level of paranoia, it had to be soon. In a few days, he would know for sure. For now, he accepted his sword and cloak as the attendant handed them to him. He immediately felt better clipping the sword belt around his waist. Draping the cloak around his shoulders, he nodded his leave. They both knew there was no point hiding where they were now.

"Mikael," he was surprised when Jon called his name. Frowning, he turned back. "The Festival of the Satana," the resistance leader said softly. "That's when we'll do it."

Mikael shivered. So his suspicions were confirmed. Just as Azaroth had warned. It would all come to a head on the day of the summer solstice.

"And what do you want from me?" He didn't ask for further details. They both knew it would be too dangerous.

"The Battalion stationed here in the city is at half strength. Four hundred men—the rest are dispersed around the province. We have the numbers to take the city." He eyed Mikael. "*Holding* it will be the problem. Once the Emperor realises what we've done, he will send everything he has at us."

"You want the clans to join you?"

He nodded. "The Gurrians grow tired of war. After ten years in Ressi, their Legions are depleted. With the support of the Highlands, they could not match our armies. Skarta and the Highlands would both be free."

Mikael exhaled, turning this fresh information over in his mind. "I'll see what I can do," he said with a final nod.

He needed to talk with Jaxon, before he made any commitments. He had made a promise, after all…

22

The pain came before Isabel's consciousness even returned. Like the burning fire that had consumed her mother and left the scars on her face, it embraced her like an old friend, its touch almost soothing. What did Isabel Fields know better than pain? Had she not suffered it all of her life?

But then the claws drew back and their needle points sank deeper, tearing through the barriers she had erected in her mind, sinking deep into her spirit. Isabel screamed then, screamed until she could feel her throat tearing and taste the blood in her mouth.

And finally she woke. She tried fighting then, of course. Mana filled the room, swirling with its flickering lights. She reached for it instinctively, desperately—but whoever her assailant was, their Mana abilities were far greater than her own, for the little scraps of Mana were torn from her grasp before they could be used.

Next she flexed her *Enforced Body*—only to find her limbs bound by unshakeable bonds. Not even the cold steel table beneath her bent as she strained against it.

And when she reached for her Aura, she finally recalled how she had come to be here. Isabel's desperate attempts to keep the wounded man alive had so drained her Aura, even now it burned low, a feeble glow within.

By Ryntirax, if she ever saw that Kat again, she was going to teach the little street rat a lesson. For now though…

…she strained against her bonds again, desperate, and thought she found a little give in them this time. Hope flickered in her chest…until she heard the laughter.

"So she's finally awake," a voice whispered. Footsteps followed as Kat cracked open her eyes to find the stunning face of a woman looming over the table. "Good. I find it so much more satisfying when my playthings squirm. Now, let's start with a name."

"Please," Isabel rasped. "I don't—"

A hand closed around her wrist—and the pain returned. Only now there was no dulling the lashing of those claws. She felt every moment of agony as her assailant's Aura poured into her body, filling it with the poisonous, acrid burning of another soul. This was like her own *Healing Touch*, only reversed, an attack on her very nature that left her sobbing in the broken void of her own body…

…the pain ceased as quickly as it had appeared as the woman withdrew her *Ardent Onslaught.*

"Now, dear," the woman continued as though they were still exchanging pleasantries. "You weren't thinking of lying to me, were you?"

"Isabel," she spat, her body still spasming from the attack.

"Nice to meet you, Isabel. I am Alyina Sorulus."

Isabel flinched and the woman laughed.

"Good. I see from your reaction you have heard of me. That should make this easier."

She had. And none of it was good. Another piece of her courage crumbled, and to her shame, a whimper left her lips.

"Oh dear, oh dear." A cold hand stroked her cheek. Isabel shuddered, though this time the pain did not follow. "Do not worry. All I want is the truth." The fingers hardened and Isabel felt the faintest breeze brush against her soul.

A brush, followed by a dagger. She sucked in a breath as the pain spread like a wave from where the hand rested, rippling outwards to fill her. There was no bracing herself against this torture, no fleeing into the darkness. All Isabel could do was arch her back and strain and scream until her throat bled…

She slumped against the steel table as the pain retreated. It had lasted longer this time. In its absence she found herself sobbing.

"Please," she rasped. "I'll tell you anything, just, please…"

"Oh, I know you will, my dear." Alyina sat casually on the table, legs crossed and reclining slightly so she could look Isabel in the face. "But you can't blame a girl for wanting a little fun before we start, can you?" She tapped a finger against her chin, before letting out a little sigh. "Very well. You can start by explaining why I found you lying in a pool of blood beside the unconscious Governor of Skarta."

Unconscious? That was good—at least her efforts had not been in vain. Though…that had been the *governor*? Godsdamn Kat, the street urchin had played her for a fool!

"I didn't know he was the governor," she rasped, "I came for my father…"

"Oh? And who is your father, my dear?"

Isabel swallowed, her throat thick with dread. "Jasper Shore."

There was a long silence. "Your father is Jasper Shore?" There was disbelief in the woman's voice.

Isabel managed a nod.

To her surprise, Alyina began to laugh. "Well, isn't that delicious? My father's saintly chancellor with a bastard daughter." She chuckled, before her face hardened once again. "In that case, I guess I need to adjust my question: *Why did I find you lying in a pool of blood beside your unconscious brother?*"

Isabel's heart practically lurched to a stop in her chest. "*What?*"

Her brother was the Governor of Skarta? And Kat had tried to *kill* him? Wasn't the man meant to be a powerful Pathfinder? And in that case, how in the Seven Hells had a *Copper ranker* even managed to hit him—let alone cause such a terrible wound that it had taken all of Isabel's power just to keep him alive. None of this made sense.

And meanwhile, Alyina was touching her again, one finger tapping gently against her breastbone. "I'm beginning to think you're a slow learner, my dear," she said, no longer sounding so amused. "I suggest you elaborate, quickly, before my patience runs thin."

Elaborate? Isabel barely knew what was going on herself! So she spat out the first thing she could think of.

"It wasn't me!" she gasped. "I didn't try to kill him. *I* tried to *save* him!"

"I see. So it was your friend. Tell me who she is."

Isabel opened her mouth to blurt out everything she knew about the girl—when an image leapt into her mind. She saw the smiling faces of Marta's children as they gathered to eat, the old woman at the head of the table, the dancing light of the lanterns as the makeshift family laughed.

Then she imagined soldiers bursting through the doors, the screams of the orphans as the blades fell.

"I do not know," she gasped instead. Blood pounded in her ears, but however she might loath Kat in this moment, she could not let them know about the boarding house. This woman did not have a speck of mercy anywhere in her soul. "A street urchin I was using as a guide. She could be anywhere."

"You're lying," Alyina said softly. "You're protecting her."

"*No!*" she all but screamed, desperate as the pale fingers slid down her belly.

Alyina paused. "Hmm, not the girl then. Someone else." She circled the table, her fingers still trailing across Isabel's flesh. "Tell me who you're protecting and I promise you a quick death."

Isabel shuddered, picturing this woman striding into the room full of children. She imagined their looks of surprise as Alyina Sorulus approached, followed by their terror as the princess unleashed her power.

And some of Isabel's old rage flared in the pit of her stomach.

"Torture me all you want," she spat, baring her teeth. "When the Darkstrider finds me, he will hunt you down and make a trophy out of your skull!"

"Jaxon Daniyal?" Alyina asked in surprise. "He's involved in this? My, my, I didn't think he still had it in him!"

A terrible fear filled Isabel as she realised her mistake. She clamped her mouth shut, but it was too late. She had already doomed her friends. Her family.

"Oh don't go quiet on me now, Isabel. Not when we're finally making progress."

Coming to the head of the table, Alyina leaned over Isabel, so they were eye to eye. Clamping her mouth shut, Isabel glared at the hateful woman. She had already said too much.

"That is a shame," Alyina said softly. Her hand stroked Isabel's cheek. "Here I was, beginning to think you really didn't have anything to do with all this."

"I did not, I swear," Isabel choked. "Jaxon either. It was just a terrible—"

She did not get to finish the words, as the torrent came flooding back. There were no questions this time, and no darkness into which to flee. Only a brilliant, shining red of the woman's murderous intent. Isabel wasn't even sure when she started to scream, or when the bindings cut into her flesh, or how long the *Onslaught* lasted this time.

All she knew was that when the agony left her, and she felt herself slipping into darkness, she welcomed it with open arms.

23

Six weeks before the Festival of the Satana

On the gently swaying docks of Pine Harbour, steel blades clashed as Conner and the chieftain of the Fushore did battle. From the very first exchange of blows, he knew he had underestimated the woman. It was not just that she was a Pathfinder—she was also a skilled swordswoman.

And in those first few heartbeats, as she *Surged* across the wooden planks, she had almost had him. As promised, there was no holding back. The crew of the Fushore ship docked at the wharf screamed as a blow from Yiva tried to cave in his skull.

He batted it aside with the flat of his sword, but the power behind the attack knocked him off-balance. The world sped up as Conner used his own *Movement Surge* ability, channelling the power of his body into a few heartbeats of speed. He recovered, regaining his balance in time to deflect the next attack.

Salt tinged the air as a wave crashed against the wooden supports of the wharf, sending water crashing over their feet. Droplets gleamed on Conner's greatsword as he switched up the pace, bringing the fight to Yiva. His *Enforced Body* powered a feint for her head—then shifted to target her legs. She skipped back, narrowly avoiding losing a foot.

A wild grin twisted her lips as she watched him. "You're *scared*, Conner," she hissed. "I can see it in your soul. Throw down your sword, and all you lose is your honour. No need to lose your life as well. Not for that bastard."

Conner pressed his lips together, resisting the urge to respond. He *was* afraid, though not of Yiva.

He was afraid of failure. All his life, he had lived for a moment like this, to fight for his people, to put his strength and skill to the test in defence of the Highlands. It was all he had ever wanted—to follow in the footsteps of his father and grandfather before him, to carry the greatsword of the Malesie into battle and emerge victorious.

Now Conner feared he was not strong enough.

So he answered the chieftain with steel. She danced away from him, stepping easily on wood slick with water. Conner followed with greater care. The watchers jeered down at him, but he ignored the taunts. He kept focused on Yiva as she came *Surging* back at him.

Planting his feet, Conner let her come. Her blade descended, but his greatsword was already there. Sparks flew as they came together with enough force to cleave a man in two. Metal shrieked, and Conner could almost hear Maisiwan's voice in his ear, reprimanding him for destroying such a fine blade. The chink such an impact would leave…

Yiva came again, still *Surging*. She must be draining the energy of her body at a prodigious rate to continue such an onslaught. Conner was forced on the retreat, though he chose his footing carefully as another wave crashed over the wharf.

Yiva's raven hair swirled as the wind swept around them. The sailors had fallen silent, their breaths held in expectation. They realised now this would not be an easy win for their chieftain. Conner was confident that Yiva was Steel rank, like himself. They should be evenly matched.

Except she had given something away—her *Aura Sense*. Useful as it could be against an inexperienced fighter, Conner had been trained by the Darkstrider. Jaxon had spent many weeks drilling him in Aura control. His soul would only reveal what he wanted it to show.

Yiva did not seem overly bothered. She kept at him, blow after blow, some even landing, slashing through the resistance of his *Enforced Body* to open shallow cuts in his skin. He ignored them, concentrating on his own form, deflecting the more dangerous and evading the rest.

And he watched.

As the contest wore on, his opponent finally began to slow, the repeated use of *Movement Surges* taking their toll. The contest continued, but he had her measure now. Jaxon's training had served him well. While Yiva was flagging, Conner had reserved his strength. He had also held back one ability, waiting for the right moment.

When it came, he didn't hesitate. There was the slightest opening—a second where Yiva's boot slipped on the slick wharf. She flung out her sword, trying to close the gap, but that only opened a different one.

Energy gathered within Conner as he activated *Might*, the power of his body coalescing, building to a crescendo that thundered in his ears. With a shout, he brought down his greatsword, all the collective strength of his body concentrated into one blow.

Steel clashed as he struck Yiva's extended weapon.

With a shriek, steel shattered.

The chieftain of the Fushore staggered back from him, horror dawning on her face as she saw the ruined blade. Half her sword remained, twisted and broken, ending in a jagged point. It was over. Conner lowered his sword, ready for her surrender. Then he saw the change come over her face. Her jaw hardened and her eyes glinted as she looked at Conner.

He saw the truth then. Yiva would not surrender. Her hatred for his father was so great, she would never allow herself to serve him, not even if it cost her life. She would go to the grave before she allowed the Fushore to march to the aid of his people.

And looking into her emerald eyes, Conner realised something else.

He could not do it. He would not be his father's executioner.

His greatsword made a *thud* as he let it fall to the boards of the dock.

"I surrender," he said quietly.

Silence. Nearby, the crew of the ship stared at him, their faces a mix of shock and disbelief. Yiva too stood with her eyes wide, lips parted as though she was preparing to hurl a profanity. Sweat beaded her brow, and her face was red with the heat of their contest. She still looked like she was gathering the strength to throw herself onto the point of his sword. It took a long while for his words to seep through her rage.

"Why?" she rasped.

"What did he do, Yiva?" Conner asked instead. "That you hate him so?"

For a moment, he thought she would rebuff him again. She watched him with those emerald eyes, dark with the weight of the past. It seemed she was weighing him up, appraising his worth.

"Nothing," she said quietly. Conner frowned, but she shook her head and continued. "My father warned Denether about the Deti. He told Denether that someone was arming them. That they were growing bold. A year before the great invasion, he sent a message to Furness, begging the Malesie to help deal with the threat. Your grandfather was still Highking then, but he was old, infirm. Denether handled most business for the clan. He refused to help us." She drew in a shuddering breath. "A few months later, my father was dead—killed in an ambush by Detian raiders."

Conner swallowed. "I'm sorry…" he exhaled. "My father, had he known—"

"Oh, he knew," Yiva cut him off. She was looking out across the ocean now. "They were rivals for the throne," she said quietly, before snorting. "Such a pointless thing, but my father and yours, they both wanted it. And my father had the respect of the Izolu, for his battles against the Deti. If he had not died before your grandfather, they would have made *him* Highking."

Conner frowned. "You're not saying…that my father had a hand in it?"

Yiva met his gaze. "A year after my father's death, the Deti invaded," she continued. "I was chieftain by then, but in my rage and grief, I refused your father's call. But that only served his purposes further, did it not? Because there he was, finally battling the Deti before the gates of our greatest city." She snorted. "The Izolu liked that, oh yes. When your grandfather finally passed away, we all knew who would have the votes to succeed him."

Yiva's words settled like a boulder on Conner's mind. "You cannot…"

"It is all a game to him, Conner," Yiva whispered, "all of us his playthings."

He wanted to object, to defend his father, but…guilt churned in his gut. He knew Denether. In public, he was the light-hearted, benign ruler of the Malesie. The even-handed judge of the Highlands. But in private, his father was another man. Cold, calculating. But would he have gone so far as to betray his own people?

Conner honestly could not answer that question. Which

might have been all the answer he needed.

"I'm sorry," he whispered.

"I do not need your sympathy, Conner," Yiva's words were weary. "Nor your apologies. I am only telling you who your father truly is." She looked away. "And why I cannot help you."

A knot tightened in Conner's chest. Without thinking, he took a step closer to Yiva, the breeze ruffling in his hair.

"I am not my father, Yiva."

Her lips turned downward. "No, you are not," she said softly, "but Denether rules. What would you have me do?"

Conner swallowed. He had dropped his bag when the fight started, but he retrieved it now and reached inside. The cloth was soft in his fingers as he drew it out. The cloak that Mikael had prepared for this very purpose. A replica of the one Jaxon had given him before the battle for Sarton.

You rejected this once, Conner, because you said you weren't worthy. But someone needs to unite the Highlands. Maybe you're worthy, maybe not. But there's no one else.

Rising, he held up the tri-coloured cloak for Yiva to see. Malesie blue. Izolu red. And Fushore green.

"We cannot change the past," he said, swinging the cloak around his shoulders and clipping it in place, "but we can change our future. Let my father sit and sulk in the shadow of Ryntirax. From today, let us begin a new chapter—you and I, and all the Highlands."

Sunlight rippled off the waters of the harbour as Conner held Yiva's gaze. Her jaw was clenched, her fist still balled around the hilt of her broken sword. Finally though, she turned away, her eyes settling on the horizon. Her face softened, and he felt a wave of relief as she nodded.

"Very well, Conner," she said, her voice heavy with past agonies. "My people and I will follow you. Let us see where this path leads us."

24

"We have to talk."

Jaxon looked up from his plate of fried potato and egg to find Mikael standing over him. A frown touched his lips. He hadn't seen the Offworlder return last night—and now he looked about as rough as a man could look an hour after sunrise. Which meant…

"Let me guess, you had a busy night?"

Groaning, Mikael sank into the chair opposite Jaxon and rubbed his brow. "You could say that."

"Well, the innkeeper's been looking for you," Jaxon said, gesturing toward the man behind the counter. He'd been pestering Jaxon earlier about a bag of supplies behind the counter. "Says he got the stuff you asked for in the market."

Mikael frowned, and it took him a long time to piece together his thoughts. "That's good, but they'll have to wait," he said, rising again. "Come on." He hesitated. "I'm going to be honest, there's a *bunch* of stuff I need to come clean with you on, and I don't want this being overheard."

Grunting, Jaxon shovelled the last few morsels from his plate into his mouth and followed Mikael outside. They wove their way through the early morning crowds, out onto the beach where they had been practicing most days since their arrival. Only then did Mikael tell him about his latest encounter with the leader of the Skartan Resistance.

"You showed him your Offworlder power?" Jaxon asked when the story finished.

They sat together on a quiet bank near the edge of the river. The sluggish waters swirled past beneath their feet, not so black as the canals in the city, but still a murky brown. Several of the enormous leviathan lay sleeping on the sand a few hundred yards away. Mikael kept glancing in their direction, then back to the packet of noodles he'd bought from a street vendor on their way through the city.

"I kept things deliberately vague," he said through a mouthful of food. "I'd rather leave him guessing than put all my cards on the table."

Jaxon took a bite of his own noodles. It was good—though Mikael said it lacked spice. Jaxon would have preferred a touch of lamb or beef mixed in, but the Skartan diet was more grain and plant based.

Puffing out his cheeks, Jaxon nodded. He didn't really understand the turn of phrase, but he was getting used to deciphering Mikael's mannerisms.

"So what did you find out?"

"The resistance is planning an uprising for the Festival of the Elohim," Mikael said so quietly that even Jaxon had to strain to hear him above the babbling of the river.

"That's in two days."

"Yep, and I'm guessing the governor won't have an answer for us before then either."

"Which means we're going to get tangled up in the entire mess." He cursed. "*Damnit.*"

Mikael was looking out over the waters. "There's more."

Jaxon stifled a groan. Of course there was. What else could he expect when Mikael Heaton was involved.

"What now?"

Mikael drew his short sword from its sheath, then reversed the blade and offered it to Jaxon hilt first. Jaxon raised his eyebrows, but accepted the offering without question. Mikael watched him, as though waiting for something to happen.

"What is it?" Jaxon grunted, growing impatient.

"You don't feel anything?"

"No, Mikael." He offered the sword back. "Enough with the games. Talk."

Mikael rested the sword in his lap. "You know I regained most of my memories, after the battle for Sarton."

Jaxon nodded. They hadn't spoken much about it, but it had been impossible not to notice the change in the young man.

"Well, I also remembered how I got here."

That was new. Clenching his jaw, Jaxon waited. Mikael liked the sound of his own voice. He would elaborate given time.

"It wasn't by accident," he said softly. "I made a machine. A construct that would help me forge a bridge between worlds."

Jaxon frowned. "Why would you want to do that?"

"The reason…still escapes me," Mikael sighed. "But that's not important right now. What *is* important is that *the machine came with me through the portal*. It's been with me since the day I arrived—first, hidden as a part of my Aura. And then…" He nodded to the sword. "It was reforged on The Day That Never Was."

Jaxon's stomach churned. That had been the day the Elohim had descended from the sky—and the day he had died, if Mikael was to be believed.

"How was it reforged?"

"It was turned into a pair of blades. This is one of them."

Furrowing his brow, Jaxon picked up the sword again. "It looks like any other one of Maisiwan's swords," he said carefully. The edge had been honed and polished with a careful hand, but he could still see the occasional mark or dent from heavy use, most likely from the battle for Sarton.

Just to be sure though, he opened his *Aura Sense*. Only living things could hold an Aura, so he would see nothing more, but...

...Jaxon frowned, focusing his *Sense* closer. That...it was barely discernible, invisible unless he'd been looking for it, but there *was* the faintest glint of something there.

"You see it?"

"I see *something*," he muttered. Blinking, he let his vision fade before handing the sword back. "You said there were two?"

"Yes. They...weren't happy with me having the construct, so the other half was taken from me."

"Very well," Jaxon replied, "and why are you telling me all this? Why now?"

"Well, I think I know why the...Elohim were so touchy about my construct," he explained. "I went to the library to find out more about magical weapons, whether any had existed in this world before. And I found—" he cut himself off with a curse. "Crap, I almost forgot. There's something *else.*"

Jaxon actually groaned this time. "What?"

"When I was in the library, I met someone..."

"*Who*, Mikael?"

"Why, he met *me*, my dear." A voice came from behind them. "Who else?"

They spun as a woman laughed. And there, dressed in a scarlet dress of swirling silk, looking as stunning as the day they had parted, was Alyina Sorulus. Princess and General of the Gurrian Legions.

And Jaxon's former lover.

"Alyina," he rasped.

Beside him, Mikael was glancing from Alyina to Jaxon and back again, looking like he had seen a ghost.

"Mikael, so nice to see you once more," the princess said as she approached. "And my dear Jaxon, you're looking…" She wrinkled her nose. "Old."

"What are you doing here, Alyina?" he growled.

A quick pass over her spirit confirmed his fears. When last he'd seen her, Alyina had been Gold rank and he himself Silver. Now…now she was pressing on the limits of even her father.

"Why, I was hoping Mikael and I might continue our chat from last night," she said brightly. "It was quite productive, all those juicy little hints he was dropping." Her eyes danced. "I can see why you kept him around."

"You two know each other…" Mikael said, finally seeming to recover some of his wits.

"She's the woman I mentioned," Jaxon growled.

"Oh my, have you been talking about me behind my back?" There was a twisted grin on Alyina's face as she circled them. "Only good things, I hope."

"What do you want—"

"*Do not be rude*," Alyina snapped, flashing him with a wild glare. "Really, Jaxon, you could be nicer to the woman you left at the altar."

"*What?*"

"I didn't—"

Her laughter peeled across the waters. "Oh relax, silly, I'm not here for you." She came to an abrupt halt, eyes fixed over Jaxon's shoulder. "I'm here for *him*."

Jaxon gritted his teeth, but Mikael placed a hand on his shoulder before he could speak.

"Maybe the governor didn't pass on my message," Mikael said as he stepped alongside Jaxon. "My secrets are for my friends alone."

Alyina pouted. "Are we not friends?" she asked in that deceptively sweet manner of hers. "After the other night, you certainly *seemed* to like me."

At Jaxon's side, Mikael's face had gone red. "I…ah…"

The laughter came again. Alyina had a mad look in her eyes as she took another step closer. "Besides," she murmured, "your secrets didn't seem so precious when you were whispering them in my ear."

"Alyina, I'm warning you—"

"Are you?"

Jaxon practically swallowed his words as the princess swung on him again. This time there was no missing the rage in her eyes. A long silence stretched between the three of them as they stood alone on the sands.

Alyina was the first to break it. "Oh, enough of this," she muttered. With a wave of her hand, her anger seemed to fade away. "I didn't come to make threats. I came with an offer." She smiled sweetly. The look was pure poison on those lips. "Peace."

Jaxon snorted. "What's the catch?"

"Careful, Jaxon," Alyina warned. "Why look a gift horse in the mouth?"

He just glowered at her at that.

A grin split her face in two. "Oh, alright, you got me. Don't worry, its nothing too onerous. My father just needs some assurances that the clans will behave. A Legion stationed in Furness ought to do the trick."

"You cannot be serious."

"Eighty Gurrian soldiers are dead, Jaxon," Alyina reprimanded. "I am deadly serious. Think about their families. You think my father could ask for less? We simply cannot have savages roaming our borders, freely killing whoever they like."

"Denether will never go for it."

"And you decide things for the king of the Highlands now, do you?" Alyina asked pointedly.

Jaxon clenched his fists. If his eyes could shoot fire, Alyina would have been a smoking pit in the ground. What she was offering…he knew Alyina. It was never *just* the devil you could see with her. There was always something more going on behind the scenes, some added layer to her scheming.

"You're offering Denether an army, aren't you?" Mikael said softly.

For just a second, Alyina's eyes widened in surprise. The look was quickly concealed, replaced by an innocent smile.

"Whyever would you say that?"

"Because it's obvious." Mikael took a step towards her. "Jaxon's right. The Malesie would never go for an offer like that. But *Denether* might. I've heard the rumours. That he has ambitions. Accepting a foreign army into the Highlands…it would start a civil war. And then who do you think has Denether's back against the other clans?" He pursed his lips. "It's classic divide and conquer."

Alyina snorted in derision, but Jaxon noticed she did not refute the Offworlder's words. And as for Jaxon himself…

…his stomach twisted. Could Mikael be right? They had placed their faith in Denether to unite the Highlands when they came here. Would he betray them at the ninth hour? Jaxon wanted to say no, that the man was loyal to his people, but he also knew Denether better than anyone. The man was as cold and calculating as they came. If he saw this as a chance to spare the Malesie a war he thought they could not win…

"It doesn't matter. We're rejecting your offer," he said quietly.

After the things Jaxon had done in Gurria, the mistakes he had made, the lives he had taken on behalf of this woman, he had promised to never place himself in a position of power again. That was why he had retired to Sarton in the first place. But now, well, he could no longer sit by and watch as others rode the world over a precipice.

"Oh dear, are you meant to be in charge of negotiations?" Alyina asked sheepishly. "My, this is awkward. You see, that offer was sent to Furness *weeks ago*. We're expecting Denether's reply by the time of the festival. Don't worry, though. I'm sure you and the highking are of the same mind."

The look she gave Jaxon was like a dagger in his guts.

"What about me then?" Mikael pressed. He pushed past Jaxon to stand before the princess. Despite his greater height, there was no mistaking the disparity between the pair as Alyina met his golden eyes. "You said this was about me, right? Was your invitation just a trick after all, or does your father have an offer for me as well?"

The dagger twisted. *What game are you playing at, Mikael?*

"Yes," Alyina said simply. "He would like to make you our honoured guest in Gurria."

"Honoured guest?" Mikael quizzed. "And would that by any chance involve a damp cell and iron chains?"

"Of course not!" Alyina laughed. "In Gurria you would be treated to the richest of accommodations, the best of our food and wine." She stepped closer, pressing herself up against him. The dagger tore a hole right through to Jaxon's spine. "The finest of our women, too."

"And if I refused?" Mikael said, somehow resisting her advances.

"Forgive me, Mikael, but that was not an offer," Alyina said, the smile falling from her lips.

Jaxon was impressed to see the Offworlder hold his ground. "If you could take what you wanted from me by force, you would have done so by now," he replied, calm as the waters of the sluggish river.

For a moment, Alyina said nothing. Then…

"You are right, of course," she murmured, reaching up to stroke Mikael's cheek. "Trying to take the information from you would be risky, it's true. It could become corrupted."

Suddenly the Offworlder stiffened, as Alyina's Aura flared with spent power. Jaxon started towards them, hand outstretched, only to stop dead as an invisible force struck him like a hammer, hurling backwards as though he weighed no more than a toddler. He recognised the attack—*Kinetic Force*. Alyina must have acquired the ability when she advanced to Royal.

"And like I said, I am not here to make threats."

Mikael still had not moved a muscle from where he stood, frozen on the sand. Beneath the surface, his Aura was raging, struggling and failing miserably to fight Alyina's *Ardent Onslaught*. The ability harnessed the power of Aura to attack the body—making it extremely difficult to counter. Only Pathfinders with a powerful Aura of their own could hope to resist such an attack, and only then against someone of similar rank.

"So believe me, Mikael," Alyina continued, "when I say this is a *promise*. Reject my offer, and I am *more* than happy to take that risk. In fact, it would be my gods' honest *delight*."

With a final flicker of Alyina's fingers, Mikael collapsed to the sand, moaning and clutching at his stomach. Alyina wore a sneer on her lips as she watched the Offworlder. Slowly picking himself up from the shore, Jaxon took a stumbling step towards her. Her eyes snapped up.

"You know our terms, Jaxon. They're a packaged deal—so you'd best make sure your friend is in the central plaza in two days' time." She smiled coldly. "Or I will personally ensure every single member of your pitiful clan is cleansed from this

Realm." With that, she turned and started away, only to pause and glance back at him. "Oh, one more thing."

"What?" he snarled, panting despite himself.

"Isabel Fields—who is she to you?"

It was like the warmth had drained from the world. Suddenly there was a roaring in his ears and a panic rising inside him, a fear unlike anything he had felt in so, so long. Isabel…he stared at Alyina, unable to believe the name had come from her mouth. It couldn't be…how could she…Isabel was in *Furness*, five hundred miles from here! She couldn't be… he couldn't…

A minute passed and still all he could do was stand and stare. It was apparently enough for Alyina.

"Ah, good," she said with a smile. "I thought so. Two days, Jaxon. The central plaza. I'll make sure your sweet Isabel is there as well."

Then she turned and walked away.

25

Five weeks before the Festival of the Satana

The sun was setting by the time Lunden wrapped up training with the latest group of Malesie recruits. More were coming in every day now, and his initial few had quickly swollen to hundreds. By the time summer arrived in earnest, their number would hopefully be approaching a thousand.

Not enough on their own, it was true, but there would be others who came when the battle arrived. Despite his success with Renard and his friends, not everyone saw the virtue in Mikael's plan. Many were reluctant to leave their lands and families for so long. But if the Gurrians really did come, Denether assured him they could count on several thousand more. They would be untrained, but with this small fighting force forming their core, hopefully it would be enough. Especially if the Izolu and Fushore clans joined them, as Mikael hoped.

Not that he had seen much of Denether over the last several weeks. The messenger from Gurria was still in the city, as far as Lunden was aware, but no one had heard anything about the man's purpose in Furness. Only that he had met several times with the highking.

Dismissing the latest recruits, Lunden wandered away through the lines of tents. The camp seemed to grow everyday now. He was already considering ideas to make the process more efficient. When he'd fought with the Ressian army, breaking and setting up camp had taken hours, robbing them of precious marching hours. Perhaps if he assigned everyone a given role to practice…

Moving through the camp, Lunden kept his eyes peeled for Maria or Scott or any of the others from Sarton. He had given the warriors from Sarton leadership positions beneath him, placing them in charge of units of fifty soldiers who would sleep, eat, and train together. By the time the war arrived, they would know one another better than siblings, and hopefully fight all the better for it. They would grieve together as well, Lunden knew, but that was the price of war.

Since he could find no trace of his friends, Lunden assumed they were already eating with their units. He emerged alone at the edge of the camp and watched the scarlet glow fade from the sky above Ryntirax. Here at its base, the mountain seemed like a dagger pointed at the heavens, as though the fallen god even now threatened to rise again and restart his battle against his treacherous sibling.

He moved away from the lights of the camp before lowering himself to the grass with a groan. Drawing in a deep breath, he savoured the crispness of the spring air. Soon summer would arrive. The season of war, where armies could march long leagues without fear of becoming bogged down in mud or snow. But it was a double-edged blade for the soldiers, who would be forced to walk day after day beneath the strength-sapping sun.

Darkness fell over the landscape as he sat there, lit only by the distant flicker of lightning. A spring storm. He knew from experience how harsh those could be in the Highlands. There was no thunder yet, but the energy in the air promised a ferocious night. But he had time yet before it struck, so for now Lunden remained where he was, enjoying the solitary moment.

Until a familiar voice spoke from the shadows.

"How goes my children, son of Ressi?"

Lunden turned to find the old seer woman of Sarton, Vinnie, standing on the hillside. A smile touched his lips and he started to rise, only for her to wave him back down.

"Do not stand on behalf of this old creature," she cackled.

He paused, then with a shrug, settled back on the grass. Still chuckling, she wandered over to him and leaned against her twisted staff.

"Such manners, you Ressi. My sister taught you well. Far better than I taught my own."

"You speak of the Malesie?" he quizzed.

The woman was somewhat of an enigma, even amongst the Sarton villagers like Maria and Scott. Many scoffed at her premonitions, claiming they were outlandish and never came to pass. Others, though, whispered of little prophecies she had given them that *had* come true. She had even come to Lunden himself and warned him of the battle, that the Malesie would need him and his men.

His own people, the fallen Ressi, had a great respect for seers—and a great deal of warnings about ignoring them. Some even claimed their last king had shouted down a prophecy given by an old seer before launching his war against Gurria.

"It's taking time," he said in answer to her question. "Your people are natural warriors. It makes me wonder what might have happened, had the Highlands fought with Ressi against the Empire."

The woman offered a dry chuckle. "It is ever the curse of humanity to wonder over *what if*," she said quietly, "it matters not whether the harbingers warned of what would come to pass. Still they must question: could I have done something differently?"

Lunden grimaced. "Perhaps you are right," he sighed. "So, honoured mother, what warnings do you bring today?"

The old woman's pale eyes seemed to shine in the darkness—until she threw back her head and howled with laughter. Lunden practically leapt out of his skin.

"Ah, but I knew I liked you. Perhaps I should have chosen you from the start." The laughter failed, her eyes becoming grim. "Very well, son of Ressi, you wish for an omen? Then tell me, do you still follow the path of the Voidlight?"

Lunden grimaced. Mikael had warned him of the old woman's dislike for him—and the name she had granted him.

"I do not see any other path to defeating the Gurrian Legions."

"There is always another path," the old woman said, "though I admit, it was my own hand that nudged my children along this one. And now it is old Vinnie that questions: *what if?*"

"The clans will fight for their lands," Lunden replied, hoping to offer some comfort. "This I know. Alone, they would have died by the score, but they would have fought. And lost. But Mikael has given us a weapon. I cannot say if it will be enough, but I plan to use it."

Vinnie fell silent, those blind eyes regarding him, as though she saw more of Lunden than any natural sight might glimpse. Finally, she sighed.

"There he is: the General. I wondered if he had lost his nerve, following this path."

Lunden frowned. "I am no general, honoured mother."

"Not yet, son of Ressi," she said with a smile, "but the time will come when the Malesie need one."

"The Malesie have their king."

"Perhaps I am wrong," she admitted. "Many months have passed since the mists last parted for me." She sighed. "But if the day does come, will you have the strength to stand up and be the leader they need?"

Looking into the woman's eyes, Lunden swallowed. The last time he had agreed to one of her requests, he had ended up fighting for his life in a valley outside Sitton. And now…

"Why me?" he whispered at last.

She smiled at that, a crooked, mischievous grin. "Because you were born in dark times, my friend," she said sadly. "And in dark times, the world needs men like you to stand up to evil. I know that is not the answer you wanted, but it is true."

Lunden nodded. It was enough. "Then I will do it gladly."

26

Present Day

Kat was in trouble. She had been quick, making it to the rope on the wall in mere heartbeats. It should have been enough! She'd even made it to the top of the wall unscathed. But of course she'd been a godsdamn idiot and looked back. A part of her had been hoping to see Isabel following.

Instead, she'd copped an arrow in the side, as one of the guards in the gardens spotted her and let loose with his bow.

That was some godsdamn shot. It had almost been the end of her, as she'd just about toppled back into the garden with the sudden shock of pain. Only through sheer desperation had she managed to haul herself over the other side and slide down the rope. From there, she had escaped into the canals, where the pain of the wound had eventually caught up with her and she had collapsed into a pile of garbage somewhere around Eastside.

Kat had spent the day there, hidden beneath folds of discarded cloth and half-rotten cabbages. The arrow she'd managed to remove in a moment of courage. She'd lost a couple more hours then, as a wave of red agony overwhelmed her. Thankfully it didn't seem to be bleeding overly much…

…hell, even the pain had lessened. It was no longer a sharp, stabbing agony, but a warm heat that seemed to wash through her. It was almost pleasant, casting back the chill night air. If only her head wasn't so light. Every step she took, stars sprung across her vision, almost blinding her. She had fallen twice already, on her way to the soup kitchen. It had to be the hunger. She hadn't eaten in two days. There'd been worse days, before Marta, but…

She staggered forward as the man in front of her shuffled closer to the counter. Just three more people in the line. She drew in a deep, shuddering breath and her knees steadied. Almost there.

Knowing they would be on the lookout for her after what had happened in the governor's manor, Kat couldn't risk going anywhere near Jon, or the resistance, or Marta's house. If she led the authorities to her friends…

That was why she was here, in one of the food kitchens provided by the Gurrians. In their boundless generosity, they had seen the poverty their conquest had caused among the Skartan people, and had nobly set up kitchens where the poor could go for free food—at least until they ran out for the night.

Two more, Kat thought as the line shuffled forward again. *Please still have food.*

They were horrible, these places. Engrained with such a feeling of despair and hopelessness that only the most desperate came. Kat certainly wouldn't have been here if not for the burning in her stomach…or was that the arrow wound?

She sucked in a breath, bracing herself as the stars returned. Pinpricks of cold sweat leapt to her skin as she swayed, and for a second she thought the pain would swallow her. Thankfully, just as the stars reached their brightest point and all she could see was red, they began to recede again, the tide retreating.

"You gonna move?"

Kat flinched as a gruff voice came from behind her. It took a second to realise the line had advanced again. Nodding, she quickly shuffled forward. There was just the one man left now. Three women were preparing plates for those already at the counter. Unlike their filthy and unkept patrons, these three were well kept, with splashes of makeup on their cheeks and fine silk dresses. Gurrian nobility. Apparently they liked to come here and volunteer their time. Must make them feel better about themselves. Gods she hated them. Maybe if she drew the sword…

She froze, her hand halfway to her belt. Quickly jerking it back, she pulled her cloak tighter about herself, praying that no one noticed the bulge of the sword beneath the heavy fabric. A Skartan caught carrying a sword would be punished with ten lashings in the central plaza. A Skartan caught with the same sword that had been used to strike down the governor…

"Next!"

Kat almost collapsed with relief. She stumbled up to the counter, stomach rumbling. Steam wafted from the food trays, which seemed to hold a kind of watery broth, but in that moment Kat didn't care. She just had to make it through one more night. One more horrible, dangerous night. Then the revolution would begin and it wouldn't matter if she had tried to kill the governor. The Gurrians would be gone.

A smiling face greeted her from behind the counter. Probably the daughter of some Gurrian dignitary, if Kat had to guess. A wave of hatred swept through Kat as the girl jabbered on about how lovely the nights were here in Skarta and how she hoped Kat had a place to sleep tonight. By the Elohim, these heathens could drown in the waters of the river for all she cared.

"Just…gimme…the food," she slurred.

A frown crossed the woman's face as she paused, an enormous spoon midway between the tray and plate.

"Well that wasn't very polite," she scolded. Then, apparently seeing Kat properly for the first time, the scowl turned to a look of concern. "Are you alright? You look like you're about ready to collapse."

Kat just stood frowning at the girl, struggling to process her words. Was she alright? *Of course* she wasn't! But what did this snivelling Gurrian care if a Skartan lived or died?

"Please," she rasped, reaching for the plate. "I just…need some food."

The frown on the girl's face deepened and she hesitated, before reluctantly filling the plate with broth and passing it across the counter. Kat didn't give the girl another moment's thought. Taking the tray in trembling hands, she staggered across the room to a bench and sat. Only at the last second did she have the presence of mind to tuck her cloak so it covered the sword.

Unfortunately, the movement was awkward, and a fresh bolt of pain tore through her side. She stifled a moan, praying that no one would notice. Thankfully everyone in the kitchen seemed too occupied with their own misery to care about the injured young girl in their midst. She was just another nobody orphan like all the others in Marta's care. No one cared what happened to her, so long as she didn't go making it their problem.

The broth was gone before she even tasted it. Probably because there was no taste. Either way, it was gone, and the hole in her stomach was exactly the same. Her heart sank and she glanced at the line for the food, but it had only grown. No way she had the strength to stand there again. She was just summoning the will to stand and leave, when a voice spoke from right behind her.

"Excuse me, miss." Oh gods, it was the girl from the counter. "Are you okay? It, ah, you seem to be bleeding."

The words were like a blow to Kat's gut. Another one, that is. Looking down, she saw the drips of scarlet liquid on the ground leading to her seat—and on the bench. Suddenly her heart was racing. There were three guards in the room. And all of them were now looking directly at Kat.

"Sorry, sorry," she muttered, struggling to rise. "It's nothing, sorry."

Making it to her feet, she shuffled towards the door. Damnit, she should never have come here.

"Wait, it's okay, we have supplies," the girl made a grab at Kat.

She bolted.

The guard nearest the door tried to stop her, but the little strength Kat had left carried her out into the street before he could block the exit. Shouts chased after her, even as she staggered, another wave of nausea sweeping over her. She forced it down. No time for weakness. Where could she go?

She didn't slow. The pounding of boots chased her as she ducked round a corner and charged across a bridge. Shouts echoed from the walls, followed by the *twang* of a crossbow. Kat ducked, her heart lurching, and sparks flew from a nearby wall as the bolt struck.

The shouts were growing closer. She couldn't get away. She was too slow. Too weak. She glanced back and saw the pair of shadows trailing her. There were only two. Could she take them? Kat wasn't a fighter, but the sword…

She darted down an alleyway and staggered to a stop. The blade was heavy on her waist. She hadn't drawn it since…but she had felt its weight, the power lingering within the cursed thing. It…called to her. Using it had filled her with such a strange rush of power, like some part of the governor's soul had been drawn out and given to her…

With her *Aura Sense*, she watched the men approach. They were only men. She could see their life burning within, rich with light, but decidedly normal. The hunger in her stomach grew as her hand clutched to the hilt of the sword, still hidden beneath her cloak. She had to be careful. They still had the crossbow.

Carefully, she pressed herself against the wall of the alley. The shadows swallowed her up.

Only then did she draw the blade.

Somewhat to her surprise, there was no rush this time, no void that swept her away. She felt a pang of concern. What if it hadn't been the sword at all that had almost killed the governor? What if this was just a normal weapon and she was about to take on two fully grown, armed men, by herself?

Unfortunately, there was no time to reconsider her course of action, as the flickering glow of the men's Auras entered the alley. They were moving slowly in the dark, being cautious. A pang of irritation touched Kat as they crept closer. Why couldn't they hurry up? She was hungry!

Patience…

The men neared, their mortal eyes struggling with the darkness. Clouds obscured the moon and stars. They would never see her in the deep shadows. Her heart slowed, a calm as deep as the western ocean falling over her. They were just three steps away now. Then two. One…

She threw herself at the first, death striking from the void. Her blade flashed for his stomach. She felt no resistance as it struck, sinking deep into his flesh. And then…

…by the glow of her *Aura Sense*, the world shifted. The blade in her hand *sang*, the note a high-pitched shriek, as it became darkness, the antithesis of the glowing Aura that made up the rest of the world. It *was* the void, an endless pit of hunger.

The man she had struck had one moment to scream. Kat

glimpsed the terror in his eyes, the moment of understanding there, that something terrible was about to happen. That this was the end.

And then the flickering glow that was his Aura just snuffed out.

It was not a normal death. Kat had witnessed more than enough of those to know what they looked like. The way the Aura lingered in a person, like their soul still clung to this world, desperate to continue. They could splutter for long minutes, sometimes even hours, before the last spark vanished.

But what happened to the poor man she had struck, this was a true ending. Absolute death. The energy, the potential of everything he was and could have been, all of it, just gone.

And in the next moment, it was Kat's turn to scream, as an energy unlike anything she had ever felt came crackling from the sword into her soul. It was restoring, reenergising as it filled her up, casting off her exhaustion and pain and despair—until it became too much. Then it began to sting, to burn like a fire in her chest she could not put out.

She realised then what it was. Aura and Mana, the fabrics of the soul and the universe, entwined like an ice-fruit smoothie stolen from the Skartan marketplace. Only this was far too much, too fast. And just like a smoothie chugged too quickly, her skull felt as though it were splitting in two—along with every other part of her body.

Though that was nothing compared to what happened to her victim. The black blade was buried deep in his body, but there was no blood. Instead, his skin turned dark, and even as the scream died in his throat, his flesh began to rot. His face sank inwards, his eyes rolling back in his skull, as veins of darkness pulsed beneath his skin.

The *thump* of his body as it hit the ground was like thunder in the sudden silence.

Kat stood, staring as the husk of what had been a man

crumbled to dust. The second guard was staring as well, his face drained of colour, his mouth wide with horror and disbelief. Slowly though, his eyes swivelled to Kat. And he saw her.

The void blade was still in her hand.

A second later, a second husk struck the ground, all the Aura and Mana and *life* of the man he had been drained away. Strange, the energy did not burn so much this time. This time, it was more like one of those spicy dishes from the south. Hot, burning even, but with a certain pleasantness to it, like a cool breeze blowing on a hot summer day.

Exhaling, she straightened and stretched her limbs. The food at the homeless kitchen could not have been so bad after all. There was still an emptiness to her stomach, but the strength had returned to her limbs, and she moved with a vigour she hadn't felt in years.

There was a smile on Kat's lips as she turned to leave the alley—only to find the flickering glow of a third figure standing in the shadows. But it wasn't one of the guards. It was the girl from the counter of the soup kitchen. She stood, face drained of colour, staring at Kat as though one of the Satana themselves had stepped through a rift from the hells.

Kat felt a strange sort of satisfaction, seeing her fear. This was the girl who had called her out in front of everyone, who had made her run in the first place.

"Did you come to watch them beat me?" she asked, taking a step towards the terrified Gurrian.

The girl was so terrified, she barely managed to shake her head. "No…"

"To kill me yourself, then?" Another step. The naked blade was still in her hand. No blood dripped from its dark steel. It had all been consumed.

"Please," came the trembling words. "I was just trying to help…"

"Of course you were," Kat snarled. There was a thrumming in her ears. "That's all you Gurrians ever wanted to do, right?" She was so hungry… "Well, I don't ever recall asking your kind for your help."

Finally the girl overcame her terror. Screaming, she turned to flee. Only the long black dress she wore was not made for the alleys of Skarta, and its hem caught on a stray piece of stone. Thrown off-balance, she crashed to the ground. On her hands and knees now, she crawled toward the street, where the false protection of lanternlight beckoned.

Kat allowed her to scramble onwards, shadowing her movements, drinking in the girl's horror, savouring her distress. It was good, to see her kind on their knees. Tomorrow, when Jon was done with them, perhaps the others would bow down as well.

Finally the girl seemed to give up. As exhaustion or terror or some mixture of the two claimed her, she collapsed to the filthy ground and curled into a ball, sobbing and rambling and pleading. Kat lingered, lips drawn back in a sneer. This girl wasn't even worthy of her time. She should go, before others came…

Only, as she turned to leave, another pang came from her stomach, and she felt again the rush of hunger. It was like those days on the street before Marta, the hollow, barren, wasted days of her life where she could barely think for the pain of the void within…

…just like that, a fresh burst of energy came rushing into Kat, filling her, casting back the hunger. She sighed, relief welling in her soul, even as the sheer ferocity of the power burned her and sent stars dancing across her vision.

Only as it cleared did she return to the alley. The night was deathly still now, without a single breath of wind. The girl must have fled, for the screaming had stopped. Except, except, there was another husk at her feet…twisted, blackened and mishappen, but smaller than the others.

Kat frowned. Had she done that? She couldn't even remember swinging the sword. But, she supposed it had to be done. The girl was Gurrian after all…wasn't she?

Suddenly Kat's legs gave way. Slumping to the ground, she gasped in great breaths of air. What…? Struggling to sheath the sword, she swayed where she lay. Her hand touched her side and came away wet with blood. And she was hot. So hot. Her mind swum. What was happening to her? She was no longer hungry, was filled with energy…but her body was failing! All this power, and she couldn't even heal a little scratch in her side? Her stomach twisted and suddenly she was hurling up the meagre broth from the shelter.

As the bout of nausea passed, she found herself crouched on the ground. The blackened husk of the girl lay beside her. Something caught in her throat. Her soul trembled. The girl hadn't meant her any harm. She was barely older than Kat herself…

I was only trying to help…

THE BLADE HISSED AS IT CUT THE AIR. A CRISP, CLEAN STRIKE, the same one Arimus had practiced every day since he had been a boy. Today though, it was wrong. Off. Like his body was not entirely in sync with his soul. Gritting his teeth, he sliced again. *Better*, he thought, before continuing the drill. It was an old pattern, a technique handed down by the ancients, one designed for a Pathfinder facing multiple opponents of similar rank. Few practiced the old patterns these days, especially the powerful. Pathfinders of Silver and above rarely found themselves facing multiple enemies of equal power. There just weren't enough of them left in modern times.

Arimus still found value in the old teachings, though. He might rely on his powers as much as the next Pathfinder, but he would not allow them to become a crutch. Even at Gold, there had been battles in the Ressian conflict that had stretched out hours or days, and even his Gold rank stamina had been pushed to the brink, leaving him reliant on his own mortal strength.

And after the attack…

His stomach twisted as he recalled the feeling of helplessness when the girl had swung the blade from the canal. He'd tried to block the blow, of course. Between his *Enforced Body* and *Shield* abilities, it should have been easy to stop her.

Instead, the dark sword had cut straight through the wall of *Mana* that sprang up between them and buried itself in his chest. It was as though his power meant nothing. Less than nothing, for he had felt it *feeding* on him then, sensed its enormous appetite as it drank upon his Aura and his Body. For a second he had been able to resist, putting all his formidable strength into keeping the black tendrils from his soul. But that had been all he'd managed—a second. After that, he had been swept away, a speck of sand drowned by the might of the ocean…

…until he woke late the next day to Alyina at his side.

She had explained what had happened. How a pair of assassins had snuck into his manor and attempted to kill him while he slept. One had escaped, slipping into the night with the dark sword that had nearly ended his life. And the other…

His stomach twisted and Arimus wove his way through another old pattern. The other had *saved* him. He remembered that much, at least—though only in flashes. Her face, etched in concentration. The warmth of her Aura, filling the holes the darkness had carved from his soul, healing his flesh. She had put everything she had into the effort. So much so, she had not even attempted to flee when the guards came.

Why?

"She's your sister, apparently."

Alyina's words had been like a fresh blow to his soul. The princess had seemed to enjoy his surprise. She was like that, sometimes. Rejoicing in other people's suffering. But she had sworn his assailant would be caught. Even now, she had soldiers scouring the streets for the girl and her friends in the resistance.

And she had the other one in custody, awaiting his verdict…

His sister…

It was impossible, wasn't it? He hadn't questioned the young woman himself yet. He was still regaining his equilibrium, after the attack. The wound in his chest might have been healed, but the muscles still felt tight. And his Aura ached, like the blade had left a scar on his soul.

But why else would an *assassin* have healed him?

Sweat dripped from his brow as he spun through the dance of death. It was just his regular blade now, of the traditional longsword variety of Gurria. The other had been taken by the assassin. More questions. The girl had reportedly only been a Copper, while the imposter lying in his personal cells was Bronze. Even together, they were nowhere near a threat to him under normal circumstances. Had they known about the void sword, or had they been planning to cut his throat while he slept, as they so nearly had?

Letting out a sigh, he lowered his sword. There was only one place he would get his answers. So why was he avoiding her?

She's your sister.

His father's daughter.

Arimus's stomach twisted. His father, Jasper Shore, the chancellor. The right hand of the emperor, who together had laid the foundations for the Gurrian Empire. He was the man people came to when there was a problem that needed cleaning up. In fact, Arimus was fairly certain he *had* been in the Highlands a quarter-decade back, to negotiate the last peace accords. That had been when Gurria was still warring within itself, struggling for control over the newly acquired provinces of Skarta and Yarrin.

His flawless father, for which nothing was ever good enough. Not when Arimus had become a soldier like the man before him, nor when he'd risen to General, or became the youngest Pathfinder to reach Gold in a generation. It was never enough for the perfect Chancellor of Gurria.

And now, it seemed, he was not so perfect.

Even as his wife had been serving his household back in Gurria and raising the young toddler, Arimus, Jasper Shore had been in the Highlands, fathering a child with one of the savages.

The thought actually brought a smile to Arimus's face.

He had a sister. It was about time he met her.

<h1 style="text-align:center">27</h1>

The *bang* of a door slamming startled Isabel awake. Not that it mattered—awake or unconscious, she had no means to defend herself. Chains rattled as she strained against the manacles, more to stretch her contracting muscles than in any real hope of freedom. For two days and nights now, she had lain bound to the cold steel of the table, unable to sit up or even really move. A servant had brought her a sip of water a few times, but there had been no food. With the scraps from Marta's as her last meal, she was beginning to understand what true hunger felt like.

Though Isabel forgot all about that when she saw who was standing in the doorway. It was the man from the manor. The one Kat had tried to kill—and who she had poured all her Aura into trying to keep alive.

Her brother.

"What are you doing here?" she croaked, the words scratching in her throat.

A frown touched the man's lips as he stepped away from the heavy wooden door. He didn't speak, just stared down at her bound to the table, until Isabel felt her cheeks grow hot.

They had left her with her clothes—not that nudity normally embarrassed her—but there was something about the way he looked at her that went deeper than clothes, or skin…

"I wanted to know if it was true."

"If what was true?"

"That your father is Jasper Shore."

Isabel's jaw hardened. "Of course it's true," she snapped.

"How do you know?"

"My mother drew a painting of him. I would remember his face anywhere."

The lines in the man's brow deepened. "Sometimes women lie about such things…"

"My mother did not lie," Isabel snarled. How dare this man question her mother? "She never wanted anything to do with your useless father after he left."

"You know who I am then?"

Isabel swallowed, her gaze flicking to the door. Alyina had not returned, but their time together had left a terror in her soul that would not easily be dislodged.

"I know he is your father too," she rasped.

He nodded. "My name is Arimus Shore. I am the Governor of Skarta."

"I…did not know, before we…came."

"Doesn't seem like you had much of a plan."

Isabel said nothing. He was right though. What had she been thinking? Stupid fool that she was, she had trusted Kat without question, thinking the girl was her friend, a twin soul suffering in this cruel world. But in the end, the street rat had only been out for her own selfish desires. Which, now she thought about it, was the same attitude that had brought Isabel to this man's doorstep in the first place.

"I just wanted to look my father in the eye and tell him that I exist," she said at last.

To her surprise, the man nodded, as though *he* of all people understood. "You're telling the truth, aren't you?"

He stood there a moment longer, still staring, before shifting on his feet. Almost as though he was nervous.

"Why did you do it?" he asked suddenly. "Heal me, that is. You must have known I wasn't your father. I can't be more than a few years older than you."

"I did not come here to kill anyone," she said, struggling to lift her head to keep her eyes on the man.

"No, but you didn't need to save me, either." There was a wooden chair in the corner. Arimus dragged it to the table and sat so she did not have to crane her neck to look at him. "Doing so cost you your freedom."

"I thought…I do not know what I thought. It just did not seem right, cutting down an unarmed man."

"So, this girl. She was not your friend?"

"If I ever see her again, I will wring her throat myself."

To her surprise, the man grinned. "Maybe we are related after all," he muttered. Leaning back in the chair, he regarded her. "You know, you've put me in quite the predicament, Isabel."

"Really?" Lifting her arms, Isabel rattled her chains. "I was kinda thinking I was the one in the awkward position."

Arimus's smile turned into a chuckle. "Indeed." He pursed his lips. "I suppose—"

"*Sir!*" Behind them, a door burst open, emitting a man in the violet uniform of a Gurrian soldier. "Thank the Emperor, you're awake…" He trailed off, seemingly noticing Isabel tied to the metal table.

"Lieutenant Bolt," Arimus said, rising from his chair. "I'm a little occupied at this moment."

"Ah." Bolt's eyes lingered on Isabel, before he tore them away. "Sorry, sir. I've been trying to reach you, but your attendants told me you were indisposed. I have news."

"Then speak it man."

"What about…" The man swallowed, glancing again at Isabel.

Arimus waved a hand. "She won't be repeating anything she hears." Her heart fell at that. She did not like the implications.

"Ah, well, yes, it's about the Offworlder."

Isabel's heart lurched in her chest. The words seemed to reverberate around the room as she lay splayed out on the table, struggling to process what she'd just heard. The only thing that kept her from screaming at the newcomer was that he continued to speak.

"I followed him, just like you said, sir. It was difficult. He's a pretty skilled Aura user, but I don't believe I was seen."

"Good," Arimus grunted, "now get on with the report. Who did he meet?"

"Princess Alyina, for one."

The roaring in Isabel's ears grew louder. *This was all her fault!* She'd told the princess about Mikael and Jaxon. Now they were paying for her folly. She scrunched her eyes closed, a lump of regret welling in her throat to choke her.

"That doesn't surprise me. She's interested in what he knows. I'm more interested in who his *true* allegiances lie with."

"Then you may be interested to learn that he *also* met with a member of your council, sir. Well, not exactly *met*. More like…taken against his will." The man hesitated. "He walked out on his own though."

Arimus's eyes narrowed. "Who was it?"

"The dean, sir, of the university. Jon Sorrow."

A silence followed. Isabel lay on the table. The thundering was deafening by now, though the source of her fears had shifted. What in the Seven Hells was Mikael up to now?

"Thank you, lieutenant, that's good work," Arimus murmured at last.

"If I may, sir?" the soldier trailed off, looking uncertainly at the governor until Arimus waved for him to continue. "Thank you. It's just, this is it, isn't it? He really is working with the resistance to undermine us, just like you suspected. We've got them red-handed!"

"No!" Isabel cried, before silencing herself with a curse. Her cheeks flushed as the two turned to look at her.

"You have something to add, sister?" Arimus asked.

Isabel clenched her teeth. She could feel the sweat on her brow, the ache of terror in her chest.

"Mikael has nothing to do with your resistance," she whispered.

The governor arched his eyebrows. "And why should I trust you?"

"I saved your life."

"True," he mused, "but only from an assassin you yourself let into my house."

The pain in Isabel's chest was growing. She glared at her captors, willing her rage to take life, but her caretakers had been thorough. Someone visited her cell regularly to drain any ambient Mana from the stale air.

"What if I gave you her name," she whispered.

Something twisted inside her. It felt like betrayal, even after the girl had abandoned her. But what else could she do? Mikael and Jaxon were her family, and they were in trouble. She had to try and help them, even if it was only the sliver of a chance.

Arimus arched an eyebrow. "I'm listening."

She closed her eyes. "Her name's Kat. She really is a street urchin. That's all I know, I swear." She couldn't give up Marta and the children, not even for her friends. Hopefully Kat's name wouldn't lead them back to the orphanage.

"Very well, I'll look into it. In the meantime," he continued, turning to the soldier. "Lieutenant Bolt, why don't you organise for the dean to pay me a visit. I believe the cell next door is available." He paused. "Take a full Force with you. As I recall, he is not a Pathfinder, but we know there are several working for the resistance. Eighty men should be enough to deal with any tricks he might have up his sleeve."

"Yes, sir!" the soldier saluted with a grin. "It will be my pleasure!"

There was a thump of wood against iron as the man retreated into the unknown beyond the wooden door.

"Thank you," Isabel breathed when the man was gone.

Arimus pursed his lips. "For what?"

"For leaving Mikael out of this."

For a long time, the man they called the governor said nothing. His eyes watched her closely, as though still searching for something in her, some piece of a puzzle he could not quite put together. Finally though, he gave a shake of his head, as though offering defeat.

"I did not do it for you," he said quietly, "and I am not leaving him out of this."

"What?" she asked, her pulse quickening again, "but—"

"I am leaving him alone—for now—only because Alyina Sorulus has commanded it," he continued over her protests. "So I cannot touch him; not without absolute proof of his involvement with the resistance." He pursed his lips. "But I know he *is* involved, somehow. All of this, you, the Offworlder, your friend Kat and Jon Sorrow, it's all connected. Someone is pulling strings in my city, my dear sister. And I'm going to get to the bottom of it." He grimaced. "And when I do, whoever is responsible is going to wish they had never been born."

THE BLADE WAS HEAVY IN KAT'S HANDS. IT WAS…IT HAD DONE something to her. She wanted to hurl it away. But…but it was her only means to defend herself. And now she could hear other voices. People searching. Coming for her.

Sheathing the void blade, she struggled to her feet and stumbled away from them. Her *Aura Sense* was flickering, struggling. Hand clutched to her side, she kept going. The blood made her fingers sticky and the pain…sometimes it was so bad, she just wanted to stop and beg the hunters for mercy. At other times, she barely felt it through the spinning in her head.

There were people ahead of her. Pathfinders this time. A Copper and an Iron. More behind. There was a tiny gap between two poorly designed buildings. She slipped through, evading their net, even as she tried to control her Aura, blending it into the sleeping souls occupying the nearby buildings.

Another Pathfinder. How were there so many? And soldiers as well. It had to be the sword. They were after it. They wanted what was hers! Kat gritted her teeth, checking that it remained in its sheath.

She kept moving. The light was growing. Dawn. As people began to move in the streets, it would become impossible to track her Aura. But the hunters were so close now. And she was injured, her clothing stained with blood. Someone was bound to notice.

Where could she go? Distantly, she recalled the festival. The day had come. Just a few more hours. Surely she could risk it…

…she stumbled on, no longer thinking where she was going, only of the Pathfinders chasing her. So many. Dozens. *Hundreds?* They could not all have come from Skarta. Where…where…

She didn't know. Her mind was failing. Her *Aura Sense* flickered. Using it for so long, her Copper Aura was burning low, even with the energy the void blade had given her. Instinct alone carried Kat through the streets, always just one step ahead of her pursuers, as the sun rose higher and somewhere, someplace, someone began to scream. She was too far gone by then to know what that meant. All she knew was, at some point, the Pathfinders hunting her seemed to fade away.

And then she was stumbling up a familiar set of stairs and an old ornate door was opening to reveal a harrowed face.

Marta.

"Help…me…" she rasped.

"Ah, child," the old woman whispered. "So the shadow weavers finally gotcha." She stared down at Kat for a long moment, those old eyes piercing her soul, before she stepped aside and gestured. "Well, come on then, don't just stand there. Others be about."

Kat tried to cross the threshold, but an old hand stopped her. "Why don't you drop that thing first, lass? Something like that'll do no good for a girl like you."

Anger flared in Kat at the request. And fear. Fear it would be taken. "*No!*" Then, realising who she was speaking too. "I…I can't…"

Kill her!

Darkness swirled, burning with anger, hatred. The void screamed to be used, to hack into the creature before them, the woman that was not mortal or Pathfinder, but something… else. Something tasty. But as Kat reached a trembling hand for the black hilt, she looked up into the kindly eyes of the old woman.

"I think that you can, Kat," Marta said softly.

And Kat was struck by a realisation: she *could*. Silently, she undid the belt from around her waist and allowed the blade to fall. As she did, the darkness on her soul lightened. Not vanished, but suddenly she *was* lighter. So, so light.

So light, a fresh darkness rose within her. This time though, it was filled with peace instead of hunger.

She embraced it gratefully.

28

Four weeks before the Festival of the Satana

Fatigue weighed heavily on Fiachson's shoulders as he climbed the winding path. One step after another, they had made the trek from Eastmore up into the wall of mountains the Izolu claimed as their territory.

Eastmore itself had been a disappointment. The fortress town was built in the confluence of two mountain tributaries and dated back to when the clans had still warred amongst themselves. Centred around a mighty tower, its purpose had been to watch for incursions from the Izolu into Malesie lands. with those days long forgotten, the place was all but abandoned now, a relic occupied by a handful of families left over from the old days.

They had not lingered long, staying just a single night before starting off on the final leg of the journey. Now, after weeks spent scrambling up scree slopes and scaling false summit after false summit, they were finally nearing their destination. Apparently.

Stone cliffs loomed all around, but Fiachson's eyes were

fixed on a breach in the sheer stone, a slit between the mountains. Surely this must be it: the pass his mother had told him to watch for. Her voice came from below, chatting merrily away with one of the guards the king had sent with them. Sucking in another lungful of air, Fiachson blocked out the noise. His mother was a warrior and a Steel Pathfinder. This might as well have been a stroll in the woods for her.

But for him, every day had been a battle, every night a struggle to stay warm as the cold crept through the canvas tents. His teeth were clenched against the pain of his aching muscles, his lungs screaming in the thin air, but still he continued, eyes fixed on the stones beneath his feet.

Step after step.

Until, suddenly, the ground was no longer sloping upwards.

Fiachson blinked, realising he stood in the shade. Relieved from the burning sun, he looked up to scout the way ahead. Steeped in shadow, he stood in a narrow passage that led through the stone. To the other side.

He lingered a moment, drawing in great mouthfuls of air, recovering his breath. The voices of the others grew slowly closer. He watched the group pick their way up the trail. The pair of Malesie warriors were both Copper like Fiachson, but *unlike* him, each had the *Enforced Body* ability, making them resilient to the conditions.

Fiachson found himself smiling. Despite their advantages, *he* had reached the pass first. And he would be the first to enjoy the view on the other side.

Drawing in one last breath, he set off through the crevice. In these deep shadows, the air was cool and his breath misted in front of his face. The path was flat, although the ground was broken and uneven, as though someone had taken a chisel to the stone to open this passage. His heart quickened. Maybe they *had*. Would the Izolu tell him that story? Excitement touched him as he imagined the possibilities. What other secrets could be contained in their songs?

Light appeared ahead, the promise of warmth beckoning him on. A few more minutes of scrambling and he emerged on the other side of the mountain.

The breath caught in his throat. Before him, the ground fell away in sheer cliff, plunging down, down, down into crystal waters far below. The mountains still stretched around him, their snow-capped peaks looming above the deep blue depths of the fiord. A distant, echoing roar carried up from a dozen waterfalls that ringed the bay, their swirling currents filling the air with a fine mist that settled into the lush forests covering the lower edges of the mountains.

Much to his surprise, there were sails on the waters of the fiord. For a moment, Fiachson thought they must be Deti, until he saw that they flew the scarlet red of the Izolu, rather than pirate black.

"How——" he began, before the rattling of stones came from behind him.

He turned, expecting to find his mother and the others approaching. Instead, he froze as a blade of icy steel touched his throat.

"Hello," a voice greeted him that was far too cheerful for the circumstances. "Do you realise you're trespassing?"

Fiachson swallowed. A young woman in a heavy fur cloak stood before him, a longsword of polished steel extended. Her face was pale and freckled, her hair a fiery red that matched his own. She wore an easy smile that was a complete mismatch to the deadly weapon in her hand.

"Ah…I was looking for the Izolu clan."

"Then you found us!" the woman said happily. The blade did not so much as quiver. "How can I help you?"

"I was…" Fiachson stammered, before realising how ridiculous the entire situation was. He was here on behalf of the Highking, damnit! Drawing himself up, he met the girl's sapphire gaze. "I was sent by Highking Denether to speak with your chieftain."

"That's nice," the girl said matter-of-factly. "If you tell me the message, I'll be sure to pass it along."

"I…" Fiachson trailed off, finding himself at a loss for what to say next.

Thankfully, footsteps from the passageway saved him, as first his mother, then the pair of Malesie warriors appeared. He almost sighed in relief—before he felt the self-loathing swelling within as he once again needed rescuing by his mother…

…except instead of charging to his rescue, Maisiwan came to a stop in the path and looked from the girl to Fiachson, one eyebrow arched as if to say: what have you gotten yourself into this time, son?

For her part, the girl seemed to be ignoring the new arrivals at the expense of Fiachson's very vulnerable throat.

"Well?" she pressed. "Let's have it, the message."

Silence. One of the men at his mother's side coughed. Anger flared in Fiachson as his cheeks flushed red-hot.

"The Highking's message is for the ears of the Izolu chieftain and the Izolu chieftain alone," he snarled. "If you are truly Izolu, then you will obey the command of your king and bring me to him. Now, please," he added, almost apologetically at the end.

The young woman stared at him for the longest time, before throwing back her head and unleashing a howl of laughter. Fiachson flinched, and felt his heart lurch as he found his foot slipping on the ledge—

Suddenly a rough hand was grabbing him by the front of his jacket and hauling him back. "Easy there, lowlander," the Izolu woman said, her eyes glinting with amusement. The sword had vanished back into its sheath. "Can't have you tumbling to your death before passing on your message!"

Fiachson's heart was pounding so loudly in his ears he barely heard the words. Licking his lips, he stared down at the chasm, his over-active imagination lingering on what would have happened if she hadn't caught him…

"I…ah…" He shook himself and tore his eyes from the distant fiord. "Yes, good, so you'll take me?" He glanced at the ships below. "How do we…ah…get down to them?"

He assumed the Izolu settlement must be hidden some-where in the cove below. There was nowhere else to go. They stood on a wide ledge, sheer cliffs in all directions. They would surely need rope and no small degree of good luck to traverse their way down to the fiord.

"Down?" the young woman asked quizzically. "Why would you want to go down?"

"Ah…"

The Izolu woman laughed. "Hold on, kingsman, I'll call us a ride."

And then she began to sing.

Fiachson could only stare in disbelief as her words rose above the howling of the wind. Her song rang from the cliffs with an echo that almost seemed to form a part of its own, like a second voice joining in with the first. The verses began to thread their way together, forming a story in his mind. The melody told the tale of two peoples, united by time, living as one in defiance of the gods…

Partway through the melody, a sound carried from above. A strangely rhythmic clip-clopping of hooves. Fiachson swung around in disbelief. No horse, not even the rugged mountain ponies favoured by the Malesie, could survive out here…

Then he saw it.

"Is that a *goat?*" he asked before he could stop himself.

It was.

Fiachson stared, mouth open, eyes bulging as an enormous mountain goat made its way down the mountain—down the apparently *sheer cliff*, to be accurate. Somehow, its delicate hooves found purchase in the stone, never faltering or stumbling or placing a foot wrong. A second followed, then another and another, until five of the bizarre creatures alighted on the ledge before them.

"You will have to forgive my son," his mother finally spoke up, stepping forward with a grin as wide as the bay below. "I am afraid I neglected to teach him the ways of his father's people when he was a child. My name is Maisiwan. I visited the Izolu many years ago."

"Maisiwan!" The young woman leapt at his mother, enfolded her in an embrace. "Welcome back, sister of the Izolu! My father has long mourned the loss of Hanequin." Releasing her, she turned to Fiachson with a frown. "Then this must be your son...Fiachson?" She waved to him cheerfully. "Nice to meet you, Fiachson. I'm Princess Moira!"

"Princess?" Fiachson blinked.

"Yeah."

"But...how..." He was utterly confused by just about everything now. The strange goats were still standing nearby, *baaing* happily at each other. They seemed to have some sort of harness on their backs. Probably to carry goods, he told himself...

Moira just shrugged. "My father is chieftain. I am his daughter. I am told that is what you lowlanders call a princess!"

"A princess is the daughter of a *king*."

"...and so he led them into the heavens, the free peoples," Moira began to sing again, the notes forming that strange harmony as they rang from the cliffs, "and they named him king upon the world, beneath the endless stars..." She paused, pursing her lips in thought. "I suppose some would translate it to 'leader'." She shrugged. "Perhaps that is the confusion. Dad warned me you lowlanders can get a little funny with your jargon."

Fiachson stared at her, completely speechless by this point, while at his side, his mother burst into laughter.

"Son, close your mouth, before you insult the princess."

He slammed his jaw shut and shot his mother a glare. She flashed him a knowing smile. Gritting his teeth, he pushed her to the back of his mind.

"Well, well met—," he started again formally, at which point the young woman tackled him in a hug with the force of a small sheep.

"Welcome home!" she exclaimed. "We have been waiting for the son of Hanequin to return for a long time. Your father's histories await you!"

"His songs?" Maisiwan's head jerked up, her voice suddenly hushed. "I thought they were lost with…when I lost him."

Releasing Fiachson, Moira offered his mother a tender smile. "His newer stories perhaps, though as his partner, you could help fill those gaps, Maisiwan." She looked back at Fiachson. "The rest are preserved with the Librarian, who guards all the stories of the Izolu. In fact, he has been teaching his apprentice the songs of Hanequin in preparation for your visit."

Fiachson found his heart hammering strangely in his chest. His father's story? The story of his family, his research, his interests. He clenched and unclenched his hands, excitement racing in his veins. His father had been an enormous, empty hole in his life, the mystery man his mother had so clearly loved, yet of whom she would not speak. Even his name seemed strange upon her tongue, she had spoken it so rarely.

Hanequin.

And now…

Making an effort to contain himself, Fiachson cleared his throat.

"Are you sick?" Moira asked, turning to him with a frown. "We have a great remedy for colds…"

"No, ah, I was just wondering, who, this ah…" Damnit, why was she looking at him like that? He cleared his throat again. "Who is this apprentice that would teach me my father's histories?"

Moira's face brightened. "Me, of course! My father, as chieftain, is Librarian." She blinked, as though remembering something. "Speaking of which, we should really get moving. He'll be waiting for you!"

"Wait, why would he be waiting for us?"

"He's been expecting you, silly."

Fiachson blinked, looking from Moira to the sword on her belt. "Then why…"

"Now, the path to Haven is treacherous," Moira said, ignoring his question entirely, "but don't worry, Larry's going to carry you. He knows the way like the bottom of his own hoof!"

And just like that, Fiachson forgot all about his questions. He looked from the young Izolu woman to the goat she was pointing at. A pit settled in his stomach. Even the pair of Malesie warriors were suddenly looking *very* nervous. Only his mother wore a grin—and it was a very knowing one at that.

"And Maisiwan, John will carry you." Moira paused, glancing at the others. "Sorry, only Izolu are allowed into Haven. You'll have to wait here."

The pair of warriors at least had the good grace not to let the relief show on their faces—even if Fiachson saw it in their Aura.

"Are you, ah, sure we can't walk?" Fiachson asked without much hope.

"I wouldn't recommend it," Moira replied with a laugh.

His heart sank. He stared at the creature in front of him. It stared back from beneath a fringe of curly white hair. What had she said its name was? Larry? It probably didn't matter. His mother was already climbing onto hers, and the men from Furness were watching. With a muttered curse, Fiachson swung himself onto the strange harness that he knew now served as a saddle.

Straightening, he looked around him—and immediately regretted it. Perched atop the strange creature, their position on the ledge suddenly felt *very* precarious. And they hadn't even started up the mountain yet.

"Ready?" Moira asked brightly.

"Ah…"

The Izolu princess didn't wait for his response. Fingers to her lips, she let out a whistle.

And their mighty steeds leapt from the ledge, out into the void.

29

Present Day

This time when Isabel woke, it was in darkness. Groaning, she pushed herself up, wondering what had woken her. Her body still ached from the harsh nights she had spent chained to the table. At least after Arimus's visit, someone had come and replaced the table with a wooden slab that now served as her bed. The shackles around her ankles had been attached to iron chains as thick as her wrist, each bolted deep into the stone wall.

It was another minute before the noise that had disturbed her sleep came again. A shiver ran down her spine as the shriek of a man's voice reverberated through the wall.

Drawing her knees up to her chest, Isabel shuddered. It must be Jon; the man Mikael had met. A knife twisted in her gut. Would he tell Arimus that Mikael was involved with the resistance? It could not be true, could it?

If only she believed that.

At least it was not Kat. Despite her anger at the girl, Isabel could never have forgiven herself, knowing she had led them to the little street urchin. Besides, if anyone was going to clock the little rat a new one, it was going to be *her*.

The cry came again, a shriek torment that seemed ripped straight from the victim's soul. Isabel tried to block her ears, but it did little good. Even through the stone, the sounds were unrelenting. Another twist tore at her gut. She felt sorry for the man, truly. Pitied him. Except…

…except she could not deny the relief deep inside her. Relief that it was *him* suffering and not her. She had sensed Arimus's power when she healed him. Just his presence had been enough to suck the Mana from her cell. He might be her brother, but he was almost as frightful as Alyina Sorulus.

So whatever distracted him from Isabel, whoever suffered instead of her…

She shuddered as another shriek carried through the walls. Fear lodged in her throat. What if he *did* come back? What if he was not content with Kat's name? She had not given him *everything*. Not really. Marta's children lingered in her mind, their innocent smiles as they shared a meal and regaled her with their tales.

How much would it take for Isabel to give them up? How much more could she suffer before she broke? If not Arimus, surely it was only a matter of time before Alyina returned.

In her fear, Isabel reached out with her soul. A few scraps of Mana had collected in the barren stone—or rather amidst the bits of lichen growing in the damp places of the cell. Her heart sank. It was not even enough to light a spark.

Not that Mana-fuelled fire would have done her much good anyway. It would have to burn with incredible heat to melt the iron shackles, if they resisted even the strength of her *Enforced Body*. And then what chance did she have of escaping this cell with Arimus Shore just a room away?

Her only hope was with Mikael and Jaxon—and Isabel feared she had already failed them.

Lost in thought, she did not notice the screaming had stopped next door—not until the heavy door to her cell swung open with a squeal of rusted hinges. Her heart almost stopped when she saw Arimus. His face was grim, eyes burning with anger. Whoever was in the other room, they obviously had not given him what he wanted.

And now…now he had come to do as he had promised. Get to the bottom of the web enveloping his city. Whatever it took.

His boots clacked against the stone floor as he stepped across the threshold. Isabel's eyes darted around the room, searching irrationally for an escape she knew was not there. A cold sweat sprang out on her brow as Arimus loomed over her.

"You know who that is in the other room?"

"Jon Sorrow?" she rasped.

His jaw tightened. "One of my advisors."

Drawing the wooden chair across the room, he sat with a weary sigh. The move surprised Isabel. She crouched on the wooden bench, staring at the man who held her life in his hands. He seemed tired.

"Someone you trusted?" she found herself asking.

Arimus gave a wry chuckle. "I don't trust any of the rats that run this city—Gurrian or Skartan," he said, "but as far as this man goes, he would have been about the last man I suspected. A fat, greedy, academic. In short, a nobody. He's not even a Pathfinder." He grimaced. "So what was his altercation with your Offworlder friend about?"

"You say he's an academic? Mikael has a keen interest in the history of our world."

Arimus grunted. "Perhaps." He studied Isabel some more. "I don't understand it. Why is everyone dancing to this Offworlder's tune. His very existence threatens our world. We know this—our ancestors, our legends, even our histories remind us of it frequently. Maybe *you* can explain it to me."

Isabel considered the question. "Mikael is…" She saw his face in her mind, the hawkish golden eyes, so calculating…yet at other times, like when he looked at *her*, they became soft. And the way his lips twisted with amusement, as though laughing at some joke no one else could understand. And his hands, the way they had brushed against her as they danced…

Her cheeks flushed. None of those things were what Arimus was asking about.

"Because he wants to help people," she said at last, meeting his eyes. They were a deep, dark brown, so unlike her own, and yet the more she looked, the more she saw the similarities they shared.

Arimus only grunted. "The road to the Seven Hells is paved with good intentions," he muttered, before rising and producing a key. To Isabel's surprise, he bent and unlocked the shackles around her ankles. "Come."

Sitting up, Isabel rubbed at her ankles, wary at this sudden turn of events. Her legs were weak with disuse, and her body ached from lying on that steel table for so long. But she had no chance of fighting this man, or even outrunning him, so Isabel allowed herself to be lead from the room. They did not have far to walk, as Arimus went to the next door in the corridor and pulled it open. He gestured for Isabel to enter first.

Shivering, Isabel stepped into the gloom and felt her soul plummet into the pit of her stomach. If she'd thought her own accommodations were grim, this was far worse. Jon Sorrow hung naked from the wall by a pair of shackles. Blood ran down his arms where the iron bindings had cut into his flesh and the skin around his wrists was turning purple. It looked like he'd been there for hours.

A moan rasped from his throat as Arimus slammed the door behind them, making Isabel jump. The dean's head bobbed a little, his eyes flickering, but otherwise he barely stirred.

Growling, Arimus strode across the room and grasped him by the jaw. Light flickered between his fingers, and then the prisoner was screaming, thrashing against his bonds in an effort to get away.

"Better," Arimus snapped.

"Please…" Jon wheezed, his flabby chest rising, then falling in a strained, shuddering breath. "Must be…some kind…of mistake…"

A growl hissed between Arimus's teeth. He reached for the man again.

"Wait!" Isabel screamed before she could stop herself, and the governor, her brother, stopped.

"Why?" he demanded.

"I don't know," she whispered truthfully, looking from the tormented man to Arimus, before shaking her head. "Why did you bring me here, Arimus?"

He stared at her for a moment longer, before lowering his hand. "Because *somehow*, all of this is connected," he hissed. "The Offworlder and your clans, the resistance and this Jon Sorrow, you and your friend Kat—"

At the name, the man hanging from the chains jerked as if stung. Arimus froze, his head turning slowly back to the prisoner. A sliver of light had crept through the slot high in the stone wall, casting the prisoner in an ethereal glow.

"You know that name, don't you?" he whispered.

Lit by a scarlet glow, the fat man blinked, squinting down at Arimus. Tears ran down his cheeks and his eyes were sunken, wreathed in shadows despite the dawn's brilliance. There was no mistaking the torment this man had suffered, yet as he looked at them now, a change seemed to come over Jon Sorrow. The weakness fled as his face hardened.

"What have you done with her?" he growled.

Arimus seemed taken aback by the change in his prisoner's demeanour. Isabel stepped in quickly.

"She's gone," she said before Jon could reveal anything more. "Escaped into the city."

Her brother was still staring at the prisoner like he'd just witnessed the second coming of Ryntirax, but with her interruption, he blinked and looked between the two of them.

"Ah, that is good," Jon sighed. "She's a smart girl. They won't find her, not before…" he trailed off, a smile crossing his lips as he blinked in the brilliant light.

"Before what?" Arimus snarled. Shoving Isabel aside, he grabbed Jon by the throat. "You will tell me——"

He broke off suddenly, stiffening like he'd just been struck through the spine with a lance. Isabel shuddered as she sensed, rather than saw, the pulse of energy. Like two great forces had just come together in an almighty crash. She could see it in the faces of each man, their frozen glares, the tension in their muscles, the way Jon's fingers clutched at the steel of his manacles and the veins bulging on her brother's forehead…

With a start, Isabel realised this was her chance. They were locked in a deadly, silent battle—and no one was left to watch her. Pulse suddenly racing, she crept carefully backwards, eyes never leaving the pair. She didn't dare blink, not even breathe, least she draw either's attention. Arimus had said that Jon was no Pathfinder, but clearly he had been mistaken.

She found the door with her boot. Carefully she reached back, fingers clawing for the handle. Arimus had not locked it, thankfully. The door swung open with a harsh squeal from the rusted hinges. She flinched, but neither of the men so much as blinked. There was a roaring in her ears as she slipped into the corridor. She caught one last glimpse of the pair, still trapped in their silent contest of Aura.

Then she turned and fled.

Isabel made it just two steps before careening into a fist that came at her from nowhere. It was only slim, the pale knuckles unmarked by scars, but it struck with the force of a raging bull

—and she would know. Jaxon's old bull, Drax, had caught her in his paddock only once. Knocked flat on her ass and lying stunned on the floor, Isabel felt much as she had that day.

Only today, it was the pretty face of Alyina Sorulus staring up at her through the dancing lights, instead of Drax.

Isabel knew which she would have preferred.

"Isabel!" the princess exclaimed, her voice rich with delight. "Just the prisoner I was looking for. Now, what have you done with…" she trailed off, a frown marring her perfect face as she glanced into the nearby cell. "Wow, Arimus actually found Sorrow! I'll have to give the kid more credit in the future." She glanced back down at Isabel. "What do you think, has your brother earned a promotion back in Gurria?"

Isabel's vision was still spinning, but she managed what she thought was a pretty good glare as she spat at the princess. "Screw…you."

Alyina laughed. "Yeah, you're right. He is rather boring in that department. Guess I'll leave him. I'm sure he can handle a little Silver ranker anyway. Well, come on then. I'm off to meet some friends of yours. I'm sure they'd love to see you!"

30

Arimus was in trouble. Of the three main components of a Pathfinder's power, Aura was by far and away his weakest. Normally that mattered little—especially for a Gold ranker strong enough to crush boulders and the Mana stone to crack open the earth beneath his feet.

But he had been lured into a trap by a man who, until ten seconds ago, Arimus could have *sworn* up and down the river Skarta had not been a Pathfinder. He had even double checked when the soldiers first brought him down to this private cell. Jon's Aura had been fuzzy and weak in his *Aura Sense*, no different from any other citizen wandering the streets of the city.

Except it had been a trick, a subtle use with the *Mute* ability to fool him into a false sense of security.

And none of Arimus's strength and power mattered a jot, as all his concentration was consumed with keeping the necrotic power of the man's Aura from tearing apart his soul. Under different circumstances, he might have even been impressed by the man's dedication. For half the night, the man had endured Arimus's *Ardent Onslaught*. He had allowed his soul to be flayed, when all the while he'd had the power to rebuff Arimus. All so as not to give away the truth about his role in the Skartan Resistance.

Except, *something* had clearly changed, if he was now willing to give all that away.

Not that any of this mattered to Arimus, if he couldn't survive the next few minutes.

Fortunately, while Jon Sorrow had clearly mastered the arts of the spirit, several advantages remained in Arimus's favour. First was the man's rank. He'd sensed it, just moments before the Aura attack began. Silver versus Gold meant Arimus had a deeper well to draw from, even if his mastery of Aura was inferior.

This fed into his second advantage. Jon Sorrow remained bound to the wall. Aura abilities could only be applied through touch, which meant all Arimus needed was a moment's break in the Silver ranker's concentration, and he would be free.

So Arimus held his cool, maintaining the protections around his soul as Jon Sorrow hurled everything he had into his attacks. Daggers of noxious Aura stabbed at Arimus's spirit, only for walls of fire to leap forth and burn them away. Vines twisted around the flicking light within, squeezing, twisting, driving thorns deep into the fabric that made up who he was, but Arimus hacked at them with an axe of burning light and they crumbled.

Again and again, the traitor came at Arimus, and again and again, he was rebuffed. He didn't try to retaliate. That would only exhaust him in return. And besides, there was no need. Once he broke free, Arimus could crush the man's throat with a single squeeze of his fist. With an Aura this strong at Silver, Jon's body was bound to be almost as weak as a mortal.

Finally, the moment came. The invading light of his enemy's soul grew fainter, a breach appearing in the veil that had trapped him within his own body. Arimus snatched at it with all the might of his soul—and he was free.

Gasping, he staggered back from the prisoner, who slumped back against his chains, gasping for air, his face slick with sweat.

"By the Emperor," Arimus snarled. "How long have you hidden amongst us with that deceitful ability?"

The muscles in Jon's face spasmed as he suffered the aftermath of their silent battle, but after a long moment, his head lifted, a smile twisting his lips.

"Decades," he rasped. "You Gurrian mutts cannot see beyond your own arrogance."

Arimus swallowed, unsettled by the zealous glow in the man's eyes. "It's over now."

To his surprise, the man laughed. "Over?" he wheezed. "Why yes, governor, I do believe you're right. It is over."

Anger touched Arimus then, that this man dared laugh in his face. He advanced a step, though not so close that the man could grab him from his chains. No need to put himself through that again.

"What are you laughing about?"

"You," the fat man spat, still cackling madly as he hung from the chains. "And the princess and all your Gurrian nobles here in Skarta. Today is the day you all die, Governor." He lifted his head to look Arimus in the eye. "Don't tell me you hadn't worked that part out yet?" He smirked. Outside, a bell began to ring. "Today comes the revolution."

Then as the last tolling of the bell faded, Arimus heard it. Like a familiar call beckoning him back to the days of glory.

Somewhere outside, steel blades clashed, and men began to scream.

31

Four weeks before the Festival of the Satana

A cold sweat dripped down Fiachson's back. Moira had been true to her word. The mountain goats sprang from ledge to ledge, defying gravity as they scaled the sheer cliffs as though it were the most natural thing in the world. He clung to his goat's back for dear life, fingers digging into its coarse fur. One wrong move, one misstep, and they'd plunge hundreds of feet to their doom.

The mountain goats didn't seem perturbed. They moved with surefooted grace, effortlessly navigating the sheer stone as the winds swirled. Moira rode ahead, seated so casually on her mount that Fiachson's heart was in his throat for the entire journey.

He would have preferred to make the journey under his own power, but he had to admit, this climb would have been beyond him. It made him wonder; what kind of madmen would live in such an impossible location—let alone build a city there! It was madness, surely.

The wind picked up strength as they neared what Fiachson

prayed was the summit. To his surprise, the gusts did not bring fresh chills, but a strange warmth that soon had him sweating beneath his heavy furs. Which was…impossible, surely? They had to be at least three thousand feet above the waters now!

"That's the zonda winds!" Moira called back in her cheerful tone. "They bring the promise of summer—but don't let them fool you. Tonight, winter's snow will surely return from the high mountains."

"Aren't *these* the high mountains?" Fiachson called back, trying to keep the tremor from his voice—though he tucked the snippet of information away to consider at a time he wasn't dangling over the side of a cliff.

"Of course not." Moira laughed. "You can't grow food in the high mountains. It snows too much. Our farmers will be readying themselves for a busy night protecting their crops."

"You have crops up here?"

Moira only laughed. She seemed to be enjoying this entire experience *far* too much.

Finally they reached the summit, their mounts leaping over a ridge to alight on a broad plateau. Fiachson sucked in a breath as he was greeted by a sight so utterly unexpected, he thought he might be hallucinating in the thin air. That happened, didn't it? He remembered reading the story of a Malesie mountaineer who tried to summit Ryntirax, only to return after witnessing shining lights in the sky that no one else had seen.

But this…this was real. A verdant plateau of brown and green stretched out before them, a little pocket of life amidst the towering peaks of stone and ice. Terraced fields rose in tiers, each constructed of carefully placed stones that lifted each terrace a few feet above the last. The entire structure seemed designed to capture moisture, then funnel it through the entire system rather than being lost to the ground. It was… ingenious! Fiachson did not recognise the crops, but he did spy several more of the enormous mountain goats, along with a small flock of sheep further up the plateau.

Dismounting from her trusty steed, Moira gestured for them to join her. Legs trembling, Fiachson was relieved to follow the young Izolu woman along the path through the terraces. Here, men and women were placing braziers stacked with coal at regular intervals amongst the plants. The sight brought a frown to Fiachson's face, but Moira had the answer —in song form.

"When the warm winds blow, let the fires of night be lit and the Izolu dance, for brighter days approach," she sang.

The dark rock of the mountains rose ever higher into the sky, seemingly without end. Fiachson began to fear they had yet more to climb, but as they reached the last terrace, they came upon a collection of low-roofed buildings placed near the base of the next cliffs.

A dusty trail led to the largest of these buildings, which unlike the clay-bricks of the Malesie, seemed to be constructed from the raw materials of the mountains. Jagged rocks of all shapes and sizes had been stacked haphazardly like a jigsaw puzzle, and then pasted together by some form of plaster.

Voices carried from the entrance of the building as Moira gestured for them to enter first. Fiachson hesitated, glancing at his mother, who had been unusually quiet since arriving in the village. Her eyes had that distant look they got whenever her father was mentioned. She didn't seem to notice his unspoken question. No matter. He needed to take the lead anyway. The highking had sent *him* to deal with the Izolu, not his mother.

Straightening his shoulders, Fiachson strode inside—and entered a large, circular chamber that conformed to the shape of the building. Several dozen men and women sat cross-legged around the room, while a giant of a man stood at its centre, garbed in a great fur cloak of the deepest emerald, his arms raised to the ceiling as his voice boomed over the crowd.

"…and so mighty Ryntirax raised his sword—"

The man was in the midst of some great story, but he broke off at Fiachson's appearance, Maisiwan just a step behind him. A great smile split his face and his voice boomed out once more.

"Maisiwan Payne! People, our sister has returned! Let our voices rise in joy!"

A cry came from the audience as they came to their feet and joined the performer in the middle of the chamber. Fiachson stood frozen with sudden indecision, until a subtle nudge from his mother's elbow pushed him forward. The movement drew the giant man's attention, who raised a hand. The others broke off, their eyes turning in Fiachson's direction.

"And this…this must be Fiachson Payne," the man said softly, before dropping into a bow. "Welcome home, lost son of the Izolu."

A flush of heat spread across Fiachson's cheeks as all the others in the room did the same—even Moira. In that instant, he wished he could be anywhere else. Thankfully, the moment was brief, as the man who had addressed him straightened once more. Then, stepping forward, he swept Fiachson into a bear hug and spun him around, before finally placing him back on his feet.

"I am Lachlan, chief of the Izolu people!" the man declared formally, "and I welcome you, son of Hanequin, to the home of your father. To Haven!"

Struggling to regain his composure, Fiachson returned the earlier bow. "Thank you, Lachlan. I have come a long way to speak with you."

"Of course, of course. Long have I waited to meet the son of Hanequin. What have you come to say, Fiachson Payne?"

Fiachson swallowed, his mouth suddenly dry. He hadn't expected the conversation to leap past pleasantries so quickly. Hells, he hadn't really thought much about what he was going to *say* to this man to convince him to answer Denether's call to war. Looking around the room, at the silent faces of a people who lived so far removed from the rest of the world, he wondered what he *could* say.

"Denether, Highking of the clans, sent me," he rasped finally. "The Empire to our south has marched an army into our lands. More will follow. He calls upon the clans to unite as they did beneath his father and rebuff these foreign invaders."

A sudden silence came over the room. Two dozen pairs of eyes focused on Fiachson with the power of a magnifying glass. Of them all, however, it was Lachlan that he watched, waiting for a hint of the man's response, for how his words had been taken. The chieftain's face did not seem to register the importance of Fiachson's words, though, for the easy smile remained.

"Moira brought you here, did she not?" he asked abruptly, gesturing to where the young woman stood behind him.

"Ah, what? Did you not—"

"And what do you think of Haven?"

"It's…" Fiachson struggled for words. "It's an interesting home?"

The chieftain chuckled. "Indeed." He laid a massive hand on Fiachson's shoulder. "And what do you think it would be like, for an army to march on our city?"

Fiachson's eyes widened as he took the man's meaning. *It would be impossible.*

Lachlan must have read the thought in his eyes, for he grinned. "I think not all the armies of the world could take Haven from us," he said lightly.

"I understand," Fiachson said quickly, "and perhaps you would be safe, for a time. But not even the Izolu can resist alone forever. Not even in a place like Haven. That is why we must stand together *now*, while we still can."

"Ay, perhaps that is true," Lachlan said, "though perhaps that is not *all* of the truth." He eyed Fiachson. "We hear rumours, even up here in the clouds. Rumours of your lowlanders and your squabbles. Of the forces you toy with."

Fiachson swallowed. He thought he knew what Lachlan was talking about, but… "What do you mean?"

"We have heard the whispers, the distant songs. That another has entered our world. One carrying the light of the void."

Damnit, how could they know? Fiachson was used to people reacting to Mikael like this by now. Fortunately, such was Mikael's charm and sheer iron-willed determination, he would inevitably win them over. But Mikael wasn't here this time. It was up to Fiachson.

"His name is Mikael Heaton," he said quietly, "and he is not the enemy you think he is."

The chief grunted. "And it was this Mikael Heaton who sent you here, to draw the Izolu into his conflict?"

"I asked to come," Fiachson retorted.

Lachlan studied him for a long time. The silence was pulpable, as though every watcher held their breath, waiting for the response of their chief. Even Moira remained motionless, her face uncharacteristically tense as she watched her father.

"I see," at last, Lachlan spoke, and the room breathed. "In that case, young Fiachson, it would seem I have much to consider." He smiled, his face lightening. "In the meantime, I understand you were never taught your father's songs. Moira knows these histories, if you wish to learn them."

Frustrated at the lack of an answer, Fiachson opened his mouth to argue, but his mother beat him to it. Stepping between him and the chieftain, she offered a bow of her own.

"He would be honoured."

32

Mikael watched as Jaxon Daniyal strode past his perch on the side of the fountain, his feet stirring up dust as he paced. It was utterly unlike the gold ranker to show such nerves. Seated on the side of the great fountain, Mikael lingered in the shadow cast by the bronze statue of the emperor. Dawn was about to break and the air was cool, despite the humidity clinging to his skin. He glanced at the sky, where a red glow still stained the horizon. The statue of the emperor was reduced to a silhouette in the growing light.

The Festival of the Satana had finally arrived.

They were waiting for Alyina, as instructed. He had even sent a note to the citadel with a stable boy from the inn. The message she wanted to hear more than anything.

I will give you what you want.

Mikael's hands began to shake as he watched the light brighten above the slate roofs. He couldn't control it. His terror. Alyina's power was unlike anything he had felt other than the Elohim and Satana—and the woman had no aversion to using it. Only his knowledge from Earth protected him. But now she had Isabel…

Leaning over the side of the fountain, Mikael splashed water in his face. Internally, he was screaming. How was Isabel even *here*? He could feel the panic welling inside him again, the dread that shouted he would doom them all.

He exhaled, and with an effort of will, controlled his runaway thoughts. Power was not everything, not even in this world. If he had to trade his knowledge for the lives of his friends, he would do it…

But it would not be his first choice. More like third.

His fingers tightened around the pack he wore strapped across his back. His plan B. Saltpetre, charcoal, sulfur. Had he gotten it right? There had been no time to test it—and even if there had been, he couldn't risk it. If Alyina found out…

He clenched his jaw, his gaze drawn again to Jaxon's pacing. The man's face was grim. Mikael could understand why. They didn't know where the Gurrians had taken Isabel. If this went wrong, they risked losing her forever.

But they couldn't turn back now. There was too much at stake. The Malesie. The Highlands. Skarta. Their own lives. Everything rested on today.

The streets bordering the plaza were busy, even in the predawn, as labourers set about erecting stalls for the festival. With their carts and stands packing the roads and even the canals in places, passage through the city was difficult, and shouting could already be heard as fights broke out amongst the visitors to the city.

The gates had opened an hour ago with the first hint of light, beckoning inside farmers from across the province to celebrate the solstice and prepare for the darkening again of the world by the demonic Satana. That was the old story, at least. As far as Mikael was aware, the Satana had as much to do with the turn of the seasons as astrological signs had to do with personalities.

But the bustle about the city was good, and the excitement in the air. Like the clans with their winter festival, there would be a feast later, and dancing in the cool evening twilight. A few Gurrian soldiers were stationed around the plaza, but none seemed the wiser that anything was amiss.

So far, so good, for plan A.

"Are you sure about this, Mikael?" Jaxon asked, coming to a sudden stop.

"Sure?" Mikael lifted his eyes to the sky. "Not at all. But what choice do we have?"

The Gold ranker grunted. "Not much."

He'd told his friend about the rebellion. Jon Sorrow had been confident he had the numbers to deal with Alyina and the governor, but words were easy. Alyina was powerful. Mikael had to assume there was a chance she would escape—or kill them all before numbers overwhelmed her.

Mikael watched as Jaxon resumed his pacing. His stomach churned at everything *else* he was keeping from the man. About the device in his pack. And the dark spirits that had haunted him since he'd torn open the rift between the worlds.

Somewhere in the distance, a bell began to toll.

Exhaling, Mikael rose to his feet. *Game on.*

A breeze blew across the square, sweeping away the stench of stale water and sewage and replacing them with the sweet scent of wildflowers. Mikael and Jaxon turned together to find Alyina striding towards them. Today the princess didn't wear one of the flowing silk and cotton dresses Mikael had seen her in on their last encounters, but a thick leather breastplate and greaves, with a Gurrian longsword on her waist. Mikael's hands tightened into fists. She had come dressed for war.

"Boys," she greeted. "Nice to see you. Season's greetings and all that."

Jaxon only growled, his face dark with anger. Whatever the pair had shared between them, it had died long ago. Mikael faced the princess. They still needed a few more minutes.

"Where is Isabel?"

"Close," she replied with a thin smile.

"I want to see her."

"I don't think a man in your position should be making demands, Offworlder."

"You want what I've got in here, don't you?" He knocked his skull for emphasis.

Alyina rolled her eyes, but with a gesture, the thumping of boots carried from a nearby alley, where a unit of soldiers emerged. Mikael's stomach twisted into a knot when he glimpsed Isabel's jet-black hair. The fiery clanswoman looked to have seen better days. Her face was pale, and shadows ringed her eyes, while iron shackles bound her hands and feet. But as their eyes met, he saw a flash of...something. Hope, maybe?

With an effort of will, Mikael tore his eyes from his friend. He had to focus. Alyina couldn't know what was coming, or she would kill them all in a heartbeat. Well, she would kill his friends. For Mikael, she no doubt had a special kind of treatment reserved.

"Release her," he demanded, trying to force every inch of authority he possessed in his fragile Steel ranked body into the order.

"You really think she's going anywhere?" Alyina chuckled. Moving between her guards, she grabbed Isabel by the hair and dragged her forward. "Oh no, now I know how much she means to you, I'm afraid the lovely Isabel will be joining us in Gurria."

"That wasn't the deal."

Isabel's scream was like the crack of a whip in the bustle of the plaza. The crowd flinched instinctively away from the disturbance. A heavy silence fell over them as they saw the stunning woman garbed in armour, holding the dark-haired clanswoman aloft. They saw her laugh as her victim screamed again…and they began to whisper a name feared by every Skartan alive.

Alyina Sorulus.

Mikael didn't blame the people that began to slink away.

He noticed, however, that others edged towards them.

Somewhere in the distance, the bell tolled for a second time.

Fingers gripped around the hilt of his blade, Mikael advanced a step towards the princess. "I said let her go."

Alyina wore an easy smile. "I think it's time you learned your place, Offworlder." She held his gaze as Isabel's cry cut off, her iron-fingers tightening around the clanswoman's pale throat.

The thundering had returned to Mikael's ears now. He could barely hear himself think. Had the third bell tolled? Something was pounding inside his chest, so hard it felt like the creature from Alien was about to burst out of him. They didn't have those here, right? What if he'd eaten something…

"Okay, Alyina," he whispered. Releasing the hilt of his sword, he raised his hands.

The smile grew on the Alyina's face. She held Isabel for a few seconds longer, even as the clanswoman batted weakly against her arms. Only when her hands fell and her head lolled limply to the side did Alyina release her. Isabel struck the dusty bricks with a thud, unconscious.

"Good, so you *can* learn," Alyina smirked. "Now, why don't you toss away that sword? If its anything like the one Arimus had, well, it would explain a lot."

Mikael's heart lurched. "*What?*"

The princess arched one eyebrow. "You didn't know?" she tisked. "Well, that *is* something."

A curse was on Mikael's lips. The other sword was *here?* It had to be, if Alyina recognised the power of his own. *Damnit.* If he'd known, he could have looked for it! Surely together, the weapons would hold enough power to deal with whatever the Satana threw at him…

…but it was too late for that. And now Alyina knew his blade was the source of his protection. Without it, he would crumble like fresh bread under the assault of her powers.

Which meant he *really* needed Jon to come through now.

"Okay, Alyina," he said. "You win."

He reached with one trembling hand for the clasp of his sword belt.

The third bell tolled.

And all hell broke loose.

The streets were chaos. Somewhere overhead, that damn bell was tolling. Men and women ran screaming in every direction, and in their midst stalked killers. Skartans with swords. And axes and knives and just about every weapon imaginable.

Arimus couldn't understand it. He snarled as one of them came at him with a massive axe. The man was unskilled, a farmer probably from his clothes. Arimus's blade slashed across his throat and he died choking on his own blood. But already others were coming. Dozens. *Hundreds.*

Arimus moved on before they could surround him. He might be more powerful than these treacherous Skartans, but he was no fool. He would cut down dozens of the bastards before they overwhelmed him, but overwhelm him they would, eventually.

He had left Jon Sorrow hanging from the wall of his cell. It had been tempting to kill the man, but if the man really was behind this treacherous revolution, then he needed to live, so he could name the other members of the resistance that served him. And besides, his chains were forged to hold stronger Pathfinders than a Silver who had concentrated all his development on Aura—and Aura couldn't melt chains. The man wasn't going anywhere.

Not like Isabel. He felt a pang of betrayal at the girl's escape. Foolishness. *Of course* she had run when the chance presented itself. They were enemies, weren't they?

She's my sister…

Arimus threw off the thought. The crowds were growing thicker as he neared the central square. That was where Alyina was meant to be, negotiating the surrender of the Offworlder. *Damnit.* He cursed the woman and Mikael Heaton both. This had to be his doing—and Alyina's fault for letting him live. The clans had clearly been channelling funds to the resistance for months, if not years.

Now, if he did not act quickly, the entire province could fall. It might already be too late.

They only had a half Battalion stationed in the city. Four hundred men. And these were distributed throughout the city, ready to keep the peace for the festival. The resistance looked to have *a lot* more than four hundred men.

Another traitor came at him, a woman this time, red-faced and snarling as she tried to stab him with a pitchfork, the points of which had been sharpened into daggers. In the press of the crowd, the swing of his longsword was hindered. He barely got the weapon around to block the attack. It became trapped as she twisted the piece of farm equipment. If not for his *Enforced Body,* Arimus probably would have lost it.

As it was, he simply tightened his grip and drew Mana from the air, then channelled it downwards. The ground *shook,* then split open, shattering bricks and filing the city with a rumbling. The woman cried out as her legs were swallowed up.

She was still struggling to free herself as his blade flashed, removing her head in one clean swing.

The governor pressed on through his raging city.

ALL AROUND THE PLAZA, CHAOS DESCENDED AS BLADES WERE drawn from wagons and beneath market stalls, and roaring farmers fell upon the soldiers of Gurria. Screams echoed from the nearby buildings as those who knew nothing of the plot fled, struggling to avoid the sudden press of armed men roaming their streets and plazas. Some even leapt into the waters of the canal that ran behind the fountain—though the river was high today and the currents quick.

The Gurrians were offered no quarter by their Skartan counterparts. Civilians and soldiers alike, if they wore the violet of the empire, they were swarmed, blows raining down to tear through leather armour and silken robes and flesh alike.

It was a bloody slaughter that only continued as Gurrian reinforcements arrived, racing into the plaza in search of the commotion, only for the resistance to fall upon them anew. There was a splash as a body tumbled into the fountain. His blood quickly turned the waters red.

As he watched it all unfold, Mikael had to admit, Jon had obviously prepared his people well. The dangerous were disposed of quickly, while Skartan citizens were directed back to their homes. And once control of the square was established, a group even donned their weapons and splashed across the fountain to fall upon the statue of the emperor, hacking and smashing at it with hammers they took from their packs. In mere minutes, the soft bronze cracked beneath the weight of their blows, crumbling into the scarlet waters.

Alyina Sorulus stood watching it all unfold, arms folded across her chest. The princess had quickly lost her arrogant smile, but to Mikael's surprise, she hadn't tried to intervene. A ring of Skartans surrounded them, twenty at least. With his Aura Sense, he could see most were some rank of Pathfinder. Along with himself and Jaxon, they were clearly meant to deal with the threat she posed. Mikael hoped it would be enough.

Though given Alyina was yet to draw her sword, maybe a fight wouldn't be necessary at all. It seemed unlikely, and yet…

"What were we talking about again?" he asked.

Arms folded across her chest, Alyina arched an eyebrow. "I believe you were in the middle of an unconditional surrender."

Mikael chuckled. "Ah yes, well, given the circumstances." He spread his hands to indicate the soldiers. "I've decided to decline your offer after all, Princess." His face hardened as he advanced a step towards her. "You see, I would never ally myself with a murderous psychopath intent on world domination. No offence, you understand."

"That's too bad."

"I do, however, have a counterproposal," Mikael mocked. "Surrender yourself into our custody and I'll make sure the Skartans don't tear you limb from limb."

It was not an idle threat. Alyina was powerful. But like all Pathfinders, she was not *invincible*. In a fair fight, one after another, she probably *could* take on every Skartan in the city. But this would not be a fair fight.

Alyina did not reply. Instead she stepped forward to where Isabel lay unconscious and placed her foot against her throat.

"The way I see it," she growled. "Nothing has changed."

This time, though, Mikael held her gaze, even as his heart thundered in his chest. "If you touch another hair on her head, I swear to you, Alyina, I will use every iota of power I can muster to destroy you."

The slightest of smiles crossed the woman's lips. "Spoil sport," she sighed. With a wave of her hand, she removed her boot from Isabel's throat.

Mikael scowled. "Now, are you going to surrender."

"You really think you can take *me* prisoner?" Alyina started to laugh. "By the old gods, if this is your plan, Mikael, you are more of a fool than I thought."

Something in her words gave Mikael pause. "You're all alone, Alyina," he said softly. "Give it up. There's no need for anyone to die today."

Arimus was breathing heavily by the time he reached the plaza and found Alyina confronting the Offworlder and his Skartan rebels. He spied Jaxon Daniyal amongst them, along with several Skartan Pathfinders that had come out of the woodwork. Alyina stood alone, her guards already dead. Those were bad odds, even for her rank.

So it was strange that Arimus found himself smiling as he approached. This might all be a disaster, but he had to admit, things had certainly turned more lively since Mikael's arrival.

"You're alone, Alyina," he heard the Offworlder say. "Give it up. There's no need for anyone to die today."

He snorted, then shouted through the crowd to make himself known. "Oh, she's not alone, Offworlder."

A ripple spread through the crowds packing the plaza as Arimus strode through their ranks. He'd seen the resistance trying to clear people from the streets earlier, but there were still plenty of citizens packing the plaza here, lingering beyond the ring of traitors that surrounded Alyina Sorulus. More fool on them. If a battle between Pathfinders really started in earnest, there was sure to be collateral damage.

Surprise showed on the faces of the Offworlder and his Skartan allies as Arimus approached. He smiled at the reaction. His arrival certainly changed the equation. They may be surrounded, but a pair of powerful Pathfinders were a great deal more difficult to bring down than just one. The Skartans would pay a grave cost indeed if they wanted any more Gurrian lives.

"Arimus, so nice of you to join us," Alyina said. She kicked a body at her feet in his direction. As she sprawled on her back, Arimus saw it was Isabel. His heart dropped into his stomach. For a second he thought she was dead—until he noticed the gentle rise and fall of her chest.

"Isabel…how?"

Alyina snorted, her eyes still fixed on Mikael Heaton. "I trust you enjoyed your time with Jon Sorrow."

"Wait…" Arimus blinked. "How do you know…"

"Governor!" Mikael Heaton's voice carried across the square. "Maybe you could talk some sense into the good princess and surrender."

Shaking himself, Arimus focused on the task at hand. "I don't think so," he growled. "I think if you want our lives, a great many more people are going to die before this day is over."

He met the Offworlder's eyes, and saw the frustration there. Mikael Heaton had been hoping his little show of force would be enough to win the day. Well, they weren't done just yet. Readying his sword, he started towards their foes. The golden eyes of the Offworlder hardened as he reached for his own blade—

A hand settled on Arimus's shoulder. "Oh, that won't be necessary, Governor."

Alyina Sorulus stepped past him, a smile on her lips. "I'll admit, I'm disappointed in you Mikael," she laughed. "I really thought you would come to your senses with all this."

The Offworlder seemed suddenly uncertain. "All I have seen of your so-called empire is cruelty and violence," he snapped. "In my world we favour a less tyrannical approach to government."

"That's a shame. Still, you seem like the talkative sort. I'm sure we'll get *something* useful out of you on the torturers rack."

Mikael's frown deepened. "You're surrounded, Alyina. Jon has a thousand fighters in the city. You can't win."

"Ah yes, Jon Sorrow and his army of farmers." The princess began to laugh. "I'll admit, the man was a useful fool." She tisked, her eyes surveying the armed men and women that surrounded her. "Look at all these dead traitors. So convenient of you to gather them all here like this."

Arimus's jaw went slack. *She knew!* Not just that. His face flushed and his body felt heavy as the pieces clicked into place. It wasn't just that she knew. Looking at her now, he realised the truth. *She* was the one behind Jon Sorrow, the secret force helping fund his resistance. This had all been a game to trick them into revealing themselves.

Everyone in the city had been dancing to her strings, even him. And none of them had been the wiser.

On the other side of the plaza, Mikael Heaton seemed to be experiencing the same realisation. "No," he rasped, the colour draining from his face. "It can't…"

Alyina gave a sad shake of her head, though she wore a wicked grin on her lips. "Yes, look at all these dead men," she tisked. "I guess it's time to go to work. Sergeant, bring me their heads!"

Somewhere in the tower overlooking the square, a horn began to blow.

Awooooogh!

And all across the plaza, the bystanders began to throw off their hoods and cloaks, revealing hardened leather breastplates beneath. Steel whispered against leather as longswords sprang to their hands. Grinning, the men advanced on the poorly armed resistance fighters.

The horn blew again.

Awooooogh!

The thump of marching boots rumbled from the stone walls. Within seconds, a column of soldiers appeared in a nearby avenue. These wore the purple colours of the Gurrian Legion. There were hundreds—more than all the soldiers Arimus had in the province. Drawing silver blades, they screamed a Gurrian battle cry and charged at the flank of the Skartan freedom fighters.

And the slaughter began.

33

Jaxon had to admit, Mikael had really screwed up this time. Not that this was entirely the Offworlder's fault. He should have known something was up the *second* he'd seen Alyina on that beach. The woman was far, *far* more than she appeared. Powerful? Of course. But beautiful, manipulative and cunning as well—cunning most of all.

"What have you done, Alyina?" he asked softly, moving alongside Mikael and placing a hand on the young man's shoulder. He felt a shiver run through the Offworlder.

"You don't recognise your old friends, Jaxon?" the princess taunted. "The Fourth Legion came with me from Yarrin. They've been waiting patiently for today, camped south of the city. You *do* remember them right, my dear? They've so been looking forward to seeing their old general again."

Jaxon's stomach twisted into a knot. The Fourth was his old Legion, the ones who had put the town of Minefield to the torch under Alyina's command. Under *his* command. Looking into her eyes, he saw the amusement there. And the hate. She was enjoying this, watching his suffering. She *wanted* him to fight, to see the despair in his eyes as she snuffed out everything he cared for.

A Legion. Four thousand men, highly trained, veterans of the Ressian campaign. The Skartans had never stood a chance.

"How?" Mikael croaked.

He looked as though the ground had opened beneath his feet, frozen, unable to react while the soldiers fell upon the Skartan Resistance. They fought back, of course; a few of them were even skilled. And they had Pathfinders of their own. But it wasn't enough. Not when their opponents were better armed and had trained for years in the art of war.

It was a bloody slaughter.

"Who do you think gave Jon his little weapons?" Alyina snorted. "What, you thought all those swords and battle-axes could go unnoticed? Over *years?* They always think they're so clever, these freedom fighters. But they're really quite simple-minded creatures. Put out word of a few secret arms deals, and well, suddenly you know *all about* their secret plans."

Jaxon watched the soldiers surround a man. He battled bravely, but the longswords descended none the less, hacking and slashing until he fell. A pit formed in his stomach, the pain of the past digging at his gut. A *whoosh* came from a nearby building as a flaming torch was tossed through its window. He had seen this before, this slaughter. Had been a part of it. Alyina wouldn't stop with the rebels. She was here to make an example.

"And to think, all because your friend Jon Sorrow thought he was smarter than everyone else." She bared her teeth. "He wasn't, of course. And nor are you, my poor Offworlder."

"Why?" Jaxon rasped. "Why wait? Why let it continue?"

"So she could get them all," Mikael whispered. "I...I should have seen it."

Alyina grinned. "These rebels are like a cancer. Kill one,

and another pops up someplace else. Better to dig them out by the roots."

"And us? Why bring us here now, if you knew this would happen?"

"Consider it a test, Mikael," she said lightly, even as she flicked an imaginary piece of dust from her grieves. "I thought you might betray us, so I dangled the chance in front of your eyes, just to see if you would take the bait." She grinned. "And you did. Hook, line, and *sinker*."

"So there was never really a peace deal?" Jaxon growled.

"Oh, *that much* at least was real," Alyina replied, flashing him a sweet smile. To Jaxon's shame, it still sent butterflies dancing through his stomach. "Only, I might have lied about *when*. Denether signed the deal a few weeks ago, long before either of you set foot in Skarta. After this, the Fourth will march north to Furness. Just in time for Denether's crowning ceremony. He is to be our vassal king of the Highlands. Peace, just like you wanted, my dear."

"I won't allow it," Jaxon grated out the words.

"Oh don't worry. Denether was quite clear in his terms." Alyina's face hardened. "This time, the Darkstrider is not to return home from his journeys in the south."

Jaxon reeled at her words. There it was—the final betrayal. For some reason, he felt a strange kind of peace. He no longer carried the weight of his people on his shoulders, nor the pain of the past. He saw now Alyina for what she was—an evil creature, incapable of empathy, adept at twisting everyone around her to her will. She had used him, just as she would use the next man, and the next, on her path to power. And then she would discard them.

He would not be leaving this city alive.

All that remained was to choose the manner in which he left this world—and it would not be on his knees. So long as he had his strength, he would fight, futile though it might be.

Before the eyes of Gurria and Skarta, he would resist Alyina and her tyrannical father, and pray to whatever gods were listening that it made a difference.

A groan came from nearby, where Isabel lay forgotten. Mikael remained at his side, failure written across his face. He had taken a terrible gamble—and lost. His heart ached for the young man and Isabel. They were the closest thing to children he would leave behind.

But maybe, just maybe, he could protect them this one last time.

"Mikael," he said evenly as he reached up to draw the greatsword from its sheath on his back. "Time to go."

"*What?*" Mikael startled.

Jaxon stepped past, placing his back to the Offworlder, but he could imagine the shock on the lad's face. Sadness touched him. He wouldn't get to witness the end of the young man's journey; whether he became a force of good in this world, or something else. He hoped it was the former, but that was all he had now. Hope.

"Go," he repeated. "Take Isabel and get out of this city. Find Maisiwan and Marcs and the others. You're the only chance they have of resisting Denether now."

"No!" Mikael gasped. "This...this is my fault. It should be me."

"Probably," Jaxon grunted, "but last I checked, she's *my* ex. *Now go!*"

Then, drawing Mana from the death and fire swirling about the square, Jaxon charged at Alyina and the governor with all the power his Gold ranked Essence could muster.

34

Three weeks before the Festival of the Satana

The morning was still dark as Lunden entered the gates of the Furness. Denether's summons had arrived early, and the nights were still long, despite summer's inevitable approach. His breath misted on the air as he followed the paved streets to the longhouse of the highking.

Once there, Lunden was forced to wait while a guard went inside, rubbing his arms in the chill. By the time he was emitted, the first rays of sun were streaming around Ryntirax, offering their warming light. Even so, he found himself in a foul mood as he entered. With the arrival of morning, his recruits would already be breaking their fasts in readiness for the day. Most of their training was arranged within units now, but Lunden still liked to be there to oversee the start of each day. Hopefully he could be done with whatever matters the king wished to discuss quickly, before more of the day was wasted.

"Marcs," Denether greeted. The man sat in his usual throne at the end of the chamber, though strangely the pair of chairs that usually sat alongside the throne had been removed. At this hour, the room was empty but for the highking and his personal bodyguard, Brandon. "Thank you for joining me. I am afraid we have much to discuss."

"What was it you wished to speak of, sir?" Lunden asked. Approaching the throne, he grimaced. "Is it Mikael and the Darkstrider?" The pair would be nearing Skarta by now. "Have the Gurrians betrayed them already?"

That would make sense. If the Gurrians had broken the truce, it meant their time was already out. It gave them less preparation that would have been ideal, but more than he'd hoped for, if Lunden was being honest. Denether would have to summon the rest of the Malesie and prepare to defend the south against invasion. Having fought more than his fair share of Gurrian Legions, Lunden was not savouring the prospect.

"Actually, it seems their journey may have proven pointless," Denether declared, rising from his chair. "For the past few weeks, I have been in deep discussion with a dignitary from Gurria. I am pleased to announce that an agreement has been made. There is to be a new peace between our peoples."

"*What?*"

Lunden couldn't quite believe his ears. He stared at the man, wondering if he was dreaming. Gurria and peace were like oil and water—mix them all you like, but it would never stick. There could be no peace with a nation like Gurria. Not for long. If they wanted peace, it was for their own reasons.

"There are conditions," Denether continued as though Lunden had not spoken. "The Gurrians will send a delegation to hash out the terms and ensure their soldiers are settled properly."

"Soldiers?" Lunden was still struggling to process the king's words. "As in Gurrian soldiers?"

Denether grunted. "Yes. I have agreed to allow a small

force to be stationed in Furness, as a show of good faith that we mean the empire no harm."

That…that was madness. Gurrian soldiers? On Malesie soil? How could the man even be *considering* it? That was exactly the outcome they had all been working to *avoid*.

"Sir…" Lunden trailed off, wondering if it was best to speak his mind, but…Jaxon and Mikael weren't here. Someone had to be the voice of reason. "Sir, the Gurrians cannot be trusted. Allow their soldiers into the Highlands and they will use it to learn everything they can about our army—if not worse."

"That will not be a problem," Denether replied. "The army is to be disbanded. I never should have entertained my son's ridiculous notion in the first place." He snorted. "We are Highlanders. Free men and women. We do not pay taxes so that others can till our lands."

"Disband the army?" Lunden gaped. "Sir, you cannot be considering—"

"You are right, Marcs," Denether spoke over the top of him. "I am not *considering* this—I have made my decision. The Gurrians have offered us the chance to avoid a terrible war. I had thought *you* of all people would understand my position."

"My king tried to make peace with the Gurrians," Lunden snapped. "They killed him for it. You cannot do this, sir."

"I do not recall asking for your opinion, foreigner," Denether snarled. He strode towards Lunden, until they stood face to face. "You are not even Malesie. The only reason you are standing here is because my people respect you."

"Sir, with respect—" Lunden tried one last time to argue.

"With respect, *Ressi*, this experiment is over. Do you understand?"

Lunden opened his mouth to tell the king just what he understood, but bit back the words. This was not the time or place to start a fight. Denether was right. He was the highking, while Lunden had no real power in the Highlands. Whatever connection he felt for this land and its people, he was still an outsider in the eyes of most.

Vinnie was wrong. He was no General.

"I understand, sir."

"Good." Denether drew in a breath, making an obvious effort to calm himself. "Now, as I said, you have earned the respect of the men and women you have trained. That is why I called you here, so you might be the one to give them the news."

It was like swallowing bile, but Lunden nodded. "Yes, sir. I will tell them."

"Good," there was a ring of finality about the king's reply. "You have a week to disband the camp and send them home." With that, he strode back to his chair and sat with a groan.

In that moment, Lunden glimpsed the face of the man behind Denether's chair. He was surprised to see anger in the bodyguard's eyes. It was gone as quickly as it had appeared, returning to a vacant stare, but Lunden was appeased to see he wasn't the only one upset by Denether's decision.

"What are you still doing here, Marcs?" the king growled. "I have a long day of meetings ahead of me. So unless there is anything else—"

"Actually, there was one thing, Your Majesty," Lunden interrupted. Hopefully the honorific would stay the man's patience.

Letting out a sigh, Denether waved for him to speak.

"Mikael and Jaxon," he said quickly. "If their presence is no longer necessary in Skarta, when will they be returning to Furness?"

Denether snorted. "Never, I would guess. The Offworlder has decided to visit the Gurrian capital and learn more about their civilisation. The Darkstrider is to accompany him."

A chill ran down Lunden's spine, though he was careful to

keep his face composed as he bowed. "Thank you, Your Majesty. If you'll excuse me, I will bring the news back to camp."

The king waved a hand, his thoughts clearly elsewhere already. But as Lunden straightened, he met the eyes of the king's bodyguard again. In that moment, an understanding passed between them, a shared rage—and helplessness. This man understood as well as Lunden what had just happened.

This was no peace agreement.

The Malesie had been betrayed by their own king.

35

Three weeks before the Festival of the Satana

"Well, the Fushore have gathered. Are you sure this plan will work?"

"Yes, ma'am."

Connor held his hands out to the coals glowing in the hearth. Several weeks had passed and the last of his bruises from the fight had faded. He wished he could say the same for his soul. His mind still lingered on Yiva's story about his father, on her accusations. And the letter that weighed heavily in his pocket.

Though summer was approaching, the nights were icy this far north, especially with the ocean winds. The howl as they swirled around the timber walls of the Fushore house was almost deafening. At least there was no chance of them being overheard.

"I still think its suicide," Yiva muttered.

The woman lounged in a sofa, nursing a glass of whiskey she had poured from her personal stores. Conner's sat untouched on the mantle above the fireplace.

"Not if things play out according to Mikael's plan."

"Ah yes, the infamous Offworlder. You realise the last kingdom to follow one of his kind ended up shattered into a thousand pieces."

"Yes, I'm aware of the history of the Detian Isles," he muttered, turning from the flames to look her in the eye. "But what is your alternative? The Gurrians will come. Whether it's this summer or the next, they will not stand for a free nation on their northern border."

"So instead you would have me sail my people into the abyss?"

Conner held her gaze. "I would have you trust me."

Yiva was the first to look away. She had the tricoloured cloak that Conner had presented her draped across her lap. Her fingers stroked it absently, running through the thick cloth.

"My father dreamed of standing with yours on the Northern Ocean and battling the Deti." She sighed. "I do not know if he would have liked your plan, Conner." She straightened in her chair. "And you're sure we can take those bastards?"

"Alone, not a chance." He smiled. *"But we will not be alone."*

A rasping laugh came from the Fushore chieftain. "Right. The Izolu. How many warriors do you think they will field?"

"The Malesie will fight as well. They are being trained as we speak."

"Right, by this Lunden Marcs. A Ressian man. Just how many links are in this chain of yours, my friend?"

"Enough to make a noose to hang the Gurrians by."

"Your metaphors need work," Yiva chuckled. "Though this one works: what if there is a weak link in your chain?" She eyed him. "Like your father."

The knot in Conner's stomach twisted. Did she know? His fingers clenched around the parchment. The letter of betrayal his father had sent. But no, he had shared it with no one.

Exhaling, he unclenched his fist and reached for his glass. Whiskey was a specialty in these parts, since the lower altitudes of the northern coast was the only region in the Highlands where grain could be grown. There was a rich, earthly taste to the burning liquor, which he savoured while he gathered his thoughts.

"Whatever his faults, my father loves his people and this land. I cannot believe he will betray us," he spoke the words with as much confidence as he could muster, though...did he still believe them? "But if the day comes when I must choose between the Highlands and my father, I will choose the Highlands."

Yiva studied him, eyes dark in the gloom. Finally she rose and placed her hands on Conner's shoulders in a gesture of respect.

"Then you have your ships, Conner Spears," she said, then grinned. "And may Ryntirax help us all!"

Later, in his room, Conner drew out the note from his father, just as he had done so many times since it had arrived three mornings ago.

Gurria is no longer our enemy. They have offered the Malesie peace and protection in exchange for the Offworlder. You are to return to Furness immediately. Say nothing of this to the Fushore.

It was signed by His Royal Highness, Denether Spears. Not Highking. Not Malesie chieftain. A lump lodged in Conner's throat. It did not miss his notice that Denether mentioned only the Malesie—and nothing about their rival clans.

Could it really be as Yiva said: that Denether would betray the others to advance his own ambition? Conner had not believed it before, not on the word of a woman he hardly knew. The very notion of his father sacrificing hundreds of Fushore and Malesie lives so he could become Highking was simply outlandish.

Yet here was the proof of his callousness. Mikael was one

thing. Denether had been reluctant to accept the Offworlder from the beginning. But what had the Gurrians offered that he would betray the other clans?

His Royal Highness.

Conner's stomach clenched, his eyes burning with unspilt tears. He had been given an order by his chieftain. It would be treason to disobey. And yet…yet if he did, everything he had said to Yiva would turn to ash on his tongue. He would be named a liar, his honour forever stained by the deed. Worse, he would be betraying Mikael, the man who had saved his life. Jaxon as well, since the Darkstrider would allow Denether to trade the life of his friend for an unstable peace.

He sat there for a while longer, the note held loosely between his fingers.

Could he really do it? Go against his father, the man who had raised him, shaped him in his own mould? Many a time, Denether named Conner his future, the one who would continue his legacy when he was gone. And now…

In the end, it was an easy decision. The flames leapt hungrily at the parchment, crackling as the wax layer burnt away. Conner watched the paper darken and curl, before finally collapsing in on itself.

Denether might have tried to shape Conner in his image, but it was Jaxon Daniyal that had won his respect, who had taught him to be his own man.

And for better or worse, Conner Spears would stand with the rest of the Highlands against the approaching evil.

36

No, *no, no!*

For just a second, Mikael stood frozen, reeling from Jaxon's sudden charge. Even Alyina and the governor seemed taken aback by his recklessness. They were slow to react. Slow enough that he had a chance. One moment to act.

He took it.

Sprinting across the bricked ground, he scooped Isabel into his arms. All around, soldiers were closing in, and from behind him came a *boom* as two forces of incredible power connected. The shockwave almost hurled him from his feet. As it was, it sent him stumbling towards the bloody waters of the fountain.

Footsteps came from behind him. The soldiers were coming. There was nowhere to go. Unless…

…his eyes fell on the canal that ran behind the fountain. Earlier, he'd seen men and women topple into those currents and vanish, dragged away by racing waters. There was no other choice. Mikael hurled himself over the side. He heard

"

shouts, but they vanished as his head slipped beneath the surface. He clung to Isabel, praying she would be okay.

And then the power of the river sucked them away.

Mikael struggled in the darkness, his powerful body pushing out for what he hoped was the surface. But all was dark now and he could no longer tell up or down. The weight of his pack and the unconscious Isabel dragged him down, but he struggled on, desperate lungs screaming, red stars dancing in his vision…

He gasped as his head suddenly broke the surface, air filling his lungs, then dragged Isabel up beside him. The darkness remained—they must be in a tunnel beneath the buildings. At least the current had slowed, ebbing gently against unseen walls. In the distance he could still hear the occasional *boom* as Jaxon did battle…

An iron vice gripped Mikael by the chest. He scrunched his eyes closed.

You failed.

His mind raced over what had happened, trying to find a way out, something he could have done differently. Should he have gone straight for plan B, and to hell with the risks?

From somewhere overhead, he heard the clashing of weapons. A scream as someone perished. Flames crackling. The city was burning.

There was nothing you could have done.

A Legion. That was Alyina's ace. She might not have played a perfect hand, but four thousand men was one hell of a trump card.

Finally his calm began to return, and with it, his sanity. He shivered, seeing again Jaxon charging at the princess. One Gold against all the might of the empire. A lump lodged in his throat. It was suicide. But it had given Mikael the second he needed to slip the noose from around his neck. Now he stretched out his *Aura Sense* in the direction of the square, hoping to sense his friend, but they were already too far away, the weight of stone and water cutting off his vision.

But he saw the rest. The harsh scarlets of soldiers marching through the streets. The emerald panic in the rebels as they fled. The navy blue terror of the innocent as they huddled in their homes.

He swum on, unsure what direction he was heading. It hardly mattered now. He had failed so utterly, Mikael didn't know where to go from here. Jaxon might have sacrificed himself for them, but what good was that if they couldn't even escape the city. Even if they did, Denether had turned the Highlands against him.

It should have been me.

His eyes stung as he thought of his friend. *Jaxon* could have done something, if he'd escaped. He could have united the Highlands, resisted Denether. He could have fought for his people, granting them courage in the dark days to come.

All Mikael could do was destroy.

He deserved to die here in the darkness.

The soft whisper of water on stone carried through the world beneath the world, and the scents were strangely muted, though he shuddered to think what this water contained. His sword belt weighed him down, and the pack, but they were all he had left. Isabel, he managed to keep on her back. Despite their predicament, her breathing seemed to have eased. Small miracles.

He wasn't sure when exactly he noticed the change. The way the water no longer seemed to move as he swum. There were no ripples, or whispers either. It wasn't like he drifted in water at all anymore, in fact, though the darkness went on and on, emptiness instead of water…

…but he noticed when the laughter started.

"Who's there?" Mikael spoke the words without thinking. They echoed through the nothing, rebounding, growing louder instead of fading, until it seemed he was shouting at himself.

Then the darkness parted and a terrible head rose from the black depths. It was one of the creatures from the riverbank. A Leviathan. But Mikael knew instantly this was not one of those gentle giants.

This was another of the Satana; the one Azaroth had warned him about.

"Leviathan," he breathed.

He had not thought that terrible, twisted face could grow any more terrifying. Until it smiled. Row upon row of long, curved teeth were revealed, glinting in the darkness.

"Good, so you know me," it rasped, though the words, like the laughter, did not seem to come from its mouth. "I thought it time we met."

Mikael struggled to find the words to respond. This creature could snuff him out like a bug. And according to Azaroth, it had every reason to do so. He hung there, suspended in the nothing, waiting for his doom to come…

…and when it didn't, he knew the truth.

"Yes, I had been hoping for a meeting myself," to his surprise, he spoke the words without so much as a tremor in his voice.

Silence.

"Say what?"

"I know we could go through the motions of me being terrified and all that, but to be honest it's been a long day. So why don't we just get to the point?"

The silence was longer this time.

"You, ah, know I could explode you into a thousand pieces right now, right?"

"I know you have the *power* to do it," Mikael countered. "I also know you have a substantial amount of credits riding on my death." He drew in a breath, doubt lingering in his mind. *Here goes.* "Which means, if you could kill me right now and get away with it, we would not be having this conversation."

This time the silence was deafening.

"Listen here you little sh—"

"NO," Mikael snarled. "No, I'm done playing along to your little games. The both of you, Leviathan and Azaroth. So why don't you go ahead and smite me right now."

The dark shape of the Leviathan twisted in the darkness, scarlet eyes glaring down at him. Finally though, it snorted. "I see why Azaroth is so fond of your chances. You have balls, mortal, I'll give you that." Laughter rattled through the void. "But it doesn't matter. I have no need to vanquish you here. You are surrounded by enemies, betrayed by your allies, your friends scattered or facing perils of their own. In a few hours you will be dead."

"It would seem that way," Mikael admitted. "Though since you came to gloat, there's something I would like to point out."

"And what is that?"

"I've been thinking over a few things. Like what exactly is happening here. Azaroth, when he came the first time, he talked about things. Producers. And getting in trouble for…things."

"You are not supposed to remember that."

Mikael waved a hand, though it was so dark he couldn't see it. For all he knew, he wasn't even really here. "I'm not supposed to do a lot of things. Too bad. My point is, even your presence, here, now of all times, tells me something. You can freeze time, but you came to gloat here, in the darkness." He grinned. "Where no one is watching."

The eyes closed and Mikael heard a sigh. "Yes, fine, as you've obviously worked out, we have to be careful when interfering. Can't go breaking the public's suspension of disbelief."

Mikael's heart was pounding and he struggled to keep his composure. This immortal creature could probably see through him like a pane of glass anyway. He did, however, have one last card to play.

"Good, good, just as I suspected." He paused. "So if I were to emerge from this place, shouting about how Azaroth and Leviathan of the Satana are playing games and betting on my death, I'm sure there wouldn't be any *consequences* for that now, would there?"

Now Mikael *knew* he had poked a nerve. Before, the demon had seemed amused, if a little taken aback by his talk. This time, Mikael felt the weight of an Aura hit him like a jumbo jet. He opened his mouth to scream, but suddenly there was no air, no oxygen, no…nothing. The darkness truly was a void, a pit of emptiness that went on and on. His lungs screamed and stars burned in his eyes as he thrashed, but there was nothing to grasp, nothing to save him. This must be what space was like without a suit to protect you. He could feel himself dying, his body atrophying, his soul being crushed in the vice of this creature's power…

…and yet he did not die. He just went on and on, in agony without an end, unable to see or scream or breath, until…

"I could leave you like this, you know," the voice whispered. "It would seem an eon to you, mortal. An everlasting death. But only a moment will have passed outside."

There came a *snap*, and the pain was gone. The red eyes glowered down at him. Mikael sucked in a deep, shuddering breath, his heart racing, a sob on his lips, tears burning in his eyes. That…that had almost broken him. The fear, the agony, the terror it would never end. His mind had fractured, slivers of glass sliding through his world.

"Do not think to threaten me, mortal," the voice whispered in his ear. "Or I will throw you back until your soul wilts and your mind crumbles."

Drawing in one last, shuddering breath, Mikael finally straightened. Every fibre of his being screamed to succumb, to bow and plead and do whatever this creature said. Every fibre of his being, except one tiny fragment, a flicker of flame that burned still in the darkness. *Pride.*

"Do it," he rasped. "Throw me back. Break my mind. But when I stumble from this place rambling like a lunatic, there'll be questions." He offered a grim smile. "And once they start digging, guess who they'll find?"

He sensed surprise from the demonic creature, and a flickering of something. Respect? It passed like a moment of stillness on a spring day. Rage replaced it, though it was tempered this time. Mikael clutched at the hilt of his blade, though he knew the broken construct could do nothing to protect him from these creatures.

Finally there came a long hiss, as of an exhaled breath.

"What do you want?" the voice rumbled.

Mikael almost collapsed with relief, almost showed his hand. But this wasn't done yet. Not by half.

"The other sword," he said quietly.

A pause. And then the laughter began again. "The sword?" Thunder rumbled through the darkness as the enormous head bellowed its mirth. "That's it? You think the other half of your cursed construct will save you? You don't even have the power to wield the half you have."

A ripple ran through Mikael's soul. The fractures shook, threatening to tear him apart. If this didn't work, he was truly doomed. But he couldn't back down now.

"The governor had it," he said. "It must be close. Better that I have it, than my enemies." He glared at the creature. He suspected he knew how it had fallen into Arimus's hands in the first place.

The laughter died away as the burning eyes lowered themselves to look Mikael directly in the face. "Are you *sure* about that, mortal?"

Mikael swallowed, struggling to hold his nerve before the infinity he saw in that gaze. "I am."

"Ha!" The twisted head lifted again. "So be it. The producers will be pissed, but it wasn't me that left those things lying around. Besides…" The lips of the enormous jaws drew back, revealing row upon row of jagged teeth. "…this is going to make a great show. *Does the Offworlder have what it takes?*" It laughed. "Yes, I like it. And even if I lose, well, Azaroth won't be able to collect if he's in the Seventh inferno. Not that I'll lose."

Mikael swallowed. "Where do I find it?"

"Ha! Where? You know what, mortal, they shouldn't notice a little shift. Here."

A *snap* echoed through the void.

And Mikael woke, gasping, as his head thumped into the side of the canal. The sun still shone high in the sky, though it was darkened by thick columns of smoke. The taste of burning was heavy in the air. He could still hear distant screams. Wherever he was, though, all seemed calm.

Groaning, he shifted in the water. Isabel lay beside him, only half-submerged in the nearly empty canal. There was barely ten centimetres of water left in the bottom. He pushed himself upright, grimacing as his arm plunged deep into the mud on the bottom. He would need to visit Jon Sorrow's bath-house when this was all over. It didn't sound like the man would be using it himself anymore. Grasping the lip of the canal, he pulled himself up, dragging Isabel with him, until they flopped onto the footpath.

Only then did he get a good look around.

The neighbourhood seemed to be abandoned, but his eyes were drawn to a manor rising amidst the squalor. It was old, and had been great once, but now it was little more than a boarded-up ruin, abandoned by the world. Or so it seemed.

Mikael's *Aura Sense* could see the souls hiding within. Dozens of them. Children for the most part, as far as he could tell. But there was one bright soul amongst them, a Copper ranked Aura he recognised.

Katherine Delinghy.

37

The soldiers died easily. Strange, how that had always been the case. Dealing death was a part of Jaxon's nature. Why had he tried to deny it? One swing of his enormous greatsword was all it took. It didn't matter what armour they wore or how fast they moved. No one escaped the Darkstrider's blade.

And so the soldiers came, and they died.

He still took blows—Jaxon was not immortal, after all, and Alyina had brought *a lot* of soldiers. They leapt selflessly between their princess and her assailant, almost eager to throw their lives away for a woman who thought them less than dogs at her feet. And they managed their hits. A glancing blow from the shield of an Iron ranker, a shallow cut across his arm by a regular soldier, a punch that must have shattered someone's hand as it rocketed from Jaxon's granite chin. None were given a chance for a second shot.

One by one, they crossed the veil into the embrace of the Elohim.

For the first time in years, Jaxon Daniyal revelled in his strength. He alone had the power to hold back this tide, to turn aside the enemy that would do harm to his friends. For a few minutes, the clock was wound back and he stood again as the Darkstrider, warrior of the Highlands, protector of the weak against the evil strong.

He knew now the error he had made. In a moment of weakness, he had been corrupted, drawn down the path of temptation. Thousands had died for his mistake, an entire town put to the sword. For that crime, Jaxon had bound himself in unbreakable oaths. To his king, to his people, to an ideal that could never be achieved. And in doing so, he had put his power in the hands of others.

But they, too, had been unworthy.

Now death approached and Jaxon was free.

Through his desperate battle, Alyina had not moved—not even when Mikael fled with Isabel flung over his shoulder. She only stood, arms folded across her chest, that twisted smile on her lips. She could end all this in a moment, he knew. She could have saved the lives of her soldiers. But she chose not to. She preferred to see him suffer, to watch him struggle, all the while knowing he could never, ever win.

Until, at last, she grew bored.

"Oh, enough of this," her voice rang across the square. The soldiers drew back instantly, showing that the iron discipline of the Gurrian Legions had not been lost.

Jaxon lowered his blade as the soldiers retreated. "Giving up already?" he puffed. More than a dozen soldiers lay dead around him.

Alyina snorted but did not reply. Instead, she turned to Arimus Shore, laying a hand on the governor's chest. "Time to show me you're the better man, my dear," she said, a sweet smile lighting up her face. "You did say that you'd deal with Jaxon Daniyal if it came to it, didn't you?"

Arimus's face was rigid, his entire body tense. Jaxon couldn't blame the man. Alyina had manipulated Arimus, leaving him jumping at shadows chasing the resistance when she had been the one pulling their strings all this time.

"What about the Offworlder?" Arimus growled. He had tried to go after Mikael earlier, only to be stayed by Alyina's hand.

"He's *mine*," Alyina replied with a smirk, her eyes mocking as she looked at Jaxon. "Don't worry, the pair won't get far."

Something seemed to flicker in Arimus's face as Jaxon watched. Then it was gone, and the young warrior was striding towards him, Gurrian longsword in his hand. He moved with the grace of a warrior, muscles rippling, dark eyes watching Jaxon with the keen intent of a predator.

"Alyina," Jaxon barked as he saw the princess turn away.

She glanced around, eyebrows lifting in surprise. "What is it, Jaxon?"

"You're not going to stay and watch me gut your new toy?" He had to try and delay her.

Her laughter tolled like funeral bells across the square. "Oh, I have missed your banter, my poor, dear Jaxon. But no, I'm not going to stay." Her face twisted in a smirk. "I'm going to go hunt down your little Offworlder friend and tear off his wings. Then, if she's still alive, I'm going to drown your precious Isabel in the canals of this filthy city. So if you don't mind…" Waving her hand, she turned her back on him.

Roaring, Jaxon leapt at her—only to hurl himself aside as a longsword flashed for his face.

Then the battle was joined, and Jaxon could no longer spare a second's energy on Alyina Sorulus and her prey.

Mikael and Isabel were on their own.

38

Two weeks before the Festival of the Satana

"…With the dawn's light, the star descended, grace made light. Hearts filled with glory, the people of Izolu bowed before the presence of Ryntirax. And he, most mighty of the heavens, bestowed upon them his gift. Not of magic or power, for those can only corrupt the minds of feeble humanity. Within their souls, the music woke. Born of life, of love, it brought wisdom to the Izolu, that they might never stray from the path of righteousness…"

Moira's voice trailed off, but Fiachson did not notice as he took a sip of his tea. He was distracted. Two weeks had passed since their arrival in the village, and the chief was yet to say… anything. Fiachson had been so excited to reach this mystical place and speak with his father's people, he had never really considered they might reject his appeal. Now Moira was laying bare the histories of the Izolu for him, and Fiachson found he could hardly concentrate…

He sat bolt upright in the wooden chair when he realised silence had fallen over the chamber. Moira stood beside the flickering peat fire where she had been narrating her tale, arms crossed, a dark look on her face.

"Do you know the punishment a Librarian deals out to Izolu children who flout their histories?" she asked, her voice stern.

"Sorry," he groaned, exasperated. "It's just…your father. It's been two weeks. Mikael needs us!"

The disappointed look remained fixed on Moira's face. "I thought the son of Hanequin would be brighter than this. Maybe there was a mix up, you know, when you were a child?"

"Hey!" Fiachson almost choked on his tea. "My mother—"

Moira's face cracked as she burst into laughter. "You really have spent too long with the lowlanders," she cackled. Relenting, she wandered over and offered him a hand. "Come on then, let's go for a walk. Maybe that will clear your mind."

"So long as we do not need to ride those damn goats again," Fiachson muttered.

Leaving the house that the Izolu had provided for himself and his mother, they followed the path through the rice fields, to where the land fell into the sky. Today there was a mist about the plateau, concealing the fiord below. Standing at the edge, Fiachson felt as though he were drifting on some great flying ship, far above the world.

Then he realised just how close he was standing to the edge and made a quick retreat.

Moira laughed. "Don't tell me you're afraid of heights?"

"Not afraid," Fiachson shot back. The wind swirled about them, giving him an unsteady feel, but he resisted the urge to retreat further. "I just have…a healthy respect."

Silence fell between them. Fiachson watched the swirling mists. The way they drifted seemed random, rising suddenly or parting for a moment with a puff of air. The strange warmth of the plateau remained despite the heavy humidity, and he realised that a touch of sweat beaded his brow.

"You look sad," Moira said suddenly. "Are your father's people not what you expected?"

"What? No!" Fiachson exclaimed. Turning to look at her instead, he stifled a sigh. How to explain? "It…it is just, I wish this visit could have been under different circumstances."

"Why did you not come sooner?"

"I was too young." He grimaced. "Too weak."

"You're a Pathfinder. I thought lowlanders considered that the pinnacle of a warrior's path."

"It is a recent development," Fiachson muttered. "Before…" He looked away. "Not even my mother believed in me. But Mikael did."

"Your Offworlder friend?"

Fiachson's hands balled into fists. "Offworlder or not, he was the only one who stood up for me. He trained me, made me a part of his team. If not for him, I would still be in Sitton, the runt of the Malesie."

"A true friend, then," she said softly. She was watching him with a strange look in her eyes. "So where is he now?"

Fiachson frowned. It was impossible to make heads or tails of the young woman. "In danger," he said at last. "He and Jaxon went to Skarta, to try and negotiate with the Empire."

"You do not think they will be successful?"

"Mikael did not think it likely."

"Then why go?"

"Because they had to try," Fiachson whispered. "And because Mikael trusted us to come through. To find them an army, in case they fail."

"I see," Moira looked thoughtful. "So your friends, you came here to ask us to help them?"

Fiachson shrugged. "I guess so."

"Well, why didn't you say so in the first place!" He almost tripped over the edge as Moira leapt to her feet with a shout.

"Wait," he stood, gaping at her. "Wait…does that mean you *will* help us?"

"Of course we'll help your friends!" Moira said. "You are Izolu, and the Izolu stand with their friends."

"But your father—"

"He told you that *we* don't need protecting," she exclaimed, sounding exasperated now. Grabbing him by the hand, she started dragging him in the direction of the village. Somewhat taken aback, Fiachson allowed himself to be led. "By Ryntirax, did no one in those lowlands ever teach you how to construct a proper argument?"

"I…ah…what?"

Tripping over his words and his feet, Fiachson could hardly believe his problem could be solved so easily. All it had taken was a little change in the wording. But the resolve on Moira's face was unmistakable.

"There's a few details we probably need to sort out," she continued as they approached the village. "Like how to make you a proper Izolu. Technically, you can't call on our help unless you're one of us."

"I thought I *was* a proper Izolu?"

"You haven't learnt your histories yet," she said, exasperated. "But…" Her face brightened. "I think I have a solution!"

"And what is that?"

"Come on," Moira exclaimed, dodging the question. "Let's go speak with my father."

39

Present Day

The sensation of waking came as a surprise to Kat. A part of her had believed she was dead. After all the suffering of these past few days—and her entire life—it had almost been a relief. So when the pain drew her back, a part of her resisted, screaming that she'd done enough, that it was time for her to rest.

But life, as usual, had no interest in what Katherine Delinghy wanted.

Instead, she woke on a lumpy pile of old clothing in a musty room. Her side ached where the arrow had struck, but it was not the same pain as before. This was crisper, cleaner, without the radiating sickness that had sapped her strength and so muddled her thoughts.

How long had she been unconscious? She tried to push herself up, but a fresh wave of dizziness brought her to a halt. Groaning, she sank back onto the makeshift bed.

"Finally awake, I see," a voice said from nearby.

Kat jerked upright—then doubled over with a gasp as fire

ripped through her side. She clutched at the wound and felt some of the pressure ease.

"Easy," the voice said softly. "I think you might be lucky to be alive, Kat."

This time she recognised the speaker—Mikael. That was even *more* confusing. What in the Seven Hells was he doing here? And where was *here* for that matter? The last thing she remembered was…

A girl's face, terror in her eyes as the life drained from her…and into Kat.

Gasping in a lungful of air, she pushed the image away. That hadn't happened. It was just a nightmare, *wasn't it?*

Something was tearing inside her, some terrible, horrible thing, but she forced herself to ignore it. To focus on the present. They were in a dark room. She could barely make out the Highlander where he sat on a nearby stool. And the smell…she knew that mix of dampness and unwashed bodies. Her heart sped up. She was at Marta's.

"Mikael," Kat rasped. "What are you doing here? What am *I* doing here?"

This was the last place she should be. She had *known* that. The pain returned as she sat up. At least her wound was no longer bleeding. Marta must have bandaged it and changed her clothes. Of course the old woman had helped her, but in doing so, Kat had put everyone in danger.

"You tell me," Mikael replied. "The old woman at the door wasn't exactly forthcoming."

She swallowed. Her eyes slowly adjusted to the darkness, bringing Mikael into focus. Only then did she notice the sword lying across his lap. *Her sword.* She could sense the power in it, or rather, the absence of power…

"You can feel it, can't you?" Mikael whispered. "The void?"

Looking into Mikael's eyes, Kat saw the darkness within her reflected back. Swallowing, she nodded.

He grimaced. "But I can't." He stared at the blade, still sheathed in black leather, before giving a little shiver. "Well, not much of it." He looked at her. "You used it, didn't you?"

Kat stood in the alley, facing the soldiers. Felt their Mana, their life force flowing into her. She rejoiced in the power of their death, watching the life fade from their eyes.

"I did," she whispered, clutching at her chest. "It's…it's terrible."

"Describe it to me."

"I don't—"

"Do it!"

She flinched at the sudden anger in Mikael's voice. No, not anger. That was desperation.

"It was like…like it drained them," she croaked. "All their Mana and Aura, even their Body, until there was nothing left."

Mikael grimaced. Reaching down beside his chair, he lifted another sword from the floor. It was the one he had used the night they'd met. Only now, Kat realised it was the same design as the void blade. Plain to the eye, for sure, but…

…she opened her *Aura Sense* and felt the subtle differences. Not an emptiness, like her own dark thing. with this sword, it was like there was *more* to it. More substance, or weight in her spiritual eye.

"They're a pair," he said quietly. "Two halves of a broken whole. Yours…" he swallowed. "I couldn't see it until I had both. The construct needed energy to function. Huge amounts. Your half provides the power…by absorbing elements of reality." He looked at his weapon. "And mine…mine should, theoretically, take that energy and shape the universe to its will."

Kat's heart began to pound. "Then…they're a weapon? We can use them against the Empire?"

"Maybe." Mikael looked away, though not before Kat

glimpsed something in his eyes that made her shiver. "Did you know?" he asked suddenly. "About Jon's revolution?"

The breath caught in Kat's throat. If Mikael knew, then… "What day is it?"

"So you did know," Mikael grimaced. "I'm sorry, Kat. It was a trap. All of it."

"What do you mean?"

"Alyina Sorulus knew all along. Jon armed the farmers, brought them into the city under the cover of the festival, but Alyina did the same. Only she brought an entire Legion. Four thousand soldiers. They were waiting for you all to reveal yourselves."

Kat shook her head. "No…" That…that couldn't be true. "We were so careful…"

"Alyina played us all for fools." He grimaced. "So, Kat, tell me how you came by that wound?" He nodded to her injury.

"Oh, yes, Kat," a voice came from behind them. Kat's heart almost fell out of her chest when she saw Isabel standing in the doorway. "Please, do tell."

FEW DAYS IN MIKAEL'S LIFE HAD GONE AS BADLY AS THIS ONE— but the sight of Isabel on her feet, eyes alive with energy, certainly added a bright spark to the otherwise terrible time he'd been having.

The day wasn't done with them just yet, though, and he could see the terror in Kat's eyes as she looked from Mikael to Isabel. It was clear they knew each other.

But the story that came tumbling from Kat's lips…well, it was unexpected to say the least. A father betrayed, a plot for revenge, a revelation that the Skartan Governor was in fact Isabel's half-brother, and an assassination attempt.

Well, let no one else claim Mikael Heaton was the only one causing trouble in Skarta.

By the time Kat finished, he knew he should be angry with her. Isabel certainly didn't seem to have forgiven her. He'd seen that look in his friend's eyes before, the fiery glow of Mana pulsing in their sapphire depths. Maybe he should even be judging Kat for the innocent girl she'd cut down in cold blood.

But he couldn't.

Because he knew now why Leviathan had laughed. Why it had asked if he had what it took. The twisted, broken thing that was the void sword still lay in his lap. The old woman had let him into the house without a single question—as though she had been expecting him—so he'd had some time to examine the sword while Kat slept.

There was a *wrongness* about it. Not in its nature. He could sense a little of the void, just like he could sense a little of the strangeness in his own sword. But with his own weapon, he could feel it pulsing back sometimes, like there was a connection between them. And there was, he knew. That was why Azaroth had left him the sword in the first place—because the construct had been connected to his soul.

But with the void sword, that connection was not there. He had tried extending his Aura into the weapon, or reaching for it like he did with Mana. Both times, rather than feeling nothing, he had felt *rebuffed*, like the weapon was rejecting him.

After listening to Kat's story, about what had happened in the alleyway, he thought he knew why.

"I'm sorry, Isabel," Kat finished, and her eyes really did seem to mean it. There was a tremor in her voice as she continued. "If I could take it back…"

She trailed off as Isabel strode across the room. Her face, already pale from loss of blood, turned ghostly white.

"Do you know what they did to me?" Isabel's voice was terrifyingly calm.

Kat shook her head violently back and forth. The poor street urchin no longer seemed capable of speech.

"Alyina Sorulus questioned me herself." Isabel towered over the girl. "She did not even ask questions—at least not at first. She just twisted her Aura through my body and soul until I screamed and screamed and screamed." She paused, fists clenched, her power radiating through the room. "She enjoyed it."

A tear streaked down Kat's cheek. She opened her mouth, but Isabel cut her off.

"Do not apologize," she snapped. "I do not need your apologies, Kat." Suddenly she crouched beside the girl, so they were eye to eye. "But I want your promise—next time you go after those bastards, we do it together."

Kat's eyes widened, clearly stunned by the offer. Mikael clenched his jaw as the street urchin offered a tentative nod. "I promise."

There was silence between the two as they held one another's gaze. Mikael broke it with a cough.

"Yes, well, about that," he said softly. "We're not exactly out of the furnace just yet."

"I take it you have a plan," Isabel asked as she rose. A smile touched her lips as their eyes met.

Despite the circumstances, Mikael found himself smiling back—before the weight of their situation stole the little piece of joy away. He bowed his head.

"I do. But it involves using these swords."

"Then take it!" Kat said quickly. "I...I don't want it." Her eyes shone and Mikael knew she was thinking of the Gurrian girl she had killed.

This sword in his lap, it was a dark thing. The yin to the yang of his own half of the construct. Separated from creation, all it desired was to consume, to destroy the world around it. A weapon fit for the Voidlight indeed.

Except he could no longer use it.

"I can't," he said quietly, his fingers tightening around the hilt. "You used its power, Kat. Now it's bound to *you*. To your soul."

It was just like Azaroth had said on the Day That Had Never Been. The construct had joined with his soul when he'd crossed the barrier between worlds. But when the Satana divided it, only half remained bound to Mikael's spirit. The other half went free.

Until Kat used it for herself.

The girl was staring at him with wide eyes. "What does that mean?"

"It means I can't use it," he whispered. "When I reach for it with my power, it rejects me." He drew it slightly from its case. Kat flinched. "But the void still calls to you, doesn't it?"

"But I don't want it," Kat whispered. Her gaze was distant, haunted. "Please…you don't know what it's like…what…what I did."

Mikael swallowed. He knew her fear well, the terror of what lay within. Of what you might be capable of, when the cards were down. He had told himself he would do whatever it took to protect the Highlands. And the power of this sword, it was their best chance of escaping the city alive. Outside the shuttered windows, the streets were crawling with soldiers. But with these weapons, who knew what he was capable of…

"There…there might be one way," Mikael croaked.

A part of him died when he saw the hope shining in Kat's eyes. "How?"

"You would have to die."

Fear replaced the hope. Mikael wondered at the person he had become.

"Please, you can't…"

"Of course he can't," Isabel snapped.

"She tricked you into trying to assassinate the governor," he said. "She led you into a trap, abandoned you to be tortured, maybe killed. Now she's the only thing standing between us and a weapon that could save your entire people." He looked from Isabel to Kat. "So tell me, Kat, why should I *not?*"

He felt cold, speaking the words. He didn't even know if he could go through with it. War was making the hard choices. But this…surely it was no different? How could he place one girl's life over the thousands he could save with that power? He watched as Kat grew tense.

"Don't," he said softly. "You're in no condition to run."

"I…I'm sorry," Kat whispered. "I didn't mean for any of this to happen."

"I know," Mikael rasped. "Sometimes we mess up."

Mikael tried not to think about what Jaxon would say. He was trying not to think about his friend at all. Isabel still hadn't asked. He couldn't face that conversation, not now. But the Gold ranker's absence was worse than the void. Ever since he'd arrived in his world, Jaxon Daniyal had been there, a shield against the forces that wanted him dead. Even against the power of the Elohim, Jaxon had stood his ground, refusing to bend.

And now…all Mikael had left of the man was a voice in his head, whispering that this was not the way.

"You tried to assassinate the governor. They won't rest until they have you, Kat. You know that."

He focused on Kat. He owed her nothing, but this decision was like a shadow on his soul. The Gurrians had taken everything from her. Now they wanted her life as well, because she had dared to stand up to them. It wasn't fair.

But that was it, wasn't it? The great meaning of life everyone sought.

Life isn't fair.

"Please, Mikael," Isabel whispered. "There has to be another way."

Mikael swallowed. He couldn't meet Isabel's eyes. She didn't know about his last option. Plan B. He still had the pack. But it was untested. Would it even be enough for the likes of Alyina Sorulus? He'd watched her brush off an attack from Jaxon *without even touching him*. And if he did use it…

…the Seventh Circle might have magic, but there were things from Earth far, *far* worse than what the Pathfinders of this world were capable of. If he did this, it could start them down a path from which there was no return.

"There isn't," to Mikael's surprise, it was Kat who spoke over his spiralling thoughts. Her head lifted, looking first at Isabel, then to Mikael. "You're right. They will come for me. Me and everyone who helped me." She swallowed. "So, I'll do it." Her voice cracked. "But only if you promise…promise you'll save them. Marta and the children. You have to protect them."

Mikael felt a lump lodge in his throat. This was it. He didn't need plan B. Didn't need to contaminate this world any further than he already had. It was all laid out before him, a path as clear as day. Kill Kat and take her sword, and he would have a fearsome weapon to use against Alyina and her army. Maybe it would be enough, maybe it wouldn't. But it certainly gave them a better chance than plan B.

Except for one thing.

It was too perfect.

"No," he found himself saying instead. "I won't do it. In the words of a hero from my world, we don't trade lives—"

He broke off. Kat wasn't listening. Her eyes were wide, her face pale. Suddenly, a brilliant light burst from her skin, burning away the shadows in the room. Mikael was on his feet in a second, grasping for his sword, before he realised what it was.

Her Aura was changing. Subtle at first, it flickered like a fire in the breeze. But eventually the breeze focused, becoming a bellows that filled the girl with a newfound power. Her Aura roared within, flickering and changing, colours swirling from yellow to red to orange. A single cry tore from Kat. Her back arched and her energy swept through the room, her Aura pressing against them, before finally beginning to retreat, coalescing, concentrating within with a fresh strength.

Finally, she collapsed gasping to the floor. Mikael shared a glance with Isabel.

"Iron," he whispered.

He didn't need to use his Offworlder ability to confirm it. Kat's decision to sacrifice herself for those she loved had unlocked her soul, allowing it to grow stronger.

Just as Mikael's own internal revelations had allowed him to advance before his fight with Conner, and during the battle for Sarton. He still hadn't found the key that would allow him to reach Bronze yet. But he would.

Gasping, Kat sat up on the floor. Sweat drenched her brow and her clothes stuck to her skin, but as she stood on unsteady feet, her eyes were wide with wonder.

"That was…"

"…unexpected," Isabel said with a grin.

Kat nodded, still looking stunned. She touched her side, eyes widening further as she realised the wound was healed.

Mikael studied her, wondering…

Activating his Offworlder ability, he examined her stats and saw the new ability listed there. He smiled.

<hr>

A SMILE TOUCHED MARTA'S LIPS WHEN SHE FELT THE RIPPLING in the girl's soul. It had begun a few minutes before the revelation, as it always did. Somehow, the soul *knew* and was already preparing itself. Her people had studied the phenomenon long ago, hoping to improve their knowledge of Aura and its connection with the world, but they had failed. Not all the collective wisdom of their generations had they been able to crack that secret.

She stepped away from the door where the three were talking. Ten thousand years of study, and that breakthrough had never been made. But it had taken only a few generations, a scant millennium, for them to create the weapons again. Last time, they had been the beginning of the end. Such power was never meant for mortal hands. When the others had left, taking their abominable constructs with them, this world had wept with joy.

But now the cursed weapons had returned. Even thousands of years later, this world still had not healed from the mutilation left by the last Destroyers. Now another generation seemed poised to take their place in the Seventh Realm.

Marta could only hope these ones would take more care with their steps.

"Who are you, exactly?"

Turning, Marta found the boy standing behind her. He held a sword in each hand and his amber eyes shone with determination. She sighed. So young, so convinced of his own genius. The hubris would be his downfall. Yet her sister had seen something about him, some glimmer of light in the grey. Maybe he would not be like the others that had come before him. Perhaps he could handle the burden.

"A friend," she said softly.

"You'll forgive me if I do not put my faith in that." He pursed his lips. "You were listening?"

"You doubt the path you have chosen," she said, ignoring the question.

He grunted. "Of course I'm doubtful," he admitted, "but they haven't left me much in the way of choice."

She laughed at that. "There is always a choice."

"And what would you do, if you were in my shoes?"

Marta felt the weight of her age in her bones, but his gall brought a smile to her face. "Can't say. Not in your shoes, am I?"

The boy narrowed his eyes. "You know that turn of phrase, don't you?"

Observant. Most people did not look beyond the mad old woman, but then, she had given him cause to suspect. She offered a wild grin. "I know when to stay out of shadow weaver business."

The boy said nothing, only stared at her, as though if he looked for long enough he might pierce her veil. Which with that particular sword in his hand, might very well be true. So Marta let the smile slip.

"Your little trick won't work on me, boy."

He clenched his jaw. "I see." A pause. "*What* are you?"

"No one," she said softly. "But the question should be, what are *you.*"

"Human," he said instantly. "They can call me an Offworlder all they like, but I am still the same man I was on my world."

"You are also the Voidlight."

"You're the second strange old lady to give me that name. What does it mean?"

"What do you think it means?"

The boy sighed. "This is getting nowhere," he said softly, glancing back in the direction of his companions. There was a resolve in his eyes when he looked back at her. *He knew.* "You're one of them, aren't you? The Satana, or the Elohim perhaps?"

Marta's heart actually skipped a beat. It had been a long time since anyone surprised her like that. "Do not insult me, boy," she hissed. "I am everything they are not." She snorted.

"Always fiddling, playing with their toys. They never saw the ruin they created."

"Then what are you?"

"We are what they left behind." She saw the understanding dawn in his eyes and raised a hand to fend off further inquiries. "No more questions. Your time is running out. She is almost here."

Mikael's face grew grim. "Alyina?"

"Ay. You led her straight to my door," Marta grunted. "Thanks for that."

"You had better get the kids out."

"Of course." She turned to leave, then paused. "She will try to kill your girlfriend first. That is the way of people like her."

"I know," he said grimly, "and she's not my girlfriend."

"Ha!" Marta chortled. "You mortals still find ways to make me laugh. Don't tell *her* that, lad." She paused, studying him. "Are you sure about this?"

This time, Mikael's face hardened into a resolute grimace. "As I'll ever be."

"That's more like it."

40

Two weeks before the Festival of the Satana

"**D**ad, I have fantastic news!"

Fiachson's cheeks flushed as he found himself in a room full of people all staring at him—again. He cursed beneath his breath. It looked like they had interrupted yet another performance by the Izolu chieftain. Wasn't the man meant to be considering Fiachson's plea to aid the other clans?

"Oh, and what news is that, my daughter?" at least the man didn't seem overly bothered by the disruption.

"Fiachson would like to invoke his right as Izolu and demand our aid for his friends!"

Fiachson stifled a groan. That was not exactly how he would have put it. And what was this right that Moira kept talking about? He should have paid more attention to the stories she had been teaching him.

"Is that so?" the Izolu chieftain's eyes shifted to Fiachson. "Then he has already memorised his family's histories?"

"Ah…" Fiachson squirmed beneath that gaze. "Not…exactly."

The chieftain grunted, folding his arms. "Then you are not yet Izolu, young man, and cannot claim such a right. You know this, my daughter."

Moira seemed to deflate, her usually vibrant spirit appearing to shrink. But the setback was momentary. The eager young woman was not to be deterred. Casting a nervous glance at Fiachson, she straightened, her face becoming resolute.

"Then he would like to initiate the Trial of the Ancients!"

"The *what?*" Fiachson spluttered. He did *not* like the sounds of that.

The chief's face took on a grim look as he turned from his daughter to Fiachson. "You would really accept such a challenge."

"I…ah…hold on just a minute," Fiachson stammered. "What exactly is this trial?"

Moira's father grunted. "An ancient challenge," the man replied. "One that tests the commitment of an outsider to our people and forever binds your soul to our ways." The deep eyes of the Izolu chieftain seemed to bore into Fiachson. "It is not for the faint-hearted."

Fiachson swallowed. Judging by the grim look on Lachlan's face, it was a grave challenge indeed. Hells, what exactly was Moira volunteering him for? An electric pulse racing down his spine, his eyes darted to the young woman. Did she really think he could do this?

She was nodding with her usual enthusiasm, and he felt himself calm just a little. Moira hardly knew him, but she believed in him. It was time he started believing in himself as well.

"I can do this," he said softly.

"Then you accept my daughter's challenge?"

"I do."

"And Moira, do you accept what the Trials will mean for you? That you will no longer be my Apprentice, but must forge your own path forward at the side of your new husband?"

Fiachson's heart all but stopped in his chest. "Wait, what?"

41

Present Day

Jaxon's lungs heaved as he reeled back from a blow. Normally he held back in populated areas, but any innocent Skartans had long since fled the plaza. All that remained was Arimus Shore. And the Skartan governor certainly wasn't holding back.

So nor could Jaxon.

Movement Surge covered the ground between them. His greatsword swept for the governor's neck. A burst of speed of his own allowed Arimus to escape, only to turn the attack back on Jaxon, longsword lancing for his groin.

He skipped back—just avoiding a second *Surge* as his opponent came again.

Gasping, he raised his sword, ready to fend off a third blow. This time his foe didn't follow. Instead, Arimus lowered his sword with a smile.

"Need a break, old man?"

As much as Jaxon wanted to deny the offer, he could already feel the fatigue creeping into his bones. Aura he had to spare, but he had used too much of his strength fending off Alyina's soldiers. So instead, he just grunted and relaxed his stance, putting a show into stretching his neck.

"Ay," he grunted. "Just starting to get warmed up."

Arimus smirked, his confidence obvious—and with good reason. Jaxon could not match his speed or Mana. It was only a matter of time before the younger man wore him down. Exhaling, Jaxon closed his eyes, extending his senses, seeking out Isabel, or Mikael, or Alyina.

Instead, he felt the pain of Skarta. It was more than just its people's suffering, as they yet again found themselves crushed beneath the boots of foreign soldiers. It was more than the fear, or the pain of the dying, or their hatred for the Gurrians that hunted them in their own streets.

It was like this suffering had seeped into their bones. Their subjugation had become a part of them, sucking the very life from the land, stealing away its spirit. They needed a guardian, someone to make them believe again.

"Tell me, old man," Arimus sneered. "How does it feel to be replaced?"

Drawing in another breath, Jaxon offered a smile. "There's not a man alive who could replace me, lad. Let alone a little scrap like you." He laughed. "What, did you graduate from diapers just yesterday?"

The grin faded from Arimus's lips. "Is that all you've got? Empty taunts?" He pointed his blade at Jaxon. "You're all washed up, old man. No wonder Alyina chose me."

Jaxon said nothing. He could sense the power building in his foe. He should flee, he knew. Alyina was a ways off now and Mikael's Aura had vanished—somehow—from his senses. But standing amidst the dead and the dying, feeling the sickness radiating from this place…

…he drew in a breath and raised his greatsword.

The Skartans needed a champion. Well, today they had one.

Today, the Darkstrider had returned.

And besides, when had Jaxon Daniyal ever run from a fight?

The next attack came without warning. One second, the young man was standing calmly in the street, blade held casually at his side—the next the longsword was scorching a path for Jaxon's throat. *Movement Surge.* Whatever Arimus claimed, Jaxon's words clearly needled him.

Fortunately, old he might be, but Jaxon Daniyal had not earned his legend for nothing. Arimus's blade found only empty air as Jaxon evaded the attack with a quick step to the side. He didn't bother to use his own *Movement Surge.* Each use consumed the energy of his body and Jaxon had a feeling he would need every bit of stamina he had to match the young Gold ranker.

"Sloppy," he taunted, even as Arimus shifted, his blade arcing around to slash at his neck.

This time Jaxon's great sword met the scimitar with all the power of his *Enforced Body*, slamming it aside. Sparks flashed as Arimus reversed the blow and forced Jaxon to deflect the attack with the guard of his blade. This time, though, the Highlander went on the offensive. As the longsword rang from his iron guard, Jaxon swung down, the enormous blade aiming to split his foe's skull in two.

At the last moment, Arimus shoved out with his longsword. The resulting *crash* as their weapons came together carried enough momentum to force both combatants apart. They sprang back, cobbles crunching beneath their boots as they braced themselves. Arimus threw out a hand, energy crackling as he drew mana from the world.

The city began to shake, the ground to crack.

Jaxon laughed. "Getting desperate, lad? Must be, if you need to destroy the whole city just to stop one old man."

Arimus faltered, before a scowl twisted his lips. But he lowered his hand and the ground stilled. He watched Jaxon with a wary eye as they began to circle. Even in the Empire, there were few Gold rankers, and it was unlikely he had faced more than a handful of his rank.

And none of them had been Jaxon Daniyal.

"I replaced you in her bed as well, old man," Arimus taunted as they circled.

"If that is true, then you have my sympathies, kid."

Arimus barked out a laugh. "Do I?" His blade flashed, and they stepped to the dance of death for several heartbeats.

"You do," Jaxon panted when they separated. "You show some promise. I hate to see another talented young man chewed up and spat out by the likes of Alyina Sorulus."

A snarl tore from Arimus's lips. "You're just jealous that she discarded you."

Steel flashed. Jaxon's blade rose to meet his opponent's, but as they connected he felt a jolt, as Arimus's Aura poured into his soul. He gritted his teeth against the *Onslaught*, his own Aura pressing back. It was a rare ability, but one with little defence other than the strength of your own Aura. Those who failed to defend themselves would suffer an agony that would cripple most men.

It was one of Alyina's favourites.

Thankfully, unlike so many others, Jaxon did not neglect his Aura. His soul was more than a match for Arimus Shore. His soul hurled the attack back and lashed out with one of his own, a *Spirit Attack*. Unlike *Ardent Onslaught*, it targeted the mind instead of the body, and would have left the governor quaking in his boots, if he had not desperately guarded with his own Aura.

Jaxon used the opportunity to hurl the man back from him, breaking the connection.

"Poor technique," he taunted as they returned to circling. "Did a priest teach you how to use your Aura? That *almost* tickled."

They came together again, blades thundering with all the power of their *Enforced Bodies*. Arimus's blows had become measured now, slashing at Jaxon's heart and groin and throat with terrifying speed, but without the earlier recklessness of a man seeking to end the fight quickly. His eyes burned with a silent fury and his Aura was a wall scarlet, his mind and body intent on cutting his foe to pieces.

Teeth gritted, Jaxon struggled to withstand the assault. It forced him backwards, almost into the waters of the canal ringing the plaza. He staggered onto one of the arched bridges instead. There they danced back and forth, the ring of iron echoing from the stone walls, while the citizens of Skarta whimpered behind their shuttered windows. But Jaxon could not spare them his thoughts now. Every piece of him was consumed with survival.

Arimus sought to pin him against the railings, but Jaxon twisted and lashed out with his boot, sending his foe stumbling. Now it was the Gurrian's turn to defend himself as Jaxon bore down with the greater reach of his broadsword. The younger man's weapon was like a viper, twisting away from any blow that came close. Finally, Jaxon stepped back.

"For the love of Ryntirax," Jaxon panted. "Keep your shoulders straight. I can see your attacks coming a mile away."

Laughter rumbled from his opponent's chest. "Do not seek to rile me, old man. Admit it: you're desperate."

"If I wanted to rile you, I would have called Alyina back," Jaxon said with a grin. "I'm telling you, kid, she's bad news."

"Maybe you're just not man enough for her," Arimus spat. "You know what she thinks of you? That you're decrepit, old, past your prime." He smirked. "That you've lost your nerve."

Jaxon shrugged. "Just trying to help out a fellow—"

Arimus attacked before he could finish, *Surging* forward. This time Jaxon was forced to use his own ability to counter. Pure speed filled him, and he ducked, just avoiding a swing that would have decapitated him. A dagger appeared in Arimus's other hand, drawn from his tunic. Caught out of position, Jaxon released his greatsword with one hand and caught the other man by the wrist, stopping the dagger half an inch from his chest. The point trembled as they struggled against each other.

"Are you scared of death, Daniyal?" Arimus hissed in his ear. The dagger crept forward. "Will you beg when it finally comes for you?"

Feeling the point touch his flesh, Jaxon activated *Might*. Strength rushed to his limbs. His fingers hardened around the wrist of his foe as he pushed Arimus away, sending the other Pathfinder dancing backwards across the cobbles.

Panting, Jaxon did not follow. "Death's an old friend," he said instead, gripping his sword with both hands again.

Arimus laughed. "Getting tired, Daniyal?" His face hardened. "I'm going to cut you to pieces."

"Come and try it."

It was false bravado and they both knew it. Arimus was an incredible warrior, skilled and powerful, and Jaxon was struggling to keep up. There was no avoiding it. Arimus was simply the superior fighter. But Jaxon knew better than most it was not always the better man who won.

"Come on, then," he said, rolling his head on his shoulders. "If you're done warming up, why don't you show me what the mighty Arimus Shore is *really* capable of."

A growl rumbled from Arimus's throat. "Very well."

For the next few minutes, it was all Jaxon could do to keep

himself alive. True to his word, Arimus did not hold back. Or at least, Jaxon prayed he wasn't; otherwise Jaxon really was in trouble. Twice more, he had to consume his body's strength to use one of his abilities. But Arimus was burning through energy as well, with lavish use of *Might* and *Movement Surge*. He didn't seem concerned about over-use. To be fair, he certainly didn't seem to be slowing down as the battle progressed.

Jaxon could not say the same. His clothes clung to his sweat-soaked skin and his enemy's blade had found his flesh several times already. The worst was a cut on his brow that dripped blood, half-blinding him as he struggled on. Jaxon had to admit, he had never faced a foe like Arimus. The man was a prodigy.

But he had to have a weakness.

"You're a lot like one of my apprentices, you know," Jaxon said as he narrowly avoided another blow and retreated a step. His heart was pounding. He could feel the acid creeping into his limbs. He needed rest, though he hoped Arimus would not see it. "Isabel. You met her earlier."

Somewhat to his surprise, Arimus stopped dead at the mention of Isabel's name. "What?"

Jaxon frowned at the man's reaction. "You know her, don't you?"

"She's my sister."

Well, well, well. Jaxon tried to keep the surprise from his face. "I guess that explains the similarities."

"What similarities?"

"You're both as stubborn as mules." Jaxon grunted.

Arimus lowered his sword, looking uncertain for the first time since the battle began. His eyes darted in the direction Alyina had taken, then snapped back to Jaxon.

"She mentioned you." He grimaced. "She saved my life. Never did get a straight answer why. Maybe you could explain it."

Jaxon raised his eyebrows. "I'm afraid I can't answer that, lad," he replied. "But when Isabel decides to do something, she sees it through to the end." He chuckled. "Stubborn, like I said."

There was a long silence as Arimus seemed to study him. Finally the man grunted. "I do not understand you, Daniyal. But perhaps you could sate my curiosity." He pursed his lips, and there was genuine confusion in his eyes. "Why betray the empire, after all Alyina and her father did for you?"

Jaxon sighed. "That's the thing, kid," he said, unable to keep the sadness from his voice. "I never did."

The frown creasing Arimus's brow deepened, but he said nothing, and Jaxon went on.

"Everything that has happened, it is because Alyina *wanted* it to happen. You heard her. She was funding your little resistance all along. Because the empire *needs* an enemy to fear—or it would crumble." He sighed, rolling his shoulders, readying himself for the battle to resume. "That's what Alyina does: use people. At least until their usefulness is spent. Then she tosses them aside." He eyed the young man. "She will do the same to you, eventually. But I don't expect you to believe me."

"I don't. I am loyal to my nation and my emperor."

Jaxon grimaced. "I respect that, kid," he replied. "Tell me though, what will you do when they ask for the life of your sister?"

"I barely know her," Arimus snapped, though Jaxon saw the doubt in his eyes. "Why would I care if she lives or dies?"

"Yes, why *would* you save the life of someone you barely know?"

"It doesn't matter. Isabel is inconsequential. Alyina is after the Offworlder."

"Alyina is a cruel and spiteful soul," Jaxon shot back. "She will ask for Isabel's death because she knows how much it would hurt *me*." He met the other man's gaze. "And she will ask you to do it for no other reason than because it will torment you. She cares nothing for you. Just as she cares nothing for any of her lovers. She never will. I do not believe she is capable of it."

He saw the anger flare in Arimus's eyes. But there was something deeper to it this time. This was not a rage born of insult, but understanding. He knew Jaxon spoke the truth. It seemed in that moment time stood still, the twin warriors sharing a moment of respect.

Finally, Arimus straightened and nodded to Jaxon. "Are you ready to continue?"

A grin formed on Jaxon's lips. "Whenever you are, kid."

42

Isabel was in agony. She did not show it, of course, not to Mikael or bloody Kat. But every few seconds, a wave of fiery pain would radiate through her body, like someone was taking a knife to her flesh and slowly peeling back the skin, piece by piece.

Funny, how strong she had thought herself before. She had exchanged plenty of blows with Jaxon Daniyal, and the man could *hit*. But either Jaxon had been holding back—even when he said he was not—or Alyina Sorulus was in an entirely different class from the Gold ranked Highlander.

It was probably a bit of both.

One blow. That was all it had taken. One punch—imbued with a fair bit of Alyina's Aura—and Isabel was still feeling it *hours* later. The damage to her body had been bad enough, the fractured bones in her chest and shoulder attested to that, but the *Spirit Attack* the princess had combined with it had crippled Isabel's soul, so she could not even heal herself.

Or anyone else.

The dagger in her heart twisted as she reached for her

Aura again, trying to force the shredded pieces back together. She *needed* it to work. Needed her *Healing Touch*, or…

Jaxon…

Mikael had filled her in briefly on what he had done. She scrunched her eyes closed, breath coming in ragged gasps. Kat and Mikael had already disappeared, readying themselves for Alyina's arrival.

Isabel's heart began to thunder. She was coming. That was what Marta had said, before she slipped out the back door with the kids. A very large piece of Isabel screamed that they should have gone with them. Fled into the twisting alleys and canals of Skarta. Surely there was somewhere they could hide, even from the likes of Alyina Sorulus.

It was a lie she wanted to tell herself, Isabel knew. Whatever hopes Skarta had for resistance had crumbled into dust with the reveal of Alyina's army. She and Mikael had only one choice.

Stand.

Stand, just like Jaxon had.

A tear streaked her cheek as she thought of him in the square, alone against the forces of the empire. It was how he would have wanted it, she knew. Wielding his sword and skill and magic in defence of those who could not defend themselves. To protect Mikael. To protect *her*.

Isabel just wished she could see him one last time, to tell him how much she loved him. She had been searching all this time for her father, but she had been looking in the wrong place. Only one man would have sacrificed the world for her.

Jaxon Daniyal.

The dagger twisted again. *Pain*. She drew in a breath. *Focus on the pain*. It radiated from the broken bones in her chest and arm where she had struck the pavement. It twisted like molten iron through her Aura. She clung to it, to the ache of it—anything but think of what might have been.

It hurt, but she was alive.

She was awake.

And she could still fight.

The *crack* as the front door of the manor flew backwards off its hinges was shockingly loud in the silence before. Isabel ducked as it hurtled past and smashed against the wall behind her. Planks of wood cracked and tore loose from their nails as the interior wall collapsed in on itself, revealing the dining room beyond the entrance chamber.

A ripple of fear began in Isabel's core as Alyina Sorulus stepped through the ruins of the front door, emerald eyes aglow with power.

"Isabel!" the princess exclaimed in an overly bright voice. "So *this* is where you've been hiding!" She wrinkled her nose. "Arg, it stinks like soiled diapers."

Isabel did not respond to the princess's taunts. Instead, she reached into the world. The manor was surprisingly rich in Mana, as though the energies of the universe had sunk deep into its ancient timbers, into the foundations even. It came to Isabel readily, leaping as though it had lain in wait for someone to call it.

Flames burst to life in her hand.

And Alyina laughed. "Oh, my dear girl, you don't want to fight me," she murmured, taking her first step across the threshold into the manor. Despite her fragile appearance, the floorboards creaked beneath the princess's weight. "So why don't you just tell me where the Offworlder is hiding, and I'll end that pain in your poor soul. Sound like a deal?"

A growl hissed from Isabel's lips. The flames burned hotter.

"It's strange," Alyina continued. "I couldn't sense him for a while—and then he was just *here*." She tapped a painted fingernail to her lips. "I wonder, does he have an ability I do not know about? Strange creatures, these Offworlders." Her eyes lit up. "Did you know he has a secret to destroy *worlds?* Can you imagine? The power to wipe your enemies from the map with the wave of your hand. It's like the Pathfinders of old. By my father, that's the sort of power to make a girl swoon!"

"He'd rather die than tell you anything."

"Of course, of course." The princess wore a twisted smile. "But could he watch as we burned his precious Highlands to the ground? As we rounded up your people and put them to the sword?" She took another step, and while Isabel was the taller, it seemed the princess loomed high, high above her. "Could he hold his tongue when we put *you* to the torturer's rack, my dear Isabel? He seemed awfully quick to pull you from danger, back in the plaza."

That was it. Mikael and Kat better be ready. She was done waiting.

Screaming, Isabel hurled out her hands, unleashing a stream of concentrated flame straight at Alyina's face. She might be the most powerful being in this province, but the princess was still mortal. Surely not even she could withstand the fury of such an assault.

Laughter once more filled the air, as Alyina Sorulus did just that.

"I'll admit, you've got style, girl," her voice came from the flames, eerily untouched by the heat and the smoke.

Isabel shuddered. She might not be able to use *Aura Sense* like the others, but she could still feel the inevitability about the princess. Alyina was like a force of nature, poised to fall upon this house and everyone inside.

Flames licked at the walls and floor of the entrance chamber, crackling greedily as they found ready fuel in the ornate tapestries and wooden fixtures of the ancient manor. With a *whoosh*, the fire spread. Isabel retreated backwards through the now-gaping hole into the dining hall.

Alyina followed. A slight glow shone around the princess as her shadow emerged through the fire. A gasp caught in Isabel's throat. That light, it was…*Invulnerable.* Very, *very* few Pathfinders ever adapted that ability. With it, Alyina could channel the considerable power of her body into a few moments, during which she became untouchable.

And just like that, neither Isabel's attack nor the regular fire singed a single hair on her head. The glow faded as she stepped after Isabel into the next room.

Just in time for Isabel's blade to arc for her slender neck. To her surprise, the princess did not try to evade the blow. She had not even drawn the longsword on her hip. All she did was raise her index finger to meet the oncoming blade.

And her sword stopped dead.

Isabel gasped as the blade juddered in her hands like she'd just slammed it against a stone wall. She stared at the woman in disbelief. That was…that was impossible. She was not glowing any longer. Alyina had stopped a sword with nothing more than the resistance of her *Enforced Body.* Just what-the-hell kind of Pathfinder was she?

"I'll admit, Jaxon trained you well," Alyina said quietly. "I never knew he had a paternal side." She grinned. "He was certainly never paternal with me. A force of nature, more like. Shame he had to go and get soft." She shrugged. "At least he brought me the Offworlder."

When the attack came, Isabel had no warning. One second the princess was standing there, chatting like they were sharing drinks over a festival bonfire—the next, her pale fingers were closing around Isabel's throat.

Isabel opened her mouth to scream, but the sound was choked off as a lance of terrible black Aura pressed against her soul. A warning. Alyina wore the familiar smirk on her lips as her narrowed eyes scanned the room.

"Where are you, Mikael?" she taunted. ""Come out, come out, wherever you are!" Her grip tightened around Isabel's throat. "Quickly, or I might have to do some bad things to your little girlfriend."

"Let her go, Alyina. I'm the one you want."

Isabel's heart pulsed as Mikael appeared in a nearby doorway. His face was hard, and lightning crackled in his left hand. In the other he held his shortsword. It would protect him from Alyina's Aura attacks, Isabel knew, but that would not be enough. Not even close.

"I tell you what," Alyina replied, her voice rich with amusement. "Give yourself up, and I'll let you bring her along with us to Gurria. I'll even let you share a cell in my father's dungeon."

Mikael snorted. "What happened to our deal? I thought if I surrendered, I would be your honoured guest."

"Oh, we're well past that now, Mikael."

"Agreed. So here's my counter-offer. Touch a hair on her head, and I'll kill everyone you have ever loved."

Alyina laughed. "Is that so?"

Again, there was no warning. Isabel screamed as the princess grabbed a fistful of her hair. This time she tried to fight back, lashing out with a blast of fire and grasping at the woman's arm in a desperate struggle. But the lance of Aura slashed through her already pitiful soul, and her resistance crumbled. Red-hot agony burst across her skull as Alyina tore a chunk of hair loose.

"Oh dear," she mocked, tossing the locks at Mikael's feet. "My bad. I guess you'll just have to kill me after all, Mikael."

Mikael did not react immediately. But his golden eyes burned with such a fury, it seemed that the entire world must be shaking. Finally though, he exhaled.

"I warned you."

The whisper of a boot was the only thing that gave Kat away. One moment, Isabel could have *sworn* they were alone with Mikael in the dining hall. The next moment, there was

Kat, her dark blade slashing for Alyina's throat. There was only a heartbeat to react. Not even Isabel's *Movement Surge* would have been enough, she was sure. She simply would not have been able to activate the ability in time.

But Alyina Sorulus was an entirely different kind of Pathfinder.

The princess became a blur, spinning, her hand snapping out to catch Kat by the wrist. For a second the dark blade hung suspended, poised just an inch from Alyina's throat. When Isabel had seen it strike Arimus, she had sensed the *wrongness* about this weapon. It was a distortion of their world, and Gold rank or no, her brother had been helpless against the hunger of the void it contained.

Alyina must have sensed it too, for her face lost all trace of humour. When she saw who it was though, and realised she faced only an Iron ranker, the smile returned.

"So you're the little assassin, are you?" she asked. "How nice to finally meet you."

A snarl hissed from Kat's throat, but the little urchin had no abilities that would give her the strength to break free. And once the princess had a hold of you...

...the whites of Kat's eyes grew huge as she stiffened, her entire body arching with the terrible pain only Alyina Sorulus could inflict.

But in that moment, Isabel saw her opening. Distracted by Kat, Alyina had left her unguarded. Even the spear of Aura that had been poised against Isabel's soul had vanished. Silently, she gathered herself where she had fallen to the twisted floorboards. Her Mana channels were strained, but her body was fresh. Energy gathered within. There was little she could do to harm this woman. But Isabel did not need to deal the fatal blow.

She activated *Movement Surge*.

In a burst of speed, Isabel *exploded* from the floor. The

princess had no chance to react this time, distracted as she was with torturing the street urchin. Isabel struck like the bolt from a crossbow, her fist slamming into Alyina's face. Caught off-guard, the princess rocked backwards from the blow.

Her grip on Kat's wrist slipped.

The void sword slashed down.

Alyina recovered with inhuman speed. She twisted as the blade flashed for her. It was almost enough.

But the razor tip still found its mark, slicing across Alyina's cheek. Just a scratch.

And yet Isabel *felt* the moment the sword found its mark. Something in the world flickered. Mana shivered and fled, collapsing in around the princess—only to be *consumed* by the power of the blade. Blood spouted from the wound—far too much for just a scratch—only to vanish into the black steel. And something about Alyina, something intangible Isabel could not see, but rather sensed, shivered and began to wither.

The princess screamed.

A second later, so did Kat.

Mouth open wide, eyes burning, the urchin cried out as though she were being eaten from the inside. The blade could only have stolen a fraction of the princess's power, and yet it seemed to be tearing Kat apart, ripping up her feeble Iron soul and shredding it to pieces.

Isabel herself was still reeling from the aftermath of using so much of her body's energy in a single attack. Fatigue swamped her suddenly burning muscles. She tried to take a step towards the suffering princess, but found her body would not respond.

Panic touched her. Alyina would not be destroyed by a scratch. Already the princess seemed to have recovered some of her wits, as she retreated several staggering steps, placing distance between herself and the dark blade.

And then Mikael appeared between Kat and Isabel.

"Isabel…" His earlier rage had vanished, replaced by a softness in his eyes as he looked at her. He didn't seem to be able to get out any other words.

Nor could she. Instead, she nodded, feeling the tears in her eyes. There had been no time for them to talk about things between them after she'd woken, not with Alyina Sorulus bearing down on them.

And there was no time to say what needed to be said now. No matter how much she wanted to throw her arms around him, to feel safe in his warm embrace, to hold him like there was no tomorrow that Gurria could destroy, nor yesterday when his lies had hurt her, that they could just be together in that moment, and every moment after that.

But instead, all she had was that look of recognition, the slight smile on his lips, and then he was stepping past and placing one hand on Kat's shoulder.

The effect was instant as the girl sagged in sudden relief, her knees giving out beneath her.

A brilliant light began to shine from Mikael's sword.

And the world trembled.

43

Two weeks before the Festival of the Satana

"I do!" Moira cried.

"Wait—" Fiachson tried again.

Too late.

With Moira's words, the chief's face changed. The hardness fell away, shifting to a look of pure joy. Grabbing Fiachson in both arms, he dragged him into a hug, lifting Fiachson clear off the ground.

"Then welcome, son of Hanequin, to the house of Lachlan!"

He began to spin, and all Fiachson could do was hold on for dear life as the massive chieftain swirled him around the room—while the Izolu cheered in the background.

Only when Fiachson's head was well and truly twirling did Lachlan place him back on his feet.

"By the powers invested in my soul by the mighty Ryntirax, I declare your challenge accepted, Fiachson, son of Hanequin. From this day forth, may you and Moira, daughter of Lachlan, be one soul, one house, united in marriage until death.

And it was done.

Fiachson's mouth was hanging open and he knew it. He could not bring himself to close it though. Nearby, Moira was jumping up and down, hands clutched before her wearing a look of utter joy. The crowd was still screaming their approval —which was already attracting attention from outside, as a few moments later, his mother appeared in the doorway.

Maisiwan's scarlet eyes swept the room, taking in the celebrating Izolu and alighting on Fiachson just in time to see Moira hurl her arms around him. She was much smaller than her father, but she still struck like a boulder that had just tumbled down several mountains.

"Fiachson," despite the raucous, Maisiwan somehow made herself heard. "What exactly is going on here?"

"Ah…"

His mother's lips twitched. "I believe it is customary to invite *your mother* to her own son's wedding."

"I'm…it is not…I didn't mean."

Maisiwan snorted, though when Lachlan saw her, he began to bellow his joy all over again. "Maisiwan, you missed it!" he exclaimed. "Come, come, at least join the festivities! Jordana, break open the high mead. Tonight we celebrate a new union between our clan and the lowlanders!"

"I…ah…" Fiachson was still struggling for words as his mother came alongside them and had a mug of strong-smelling liquor pressed into her hands. "I'm sorry?"

Her eyes dancing, Maisiwan raised her cup. "Well in that case, cheers to the groom!"

Fiachson did his best to stifle a groan as another mug was pushed on him.

At least he had secured the alliance Mikael wanted?

44

Two weeks before the Festival of the Satana

The first crow of the morning's rooster found Lunden Marcs already awake, though he had yet to rise from his stretcher. His heart was too heavy to stir himself. A week had passed since his meeting with the highking. Today would be the final disbanding of the Malesie army.

The mood in camp was almost as heavy as Lunden's own heart. Because he knew he had failed not just Mikael Heaton, but his new home. Now he would have to watch as yet another people inevitably fell to the greed of the Gurrian Empire.

The soldiers and their unit commanders had taken the news about as well as could be expected. Like a punch in the gut. They were angry, all of them. They wanted to remain in Furness, in case the Gurrians proved less than trustworthy. Lunden agreed, but…well the Highking had spoken, and Lunden was not Malesie.

A groan rasped from his lips as finally he pushed back the covers and rose. The noise of the camp being disbanded had already begun outside. It should be quick—he had been training them to work in different units to improve efficiency. Lunden had no desire to watch all their hard work go to waste, but he had gear of his own to pack. If a pact was struck between the Malesie and the empire, it was only a matter of time before Gurria's edict against Ressian veterans extended into this land. Which meant the hangman would be coming for him if he remained.

Not that he had any intention of lying down and letting the enemy take him. He would travel south to Skarta and seek out Mikael and Jaxon. The more he thought on Denether's words, the more he feared the pair were walking into a trap. If he found them, maybe they could return to the Highlands together and seek...

Lunden frowned as voices carried through the canvas walls of his tent. He thought he recognised Maria amidst the low whispers. Was she going to try to change his mind again? It had hurt to see the disappointment in her eyes when she'd learnt there would be no revenge for her murdered husband. Nor for Scott's brother.

He sighed, pulling on a pair of leggings and a fresh shirt before clipping on his sword. He would have to find a replacement, something with better length. Without the soldiers he'd been training around him, the shortswords were less than ideal.

His heart shrivelled, thinking of the progress they had made over the past few months. What miracles might the Malesie army have produced if given their chance to fight? Could they have crushed the Gurrian Legions and freed the continent from the emperor's iron grasp? Might they have marched all the way to the gates of Gurria?

They would never know.

The voices were rising in pitch outside now. Grimacing, Lunden yanked open the canvas flaps and strode outside, prepared to send a few of his commanders scampering back to their units.

But it wasn't just Maria outside.

It was all of them, as best as he could tell.

"What in the Seven Hells…" he muttered. "What are you doing here? You're meant to be clearing camp with your units."

The commanders looked around at his appearance, their faces grim. Maria and Scott took the lead.

"Sir," Scott said immediately. "We wanted to know what you would do?"

"What *I* would do?" Lunden frowned. "I already told you what you *have to do*. The army is done. Go back to your lands and tend to your crops."

"That is not what he means, sir," Maria said quietly. "He means, if you were our General, what would you do?"

Lunden blinked. "I can't—"

"Please, sir," Scott interrupted. "No bull. We are all in agreement. This entire agreement stinks like a Fushore swamp."

"It doesn't matter what it smells like," Lunden dismissed his words with a sigh. "Your king has spoken."

Maria snorted. "Denether can pretend to be a real king all he wants, but that is not how things work in the Highlands. He cannot just order us home—so *we are not going*." She leaned forward, until they stood eye to eye. "Now, are you going to tell us what you think we should do, or are we going to have to make it up as we go along?"

Lunden stared at the young woman, before turning his gaze to the other men and women who had gathered there. They stared back at him, eyes resolute. They would not be dissuaded. Whatever the man sitting on the throne said, these people weren't going to hand over their land without a fight.

Suddenly his heart was racing. "I would move quickly," he said at last. "Break camp and scatter, so Denether doesn't catch on. Regather…in Sarton."

"And then?" Maria pressed.

Lunden pursed his lips. "Mikael had a plan," he said softly. "A contingency plan, in case things went awry in Skarta. We were to march south and launch an attack on the city before the Gurrians could reinforce the province. With luck, the Fushore and Izolu would also join us."

There was a moment's silence as Maria and the others processed his words. One man nodded, then another, until it seemed all were in agreement. Maria turned back to Lunden with a grin.

"Very well," she said formally, "then we will follow your command, General Marcs."

45

In the minutes before Alyina arrived at the manor, Mikael's mind had been consumed. And not with what the others might have assumed. Not this time. He did not think of what he could have done differently, or whether Jaxon lived, or what he was going to say to Isabel if they survived all this.

No, in those brief minutes left to him, his mind was on an old biology lecture about observational studies, and something called the Hawthrone effect. Or observer bias. Or even the Heisenberg Uncertainty Principle in certain fields

The principle was simple: the observers of any study must necessarily create some form of reactivity on their subjects.

He wondered if Azaroth and Leviathan had paid attention to their science classes in Satanic high school—if that was really a thing.

Because what he was about to do was either exactly what one of the two demons wanted, or he was about to take a wild swerve off-road of their plans.

Considering the first few seconds after Alyina stepped into

the house, well, everything had very nearly gone wrong already. Isabel had been intended as a distraction, so that Kat could get close enough with her *Mute* ability to score a blow with the void sword. No one was exactly sure how much damage it would do against Alyina, but the consensus was it would be considerable.

They'd been partly correct. And maybe with a deeper blow, it would have killed her. But while Kat's scratch had certainly caused Alyina some discomfort, she was already recovering. Only now, she was also *pissed*.

So it was time for the next phase of the plan. The part he was *least* sure about. They hadn't exactly been able to test it earlier. But here went nothing. Laying his hand on the girl's shoulder, Mikael reached out with his *Aura Sense*—

And was overwhelmed by a *tidal wave* of energy that swept from the girl into him. So much, he had no idea how the girl had held it all inside her. Surely it should have torn her apart from the inside? And that sword…Mikael shuddered as he sensed the dark edge to the energy he received. Whatever Azaroth had done to his construct, its nature had been irrevocably changed.

It made Mikael fear what he was going to do next.

No going back now…

The energy flowed into him, and *through* him.

And the short sword in his hand became no longer just an empty piece of iron, but a construct of creation. Fed by the stolen energies of the void blade, it burned with a terrible glow. And just as Kat had described the void within her sword, so too did Mikael feel something new from his own weapon.

Through the connection in his soul, he sensed something waking, some remnant intelligence from his construct. Azaroth's magic had changed it, twisted and divided it, but now the energy had returned so too did the mind he had created to channel that energy.

Mikael felt the world shifting on its axis.

His body trembled, vibrating with the sheer power it had channelled. His soul and Mana channels felt stretched and broken, scorched. He knew then he would only get one chance to do what was needed. And if he failed…

"Kat…" he rasped. It seemed to take all of his effort just to speak. "Kat…remember…plan B."

On her knees, the girl stirred with a groan. Isabel stood nearby, frozen in fear or awe. Mikael couldn't tell. But he needed her.

"Isabel," he managed, "take Kat…and get out of here."

She hesitated at his words. Alyina had fled into another room the second she saw the glow from Mikael's sword, but he was tracking her with his *Aura Sense.* She was already stabilising. And Isabel had already used everything she had; she could offer nothing more in this fight. He needed them out of here, in case…

"But—"

"Go." He turned his back on the pair. "I'll…take care of her."

He strode through the doorway after Alyina. The room beyond was dark, the fire out front yet to reach it, but his sword glowed now with an otherworldly light. Mikael could feel its potential, though he wasn't sure he would be able to use it. Alyina was powerful and she'd had a lifetime to adapt to her power.

He had to find a way to best her.

The next room, however, was empty.

Which was ominous, because suddenly he could feel Alyina's Aura *everywhere.* It covered the entire chamber, a crushing, terrible force. He knew immediately what she was doing. This wasn't like *Mute,* which could make even regular senses overlook her presence. But she *was* blinding his *Aura Sense,* so he had no way of locating her.

"Are we playing hide and seek again?" he taunted the empty room, raising his burning sword. "I guess I'm *It* now."

"You think I'm afraid of you?" Alyina laughed, emerging from the shadows. "You're like a child playing with matches. Why don't you put down your little sword before you hurt yourself."

Despite the bold words, Alyina maintained her distance. She had certainly seen better days. The cut across her face had left a terrible mark, slicing from her nose to her jaw. Incredible, that the slightest nick had done so much damage to her *Enforced Body*. He doubted a regular blade would have even pierced her skin, judging from what he'd seen earlier with Isabel.

"I can see you straining, Mikael," she continued with a derisive snort. "Steel rank. How long do you think you can hold out, before it overwhelms you?"

Mikael gritted his teeth, a worm of doubt gnawing into his soul. Alyina was right. It wasn't that the power burned like it had for Kat. It was infused in the sword, rather than his own soul. But just holding it, sensing that presence working on his mind, he was beginning to get a taste of just what this thing was capable of.

He was beginning to see…possibilities.

It wasn't a weapon—at least not in the traditional sense. It was a tool. And given enough power, he wasn't sure there were limits to its potential. Wielded in unison with the void blade, it could rewrite the fabric of reality, twist it and pull it how he wished. If Mikael wanted to move himself to the Highlands, he could do so now in the blink of an eye—though instinctively he knew it would consume far more power than he had at his command.

"Well, Mikael?" Alyina whispered, taking a step closer. Her eyes shone in the light of the sword. "What will it be?"

Mikael hardly heard her. Now that he had considered one possibility, others presented themselves. *Infinite others*. He could attack her soul with the energy of the blade. It did not suffer the same limitations as a Pathfinder. Or he could drain the oxygen from the air. Maybe even turn the power of her body against itself. The potentials stretched out, one feeding off another, each more complex, more difficult.

More overwhelming.

He sucked in a groan. Holding the blade, he could see the world branching before him into an infinite number of paths, each screaming their merit. A tiny part of his mind, partitioned away from the power, wondered if this was where the title 'Pathfinder' came from. If it was, Mikael was pretty sure he'd skipped some steps along the way.

His mind creaked beneath the weight of what he saw. If only Jaxon were here. Jaxon would be strong enough to make this choice.

But Jaxon was lost.

Mikael was the only one left.

"I told you you'd pay if you touched Isabel," he said, fingers tightening around the hilt of the blade.

"Your toys don't scare me, Offworlder." She spread her hands. "True warriors do not need to borrow strength. Here, let me show you a glimpse of real power."

Her figure flickered, then began to shift. A shadow darted from her, then another and another, until the room was filled with shadows. Each changing, shifting until they coalesced into a copy of Alyina. Each wore the same hideous smile.

Mikael swallowed. He knew this ability, even if he hadn't seen it in action. *Illusive Image*. With Alyina's Aura permeating the entire room, not even his *Aura Sense* could penetrate the illusion.

"Tell you what, Mikael." Her voice boomed. "Take your shot. Just remember, when you miss, I'm going to break every bone in your body. And then…" The shadows all advanced a step, closing the circle around him. "…I'll hunt down your friends and make you watch as I kill them, one by one. How does that sound to you?"

Mikael looked around at the victorious faces of the princess. A leaden terror formed in his heart. He *might* be able to break the illusion with the sword and then kill her. But the more he held the blade's power, the more he grew to understand it. And in his heart, Mikael knew he would fail. The paths were incomplete, the tiny spark of stolen power not enough. Maybe he could cripple Alyina, but he would not stop her.

Even so, it was tempting. To try. To make the bold move and risk everything on one roll of the dice, and hope it was enough. Another Mikael Heaton, at another point in time, might have taken that gamble.

But it was not just *his* life he was putting on the line. If he failed, Alyina would not stop with him. The vindictive witch would hunt Kat and Isabel to the ends of this world and make them suffer a thousand times over for denying her the knowledge of his world.

You need to find your place in this world, Jaxon's voice whispered.

Mikael clenched his fists. He could choose to be the Destroyer everyone thought he was. He could unleash the unknown power of this sword upon this house and to hell with the consequences. So long as he lived, and his enemies burned.

But Mikael was not the Destroyer they thought he was.

He wanted to be more.

"I swear to guard the weak against those who would do them harm, and fight evil wherever I find it," he whispered.

A frown touched the faces of Alyina Sorulus. "What was that?"

"To never use my powers for personal gain," he continued, ignoring the woman, "nor allow temptation to lead me down the path of evil."

Her face hardened. "Enough," she snarled. "Take your shot."

"No," he whispered.

So many paths, but in the end, Mikael Heaton chose the path that was his own. Plan B. It might not be his first choice. But at least it was his. Even if it meant putting his life in the hands of others.

He lowered the blade. "You win."

The words hung over his head like a guillotine. He wasn't sure which of the demons on his shoulder this benefitted. Neither, he hoped. As far as Mikael was concerned, the pair could burn in the fires of the Seventh Hell. Azaroth no doubt wanted him to take the void blade from Kat. Maybe that would have been enough. He could have fought Alyina and drained enough of her power to destroy her. His soul would have forever been stained by Kat's blood, but what did that matter to an interdimensional hell-beast?

As for Leviathan, the beast probably thought he didn't have the stomach for murder. It was right…*just*. Had it expected them to try and use the swords together, though? Mikael supposed it really didn't matter now.

"You're giving up," Alyina asked after a moment of stunned silence. Her shadow copies each reflected her confusion. "Just like that?"

Nodding, Mikael allowed his sword to fall. As soon as it left his hand, the light flickered, then blinked out like someone had flicked a switch. He sensed a brief burst of energy, and for a moment the room seemed brighter, richer.

Then he felt it. A familiar stirring. A rippling within, followed by the bubbling of energy, a surge as *something* changed.

His soul.

Alyina surely sensed it as well, but she did not move. A Bronze ranker could no more threaten her than a Steel—and they both knew it. So her shadows stood and let it happen, each still wearing that look of bewilderment on their lips.

Mikael shuddered as the new light engulfed his soul. How strange this world was, that such an astonishing change could come from such an easy decision. He had accepted his place in this world, that he did not have to do it all alone. He could rely on others as well as himself. A simple acknowledgement, and yet a colossal one all the same.

He felt the moment the change settled, the new weight burning in his Aura. He didn't need the voice that accompanied it.

Transformation Complete. User Advanced to Bronze rank. Ability acquired: Shield.

User: Mikael Heaton. Rank: Steel. Body: 21. Aura: 25. Mana: 18. Abilities: Enforced Body, Aura Sense, Elemental Manipulation, Shield.

Was it Mikael's imagination, or was there a slight inflection to the voice now? Like it was something…more. Exhaling, he opened his eyes, feeling refreshed. The new power had restored his body and soul. He would be able to fight again, use his abilities and Aura. Even a new ability.

His heart sank. Nothing had changed. It hurt to admit it, but that was the truth. Steel or Bronze, Alyina remained far above any limits they could hope to bridge. The swords had been their only hope—and that had failed before it had even begun.

He looked at Alyina with a sad smile. "Yes," he said simply. "I am. Just like that."

Silently, he prayed to whatever gods were watching this world that Kat had lit the goddamn fuse already.

46

The end was approaching. Arimus could sense it. Daniyal had fought him every inch of the way. Truthfully, he almost lived up to the legends.

Almost.

But even Jaxon Daniyal could not resist the inevitable creep of time. Pathfinder or not, age had slowed his reflexes. Perhaps only by inches, but those inches were everything in an exchange of this calibre.

And so they had fought, and the older man had battled well, but now it was done.

Arimus was surprised the knowledge brought him sadness. Somewhere in the battle, he had grown to respect the man. How could he not respect a foe of such unyielding will? It didn't matter if he faced Arimus or the empire itself, Jaxon Daniyal would stand to the very end for the path he believed in.

Could Arimus say he would do the same? What did he *really* stand for?

He had believed in something once, hadn't he? His father had raised him on tales of Gurrian nobility, of brave soldiers defending their land from the barbarians on their borders. And then of a golden civilisation, rising from the ashes of war to spread its benefits across the world. Of a peace bound by one rule, one emperor. That was why the Ressian armies had to be crushed and their mad king destroyed, wasn't it? To restore peace.

Yet what had Arimus sought from the moment that war had been won? Another battle, another conflict, to stem the endless boredom of *peace*. He had sought enemies wherever he could find them, whether it be Skarta or the Highlands.

And all the while, the promised prosperity of their civilisation never arrived. Not for the likes of Skarta, at least.

Now this man stood before Arimus and said his rulers *did not care*. That Alyina only cared about entertaining herself with her games, and Arimus felt the rage within. Not because the Darkstrider was wrong, but because he was *right*. Arimus had been hunting the hidden forces behind the resistance, the one uniting them, manipulating events behind the scenes, directing them towards some unknown objective.

But it had all been Alyina. She had paid for the resistance, swelled their ranks and funded their attacks, expanding the misery across Skarta until it had finally come to a head.

At which point she had swiftly cut the head off the snake she herself had created.

In his heart, Arimus knew it was wrong.

But what could a soldier do but follow orders?

Jaxon grunted as Arimus's sword flashed for his chest. Arimus thought it might be over then, but at the last moment the old Gold ranker straightened, his blade coming up to catch the blow on his pommel.

And the fight continued.

But *why* did Arimus fight? He'd been waiting a lifetime for this chance, to cross swords with another Gold ranker and finally prove his worth. Yet here he was, locked blade to blade with the legendary Darkstrider, and all he felt was sadness—and doubt.

Doubt that this man could actually be *right.*

Jaxon no longer offered his taunting snippets of advice. He had no breath left to speak, only fight. So Arimus pressed the advantage, forcing him back, seeking to trap his foe against a building. Within, he sensed the Aura of fear pervading the place, the unseen eyes watching them, wondering if the pair of giants outside would come for them next. And he felt guilt.

For now, though, the citizens were safe, as Jaxon parried a blow and hurled a fist, catching Arimus in the cheek. The blow carried the taint of a *Spirit Atack,* and his soul recoiled. Fortunately, even Jaxon's famed Aura was burning low by now, and Arimus was able to fend off the secondary assault with relative ease this time. Though the blow still stung.

Carefully he wiped a trickle of blood from his lip. "You hit hard, old man."

Daniyal grunted and gestured him forward.

And so their dance continued. Arimus's blade found flesh twice more as his foe struggled on. His own body slowed as he began to suffer the aftereffects of his Pathfinder abilities and the prolonged battle.

While they fought, Arimus tried to extend his senses to the north, where he had last sensed Alyina, but Aura was not his strongest attribute and he sensed only emptiness. They were beyond his range.

His stomach twisted at the thought of his sister. Isabel. It was strange to think of his father bearing another a child—or that another woman could find it in her to love him. He had no doubt that Isabel was his flesh and blood. The similarities were too striking. Their connection could not be ignored.

Yet now he fought against Jaxon Daniyal, her mentor and the one who had trained her to be more than a warrior, to heal rather than just kill. A man she cared for greatly. And he would die—all because she had decided to heal him.

The knots in his stomach tightened. Was this really how Arimus would repay that deed?

The crack of iron striking cobbles snapped Arimus back to his senses. Even exhausted, Daniyal was not to be underestimated. He seemed to have found a second wind as he came at Arimus, swinging that ridiculously large Highland sword. But this blow was feeble and slow. The heavy blade must be sapping Daniyal's energy in this long fight, even at his rank. Arimus gave a casual flick of his longsword to deflect the blow—

And almost lost his life.

There was a terrible rending as their blades met. In that instant, Arimus realised he had underestimated his enemy after all. Jaxon's swing was languid and slow, exaggerating his exhaustion—so Arimus hadn't noticed the clever use of energy the Darkstrider had applied. Slow it might have been, but it had been powered by *Might*. Unbraced, Arimus's longsword was sheered in two by the weight of the blow—leaving the terrible blade arcing for his skull.

Movement Surge.

Arimus's body screamed as he pushed it beyond its limits, shifting himself from the sword's deadly path. The world flashed red and he staggered—but the blade missed. Stars searing into his eyes and his muscles shrieking, he spun to face his opponent's next attack.

Except it didn't come. The tip of Daniyal's sword rested on the cobbles as the man leaned against its hilt, chest heaving. Holding his broken sword, Arimus frowned. What game was the man playing at?

"Trying to catch me off-guard, old man?" he demanded, clutching his broken longsword. He was now missing an inch from the tip, but enough remained that he could fight on.

Sucking in a long gasp, Jaxon straightened. It seemed to take the man an effort of will just to manage that. Arimus wasn't buying it.

"Water break?" the clansman rasped.

Arimus narrowed his eyes. "Already?" he growled. "Things were just getting fun."

A chuckle rasped from Daniyal's throat. "Is that so?" He grimaced. "Ah, but I thought I had you there." He gestured to the broken sword in Arimus's hand. "Hope that wasn't a favourite."

"It needed replacing," he replied, at a loss for what else to say. What was the man playing at? What advantage did he hope to gain out of this?

Jaxon nodded. "She's a good lass, you know," he murmured. "I wish...wish I could have saved her. Maybe Mikael..." He sighed. "So you're her brother, ay? Imagine that. Will you look out for her, after I'm gone?"

That's it, now he *knew* the man was up to something. "Enough with the games, Daniyal!" he snarled, pointing his jagged sword at his enemy's throat. "Pick up your sword and let's finish this."

This time the big man found the strength to laugh, though his face did not lose its weathered look. The wrinkles in his forehead seemed deeper, as though he had aged several decades in the last few minutes.

"Pick it up? Don't think I have the strength left to stand without the bloody thing as a crutch, lad."

"What are you talking about, old man?"

"Really thought I had you," Jaxon muttered. "I put everything I had into that last attack. One last gamble from the mighty Darkstrider." He grimaced. "Nothing...left to fight with, I'm afraid. Burned everything my body had. You win."

"I..." Arimus trailed off as he looked at the man, *really* looked this time.

Beads of sweat dripped from Jaxon's brow and his clothes were stuck to his muscular frame. His bronzed complexion had paled several shades, leaving him a sickly grey. He still clung to the hilt of the mighty greatsword, but veins protruded from his arms, and he clung to the weapon like it was the only thing left in his life. Even his Aura was diminished, dwindling with the power he had extended.

"Isabel," the clansman repeated, "you'll look out for her?"

Suddenly Arimus's mouth was parched. "I..." He swallowed, straightening. "I will do my best for the girl, if she lives. You have my word."

Jaxon nodded, his eyes flickering. "Thanks, kid." There was a pause as he heaved in a fresh breath. "Damn, but you know how to fight. Wish we'd met when I was younger."

"You would have won," Arimus said, surprised that he meant it.

"I know," the Darkstrider chuckled, "but maybe then I could have saved you from Alyina." A sigh slipped from his lips. "You'll figure it out for yourself, eventually."

Silence fell between them. They both knew Jaxon spoke the truth. A cold breeze blew across the street. Arimus swallowed. He could hardly believe this moment had arrived. The legendary Darkstrider, defeated by his hand. Surprisingly, Arimus realised he didn't have it in him to deliver the final blow. Thankfully, in his exhausted state, Jaxon wouldn't be able to resist now. Arimus could take him prisoner. Alyina would be disappointed, but she owed him this much after her little stunt. Let her be disappointed.

"I'm going to take you in, Daniyal," he said formally. "Drop the sword." It didn't matter if he did. Arimus would take it from him if need be.

Of course, Daniyal did not disappoint. Grinning, he drew in a breath and straightened, fingers tightening around the Highland blade.

"I don't think so," he rumbled. The tip left the ground, though it trembled as the great man lifted it. "I'll not be Alyina's plaything again, not on your life."

Arimus grimaced. The man was fooling no one. He had nothing left. "Come on, Daniyal," he said, starting towards the clansman. "Surrender now and keep—"

"*Sir, look out!*"

Later, when he looked back on that moment, Arimus would tell himself that it all happened too quickly. He was almost as exhausted as Jaxon Daniyal. Certainly he didn't have enough left for another *Movement Surge.* But sometimes, as he lay awake on cold nights, he would wonder if maybe there had been a chance, a moment where he could have reacted…

…and decided it was kinder not to interfere.

Regardless, neither of them noticed Lieutenant Bolt when he stepped from the alley. Even as he shouted his warning, neither of the men reacted—and by then the spear had already left his hand. Thrown in panic, it could have missed, but Gurrian soldiers were well trained. And there was no panic in Bolt's eyes.

The spear flew true, slamming into the back of Jaxon Daniyal with all the force the lieutenant could muster. There was a moment of shock in the Darkstrider's eyes as the blade tore through his spine, as though he couldn't quite believe this day had finally come.

Then without so much as a final word, he crumpled to the cobbles at Arimus's feet.

And the Darkstrider drew his final breath.

47

Two weeks before the Festival of the Satana

The night was rich with the music of the Izolu. Their old string instruments thrummed and the rumbling voice of the chieftain spun his tale. A new story was to be added to their histories, a tale of daring and love, edged with sadness, but also hope. The notes wove together with their other stories, uniting those who had come before with this new generation who would carry the clan onwards.

Amongst it all, Fiachson danced, lost in the revelry of the moment. His face was flushed, his brow damp with sweat as the bodies surged around him, the cold night beyond the stone walls a distant memory.

And with him spun Moira, her eyes alight with the glow of the lanterns, cheeks red, a smile as large as the rising moon plastered across her face. Fiachson could feel the heat of her hands on his waist, the thundering of blood in his ears at her closeness. And he held her as well, feeling the sensual sway of her hips, the closeness of her body as the crowd pressed against them and the music told tales of what the future might yet hold for the budding couple.

Truth be told, Fiachson was not convinced this was all real. Perhaps he had caught a chill on the climb up those terrible cliffs and was now in the clutches of some terrible fever hallucination. He was not even sure what all this really meant, whether Moira had constructed a true marriage for the pair of them, or if it was in name only, in order to gain the support of her father. The glow in her eyes seemed to suggest otherwise. Though, if this really *was* a marriage, that meant…

…his cheeks grew red and his heart, already racing, truly began to pound.

The music carried them on through the laughter and the chatter of the crowd. Men and women raised glasses of mead and rice wine and shared knowing smiles as the couple swept passed.

And then, before Fiachson was ready for it all to end, the last of the revellers were bidding them good night and wandering out into the cold. Fiachson had lost track of his mother in the chaos, but he thought she might have departed early, one of those strange looks on her face. He wanted to find her, to explain, but Moira was right there, standing with him as the last of her people left, leaving them alone in the grand chamber.

A lump lodged in his throat as she sighed, leaning her head against his shoulder. "That was…fun."

"It was," he said. Words were a struggle. "Shall we…go for a walk?"

Moira nodded sleepily, though her eyes fluttered closed. After a moment though, she groaned and pushed herself straight. "Yeah, I bet the moon is beautiful tonight," she said, some of her usual energy returning.

There was a *booming* in Fiachson's ears as he led her outside. And what was wrong with his chest? It felt tight, like he could hardly breathe. Surely his heart should not be going *this* fast, even as a Pathfinder? Was he having a heart attack?

Moira's hand slipped into his as they approached the cliffs and a little of his panic eased. She gave his fingers a squeeze and flashed him a smile.

"Everything okay?" she asked.

He swallowed. The night was clear, the clouds having lifted during the celebration to reveal the brilliance of the full moon. Its white light rippled on the still waters of the bay far below, so that it seemed two moons shone their brilliance upon the night.

"This…just was not exactly what I was expecting," he said finally, deciding it was best to start with the truth.

Some of the smile slipped from Moira's lips. "What do you mean?"

"I, ah, well, when you offered that challenge, I did not realise…" He cleared his throat awkwardly. "I did not know you meant for us to marry," he finished, shifting awkwardly on his feet.

"What?" The last of Moira's smile died like a trout struck by a Malesie spear. "I thought…that was how your mother…*I thought you knew!*" she shrieked the last words, colour draining from her face.

"Wait, it's okay, just hold on!" The tightness in his chest was back.

"Hold on?" Moira cried. "I just tricked you into marrying me!"

"No!" Fiachson shouted back. "I wanted to marry you!"

Silence. "What?"

"I…ah…" Gods, why had he even opened his mouth in the first place? He swallowed, unable to meet her eyes. "I…you are so brave!" he exclaimed at last. "And free-spirited! Of course I liked you." His cheeks grew hot and he rubbed the back of his head. "I just was not sure you really liked *me*."

"Oh!"

Moira stood stunned, eyes huge in the moonlight. They were raven-black, almost as dark as her hair. He'd never noticed.

"Of course I like you," she said finally. "You're cute and strong and brave!"

"Brave? I'm afraid all the time!"

"Yeah, but you don't let it stop you!" she snorted. "I don't think anyone has ever marched up to my dad and *demanded* he give them an army." She nodded enthusiastically. "Yup, brave. Maybe not *intelligent*, but…"

"Hey!" he exclaimed, before he saw her eyes were dancing with amusement. "You're pretty brave yourself," he murmured, stepping a little closer, so they were close again. As close they had been while they danced their new story. "Tricking a powerful man into marrying you."

"I know, right?"

"I thought you said you did not realise."

"I saw my opportunity and took it—"

She broke off as Fiachson kissed her. The world fell away, the gentle swirling of the wind, the distant voices in the Izolu houses, the rumble of the mountain, all of it departed, until there was only the taste of Moira on his lips, the fiery heat of her body pressed against him, the thundering of their hearts as they beat as one.

They hung in that moment for an eternity, hands clutching, pulling themselves close as their tongues intertwined and the world was forgotten, so there was only Fiachson and Moira and that cool spring night…

They broke apart carefully, smiles upon their lips. They held each other's gaze for a time, drinking in what they had found, the moment they had shared. Until a distant shout broke the night's silence.

"Sails…in the bay!"

They both spun as one of the Izolu summited the mountain path on the back of a giant mountain goat. The man waved when he saw them, directing the great beast towards them.

"Moira!" he exclaimed. "I bring news for your father. Sails have been spotted in the bay."

Moira was at once alert. "The Deti?" She demanded.

But the man shook his head, his lips twisting in something of a frown. "Actually, no," he said, looking from Moira to Fiachson. "It's the strangest thing. They're flying emerald sails."

Moira blinked. "The Fushore?"

"Oh!" Fiachson exclaimed. "Yeah, that'll be our ride!"

The pair turned to stare at him. "What?" Moira asked, bewilderment written across her face.

Fiachson allowed himself a grin at finally getting one over her. "What, you did not think we were going to *walk* to Skarta, did you?"

48

Present Day

"What's to stop you going back on your word?" Alyina demanded.

"I imagine if I did," Mikael said slowly, "you would hunt me down pretty quick. Followed by my friends."

Alyina chuckled. "And what makes you think your friends are getting out of here alive at all?"

"Didn't I mention that part?" Mikael paused for dramatic effect. "You're going to let them go, because I'm going to show you one of the weapons from my world."

Alyina's eyes lit up with desire. Did her hunger for power know no limits? Mikael imagined the look in her eyes must be much the same as those leaders who had first dared to imagine the atomic bomb.

"Ahhh, yes, you did leave that part out." She slid towards him, seemingly more snake than human. "In that case, I'm *sure* I can find it in myself to be merciful."

Mikael could have laughed. He stood tense, renewed power burning in his soul, as the princess approached. The sword lay at his feet, but it was all but useless now its power had fled. She would take it from him if he tried to wield it again.

As for Kat and Isabel…he couldn't sense them any longer. Hopefully that meant Kat's *Mute* ability was hiding them. And that they'd managed to light the fuse…

In the meantime, he needed to stall.

"You cannot fathom how long I have been waiting for this," Alyina whispered, moving closer still. "My father has an Offworlder of his own, you know?"

Mikael's heart practically stopped in his chest at that little revelation. "*What?*"

"Oh my dear, sweet Mikael, did you really believe you were the first one in a millennia?" Laughter rasped from her throat. "There have been so many theories about how dad built our empire, but no one ever did quite figure it out. My father met him when they were both just young men, and he was still new to this world. They worked together at first, making Gurria a better place. That's how my father rose to power, all those priceless snippets from a world of war and struggle."

She sighed. "Eventually though, the Offworlder lost the stomach to do what was needed." Now Alyina's smile revealed all her teeth. "After that, father locked him away in a cell. I used to sit with him at times, when I was just a girl, to see what fresh secrets I could wheedle out of him. The things I learned…" Her eyes shone. "And now I have a brand new plaything."

Mikael's breath was ragged in his throat. The sword still lay on the ground in front of him. He fought the desire to pick it up and hurl himself at her. That would be a death sentence for Isabel and Kat. Once Alyina turned her attention back to them…

Exhaling, he managed a laugh. "You recall our conversation back in the library?" he asked. "You said you didn't believe in the Elohim."

Alyina arched one eyebrow. "As I recall, I *proved* they were only Pathfinders," she replied, crossing her arms. "Though I don't see how that has anything to do with your current predicament."

"Oh, it doesn't," he said with a grin. "I just thought it was an interesting outlook. What about the Satana?"

"Bedtime stories told to scare children," Alyina snarled. "Now, if you don't mind—"

Suddenly, she darted towards him. Instinctively, Mikael drew on his new ability. A flickering *Shield* of Mana burst into life around him. Alyina paused, eying the magical barrier, before her smile returned.

"You think that flimsy thing will stop me?"

Mikael sighed dramatically. "Probably not." He grinned. "Why don't we ask them? They're watching us, you know."

That brought a frown to Alyina's lips. "What?"

"The Satana. Maybe the Elohim too. Haven't quite figured them out yet."

Alyina stood with a strange look on her face. "All that power better not have melted your brain, Offworlder."

Mikael chuckled. "Maybe it's like you said, and they really were Pathfinders. Personally, I think you're only half-right."

"And what is the other half?"

"They were Pathfinders, sure, but I do not think they came from your world. I think they came from mine."

The lines on Alyina's brow deepened. "Why would you say that?"

"It all comes down to linguistics, just like you said. *Elohim,*" he said it slowly. "Doesn't really have any connection with *Pathfinder*, does it? So why would one become the other?"

"You're saying Elohim has a meaning in *your* world?" she hissed.

Mikael smiled. "*God.*"

Her eyes widened. Mikael would have said more. Taunted

her with the connections he'd made, the revelations from this world's past. But he never got the chance, as somewhere under their feet, a burning fuse finally reached the amphora he had stashed beneath the house.

And the world turned to fire.

"*YES!*"

Raising his elongated head to the multidimensional ceiling, Leviathan screamed his joy, while Azaroth slammed a fist full of claws down on his workbench. The machinery crackled, the screen flickering at the interference from his innate magic. Muttering a curse, he glanced at the other monitors.

They showed an infinite universe of reactions. Some viewers were screaming with rage, others sadness or joy or a strange mixture of it all, but none had quite the same level of ecstasy as Leviathan. Sure, others might have had credits riding on the outcome of this season, but they were only viewers. They didn't have a personal hand in manipulating the outcome.

Officially, neither did he or Leviathan, for that matter. They were just IT guys, not producers. And gambling amongst federal employees was strictly prohibited. How else could they maintain their neutral observer status? Writers and producers might put the various elements in play, but not even *they* could always predict the outcomes. Humans—whichever realm they were from—were unpredictable bastards. You could never quite tell when one would go feral.

Mikael Heaton, you little bastard.

Baring his teeth, Azaroth began working at the dashboard. If that earthling thought he was going to escape at the seventh hour, he had another thing coming. Azaroth didn't have long before the reapers did their business, but the infinite abyss was too good an end for the likes of Mikael Heaton. Not after Azaroth had basically *handed* him the solution! All he had to do was kill one damn girl. Was that too much to ask?

Sure, tapping directly into the forces of the twin blades probably would have torn his soul apart within a few days, but that didn't matter! By then Azaroth would have made his fortune.

Now he'd lost, and Azaroth was going to make sure the Earthling's soul suffered the consequences for it.

"Come on, pay up, 'Roth," Leviathan loomed over his station, a sickly grin on his twisted lips.

"Yeah, yeah, gimme a moment," Azaroth muttered, "and don't call me that."

"Aww, buddy, feeling a bit salty?" Webbed claws patted him on the shoulder. "I'd offer to double it again, but your little Earthling friend is looking a little crispy for another round."

A growl rumbled from Azaroth's throat, but he was concentrating on the system. It was giving him an error when trying to access Mikael's soul. Maybe because he was not native to the Seventh Realm? What if he tried Earth…nope.

He sat back in his chair, a frown twisting his demented features. "What in the Seven Hells…"

Leviathan chuckled. "Don't tell me you don't have the money." The claws tightened on his shoulder. "That would be most disappointing."

"It's not that," Azaroth muttered. "It's…his soul isn't in processing."

"What?" Leviathan growled, his enormous head looming over the station for a closer look. "Then where is he?"

The realisation struck them both at the same time. A stream of profanity tumbled from Leviathan's jaws—while Azaroth leapt to his feet with a whoop.

"*Yes!*"

In the split second before the world turned to fire, time seemed to slow. Mikael would never know if the Satana had stepped in at the last moment to make a desperate change, or if some remnant energy from the sword remained within him, or if it was just the panicked act of a brain that knew it was in its final moments.

All he knew was that he enjoyed the glimpse of shock in Alyina's face before the inferno engulfed them both.

Well, her less than him as the *Shield* he had pre-emptively activated absorbed the first wave of fire and shrapnel from the homemade explosives he'd planted beneath the floorboards a few hours ago.

Then all Mikael saw was the inferno. Miraculously, his *Shield* held. It was just as Jaxon had said all those months ago— the universe provided what a Pathfinder needed most. Of course, whether it was the universe or a demon with a gambling habit, Mikael wasn't sure, but he sure as hell was thankful.

Until the first crack appeared in his *Shield.*

The end didn't take long, after that. Within seconds the cracks spread, as the Mana began to slip through his grasp, the unpractised power spluttering...until it died. His shield splintered, and the final blast struck him with the force of a truck. He felt his *Enforced Body* breaking, his skin searing and bones fracturing, even his ear drums shattering from the sheer force of the boom...

Thankfully, the darkness took him before the agony arrived.

49

The explosion unleashed by Mikael's device was unlike anything Isabel had ever witnessed. One moment, the old manor was looming over the street just as it had since the day of its construction, its windows boarded up, walls creaking slightly with each puff of wind—the next a column of flame shattered every window and hurled the roof a thousand feet into the sky.

Hidden by Kat's power, Isabel had helped the girl to light the little wire behind the building. But only now, as the flames bloomed and the enormous house crumbled, did she realise Mikael's true plan.

A second after the explosion, an invisible force struck them where they stood in the street. Despite her Bronze rank strength, Isabel was pushed backwards a step, while Kat would have been blown away if Isabel had not caught her.

They stood for a second, staring at the ruin Mikael had unleashed. Watching everything burn, to see the flames steal another loved one from her, Isabel wanted to scream, to grab Kat and shake her, to demand answers, to curse the girl for letting Mikael do this…

Instead, Isabel found herself walking towards the inferno. Behind her, Kat screamed something, but Isabel ignored the girl. This wasn't her fault. Kat had been used by the people of this city, people like Jon and Alyina and Arimus. That was what they did, these Gurrians. The Skartans were not people to them, but tools to be used and then discarded when they no longer served their purpose.

Maybe Mikael was a little like that as well. The way he had set his friends to their tasks, their little missions that would help protect the Highlands. Protect him. All of them, just pieces in a greater machine.

But unlike the others, Mikael had done it to save them. Because he cared about them. Cared enough that he would sacrifice himself, if that was what it took. Because in his heart, Mikael knew he was too dangerous. A liability to everyone in this world. If their enemies could force him to reveal the knowledge in his head, there would be no stopping them.

But Mikael Heaton was wrong.

They needed him. The clans needed him. Not because of what was in his head, or his magical swords or his dangerous machines, but because of what was in his heart. Because where others saw weakness, Mikael Heaton saw potential. He had given Fiachson self-belief, and Conner the courage to reach for something greater than his father's shadow. He had given Isabel the heart to pursue her past, and to finally realise it was not what she sought.

A man like that was worth fighting for.

Fire.

It burned all around her now, the inferno.

Its heat did not touch Isabel, however. Her *Elemental Manipulation* held it at bay. It was not easy, but she could manage, creating a pocket of coolness around her. Just her.

The building was a different problem. The walls groaned and the ceiling cracked, threatening to bring everything down on her. She needed to be quick. It seemed impossible that anyone could have survived that blast, but Isabel would not stop until she found him, until she saw for herself that Mikael Heaton was really gone.

She pressed on, struggling to find her way in the twisted ruin of the manor. There was no longer an entrance, nor a corridor, nor a dining room. Just a churning tapestry of flame. She shuddered to think what anyone alive would be suffering in this. But maybe, just maybe…

At first she saw nothing. The floor was twisted and torn where the explosion had originated. She feared Mikael must have been consumed utterly by the blast. But she would not quit. Not until…

There!

Incredibly, his body looked almost whole—though his clothes were aflame and he wasn't moving. Isabel fell to her knees beside him. It was growing steadily more difficult to hold back the heat, but drawing power until her Mana channels screamed, she extended her influence to extinguish the flames on Mikael's body.

She grimaced at what they revealed. He must have somehow avoided the main impact of the blast, but the fire had still done its work. His flesh was scorched and bubbling, his hair burned away, and one arm and both legs were twisted at unnatural angles. Grimacing, she lifted him into her arms. If he was gone, she could at least carry him from this place, give him a proper burial.

But to her shock, she felt a spark of Aura as her arms wrapped around him. Heart suddenly racing, Isabel extended her soul. It was still damaged from Alyina's attack, but desperation did wonders and her *Healing Touch* finally activated, pouring into Mikael even as she staggered to her feet with him slung over one shoulder.

A piece of the ceiling crashed down, carving through the

floor and sending burning splinters slashing across her face. She staggered, almost dropping Mikael and losing control of her Mana. She clung on. If she lost focus now, they would both perish.

Teeth clenched, she stumbled around the burning beam, seeking a way out. The flames were so bright, they left her disoriented. But she had to move. Aura still pouring into Mikael, she felt a stirring, his soul and body coming back from the brink.

In desperation, she hurled herself in the direction she hoped was the street. She didn't care about doorways in that moment, or windows, just that the flames seemed less. Her Mana channels were straining now, the bubble shrinking around them, as the hungry flames sought to reassert themselves. They wanted to consume, to feed upon their flesh and return it to the world.

Well, the world could wait. Today, Isabel would not surrender.

She screamed when she finally burst free of the building and tumbled to the scorched grounds of the manor. Her Mana collapsed and she felt Mikael groan in her arms as the heat washed over them. She hauled him up. Even her body was giving in now, and it was taking all her soul to mend the horrible damage Mikael had taken. How he had survived in the first place…

…he would tell her when he woke.

Kat met them when they were far enough from the fire that the heat no longer burned. Isabel almost sighed when the girl's ability washed over them, concealing them from prying eyes. They were hidden now. Safe.

Her legs gave way and she collapsed to the dirt street. Mikael came with her, though she did not release him. Exhausted in Mana and Body, Isabel was still giving all she could afford of her Aura.

"How?" Kat whispered, looking down at them with eyes wide in disbelief.

Isabel shook her head. Her *Healing Touch* was doing its work, mending the worst of the burns, knitting broken bones back together. But it wouldn't be enough. Not to heal all of him. Wherever her Aura touched, she could sense the damage. The explosion had torn him inside and out. Her power would concentrate on the most dangerous areas and hopefully stabilise them, bring him to the point he could heal by himself.

But Mikael would be left with scars. Scars like her own.

She clenched her fists. At least he was alive. They both were…

…her gaze drifted in the direction of the plaza, where Jaxon and Arimus had been fighting, and her heart twisted. She didn't know the outcome of that battle. But she knew one must be dead by now.

"Jaxon," she whispered to the winds.

But whether he lived or died, she could not help him now. Not in her state. Not with Mikael in this condition. He needed her. And Kat…

"He has the sword," the girl whispered.

Looking from the street urchin to Mikael, Isabel swallowed as she saw the blade clutched tightly in his hand. She hadn't noticed. Carefully, Isabel took it from his fingers and slid it through her belt. He would want it back later.

"What now?" Kat asked as Isabel rose.

"Now we flee the city," Isabel replied quietly.

"And go where?"

Isabel turned towards the northern horizon. The sun was setting, and a haze obscured the distant mountains, but like every Highlander, she could picture the twisted peak of Ryntirax perfectly, the way it stood in watchful vigilance over their lives, a silent guardian for the world. The memory brought a smile to her face. Whoever her father might have been or wherever she had come from, there was only one place she longed for now.

"Home," she whispered.

———

Amidst the darkness, Mikael remembered. The day they had come. The day they had taken his father. The streets had been quiet when the portal opened and the light of another world spilled into the evening twilight. His father had paused, cricket bat in hand, to stare at that strange glow. Mikael had too—what ten-year-old wouldn't?

The rest was a blur. His father, stepping towards the void. A twist in time, like the world blinking backwards. The flicker of something in the light, as something dark reached through.

A conversation, unheard by the ten-year old boy. Then his father, smiling down at him.

"Don't worry, son. I'll be back soon. They promised." A sad smile. A challenge. "Look after your mother for me."

And then his father was gone.

Mikael drifted in the darkness a while after that, the memory lingering, twisting its fiery coils in his soul. They had tried to keep this from him. First on Earth, then here. What they had done. The Satana, or maybe the Elohim. It didn't matter now. They had taken his father.

And Mikael Heaton had spent every waking moment from that day forth trying to get him back.

"Thought you deserved to know, after that little stunt you pulled."

Azaroth's voice brought no fear for Mikael now, as he found the demented creature drifting alongside him in the void.

"Did you want a thank you?"

"Dunno." A pause. "Ya just about gave me a heart attack back there, you know?"

"Next time I hope it kills you." He felt strangely empty, confronting the creature after everything he'd been through. Must be how the Winchesters felt after facing their umpteenth demon.

Azaroth's chuckle held no amusement today. "Fair enough."

"I'm done playing your games."

"Now listen here, mate——"

"I said I'm done!" If Mikael had had a body in that moment, he would have taken a swing at the creature—eternal demon of the underworld or no.

Silence. "Okay, mate. No more gambling."

"Thank you."

"Can't promise it'll make a difference though."

"What?"

The monstrosity shrugged. "I don't write the scripts. And now that you two have those swords, well, things just got a lot more complicated for the producers. This world wasn't meant to get anything like those again. I'm not sure the Seventh Realm can handle that kind of power."

Mikael suppressed a sigh. "So you're saying I've pissed someone else off? What else is new?"

Azaroth's laughter regained a bit of its usual humour. "You do have a knack for it."

Closing his eyes, Mikael exhaled. Damnit. He couldn't believe he was going to say it, but if others were plotting against him, he needed to advance his own plans. And there was only one way to do that.

"What would it cost, if you were to send a message for me?"

There was a long silence at that. "To who?"

"Conner Spears."

Raising one clawed finger, the demon tapped his chin. "Hmm, how does…three months sound?"

Mikael winced. Three months was along time to survive in a world where everyone was out to get him. And if he failed…the eternal flames of whatever hell he'd glimpsed on The Day That Had Never Been waited for him.

Oh well, better the demon he knew than the ones he didn't. Which… he doubted had ever been meant literally. And it wasn't like he planned on dying. Other than the one time he'd deliberately had his friends set off a bomb in a building he was occupying. It wasn't like those circumstances came up more than every…six months, right?

"Deal."

A wicked grin spread across the Satana's jaws. "Great! So what's the message?"

50

Present day

A warning from the soldiers on watch alerted Lunden to the disturbance. The sun was just rising over the horizon, setting the plains of Skarta aflame with its light. Two weeks of hard marching, and they had come within a stone's throw of the Skartan capital just a day after the solstice. Today he planned to send scouts ahead seeking information about Mikael and Jaxon.

Or he had been planning to, until three weary figures came stumbling out of the fading darkness.

All three had seen better days—but Mikael was by far the worst. His skin was blackened, melted in places, and he was barely conscious. It looked like someone had tried to cook him alive. Isabel herself looked utterly exhausted, almost out on her feet, as though she had poured her entire soul into keeping her companion alive—which judging by Mikael's condition, she very well may have.

The last was unknown to Lunden, though she seemed in

the best condition of the three. Kat, she called herself when she told him their story. He waited until the end for his questions, though what she had to say sent a bolt of fear down his spine.

"How many soldiers in this army, do you think?" he asked when the girl had finished.

It was Mikael, though, who rasped: "A Legion, she said."

The bolt twisted deeper. "Four thousand men."

Lunden was glad he had pulled them aside. Only Maria and Scott were in attendance—his two deputies. The pair exchanged a look at the news. The Malesie army did not even number a thousand.

"We have to retreat," Isabel croaked.

Her eyes were haunted. Lunden felt for her. He could hardly believe it himself, that Jaxon Daniyal might have fallen. The man carried an aura about him. Not of a Pathfinder, but something else entirely. A sense of invincibility that screamed this man would live forever.

And now…could he really be gone?

"No, we can't," Mikael groaned.

Lunden frowned. "Why not? The Malesie are brave, but even with our preparations…"

"Because if we retreat, that Legion is going to turn around and slaughter Conner and Fiachson."

"What?" Isabel frowned. "How…" she trailed off, her eyes fluttering closed. "What have you done now, Mikael?"

"They were meant to be joining us," Lunden said quietly. "Taking Fushore ships and sailing around the peninsula to collect the Izolu, before joining us in Skarta. But…" he swallowed. "I'm sorry, all of you, but Denether has betrayed the rest of the clans."

Mikael nodded. "We know."

Lunden pursed his lips. "We weren't meant to come here at

all," he said quietly. "I imagine Denether must have sent word to the other clans as well, not to engage with Gurria."

Isabel grimaced, but Mikael only chuckled. "That's why I sent Conner and Fiachson."

"You think Conner would disobey his own father?"

"I'm betting my life on it, yeah."

Lunden shook his head. "Even if they *do* join us here, they can only have a few thousand more, at the most. We'll still be outnumbered."

"A good thing they're not coming here then."

"What do you mean?" Lunden pressed.

"Well, the princess enjoyed her surprise so much, I figured we'd spring one of our own on her. Those soldiers she brought came from the garrison in Yarrin. Without them, the city should be unprotected."

"You sent them to Yarrin," Lunden breathed. If Mikael was right, then the war had already begun. Not here, but in Yarrin, a province a hundred leagues to the east. "How?"

"How is not important." Mikael said quietly. "What's important is if we turn around and run, Alyina will be free to march on Yarrin and kill our friends."

Isabel snorted. "After what you did to her, that woman won't be a problem anymore."

"No," Mikael said, drawing every eye in the tent. His face was haunted as he met their gaze. "She's not dead," he continued. "The explosion caught her unawares, but she had an ability, too."

Isabel's face paled. "*Invulnerable,*" she whispered.

"Yes," Mikael said grimly. "I sensed it, just before my *Shield* broke. It just took her…longer to activate it. She's alive. But I don't think she's going to be in a very good mood."

STANDING AT THE RAILINGS OF HIS SHIP, CONNER WATCHED THE city slowly emerge from the mists. Behind them, the scarlet sun crept onto the horizon. From the darkness came the creaking of wood and the cracking of sails, the whispers of men as they prepared themselves for battle. Noise would travel easily over the water, and no one wanted to alert the watchers on the walls. That was something both the Izolu and the Fushore knew well—to guard for raiders with their ears, not their eyes.

So they had wrapped their weapons in wool and ordered no one to speak above a whisper. So far it seemed to be working, as the city continued its slow awakening to the first dawn of summer.

Yarrin. The pleasure house of the Empire, some called it. Once it had been independent, like Skarta or Ressi, but it had been the first of the free cities to fall before Gurria's inevitable march. Today, Conner hoped it would be the first to be freed.

"The Izolu are ready," Fiachson said quietly, joining him at the rail.

It was difficult to recognise the naïve young boy from Sarton nowadays. Fiachson had filled in over the nine months: Between training and the Pathfinder transformation, he had put muscles on his arms and legs, and his chest had filled out. No one would mistake him for a boy now.

And if you did, well, the young woman hanging from his arm would be quick to correct you. Conner was not exactly sure what had happened up in those mountains, but it seemed that Fiachson had become a man in more ways than one. He and Moira had rarely been seen apart since the Izolu joined the fleet—much to Fiachson's embarrassment.

Conner, for his part, was glad for them. Between the two clans, their fleet carried almost two thousand warriors, clansmen and women ready to lay down their lives for their lands.

"The Fushore as well," Yeti murmured, joining Conner on

his other side. Her eyes were sharp as she looked across the waters. "Looks quiet. Guess that dream of yours was real after all."

A shiver ran down Conner's spine. They could mock him all they liked, but it had been no dream. He had never *quite* been sure of Mikael's tale about The Day That Had Never Been. There was just something…off about it. But last night, one of the Elohim had come to him itself.

Light had filled his cabin and a face had appeared amidst the brilliance. It was strangely distorted, twisted, almost monstrous, but no one could have mistaken its power.

Change of plans. Go to Yarrin instead. Its gates lie open, its walls unguarded. This, Mikael commands you.

Well, who was he to disobey an instruction from the gods, even if they were only passing on word from his friend?

Now his heart was hammering as the ships drifted closer to the docks. There were still no shouts, no horns to sound the warning. The city slept on, unsuspecting to the threat that approached on silent oars.

Conner swallowed. This was it. Their last chance to turn back. No one knew they were here. They could still leave and none would be the wiser about how close the Highlands had come to starting a war with Gurria. Doing this would make him a traitor to his king, if not his people.

He wondered what Jaxon would say, if the Darkstrider was here. This was not the code Jaxon Daniyal had preached. The people in this city had committed no evil against them. They would suffer most in what was to come, not because they were evil or even because Conner wished them ill, but because they were in the wrong place at the wrong time.

It was a vile, terrible thing, the injustice of war, that the innocent suffered far more than the guilty. It was enough for Conner to question whether his father was right, that it was better to surrender their freedom in return for peace. Maybe no one had to die…

…except he knew that was not the choice the empire offered. The soldiers who had marched on Sarton had not wanted peace. They had come to slaughter an innocent village. The Empire was a monster with an insatiable hunger. It had already consumed Yarrin, and Skarta, and Ressi. Now his father thought it would spare them because they fed it rations and half-measures?

No, it was not a choice between war or peace, but a war now, or when the Gurrians decided it was time.

Conner might not be his father, but at least he did this for others, not himself. He hated war and everything to do with it. There was no glory in watching men and women he had never met die beneath his blade. People with their own hopes and aspirations, sons and fathers and daughters. That thrill had died in Sarton. All that remained now was the empty knowledge of its inevitability. Whatever the future held for Gurria and his people, it would be built on the bones of those who died today. War was a tool that corrupted all it touched.

But at least this way, they might *have* a future.

Conner thought of all the people back in Sarton, of their peaceful lives, serving their community. Of Furness and its beauty, of the soaring peak of Ryntirax, and of the Fushore, and their lives high on the verdant coasts.

All of that was worth fighting for. Even dying for. Conner would not hide behind stone walls or command those who followed him from a gilded throne. He would fight and die with his people, if that was what it took.

The shift in his soul felt almost gentle when it happened, like he had been standing on a precipice for so long now, it only took a tiny leap. A deep, Bronze glow filled him as he changed, and a smile touched his lips.

"I'm ready too," he said softly.

Ahead, the first ship reached the wharfs of the city, just as the bells began to toll.

Drawing his sword, Conner Spears lifted it to the sky and shouted a battle cry.

And the Highlands went to war.

51

Arimus gazed upon the twisted ruin of the manor. The fires must have burnt with an unnatural heat, for little remained but ash and desolation. Smoke filled the air, though its reek was not the pleasant tang of wood, but rather an acrid, toxic thing that clung to the tongue. The weaker members of the Fourth Legion had already retreated, hacking up their lungs as they choked on the chemical stench.

He alone remained. He could sense their gaze on his back, the questions on their tongues. He was the Governor, the only Gold in the city. The man they would all look too if the rumours were true.

They were waiting for him. For his orders. The news had arrived that morning by pigeon—Yarrin was under attack. No one could say by who, but Arimus knew. There could only be one culprit. The clans and their king had deceived them. There would be no peace. And it had been the Highlands who had cast the first stone.

For the fifth time in as many minutes, Arimus cast his *Aura Sense* over the ruin. And for the fifth time, he felt the chaos in the ashes, the distortion of the world, the shattered pieces of things that had once been whole. Difficult to read, but of one thing he was sure. There was no flickering glow of living Aura amidst the ruin.

No Alyina Sorulus.

It was a difficult thought to reconcile; the Gurrian Princess, dead. That she could have been killed by one so feeble, so pathetic as a Steel and a Bronze ranker…it made no sense.

And yet that was what she had sought, wasn't it? An otherworldly power, capable of humbling even the most powerful Pathfinders. It seemed Mikael had shown her his secrets after all. And all it had cost Alyina was her life.

For a sixth and final time, Arimus extended his *Aura Sense*. It was unnecessary, he knew, and yet he had to be sure, had to sift through that broken field of past lives one last time.

And to his surprise, this time he felt something stir.

It was subtle at first. A burst of scarlet amidst the twisted threads of Mana and Aura. Then a shifting of rubble, a *whisper* of movement. He focused on the source, heart suddenly pounding. It came again, darkness swirling, parting as a figure rose, emerging as if born of the ashes themselves.

Then the ash fell aside, revealing the monster hidden beneath.

Alyina Sorulus had been a vision of beauty. No more. Whatever power had saved her from death had not spared her the cruel touch of the flames. Her skin was scorched black, cracking in places as she took one staggering step, then another, and her hair was gone, the luxurious locks burnt away in the inferno that had consumed everything around her.

The only part of her that remained untouched were those emerald eyes. They glowed now with raw hatred.

She had used her *Invulnerable* skill, but the destruction of the manor must have caught her off-guard. It may have saved her life, but it had not prevented the horrible damage to her body.

Even so, the explosion must have been incredible to inflict such damage on her *Enforced Body*.

Arimus couldn't help but think her looks now mirrored the twisted nature of her soul.

He was torn as she staggered towards him. This woman had used him, cast him into her web of lies like a thing to be played with. She had been the cause of so much pain and suffering. Even now there were soldiers going house to house, smashing down doors and dragging the occupants away in chains. Skarta was undergoing a cleansing of the sort not seen in a decade—all at the behest of this woman.

And yet…wasn't that what he had wanted? To finally go to war against the resistance? To burn them out at the root?

He saw Jaxon Daniyal, lying dead in the street, heard again his final plea: "Look out for her."

His sister. *Isabel.* After this, Alyina would hunt her to the ends of the earth.

Arimus was just grasping for his sword when she reached him. His hand was already around the hilt. Yet as she stood before him, twisted, broken, pity touched him. Evil she might be, but in this moment of utter agony, even Alyina Sorulus deserved pity, did she not?

Then she reached out a trembling hand and grasped him by the arm.

Her touch was like a searing…light…his thoughts… muddled…he struggled to think…feel…faces spun in his mind, Alyina and Mikael, Isabel and Daniyal.

Protect her, the voice said. *Guard her.*

The fog swirled, the faces flashed. The warmth swelled within, washing away the disgust.

Alyina. She needed him. Now more than ever. Their enemies, they were everywhere. The foul Skartan Resistance. The Highland clans. The Offworlder.

"Well, Governor." Alyina's voice was like burnt coals, but her eyes were clear. "Will you be my guardian?"

There could be only one answer. "Of course, my love.'

EPILOGUE

Somewhere in the immeasurable cosmos, amidst the void between worlds, a conclave had gathered. Shining stars of light speared out into the ether—only to twist back upon themselves in the space of infinity, collecting, uniting until all stood before the Barrier of the Enemy.

"Where is Dagon?" Vesryn, first of the Elohim, demanded of his fellows.

"The Watcher has fallen," came the reply.

"He passed beyond the Barrier," spoke another.

Silence filled the void, thundering with the energies of the gathered armies. And slowly the void was filled, as emotions not felt in eons boiled to the surface. It was wrong, they knew, to allow such mortal conditions to affect them. Only suffering could come from those evil concepts. But this news…

"How?" At last came Vesryn's question.

"A rift. It closed."

The void shook. Emotion, that enemy of emptiness, creator of suffering, burned hotter. Anger. Hatred. Fear.

"Then the Enemy bangs the drums of war," Vesryn said, his voice thundering over the collapse of a dying star.

"No…"

"It was not the Enemy…"

"Another light burned…we saw…we saw…"

The silence returned. Vesryn pondered this news. Another? Who else was there but the Enemy and their victims? The souls of the suffering screamed out to him across the void, guarded by the Barrier, and yet one could still hear them if you listened, their whispers amidst the emptiness, the fury of their emotion, their anguish.

He and his Elohim were pledged to end that anguish, to light a cleansing fire that would burn across the cosmos, consuming all until no more suffered the wickedness of the Enemy and their temptation.

"If there is another, perhaps there is a chance," Vesryn spoke at last, and now his voice was quiet, as though fear, that most hateful of emotions, had touched him. "If there is another, perhaps the rift will come again."

"Yes…" the voices replied, and now they were touched with excitement.

Another treacherous emotion. And yet…if the Barrier truly fell, the moment was finally upon them. After an eon of waiting, the time to fulfil their vow approached.

"Join me in vigilance, brothers, sisters," Vesryn intoned. "Let the Watcher's fall not be in vain. We have but to wait a little longer, and Dagon shall light the way."

And so they gathered, those brilliant lights that called themselves Elohim. Each of them burned with the energy of a cosmos, with the power of a thousand worlds consumed, cleansed of that most vile of things—life.

An eon passed. A sun was born, brilliant, burning, lighting up the void, blooming only to shrivel once more and collapse, its time no more than the blossoming of a flower for these beings of light.

Then somewhere beyond the Barrier, a man by the name

of Mikael Heaton bore the forces of Destruction and Creation. It was only brief. Only a touch of what was to come.

But the Barrier shook.

A Breach opened.

And forces of the Elohim went charging into the abyss.

A NOTE FROM THE AUTHOR

Phew! That was a lot of point of views, time periods and story plots to intertwine, but fingers crossed it all came together in the end. I was very happy we got to check in with what Fiachson, Lunden Marcs and Conner were up to in the weeks before everything comes to a head in Skarta. Bring on the battle for book three!

Hopefully if you made it this far, you enjoyed the book! Please, please, please, if you did enjoy it, don't forget to leave your review. And don't forget to tell all your friends how awesome the series is too. The more successful the book, the faster book three comes along!

And once again, thank you to all my wonderful Kickstarter backers that made this story possible. Be sure to follow my newsletters below if you'd like to get updates on the next books (and a chance to grab the special kickstarter editions of this series!).

Write on!
Aaron Hodges

FOLLOW AARON HODGES...
And receive TWO FREE novels and a short story!
https://aaronhodgesauthor.com/newsletter

ALSO BY AARON HODGES

The Sword of Light

Book 1: Stormwielder

Book 2: Firestorm

Book 3: Soul Blade

The Legend of the Gods

Book 1: Oathbreaker

Book 2: Shield of Winter

Book 3: Dawn of War

The Knights of Alana

Book 1: Daughter of Fate

Book 2: Queen of Vengeance

Book 3: Crown of Chaos

The Evolution Gene

Book 1: Reborn

Book 2: Havoc

Book 3: Carnage

Descendants of the Fall

Book 1: Warbringer

Book 2: Wrath of the Forgotten

Book 3: Age of Gods

Book 4: Dreams of Fury

www.ingramcontent.com/pod-product-compliance
Lightning Source LLC
Chambersburg PA
CBHW070308310726
48976CB00005B/1615